Robledo Mountain

Retreat

By P.C. Allen

Copyright 2019 P.C. Allen

Dos Santos Edition

DEDICATION

For my son. One of the greatest pleasures in my life has been, "Watching Scotty Grow."

ACKNOWLEDGE-MENTS

As always, first and foremost, my thanks to my First Readers, Robert Green, Joyce Ward Kelly, and Robert Leger, who continue to give their time, creativity, and encouragement.

I owe a tremendous debt to my editors, 'TeNderLoin', 'TheRev', and 'zap292'. All of whom wade through the gibberish masquerading as prose, add in all the punctuation, discover disappearing words, and rein in the loose and forgotten plot lines. The book you are reading now is largely a result of their selfless efforts. Any issues you may have with this book remain my sole responsibility as the decisions on what to include, what to change, and what to ignore were mine.

The cover of any book is just as important as the story. My sincerest thanks to Mike Groves, another of the very talented photographers who call the Mesilla Valley home. He graciously allowed me to use one of his photographs as the background of this book's cover. I encourage you to visit http://mikegrovesphotography.com to see more of his incredible work.

Once again, a special thanks to Tatiana Fernandez at Vila Design for the cover design. She continues to astound me. Working from nothing more than a concept and a background photograph her imagination and talent are truly impressive. See more of her work at viladesign.

TABLE OF CONTENTS

NEW MEXICO TERRITORY MAP - 1854

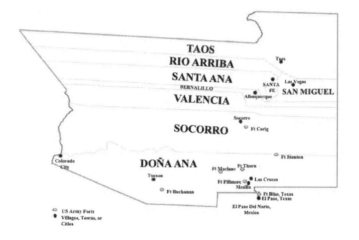

TAOS

RIO ARRIBA

Taos

SANTA ANA

SANTA FE

Las Vegas

BERNALILLO

VALENCIA

Albuquerque

SAN MIGUEL

Socorro

Ft Craig

SOCORRO

Ft Stanton

Colorado City

DOÑA ANA

Ft Thorn

Ft Machase

Tucson

Ft Fillmore

Las Cruces

Mesilla

Ft Buchanan

Ft Bliss, Texas

El Paso, Texas

El Paso Del Norte, Mexico

US Army Forts

Villages, Towns, or Cities

PROLOGUE

*...Four stones were heated by the fire inside
the sweathouse... The others sang songs
of healing on the outside, until it was time
for the sweat to be finished...
~ Excerpt from Apache Creation Story ~*

T he tired shaman straightened as he exited the wickiup, glad to be out in the fresh evening air. The worry etched deeply into every line on his face was all encompassing as he stared off into the distance.

Four times he'd failed. Four, a powerful number; he couldn't, wouldn't, fail a fifth time.

He'd had an extraordinary number of visions in the last handful of years. A long, glorious string of visions, that had proved to be accurate. More than in all the previous years combined. He thought he'd been blessed. Instead he'd learned he'd been cursed. Perhaps Raven, the great trickster, was behind these last four visions. Regardless, instead of assisting his people with spirit contact, he'd hurt them.

He'd counseled for a large raid on a white man's town. He'd been assured of a large victory, succeeding where so many others had failed, with few loses among his warriors. The victory would be the beginning of the death knell for white men in Apacheria.

Instead of victory his warriors had been decimated with nothing to show for the effort and loss. The hated white man only increased his numbers as more and more arrived to stake out the land so precious to his group; Failure Number One.

To make up for that failure he'd been given a vision of a great victory against the most hated of his people's enemies, the Navajo. That vision too proved to have been false, as again his warriors were decimated with nothing in return except the death wails of the women; Failure Number Two.

He'd been warned during a vision in the sweathouse over a year ago that his future and that of his family lay in the North. He'd convinced his leader of this even after a lengthy visit to a promising area in the South. He now knew his vision had been wrong; Failure Number Three.

The last failure was the most immediately dangerous for his people by far. He'd missed all the warning signs, signs which every shaman was trained from youth to recognize; yet, he'd missed them. And because he missed them, the leader of his people was now dead. He went to sleep last night an apparently healthy man, an old man to be sure, but healthy enough. The leader died in his sleep without a sound. If he'd been paying more attention instead of worrying about failures he could have interceded with the spirit world before it was too late and likely the leader would still be alive; Failure Number Four.

Four! A powerful number indeed.

He came out of his reverie to find his apprentice standing in front of him looking at him with concern.

Ignoring his apprentice, he stalked to the sweathouse still deep in thought. Removing his clothes, he entered the small hut, immediately breaking into a heavy sweat from the cloying heat and humidity.

As he settled himself he hoped the spirits would hear his prayers for counsel and bless him with a visit. Without thought to the activity going on outside the sweathouse he took a deep steadying breath and began the focus chant.

Almost immediately he felt himself enter the serene peaceful existence of the spirit world. A world he well knew from his previous visions. This time though there were differences from the previous visits he could remember. Subtle differences most of which he couldn't quite put his fingers on but they were there.

The difference he could identify was the ease with which he'd entered. He couldn't remember a faster or smoother transition from the world of man, to the world of the spirits. He pondered this for some time before becoming aware of nebulous presence nearing him.

Suddenly, the presence blossomed into a young maiden sitting before him.

"I am Girl-Without-Parents. I have heard your call, and am here to provide counsel if you would listen," she said mildly yet her lips never moved.

"You honor me with your presence," the shaman replied. "I am confused, and in need of counsel which only the spirits can provide."

"What has you confused?" she asked pensively, almost as if afraid of the answer.

"Four times the visions I was given were wrong. Wrong for me, wrong for my family, wrong for my people." With an imploring look he continued, "I would know what I have done to bring such bad visions from the spirit world; and, more importantly, what I need to do to regain your favor. My people won't survive another bad vision."

"I will help if I can, of course, but only the Creator knows all. So, tell me of these visions, and the results," she said solemnly.

He lost track of time, even more than usual, as he recounted the visions he'd had, his actions, and the results. Girl-Without-Parents listened patiently, outwardly calm, but with an inner anger that grew with each vision and result the shaman told her of.

They'd been sitting in silence after he finished as she reined in her anger sufficiently to begin giving counsel when they both felt a shift in the spirit fabric.

With that shift, her anger was gone, replaced by sadness.

She answered his unspoken question. "That was your mentor, your teacher, leaving the realm of man for the spirit world and the Land of Ever Summer."

The shaman gave out a great sigh of loss. In all his years he'd only gone against his teacher once. And that one time was counseling his people to move North instead of staying in the South as his teacher had advised. He should have listened to his teacher.

"Yes, you should have listened to him," Girl-Without-Parents said as if reading his mind. "The four visions you seek counsel on, were all from a spirit with evil intent. Whether it was the trickster or one of the others, I can't tell. What I *can* tell you is that you need to lead your people South and rejoin this branch of the family to the Southern branch, making the family whole once again as your teacher asked."

"This I will do as swiftly as possible after preparations are made," he promised.

"You will find another student awaiting you there. Not an apprentice but a student. That student will tell you of their need and you will strive to teach them what they seek," she commanded.

Before he could reply the presence began to rapidly fade.

"My time with you is done," she said as her form vanished. Her final words settled heavily on him in the still air of the sweathouse. "One last thing, listen to the counsel of your brother. If you have concerns discuss them with him and take heed of his words."

With a heavy sigh he gathered his thoughts examining everything Girl-Without-Parents had said during his discussion.

Hours - which seemed like minutes - later, Nan-tan, Shaman, and now leader, of the Northern Garcia Apache, left the sweat lodge. Tiredly, he directed his apprentice to spread the word. His people were to be ready to leave first thing in the morning. They had a long trip South to make.

CHAPTER 1

My head was pounding! Somehow, around the pain, I thought, 'After seventy some years, you'd think I'd remember never to mix distilled and fermented alcohol!'

I may have looked twenty years old, but I was well over seventy. Getting sent back over 160 year's in time was bad enough. Throw in losing everyone and everything I knew, and it was even tougher. Losing fifty years off my apparent age paled in comparison; but it was rough, too. Well, losing the years, both in time and age, had its good points; but still, until I'd adjusted to the reality of it, I thought I was either going, or already was, bat shit crazy.

Of course, hearing the voice of my dead wife whispering in my left ear at odd times, just reinforced the thought that I was experiencing a psychotic break.

Eventually though, with the help of friends I made over the next few years, I'd come to adjust to my situation. My new reality. I think it was Anna, my lovely Anna, that finally grounded me to the point where I could accept my new reality.

We'd been married almost a year. When I had the time to think about it, I still found it hard to believe that I'd found Anna. Okay, so Las Cruces isn't exactly Casablanca but with just a little modification, the line about, 'all the gin joints in all the world', would apply to me meeting Anna. I'd probably never have noticed or entered that restaurant, if it hadn't been for meeting her grandfather a couple of times over the previous few months.

Thinking of Anna, I opened my eyes, only to immediately shut them again as the pain in my head flared. The glare of light from the sun as it peeked over the Doña Ana Mountains streaming through the French doors, was tough to take with a hangover. When I thought I had a handle on the pain, I squinted my eyes open as I turned my head.

Anna's head was on my shoulder, her twinkling eyes were wide open and looking at me with a smile on her face.

"Good morning, mi Pablo," she said softy. "You

don't look well."

"I don't feel well," I grumbled in reply. "I don't think we'll be leaving for Las Cruces this morning my love. I'm sorry, but if this headache didn't kill me the ride would."

Anna gave a small giggle. "That's okay Pablo. From what I saw of George and the others last night, I don't think any of you will be able to make the ride, today."

Anna was right. All the men in the Hacienda were too hung over to do much of anything. Aspirin and copious amounts of liquid to rehydrate were great at helping us recover from hangovers, but they're not an antidote.

My cousin, George Pickett and I, managed to recover from the celebration enough to ride to Las Cruces the next day. We arrived in the early afternoon, with Anna and I each leading three mules. George left us almost immediately. He had six more miles to go to get to Fort Fillmore, and report back in from his leave.

At supper Anna's great grandfather, Mr. Garcia, asked if the invitation for him to spend time at the Hacienda was still open. Anna was quick to assure him it was a standing invitation, and he would be welcome any time he showed up, for as long as he cared to stay. Yolanda and Tom were there as were all the cousins, so he would be more than welcome, even if we weren't there.

Mr. Garcia thanked us, and the conversation turned to other subjects. After supper Anna, handed me my guitar and asked me to sing, as she wouldn't get to hear it for a while. I thought for a minute and played "Till the Rivers All Run Dry" followed by "Tumbling Tumbleweeds". The rest of the evening I played whatever the family requested, finally closing with "Anna's Song".

As were going over to the house, Mr. Garcia told Yolanda's father that he would take him up on the offer of a ride to the Hacienda in the morning. Anna beamed me a smile on hearing that, whispering to me that it would do him a lot of good to be around all the kids. We spent the night with the Mendoza clan enjoying soft beds and clean sheets knowing we wouldn't have those luxuries for a few months.

The next morning, we said our goodbyes and rode out to Mesilla, for a quick stop to check in with my Deputy Marshals, Esteban and Ed, as well as say goodbye to George.

The visit with Esteban and Ed was disturbing to say the least. Apparently the comancheros we'd killed on our raid a few months earlier were part of a larger group, and had been awaiting the return of their leader and the rest. The leader had taken a large number of captives and goods east to the Comancheria, to sell to the Comanche.

The gossip being spread around the cantinas and bars, was that the leader had been livid on his return to the camp and finding all his men dead, and the rest of the captives as well as the loot gone. While no one knew his name, he was described as a big man with a flat nose, which had been smashed and broken sometime in the past.

Everyone who'd seen him agreed that he most closely resembled an angry bear, both in build and disposition. He had publicly vowed vengeance on Esteban, Ed, and me during his last saloon appearance a few days ago, before disappearing into the desert.

So far there hadn't been any reports of raids on ranches or farms in the area, but they were keeping their ears open. I told Esteban to write up a report and send it to the Judge, asking for any information he may have.

Anna and I debated putting off the trip until we'd tracked down the group of comancheros, but eventually decided to continue as planned. I wrote Tom a brief note explaining the situation, telling him to put the cousins on alert to this new threat. I gave Ed the note and asked him to take it to Juan for delivery to the

Hacienda with the next delivery of building supplies. I also asked Ed to stop by the Mendozas, and let them know about the threat as well.

We said our goodbyes to George outside Fort Fillmore and reminded him that even though we'd be gone for a few months, the invitation to visit the Hacienda remained open.

Anna and I led our mules west from Fort Fillmore, finally beginning our long-anticipated trip. I was worried about the comancheros and Anna picked up on my worry. We were hyper-vigilant on the first portion of the trip not only while we were riding but at night as well, getting up numerous times each night to check the surrounding area.

We rode into Hurley, our first planned stop, exhausted and ready for a break. We spent a somewhat more relaxed two days in Hurley, 'showing the badge' after introducing ourselves to the Sheriff and Mayor.

The hotel was barely habitable and only contributed to my sense of unease. I was continuously on edge and for the first time since we'd been married I found myself snapping at Anna. When I realized what I was doing, I gave her a big hug and apologized to her.

For some reason I couldn't get my mind off

the leader of the comancheros, and his vow to get even with me. There was no telling what he would do, and it gnawed at me relentlessly. Anna did her best to comfort me, but I was worried. I was worried like I hadn't been worried since coming to this timeline. I had a bad feeling, a premonition, that both Anna and I were going to regret not delaying the trip.

The third morning after arriving in Hurley, we packed up and rode the short distance to Fort McLane. We introduced ourselves to the Fort Commander using the letter of introduction Colonel Miles had written for us. He was indifferent to my status as US Marshal, but was extremely interested in me as the owner of the Estancia Dos Santos, and our ability to regularly supply him with beef at an acceptable price.

Anna eventually negotiated a price of seven dollars and seventy-five cents a head for a contract that in every other respect was the same as those we'd signed with Fort Fillmore, and Fort Thorn. The Indian Agent for this area was on a trip to El Paso, though, and wouldn't be back for some time

I let Tom know the terms of the contract in a letter I sent from the fort, as well as instructions to have Hector contact the Indian Agent when he made his first delivery, to see about selling him some beef.

Visitor accommodations at the fort looked to be even worse than the hotel in Hurley, so we decided to leave on the next leg of our trip, instead of spending the night at the fort.

We stuck to our tried and true method of paralleling the road, staying a half mile off the road to attract less attention. The further west we rode the more relaxed I became, until it was almost as much fun as the honeymoon trip up to Santa Fe.

There was still a small part of me that worried about the situation back home, but the distance and our lack of ability to influence the outcome lessened my worry with each mile west we rode.

We knew that Apache, Yaqui, and Navajo raiding parties frequently crossed this area at all times of the year, looking for targets of opportunity, so we rode carefully and were ever watchful. This was the kind of tension we were used to though, and it caused no undue stress. We passed two different slow-moving trains of freight wagons hauling goods west, as well as a large wagon train of settlers headed for California on our way.

Sonoita proved to be a town in name only. It was really nothing more than a handful of adobe buildings, centered around a general store. There was no government of any kind. After a quick lunch at the only cantina, we left for the three-mile ride to Fort Buchanan.

The Fort Commander gave us a cordial greeting after discovering who we were, and why we were there. We spent two hours learning the fort was established primarily to stop the cross-border raiding activity of the Apache and Yaqui Indians. The Major in charge of the Fort told us that he patrolled the wagon road as often as he could, but the bulk of his forces patrolled the border area. According to him, Sonoita and the Fort were so far off the beaten path that they had very few visitors or settlers in the area. There were so few visitors in fact, that the fort did not even have any visitor's quarters. I crossed both Sonoita and the Fort off the list as a regular stop on the circuit.

Early the next afternoon we were a little over half-way to Tucson, the next stop on our circuit, when we decided to stop for a late lunch. I'd just taken a bite of my ham sandwich when I noticed a brown mass on the western horizon, stretching from side to side as far as the eye could see. Before I'd finished the mouthful of sandwich I was chewing, I knew we were in for a big sandstorm. I cursed under my breath, but Anna heard it and looked at me crossly.

I pointed behind her. "Sorry, but we're in for a sandstorm, my love, and a big one at that. We need to move quickly."

Sandwiches in hand, we mounted and rode northwest looking for a suitable arroyo or canyon to help us ride out the sandstorm. This wasn't the Mesilla Valley with its abundance of arroyos and canyons and finding one was difficult.

We got lucky and came across an arroyo running north and south. It took us a couple of minutes to find a way down to the bottom and another few minutes to find a curve to better shelter us and the animals.

Using the panniers, packs, and saddles we built a hollow square, big enough for both of us to fit inside against the western wall. I hobbled and tied the horses and mules to some strong mesquite against the eastern wall before wrapping all their heads in canvas. Finished with the animals I went back over to the western wall and helped Anna unfold our large piece of canvas.

Working together we slid one end of the canvas down between the wall of the arroyo and the pack frames we'd stacked up against it. When it was far enough down I lifted each of the two stacks of pack frames while Anna pulled about six inches of the canvas under them, before I set them back down.

The wind had picked up by now, as the leading edge of the sandstorm hit the arroyo and we hurried to tuck the sides of the canvas under the panniers on both sides. Done with that, we scurried under the canvas and I lifted the saddles while kneeling, so that Anna could pull the final ends of canvas under them.

Anna and I sat at the back of our little refuge against the wall of the arroyo between the pack frames. Anna dug through her saddlebags to find the cotton cloth squares we'd packed, while I pulled one of the small water barrels over near us and used it to start refilling all four of our camel packs. When I was done with that, Anna handed me the cloth, receiving her two camel packs in exchange.

We dampened the cloths before tying them behind our necks, making a face mask. We could hear the wind howling around us, see the canvas shaking, and hear it flapping violently. A few minutes later we lost most of the daylight as the brown roiling haze of the sandstorm raged over us.

For the next two days, we sat and waited for the storm to blow itself out. After the first couple of hours a coating of fine sand covered our hair, clothes, the packs, and saddles. Despite our face masks, the dust managed to get into our noses and mouth and, over time, irritated our throats making it uncomfortable and difficult to talk. Luckily, it wasn't summer! While the air under the canvas was stifling, we weren't sweating to death in one hundred plus degree temperatures.

The first twenty-four hours we talked for a few hours before having a supper of beef jerky I carried in a bag inside my coat, so it wasn't covered in sand. We slept uneasily through the night, and had a breakfast of more beef jerky while we talked some more about the future, our plans, what could go wrong, and what backup plans we needed to come up with.

The final twenty-four hours were maddening, as three different times the wind started to die down and we got more light leading us to believe the storm was about over, only to have it come roaring back. We held each other and waited silently for the last few hours.

We must have dozed off in our boredom as I woke up a few hours later with Anna's head on my shoulder. It took me a few minutes to realize that everything was quiet and calm, and a few moments more to realize that meant the storm was over.

Gently waking Anna, I let her know the storm was over, and we needed to get out from under the canvas. As quickly as I could shift the saddles and lift the canvas we were out from underneath it and breathing clean, clear, refreshing air.

The horses and mules seemed to have weathered the storm without much harm, and we gently unwrapped their heads one at a time, swabbing out their nostrils with our damp cloths, giving them small drinks and arranging feed bags.

It was almost dark by this time, and we spent what little daylight we had left finding firewood and pulling out what we needed to cook our first hot meal since breakfast three days ago. The last thing we did before going to bed was strip down to get out of our sand laden clothes. We washed both ourselves and the clothes the best we could using almost a full three gallon cask of water.

We finally rode out of the arroyo the next morning, pushing the animals hard, to get to Tucson as early the next day as we could. We were both looking forward with anticipation to a nice hot bath.

We rode into Tucson near mid-morning, and found it to be somewhere between Santa Fe and Mesilla in size. Asking a couple of men, we received directions to the best hotel in town, and tied up in front of it a few minutes later. We checked into a room for two nights. Discovering the hotel only had one tub, I had it sent up for Anna to use while I arranged for the care and feeding of the livestock and went to the barber shop for my bath.

I came out of the barbershop an hour later clean, freshly sheared, wearing fresh clothes, and looking and feeling much better. Anna was waiting in the hotel lobby looking like she was feeling better after her bath, too. She pinned my badge on the outside of my coat and we went in search of the best place for lunch.

We were sitting in the restaurant enjoying a leisurely cup of coffee when the Town Marshal walked in, looked around, and came over to our table. He took in my badge and without introducing himself, rudely informed me that it was customary for visiting lawmen to come to his office and introduce themselves when they got to town.

I sat back in my chair and, as I looked him up and down, I couldn't help but wonder what it was about people that made them act like assholes when they had a little bit of power. I looked over at Anna who, with a twinkle in her eye, beamed me one of her special smiles. Picking up my coffee cup, I took a drink, wiping my mouth afterwards with a napkin before asking him who he was.

My actions up to this point didn't sit well with

him and he answered tersely, "I'm the Town Marshal!"

"Well, now! That's sure enough a rather strange name to my way of thinking, but I guess you can't be held accountable for what your parents named you. What can I do for you, Mr. Marshal?"

"No damn it! My name's not Marshal, I'm the Town Marshal," he replied in exasperation.

"Well, why didn't you say so? I'm Paul McAllister and this is my wife Anna. I'm the US Marshal for this part of the territory. What can I do for you?"

"Damn it man! Are you deaf as well as stupid? I asked you why you didn't come to my office and introduce yourself when you got into town?"

I was starting to get just a little angry by this point, and looking at him with a glare I said, "That's the second time you've cussed in front of a lady. Apologize immediately and mind your tongue, or Tucson will be looking for a new Marshal this afternoon!"

The Marshal got red in the face as he lost all self-control and started to draw his pistol. Both mine and Anna's pistols were out and pointed at him in a flash.

He calmed down immediately and moved his hand away from his holster. For effect, I cocked the pistol. "I'm still waiting to hear the apology."

Looking from me to Anna, who cocked her pistol with a grim look on her face, the Marshal eventually stuttered out his apology to Anna. We both let the hammers down and holstered our pistols.

Taking a drink of coffee, I looked at the Marshal who remained standing in front of our table. With a sigh, I addressed the Marshal, "I don't know who you think you are, or what powers you think you have, but let me make a few things clear. I don't know you, I don't even know your name, since you haven't had the manners to introduce yourself. I don't work for you, and I'm not responsible to you. Where I go, when I go, and who I see; are absolutely none of your business, unless I choose to make it so.

"My wife and I have spent the last few weeks in the saddle, and two of the last three days hunkered down in a sandstorm, so we're a little out of sorts. Neither of us appreciate your rude interruption as we're relaxing for the first time since we started this journey. We may or may not see you before we leave town.

"Rest assured, however, that either me or one of my Deputies will be in town for some period of time at least twice per year. When, is none of your business. I strongly suggest you show yourself to the door with the clear knowledge that you're still alive, only because you're so slow with your gun that even my wife beat you to the draw."

Ignoring the Marshal from that point on, I turned to Anna and asked her if she'd like another cup of coffee. At her nod I poured us both a fresh cup. The Marshal finally turned and left as I was pouring.

Anna looked at me and said, "I don't think we've seen the last of him."

"You're probably right; but people like that, in positions of authority just get my dander up," I replied.

Drinking our coffee in contemplative silence for a few minutes before Anna spoke up. "That Marshal reminds me of somebody, but I don't know who."

I shrugged and said it would come to her eventually. We finished our coffee and walked back to the hotel and asked the man behind the counter where we could find the Mayor. He took in my badge, and politely told us that the Mayor ran the livery stable at the southern edge of town.

We walked back to the hotel stables to get our horses only to find the Marshal rifling through our panniers. We stopped ten feet behind him, I drew my revolver, looked at Anna, and cocked it. The sound reverberated throughout the stable and the Marshal went completely still.

"Marshal no name, please tell me why you're pawing through our panniers without our permission," I said in as reasonable a voice as possible.

"I'm looking for stolen valuables. I don't like the look of you, and I don't think you're a US Marshal," he replied belligerently.

I cocked an eyebrow at Anna who just shrugged. I looked back at the still bent over Marshal before saying, "Stand up slowly, with your hands visible."

He did as I instructed and as he turned towards us I heard a small gasp from Anna. I glanced over at her getting a look that said we needed to talk in return.

"Marshal, this is a territory of the United States. The 4th Amendment to the Constitution prohibits unreasonable search and seizure. That means that unless you have a search warrant, you are in violation of federal law, and I'm well within my rights to shoot you for attempted theft. This is the second time you've made me angry today. There won't be a next time. Have I made myself clear?"

He started to reply but stopped when Anna broke in. "Pablo, the excitement from the restaurant and now this is getting to me. Please take me back to the room to rest for a while."

Now that was interesting. She clearly wanted to talk to me as soon as possible. I motioned with my gun for the Marshal to leave the stables. He left without a word, and I tied the covers on all the panniers making sure they were tight before turning to Anna, taking her arm, and leading her back over to our room in the hotel.

No sooner were we inside and the door closed, than Anna asked me for the stack of wanted posters, descriptions, and warrants I'd gotten before we left Mesilla. Digging them out of my saddlebag, I handed them to her, curious to see if she would find something of interest.

She spent a few minutes looking through them before pulling a poster and warrant out of the pile and handing them to me. I looked down to see a picture of the Marshal we'd just been talking to.

His name was Fred Atchison. He was reportedly part of the Red River Gang, and was wanted for robbing the Overland Stagecoach near Las Vegas, killing both the driver and guard. I looked up at Anna and she handed me three more wanted posters, one for each of the Red River Gang.

The leader of the gang was Mike 'Two Hands' Stubben. His nickname apparently stemming from the fact that he was completely ambidextrous and wore two guns. There were no pictures for the other two gang members, and the descriptions were generic which didn't help us much. I looked up from the papers, and found Anna throwing her shawl on over the shotgun sling she'd just finished putting on.

I raised an eyebrow at her and in a tart tone she said, "If you think you're going up against four of them by yourself you have another thought coming."

Putting on my shotgun sling, I wondered if I'd ever win an argument with her.

Checking that our shotguns were loaded, we walked downstairs and got directions to the Marshal's office. We crossed the street and walked arm in arm down the sidewalk.

Just before we got to the Marshal's office I had Anna check for a back door and if there was one to see if it was locked. She returned less than a minute later telling me there was a back door, but it was locked. We walked into the office and found a young Deputy sitting at a desk, reading an old newspaper. He looked up, and seeing my star introduced himself and asked how he could help us.

"We're looking for the Marshal," I replied.

"You just missed him," came his reply. "The Marshal went over to the Mayor's office just a few minutes ago."

Out of curiosity I asked, "How long have you been the Deputy?"

Giving a deep belly laugh he replied, "This is my third year as a winter Deputy. Normally, I'm a cowhand, but I prefer to spend my winters in town."

I asked the same question about the Marshal, and the Deputy told us that the Marshal had taken the job about six months earlier, when the old Mayor and Marshal had been killed walking down the street one evening after a late poker game.

He also told us that both the Mayor and Marshal had just been reelected before they were killed. No one in town wanted either job, so the new Mayor agreed to take the position and had appointed his friend the new Marshal.

Without coming right out and saying so it was clear from the Deputy's tone of voice and body language that he didn't much care for either the Mayor or the Marshal. I asked him for directions to the Mayor's office and again he laughed before pointing out the window to a small adobe building across the street.

"That used to be a storehouse, and since it only has the one door, I'm certain both the Mayor and Marshal are still inside," he said helpfully.

I thanked him, and told him I'd see him a little later.

On our way across the street I told Anna to enter behind me and move at least two steps to the left with her shotgun ready. She nodded and reached down to grip her shotgun. I stopped in front of the door, pulled my shotgun around holding it by the stock with my finger on the trigger, and at Anna's nod I opened the door and entered.

The 'Mayor' was sitting at a desk talking to the 'Marshal', who was standing on the right side of the desk looking at a small ledger laying open on the desk in front of the 'Mayor'. The 'Mayor' looked up, saw me entering the door with my shotgun ready, and reached over to a pistol lying beside the ledger.

He cocked it as he was raising it towards

me and without hesitation I fired the shotgun in his direction. In the small confines of the office the blast was deafening. The 'Mayor' was thrown against the back wall before falling to the floor.

Less than a second later I heard Anna's 20-gauge shotgun go off and watched as the 'Marshal' joined his friend on the floor against the back wall. At least this time he'd managed to get his pistol out of his holster!

I took Anna in a big hug. "Are you alright?

"I'm fine," she replied, hugging me tightly before pulling back. "What's next?"

"I have no clue," I said. "I'm just making it up as I go along." After a few seconds of thought I said, "Wait here and don't let anyone in until I get back with the Deputy."

At her nod I opened the door to walk out and found the Deputy crossing the street towards me at a trot. I waved him inside and he paled slightly at the sight of the 'Mayor' and 'Marshal' laying along the back wall.

Pulling out the wanted posters and warrants from my coat pocket I handed him the two for Mike 'Two Hands' Stubben and Fred Atchison. He read them both, looked at the two bodies, shook his head, and handed the papers back to me.

"That explains the rash of stagecoach holdups over the last six months," he said shaking his head.

"Has anyone matching these descriptions been close to either the 'Mayor' or 'Marshal'?" I asked as I handed him the papers on the other two members of the gang.

He read them quickly, thought for a second, and then shook his head saying, "Neither of them had any close acquaintances in town that I'm aware of." After another moment of thought he added, "When they first arrived in town, there were four of them but the other two left town for California after the first week or so."

While the Deputy and I had been talking Anna had been looking through the ledger.

She looked up and interrupted us. "This ledger is broken into two parts. The first part shows a list of deposits and withdrawals from a bank in Santa Fe. The current balance is over $35,000. It also gives two names and the address of a boarding house in San Francisco. The other part of the ledger lists deposits and withdrawals for the livery stable, with a current balance of $18,000."

The Deputy's eyes nearly bulged out of his head at the numbers Anna gave. In 1855 that amount of money would allow him to retire at his young age, and never have to work a day in his life again if he was careful.

"Please make arrangements for the bodies with the undertaker," I instructed the Deputy. "The weapons these two have should cover the cost of burial."

He nodded and left while I searched the two bodies. Between them they had just under twenty dollars, which I gave to Anna telling her, tongue in cheek, that it would cover the cost of our ammunition. We left the office, and went to the bank to discuss the account shown in the ledger.

The bank president took in my badge and greeted us cordially after I introduced us. When he asked us how he could help us Anna handed me the ledger.

I said, "I need the answers to some questions. Is the account in the ledger still open? If so, is the current balance in the ledger accurate, if not, what's the current balance? Does the 'Mayor' have any other accounts open under any other names?"

"I'll have to check," was the unexpected response. The town wasn't so large to have many large depositors, and this was a very large account.

He started to move to the tellers' area when I stopped him. "I also need the balances of any accounts the 'Marshal' has open as well."

He nodded, clearly curious but also clearly intimidated by the badge, not asking any questions. When he came back he said, "The balances in the ledger are accurate, neither man has more than one account, and the balance in the 'Marshal's' account is just under forty dollars."

"Do you know when the last stage holdup was?" I asked after a few moments of hard thinking.

"It was eight days ago. The robbers got away with almost $4,000 in the strongbox," was his immediate reply.

"Hmmm," I said while thinking furiously. "I need to see the detailed account information for both men, immediately."

The Banker stiffened as he said, "I can't do that without their permission."

"That's going to be difficult since they're both dead," I replied with a glare.

That news shocked him, but again he surprised me. "I still can't give you that information."

I looked at Anna shaking my head in disgust before looking back at the banker. "The 'Mayor', and 'Marshal's' real names were Mike 'Two Hands' Stubben and Fred Atchison, leaders of the Red River Gang up near Las Vegas."

I took the papers on both men out of my coat pocket and handed him the wanted posters. Now he was convinced but still refused to show me the account information. I sighed heavily and handed him the two warrants which included a statement authorizing review and seizure of all bank accounts.

As he was reading the warrants I said, "You can either give me immediate access, or I'll put you in jail for obstruction of justice and you can wait until transport to Santa Fe is arranged. Once in Santa Fe you can explain your obstruction to the Federal Judge."

His face lost all color, and he gulped before handing me back the warrants and leaving to get the account information.

Anna beamed one of her smiles my way. "I've never seen so many contrary people in one place in all my life."

"Confiscation of the funds in these accounts is going to hurt the bank," I explained. "He was just trying to delay the inevitable."

He came back with the information I'd asked for regarding both accounts, and handed it to me. I compared the activity recorded in the mayor's ledger with what had been provided by the banker and when I was sure it matched I asked where the Overland Stage Office was as that was our next stop.

"It's two doors down on this side of the street," the banker replied helpfully.

Standing up, I said, "We'll be back when we're done with the stage company manager."

Anna followed me out of the bank curious at what I was going to do at the stage office. We walked into the stage office and, after confirming the man behind the counter was the manager, I introduced Anna and I.

"Now that you know who I am what can you tell me about the holdups your stage company has experienced over the last six months?"

The manager answered my questions readily. "The stage has been held up five times in the last six months. Every holdup was within twenty miles of Tucson and was done by the same two men wearing black clothes and bandanas. In every case at least one person, the shotgun rider, was killed. The total amount taken from all five robberies is $14,500."

"I see," I said thoughtfully. "What was the date of each robbery and what was the total amount taken in each robbery?"

He checked a diary and his account ledgers, before writing down the dates. I handed them to Anna asking her to check the dates against the ledger and see if she could determine if there was a pattern.

While she was doing that, the manager was looking back through the records and adding up the amounts. He handed me another piece of paper with the amount stolen during each robbery. After a quick look I handed it to Anna as well.

After a few minutes Anna said she was done. "There were deposits made ten days after each of the first four robberies."

"How much was each deposit?" I asked.

She read off the amounts of each deposit and I compared the number she gave me to the amounts stolen. In every case the amount deposited appeared to have been rounded up or down to the nearest twenty-five dollars.

"Well, that pretty much solves the robberies," I said after giving them the results. I looked at the manager. "I need you to come to the bank with us please."

He closed up the office and we all walked back to the bank, where we went directly to the bank president's office. I asked to borrow his desk, his pen, and three pieces of paper. He waved me to his chair and after sitting down I wrote out the same set of instructions three times numbering each piece of paper sequentially as '1 of 3', '2 of 3', and '3 of 3'.

When I was done I handed the three pieces of paper to the bank president and told him to read all three and after confirming they were exactly the same to sign all three. When he was done I gave the same instructions to the stage manager who had a big smile on his face after reading the first paper. When he had signed all three I signed them as well and kept the first copy giving each man one copy for their own records. I handed my copy to Anna and asked her to keep it with the ledger.

The paper instructed the bank to transfer $14,500 from the 'Mayor's' account to the Overland Stage Company account. The remaining funds were to be added to the funds from the 'Marshal's' account and a Bank Draft issued to the Judge in Santa Fe and given to me to deliver to him.

When he'd verified the transfer, the stage manager left, and I told the banker we'd wait while he prepared the Bank Draft. While he was doing that I wrote out two copies of a receipt for the Bank Draft, numbering both as I had the instructions, and signed them. I gave him the second copy when he gave me the Bank Draft.

Before we left I asked, "Did the 'Mayor' own the livery stable and his home?"

The banker shook his head. "The bank owns both, and rented them to the 'Mayor'. The house is part of the stable complex."

I sarcastically thanked the banker for his help and Anna and I left.

Anna took my arm as we walked. When we passed the hotel she asked, "Where are we going?"

"To search the 'Mayor's' house and stables if necessary," I absently responded. "There's still the money from the last robbery that hasn't been deposited yet."

Anna gave my arm a squeeze. "You know, cousin George was right." I looked at her questioningly. "It's never dull around us."

I had to laugh and agree with her.

We found the stables strangely quiet with seven horses in stalls, no animals in the corrals, and no mules anywhere. We eventually found an older man leaned back in a rocker with his feet up on the desk, fast asleep. He woke up with a startled exclamation almost tipping over backward in the rocker at the sudden noise as I loudly cleared my throat from the doorway.

When he righted himself, I introduced us both and asked him about the horses in the stable. He proved to be quite loquacious. Over the next five minutes we learned that one horse belonged to the 'Mayor', one belonged to the 'Marshal', the other five horses were rentals although nobody had ever rented them.

The stable had had no business in the last four months, as the prices had been set too high, and the only time the 'Mayor' was in the stables was to saddle his horse or give him his monthly pay. He wasn't too surprised when I told him the 'Mayor' was dead, and suggested he close up for the day and go see the banker to find out about his job and pay.

He nodded and quickly left after walking out with us. Once he was gone, we made our way to the small house sitting off to the side, and walked in the front door when no one answered my knock. There were three rooms in the house, a front parlor, a combination kitchen dining room, and a bedroom.

I started the search in the bedroom, looking under the mattress, under the bed, through the dresser, and in the small closet. When we didn't find anything there we went through the kitchen and then the parlor finding nothing.

I walked back to the kitchen door and looked around distractedly. "I'm sure the money is here somewhere. We just have to figure out where."

Anna stood in the doorway with me looking at the kitchen. After a couple of minutes, she looked up at me. "Where's the cold room?"

"I'm not sure there is one," I said.

She pointed at the table where a plate of partially eaten toast and eggs as well as a glass of what looked like milk had been left out. "There's no milk bottle anywhere," she pointed out. "The toast has butter on it but there's no sign of any butter, so both must be stored somewhere."

I beamed her one of my special smiles, and told her she was one smart lady. She snorted, gave me a light arm slap, and told me to look out the back door for a separate cold room or cellar entrance.

While Anna searched the kitchen more carefully for an entrance to a cold room I walked out the back door and around the house. The only thing I found was the outhouse and I was pretty sure the money wasn't hidden there. I returned to the house through the back door and found Anna studying the pantry floor.

Joining her we both stood looking into the pantry. "This pantry is odd. The shelves are much too narrow for the amount of floor space there is," she said pensively.

I looked down at the floor to see if there was the outline of a trap door. I didn't see a trap door but I did see a small rectangular notch just big enough for a finger to fit into a cut between two of the floorboards.

Bending down, I stuck my finger into the notch feeling for a release latch. After a couple seconds of experimenting the latch moved to the left and released a catch holding the floor down. Using both hands I lifted the floor where it had popped up, and it swung up on hinges at the back of the pantry.

With the floor up, we could see a set of stairs leading down. I looked at the trap door and saw that it had been disguised by the simple expedient of using the normal staggered floor planks joins to hide the door, much like what I had done to hide the cave entrance.

Anna left while I was looking at the door, and returned with a lit lamp. Pushing me out of the way she started down the steps before looking back at me. "Are you coming with me?"

Grinning, I said, "Right behind you, my love."

The cold room proved to be quite large. Along the right-hand wall, we saw a small milk can sitting under a set of shelves holding butter, eggs, bacon, a ham, and a small wooden box of potatoes.

Along the back wall was a large heavy work table. Four empty strong boxes from the Overland Stage Line were under the table, while a fifth opened box was on top of the table. A heavy chisel and sledge hammer were also on top of the table lying next to a shattered lock.

Against the left hand wall was a smaller table holding two neatly folded sets of clothes, all black.

I walked to the table and picked up a bag of money from inside the strong box. We'd count it later when we got back to our room, but I was pretty sure it held all the money from the last robbery.

Anna picked up something from behind the clothes on the other table, and brought me a small metal money box like we used at the Hacienda. She put it on the work table and opened it up, revealing a mix of half eagle, eagle, and double eagle gold pieces.

I put the money box and the bag of money from the strong box, inside the wooden box the potatoes had been in, before picking up the straw the potatoes had been nestled in and putting it over the top. Anna led me back upstairs, closing the trap door after I was out, and followed me out of the house.

Back in our hotel room we both counted the money, and found all $3,750 from the last robbery in the money bag as well as another $600 from the small money box. There was no way of telling where the $600 came from so I just dumped it loose in a burlap bag and put the bag of money from the stagecoach on top of it. I tied up the burlap bag and put it under the bed with our saddle bags.

I retrieved my courier bag, and suggested to Anna that we go get some coffee while I wrote up my report to send to the Judge. She thought that was a splendid idea and we walked down to the restaurant.

Anna kept me company the rest of what was left of the afternoon. I wrote out the long report to the Judge, telling him what had happened and letting him know that I was bringing the various pieces of documentation, the Bank Draft, the ledger, and the money we'd found in the cold room with us on our trip to Santa Fe in a few months.

I added the wanted posters and warrants for 'Two Hands' and Fred that I'd marked diagonally with the word DECEASED, the date,

Tucson, and Resisting Arrest. Anna read over the report and agreed it covered all the major points.

While Anna folded everything up into an envelope I wrote another, much shorter, note to Esteban and Ed, telling them to ignore Sonoita and Fort Buchanan during their circuit and to remove the two dead men from their stack of posters and warrants. Anna read the note before folding it up into another envelope and handing both envelopes to me. She'd already addressed both envelopes, so I asked the waitress for a candle to seal them with. After sealing them with my ring, I put the envelopes in my courier bag to mail out tomorrow.

Later that night, following an acceptable supper in the restaurant, Anna and I discovered that while the bed in our room wasn't perfect, it was more than adequate for exploring possibilities.

We fell asleep cuddled close together with the cool night air of early spring wafting through our open window.

CHAPTER 2

We were up early, and after breakfast, we rounded up the deputy and the stage coach manager before walking over to the bank.

The four of us walked into the banker's office over his objections. I closed the door and told him to shut up and listen, as Anna looked away to hide her smile. I asked the banker if the 'Mayor' had been up to date on his rental payments for the stable and house.

When he said that he was current, I turned to the Deputy. "I want a complete inventory of the stables to include the horses, tack, and feed. Once that's done you're to sell them to whomever wants them for a minimum price of," I stopped there and turned to Anna with a raised eyebrow.

She smiled at me and gave me a number that

seemed a little high, but I didn't question it. I turned back to the Deputy, "It's helpful to marry a girl who grew up in her grandfather's stables. Now, that's the minimum price you will accept. If you can't get that price, then you'll put up the horses and store the tack and feed, at the city's expense, until one of my Deputies comes through to take everything off your hands."

None of them liked that very much as it stopped them from buying everything for a song and forced the city to pay for the upkeep and storage. I looked at all three of them with a hard glare.

"As far as I'm concerned, you earned this for failing to notice the timing and amounts of the deposits compared against the date of the robberies, the overnight absence of both the 'Mayor' and 'Marshal' on the dates of the robberies, and the size of the deposits, for a business with absolutely no clients. You had to have known something was wrong, but turned a blind eye to it through sheer laziness."

By the time I was done they all had sheepish looks on their faces.

Turning to the banker I asked, "Do you know how to get into the cold room at the house?" At his nod, I continued, "There are two sets of black clothes with bandanas, as well as all five strong boxes from the robberies in the cold room. I recommend you have them removed before renting it out again."

We left the three of them in the banker's office, and went to buy more supplies for the long ten day trek to Colorado City, the largest of the three towns in the area that would one day be known as Yuma.

Leaving early the next morning, we were relaxed and focused as we traveled. It felt good to travel again like we had on our honeymoon. All the major tension I'd been feeling and transmitting to Anna had been overcome by our discovery in Tucson that the 'Mayor' and 'Marshal' had, in fact, been wanted fugitives; not to mention being responsible for the latest rash of stagecoach robberies in the area. The short time we'd spent in Tucson more than justified our entire trip.

We arrived in Colorado City in the fading twilight ten days after leaving Tucson. We were both ready for a few days of good meals, soft beds, and most importantly, a hot bath. The accommodations were much better than Tucson, but again, there was only one tub so I resorted to the barbershop bath house while Anna used the tub in our room.

We spent the next two days doing our meet and greet sessions with the various powers that be in town. Our reception was much better than we'd received in Tucson, and we ended up having supper with the Mayor, Marshal, and Commander of Fort Yuma, along with their wives our last night in town.

The conversation at supper was lively with Anna regaling our table mates with stories about my exploits taking on the Stevens Gang, the Comancheros, and the Red River Gang. By the time she was done even I was impressed with her version of me and I knew better.

Riding north, we left Yuma the next morning following the Colorado River for the first day before moving a half mile east to parallel the river still traveling north. When we stopped for lunch on the third day I got out the compass and map while Anna made a lunch of rabbit stew.

I shot azimuths on the two tallest peaks and marked the back azimuths on the map. I grinned when I discovered we were less than a mile from Arroyo La Paz. If mining there didn't pan out Goodman Arroyo was only a little further north and we'd check that next.

I returned to where Anna was cooking and told her the good news. She beamed me a smile and I just had to give her a big hug and kiss when she tried to hand me a bowl of stew. She gave me a small giggle along with a light arm slap when I let her go, and she sat down next to me to eat her stew.

We rode into Arroyo La Paz less than an hour after lunch, and turned to follow the arroyo in a generally northeast direction. We explored the arroyo and its branches for an hour before coming on the perfect camping spot in a side arroyo, that ended in a large bowl less than a hundred yards from the main arroyo.

One side of the bowl had caved in, leaving a gentle ramp up out of the arroyo. When we rode up the ramp we discovered a nice grass covered area surrounded by an irregular circle of hills literally covered in dense thickets of mesquite.

We set up our camp at the base of the hills nearest the ramp, and let the horses and mules graze without hobbles or pickets for the time being. With camp set up, we took the metal detector and two shovels and walked back down the ramp to the arroyo.

At the bottom of the ramp Anna put the headset on and turned on the metal detector to test it. She gave a small shriek, and pulled off the headset rubbing her ears. I asked what was wrong and she said she didn't know but the metal detector had begun a loud screeching in her ears as soon as she turned it on.

I took it from her, turned the squelch all the way down, put on the headset, and turned it on. She was right. Even with the squelch turned all the way down, the screech in my ears was loud. I swept it from side to side, getting a continuous screech, instead of the pings we were used to.

I walked all the way down to the main arroyo and back, continuing the sweep. The screech never stopped. I checked the battery and it showed it was half charged so I checked all the connections, and everything looked good with those as well. I walked up the ramp, and the screech died out to be replaced with the intermittent pings we were used to.

Turning around, the screech returned as soon as I was in the arroyo again. The only thing I could come up with was that we were standing on some kind of mineral deposit that was so big it was setting off the screech. I couldn't think of any minerals that I'd ever read about in this area, in high enough concentrations, to do that.

Taking the headphones off, I dug down into the sand, pulling up a shovel full of sand and started gently sifting it off shaking the shovel side to side. I stopped after the second shake, staring in dumbfounded amazement, as the falling sand glittered gold in the bright sunlight.

It reminded me of the fairy dust Tinkerbell threw on the Darling children in the animated Peter Pan cartoon. Looking over, I saw Anna staring in bright eyed wonder, as the slowly falling sand continued to glitter.

Coming out of my stupor, I sifted a little more aggressively until most of the sand had fallen off. I looked at the shovel full of gold nuggets of varying sizes in wonder. Pouring the nuggets in a small pile behind me, I dug another shovel full of sand out of the ground repeating the shaking action and again watched the gold dust float down, leaving the shovel blade covered in nuggets.

Waving out over the arroyo floor, I looked at Anna. "If the whole area is like this, our panniers will be full in a couple of weeks or less instead of the seven weeks we planned."

She beamed me one of her rare huge super megawatt smiles, and I decided she was pleased with the news.

I tested eight spots between the ramp and the main arroyo before finally telling Anna we didn't need the metal detector. She picked up her shovel and a burlap bag, before walking down to the main arroyo and started digging. I followed behind her and moved off to one side to start digging myself. By the time we quit a couple of hours later we had three bags of nuggets between us.

The next morning, while Anna continued digging and sifting, I walked almost three miles down our back trail to where we'd left a stretch of hard pan. I used every trick Miguel and the instructors had taught us during Scout/Sniper training to hide the trail we'd made from the hard pan all the way back to where we were digging. If someone found us, it would be by luck and expertise, not because they followed our tracks. When I walked back into camp, Anna was just finishing making lunch, and we both ate with healthy appetites. Mine from the long walk and Anna's from all the digging.

Over supper, we talked about the plan for the next couple of weeks. We calculated that we could collect, on average, 260 pounds of gold per day, with one of us digging and collecting full time during the day, and the other only digging and collecting a half day.

Whoever was digging and collecting a half day, would spend the other half of the day melting nuggets. We'd both melt down nuggets for a couple of hours every night after supper. If we could manage to pour 700 bars every day, we would be caught up roughly two days after we finished collecting the nuggets. This all rested on the premise that the gold field was as big as the metal detector indicated, but it was a plan we could work with until something changed.

Work the plan was exactly what we did, for the next eight days. By the end of the eighth day we had collected more than 2,000 pounds of gold to go along with the 400 pounds we collected the first day and a half. We had 5,600 bars all ready to go, leaving us to pour another 1,750 bars at a minimum. We spent two days melting the remaining nuggets and ended up with a total of 7,700 bars or just over the 2,400 pounds we originally planned.

We spent our final day at Arroyo La Paz rearranging and repacking the panniers with the bags of gold bars at the bottom of the panniers and the supplies and clothes on top. When that chore was done we lazed around and talked.

We had both reached the decision that we'd need to hunt on the long 500-mile ride to Santa Fe, as we'd used more of the supplies than we'd anticipated. We were a little short on meat. Hunting wasn't a problem, but I was still terrible at skinning and butchering, so Anna would do that part of the job with whatever help I could provide.

We also decided we would travel north along

the Colorado River skirting the mountains for a few days, before turning east and working our way to Santa Fe.

Things went well for the first two weeks of the trip. We rode north as planned, skirting the base of the mountains along the Colorado River, and then turned east. Anna and I enjoyed our alone time in this rugged and desolate land.

We hunted as we'd planned, and Anna began teaching me how to butcher our kills. Like my stove top coffee, I'm afraid it was a lost cause, but I did try.

On our fifteenth day of travel we stopped at the base of a hill to fix lunch, and rest for an hour before moving on. I was cleaning up after lunch and repacking what we'd used, while Anna had climbed the hill to scout out the rest of the days ride with her monocular.

I'd just finished tying the cover down on the last pannier, when I looked up and saw Anna halfway down the hill waving me to her frantically. I climbed up to her as fast as I could and, while I caught my breath, she told me she'd seen what looked like a raiding party with captives moving north. They were about two miles south of us and another two or three miles east.

We climbed the rest of the hill and laid down, so we could see over the top. Anna searched for a couple of minutes with her monocular, before finding the group again. I found them quickly after Anna pointed me in the right direction.

The distance was a little long for the monocular, so I couldn't get any detail, but the general impression was as Anna had said. A group of six or seven warriors traveling north with a group of four or five captives. We couldn't tell for sure, but we both agreed that we thought the captives were children and a young woman who may have been carrying a baby or toddler.

Damn Murphy and all his laws! So much for a nice peaceful trip to Santa Fe.

I judged their line of travel the best I could and started scanning with the monocular looking for someplace suitable to free the captives. I thought I saw a cut in a long rocky ridge that might work about two miles north of us. I couldn't make out enough detail to be sure though.

Anna and I talked about it for a few minutes and decided to see if we could work our way around the ridge to the other side. We rode north as fast as we could without raising a dust trail behind us. When we'd traveled what I judged to be two miles, we stopped at the base of another hill, and climbed up to check our position and the location of the ridge.

From this position, we could see the cut was really the end of a large miles long arroyo, which would indeed make a good spot for an ambush. We remounted and rode a little further north before turning east, and riding to within two hundred yards of the arroyo.

We tied up the animals to a large mesquite bush, and hobbled them. While Anna took our rifles out of their scabbards, I dug out my ghillie suit from the pannier I'd packed it in. Anna handed me my rifle and we went scouting for a good ambush spot.

We'd seen that there was no way out of the arroyo for at least the first mile, so I was hoping to find a fifty to one-hundred-yard stretch that was almost perfectly straight. As it turned out the perfect spot was four hundred yards from the entrance.

I positioned Anna near the northern end of the straight stretch behind some creosote where she could look down into the arroyo.

"Stay out of sight until you hear me start firing. As soon as I start firing kill any of the warriors between you and the captives," I said in a low voice.

Getting her nod of understanding, I walked south towards the entrance. I soon found a nice open spot in some creosote looking directly into the arroyo, fifty yards from Anna's perch. Digging a little depression, I lay down, arranged the ghillie suit over and around me, settled in, and waited. And waited. And waited some more.

I'd just about decided that the arroyo wasn't where the warriors were aiming for, when I faintly heard a young voice asking for water in Spanish, followed by the crack of a hand hitting skin and a cry of pain. The silence that followed was unnerving.

Less than five minutes later I heard adult voices talking a language similar to Apache but I couldn't understand what they were saying. A calm settled over me as I waited for the group to come into sight. When they finally rounded the small bend in the arroyo, there were four Navajo warriors in the lead, then came the captives in a tight group ten yards behind them, followed by two more Navajo ten yards behind the captives.

The lead warriors were bunched up, talking quietly as they walked, not really paying much attention to their surroundings. The captives were all naked, walking gingerly on sore bare feet over the hot arroyo sand. The two trailing warriors were more concerned with keeping the captives moving, than they were with what was around them.

The captives were being led by a young Anglo woman in her mid to late teens. She was carrying a baby, while talking encouragingly to what looked like a Hispano brother and sister about ten years old, and an Anglo boy about eight.

I waited for the trailing warriors to get ten yards past me, and opened fire at point blank range. Two shots and I was moving to standup, so I could get a better angle on the leading warriors over the captive's heads. By the time I'd stood up and had the rifle to my shoulder, it was over.

Anna had taken out all four leading warriors with single shots to each. The kids were crying in terror, and the young woman was looking at me like I was a monster. I told them in English and Spanish to stay there, and we'd get them some water in just a minute.

It took a couple of minutes for me to get out of the ghillie suit. When I finally had it off, I looked down and saw that Anna had already thrown them a camel pack, and was showing them how to drink from the suction tube.

While she was talking to them and calming

them down, I went back and got the horses and mules leading them back to where Anna was standing near the edge of the arroyo.

I took the coil of rope off my saddle horn and tied a bowline in one end. While I was working on the rope, Anna went over to the mules and pulled out my medical kit bringing it back with her. She opened up the medical kit, took out a sling, tied it around her neck, and told me she was ready.

The little minx laughed when I tried to hand her the rope, and instead leaned over grabbing the base of a mesquite bush growing on the edge of the arroyo. With a firm hold on the mesquite, she walked backward down the arroyo wall until she was dangling four feet from the bottom of the arroyo and let go. She landed lightly on both feet, and with a short laugh dressed the kids as best as she could using a combination of her spare travel clothes and what she could cut down from what the Navajos had been wearing. When she'd done what she could she told me to throw down the rope. I shook my head at her antics as I threw her the rope, but realized she was trying to calm the kids down even more.

Anna calmed the kids, got them into the rope, and I hauled them up one after the other. As I got them up to the top of the arroyo, I carried them to the shade of the mesquite where the horses were tied. Sitting them down, I gave them more water and a handful of jerky to gnaw on while they waited for the others.

Anna was the last one up, carrying the baby in the sling while holding onto the rope with one hand and fighting off the wall with the other. As I pulled Anna up into my arms and wrapped her in a hug, she whispered that none of the kids had eaten anything but jerky. Looking into her eyes I saw both concern and determination.

In short order she was fixing the biggest pot of stew she could using what was left of the antelope we'd killed yesterday along with some potatoes and carrots. Her plan was simple, she'd feed the baby the stew broth using one of the camel packs and then spoon feed the potatoes after mashing them well.

While she was doing that I went over the kids with my medical kit. Besides all of them having bruises on their face, arms, and backs, the only complaint they had, other than being hungry, was their feet, which were in pretty bad shape. Of course, none of the warrior's moccasins would fit any of the kids feet, not even the teenage girls.

With a silent sigh I told them exactly what I was going to do to their feet, and that it might hurt, but I would be as gentle as I could be. I started with the youngest boy first.

I washed the sole of each foot as gently as I could, removing all the sand, thorns, and slivers that I could find. I coated the soles in an antibiotic and analgesic cream, before wrapping both feet lightly with cotton cloth. I did the same for each of the rest, talking to them as I worked to learn what I could.

Most of the information I got was from the young woman, Elizabeth Saunders, who was fifteen. All of them had been with their parents in a small wagon train of six wagons that had formed in El Paso to travel to California together.

They'd been on the trip for almost two months, when they were attacked by a large raiding party just after sun up four days ago. When the attack started, she'd been put in charge of the kids, bundled into the back of a wagon with them, told to stay quiet, and not to come out until an adult came to get them. As far as she could tell, they were the only ones left alive from the wagon train when the fighting was over.

The Navajo had found them hiding in the back of the wagon. An argument broke out among two of the warriors shortly after they were found. Six disgruntled warriors left the group leading the kids north while the others stayed and looted the wagons. The last glimpse she had of the wagons was the other warriors moving south.

Mike Adams was six-years-old and the youngest of the group other than the baby. Sierra and Manuel Barela were eleven-year-old twins and the baby was 9-month-old Rose McClure. Elizabeth, or Beth as she preferred, was an only child, and was certain she had no living relatives.

Sierra did all the talking for the twins. Neither had ever heard their parents talk about any living relatives. Young Mike just shook his head when I asked him if he had kin anywhere, and Beth said she'd never heard his parents talk about relatives during the trip.

By the time I was done fixing up their feet and talking to them, Anna had the stew going and had fixed each of them some willow bark tea. As they sipped the tea I told Anna we'd let them eat lunch here before loading up and leaving to get as far away as possible before we lost daylight.

She asked about the kids and I gave her what history I'd learned. I told her when we left I would be walking, Beth would ride my horse carrying the baby, while the other three rode the mules. She started to say she would carry the baby.

I stopped her, reminding her she needed to be unencumbered as she would be the only fighter and would need both hands to handle the horse and whatever weapon she was using. She thought for a moment and then nodded her understanding of what I was telling her.

Two hours later, with everyone fed and every-thing packed back in the panniers, we were on our way. Anna led the way on her horse at a fast walk, followed closely by the kids. I followed well behind them on foot.

We managed to get back down around the ridge and headed east without any difficulty and when we were on hard pan about a mile from the cut I told Anna to keep going and I would catch up with her after I did what I could to mask the trail we were leaving. As they rode off, I cut a mesquite branch and started using it to sweep out any tracks we were leaving. The tracks got a little more diffi-cult to hide once the hard pan gave out to sand.

The tricky part was where Anna and the kids had crossed the tracks of the warriors as they headed into the cut. Luckily Anna had been paying attention, and had tried to stick to the hardpan or caliche as much as she could in that area. My efforts weren't going to fool a good tracker for very long, but it would buy us some time, if the bodies were found in the next day or two.

A mile beyond the cut I threw the worn branch aside, and broke into a trot following Anna's tracks. I caught up with them two hours later when they stopped for the night. The camp was set up, the kids were all seated near a fire waiting for supper, which Anna was cooking over a small fire. She gave me a tired smile, and handed me a cup of coffee telling me supper would be ready in a few minutes.

Exhausted from their ordeal and their bellies full for the first time in days, the kids were asleep soon after they were done eating. The baby fussed for a little longer, but she soon followed the others to the land of nod.

Anna and I put out the fire and drank the last of the coffee as we talked quietly. We both agreed that we would adopt the kids and raise them at the Hacienda. We'd ask them if that was okay in a few days, but the only one that was really old enough to object was Beth, and we'd work with her if she wanted to go it alone.

Over the next week we made our way - though a little slower than planned - towards Santa Fe. I ranged on foot all around them, doing the best I could to scout the trail ahead and look for pursuit from behind.

While I was running around, Anna was telling the kids stories about the Estancia, the Hacienda, and all the people that lived and worked there. She tried to keep it focused on the kids already living in the Hacienda and the ones she knew in the village; but she was always answering questions about the village, the vaqueros, and the farmers.

Their feet were healing well and without problems, but without shoes they limited their walking to only what was necessary around camp.

I had left the decision on when to tell the kids about our adoption plans, and how to tell them, up to Anna. She decided that she would tell Beth first. The two of them talked late into the evening after the others had fallen asleep. Every once in a while, during the talk, Beth would glance over at me looking for confirmation on something Anna had to say, and I would nod in agreement.

Beth was in high spirits the following day and that was noticed by the others. Anna broke the news to them during the day's ride, while I continued my running back and forth. When we finally made camp that night, the kids were all in much better spirits and were helpful around the camp as they had regained a sense of belonging and a certainty of their future.

After another long week of travel, we hit the Camino Real ten miles south of Santa Fe. Following our usual practice, we skirted around Santa Fe ending up at our old camp five miles north of town. After making camp, I changed clothes and hurriedly rode into Santa Fe to arrange a late-night meeting with Hiram. I did remember to check what day of the week it was with Anna. Anna laughed and told me it was Tuesday.

Hiram was happy to see me, and even happier when I told him we had a large deposit to make just after sundown. With the arrangements made, I rode back to the camp in a good mood. Anna had cleaned up the kids the best she could, wrapping their feet in fresh cotton cloth and canvas to make walking a little easier for them.

Following an early supper, we repacked the mules, while telling them all we were going into town and would be sleeping in soft beds with clean sheets for the next few days. They really became excited when Anna told them we would all get hot baths and new clothes, including shoes tomorrow, after breakfast.

If it had been daylight, we'd have been a sight riding down the street. As it was, it was an hour after dark when we rode into Santa Fe and headed to the hotel where Anna tied up her horse, while I helped the others and Beth with the baby down from the mule she'd been riding from the camp.

I left them there as Anna gathered them all up, to troop inside and get a three-room suite for a week, with stabling for the animals. I led the mules around to the alley and was met by Hiram and a guard. Hiram and I hauled all ninety-seven burlap bags of gold bars inside the bank.

After out last trip, we started opening the bags and stacking the bars on the table with the scales. Hiram's eyes got wider and wider as I emptied the bags, and the stacks of bars grew and grew. When I was done he told me to wait just a minute, and disappeared out the door.

He quickly returned with two large glasses of scotch. Handing me one, he took a large sip while eying the stacks of gold bars. He shook his head and sat down at the table to start weighing.

When he was finally done, he looked up and told me the weight came in at 38,400 ounces which I confirmed. The price this trip was the same as the last, so I had him deposit $462,000 in our personal account and told him I needed to get back to the hotel to help Anna with the kids.

He raised an eyebrow at that, so before leaving we both drank a second, much smaller, glass of scotch, in his office, as I told him the story of rescuing the kids, and adopting them.

I stabled the animals and lugged my saddle-bags, scabbards and four burlap bags of clothes into the hotel stopping at the desk to get the room number before walking upstairs. I walked up to our suite, and into the middle of an argument.

Anna had separated the kids with Beth, Sierra, and Rose in one room, and Manuel and Mike in another. Sierra and Manuel were completely against this, as they didn't want to be separated.

I looked at everyone in the room including Anna. "Sierra and Manuel aren't being separated, they're just sleeping in different beds, in different rooms."

That made no sense whatsoever to them, and it took them a minute to puzzle out what I had said.

When they started to argue again, I held up a hand stopping them. "You are in the same hotel suite, in the same hotel, in the same city so you aren't being separated. You can get up all night long and check on each other if you want to, but you'll be sleeping in different rooms. You need to get used to sleeping in different rooms, as you'll each have a separate room at the Hacienda."

That stopped the argument. They all started asking about their rooms in the Hacienda, which I left for Anna to answer. The kids slept well in their assigned rooms without problems that night, although Anna and I did spend some time 'exploring possibilities' for the first time in two weeks, so we may have missed them getting up to check on each other.

The next morning, while Anna led the kids into the restaurant, I stopped at the desk and arranged for three hot baths to be ready in the room when we'd finished breakfast. I walked into the restaurant to rejoin everyone, and found them all sitting at a large table with Hiram and Helen.

Beth and Sierra were in a very animated discussion with Helen and Anna, while Manuel and Mike were talking much more sedately with Hiram. I greeted Hiram with a handshake, gave a nod to Helen, and sat down next to Anna.

Discovering the ladies were talking about clothes shopping after breakfast, I looked at Hiram and shivered, receiving an arm slap from Anna. Hiram laughed and shook his head telling me I needed to learn to be much subtler if I wanted to get away with things like that.

The kids wolfed down their breakfast, anxious to get their clothes and shoes. They waited quietly and impatiently for the adults to finish their last cup of coffee. Helen joined Anna in taking the girls upstairs for their baths, while I gathered Manuel and Mike for our trip to the barbershop bath house.

Hiram left us as we walked out of the restaurant heading for his office, as we turned to walk down the street. At the bath house behind the barbershop, the boys watched with interest as the tubs were filled up and then with trepidation as I made them get undressed and into the tubs full of warm water.

They were decidedly unhappy with me, as I made sure they were well scrubbed and dry before letting them get dressed. We trooped into the barbershop where we all got a haircut, and I got my thin scraggly beard shaved off. We walked back to the hotel and found the ladies waiting for us. Both of the younger ladies were rather impatient to begin, and I had to force back a laugh at their attitude.

Anna and Helen took charge of all the kids and set out to turn the merchants of Santa Fe inside out, in their search for clothes and accessories. I set out on my own to report in to the Judge and then see Tom Stevenson.

The Judge was happy to see me, praised my efforts, and the results; although he did ask me to try and bring a few fugitives back alive, every once in a while. When we were done talking about official business, he agreed to meet me at the club for an early lunch. I left the Judge's office and walked down the street to Tom Stevenson's office where I was greeted warmly. He quickly agreed to join the Judge and I for an early lunch as well.

I went over to the club, found the manager, and paid for a week of visitor's membership before arranging for a private dining room for lunch. I checked the game room on my way out, and found Lucien Maxwell sitting at his usual table playing solitaire. He looked up as I walked in, and greeted me like a long-lost friend.

He pushed out a chair with his foot, so I sat down for a few minutes to talk, telling each other what had happened in our lives since last year. I was getting ready to leave when I mentioned that I had to go look for some suitable horses and tack for the kids to use on the rest of the trip home.

Lucien thought for a moment then stood up. "I know just the place. Come on, I'll take you there."

He led me out of the club and down the street

two blocks, before turning left and going an-other six blocks and stopping at a small stable yard with a large corral behind the stables. We walked into the stable just as an older man came out of one of the stalls.

Lucien greeted him loudly, whispering to me the man was a little deaf. Lucien introduced us, and we exchanged pleasantries for a few minutes, before Lucien pointed at me telling the man I needed four horses, for kids between the ages of six and fifteen.

The owner looked me over for a few seconds. "I have a few horses suitable for kids, but I'll need to know more about each child before I can make any recommendations."

We talked for a few minutes about the kids, how the horses would be used, and what little I knew of their riding abilities. We agreed that I'd bring the kids with me tomorrow morning, and have them ride a few horses to get a better understanding of how they sat a horse, before making any decisions.

Lucien and I were walking back to the club when he said, "Paul, trust the owner's decisions on horses for the kids. That old man was my head wrangler for a number of years and selected which horses my kids and the kids of others rode. He has a lot of experience and a reputation for honesty second to none."

I thanked Lucien for his help as we entered the club, and invited him to lunch with me, the Judge, and Tom which he accepted with alacrity.

The Judge was waiting for us in the private dining room and Tom followed us in a couple of minutes later. We all ordered, and while we were waiting for our food, I told them I had a long-term problem I was hoping they could give me not only advice on, but also some assistance if they felt that was appropriate. They asked for particulars, and I was about to start explaining when the food arrived. I gave a nod towards the food and told them we'd discuss it after lunch was over.

The lunch conversation turned to other mundane matters regarding Santa Fe, the law, and Lucien's vast land holdings. We turned back to the subject of my problem over our after-lunch coffee. Lucien, of course, had his after-lunch whiskey.

I explained the issue the best I could. "Gentlemen, there is a section of land in Texas about one hundred miles east of El Paso known as the Salt Flats. This land has an almost unlimited supply of salt and has been used for hundreds of years by anyone who wanted to brave the trip to harvest salt for both human and animal needs.

"The Spanish held it as common use land, and the Treaty of Guadalupe-Hidalgo guaranteed continuance of this practice. The new Texas Constitution allows the land to be bought, but prevents anyone from buying mineral rights for that land and other common use land. As you know I went into cattle ranching in a big way this year.

"When I left the Estancia a few months ago I had somewhere between 11,000 and 13,000 head of cattle along with roughly 500 horses and mules. All those animals need salt to survive the desert environment. I also have roughly 1200 people living on the Estancia counting on me to provide access to the basic necessities of life to include salt. The way things stand at the moment there is no problem getting the salt I need other than the dangers inherent in any long trip through that area."

I stopped for a moment to make sure they were all following so far, and to take a sip of coffee. From the looks on their faces I could see they all understood the current situation, and were beginning to wonder what the issue was.

I swallowed my coffee and started talking again. "You've all heard my thoughts on what I believe to be a coming war pitting the North against the South. The war will start over economic legislation in Congress favoring import taxes over export taxes. This will hit the South much harder than the North as the North is the nation's primary importer while the South is the nation's primary exporter.

"To add fuel to the fire the recent spate of civil violence in the border states will worsen and spill over into the states further east. Texas, as a southern state, will join the other southern states in the rebellion and most likely will withdraw from the United States. A state of insurrection will be declared and whoever the president is at the time will be forced to send troops to the South to try and force reunification.

"The South will lose the war gentlemen. They will win most of the battles because they will be fighting for the homes, on their land, against what they consider invaders. They will, however, lose the war because the North will be able to provide an unending stream of men and supplies whereas the South has, by far, fewer men and their supplies will be exhausted in a few years.

"When the South does lose, the North will treat the South as a conquered people and make harsh economic and political demands. One of those demands will most assuredly be new State Constitutions, removing slavery -

among other things. Men being men, I fully expect an individual or group of individuals to use that opportunity to remove the prohibitions of buying mineral rights to any land sold. It's at this point that I foresee major problems for the El Paso area, to include the Mesilla Valley."

I stopped again to evaluate the reactions and have another sip of coffee. I could see, from the thoughtful looks on their faces, that they had decided what I'd presented was at least a plausible scenario even if they didn't agree with the likelihood of it happening as I'd outlined.

I took another sip of coffee before continuing. "Eventually, one of the individuals or groups who will be moving west will settle in the El Paso area, learn about the salt flats, and buy them as a business enterprise. When that happens everyone within three hundred miles will be embroiled in more civil unrest.

"The Hispano community of San Elizario will be the focus of the unrest as the entire area relies on the money they earn for hauling and selling the salt. They will be reinforced by other Hispanos from both sides of the border that rely on access to the salt to meet their needs.

"If I need to make it clearer, think Acting Governor Bent and the Taos Revolt. This would be much worse than that little episode as many more people will be affected. Relations between Anglos and Hispanos will be stressed beyond the breaking point, taking untold generations to erase the ill will generated by such a move. Additionally, the ranching communities as far as the Mesilla Valley would be significantly impacted by the increased cost of salt."

My explanation of the problem finished, I looked at them one at a time. Every single one of the three had a look of horror on their face at the mention of the Taos Revolt, combined with the economic impacts. They all knew the Taos Revolt was small compared to what I was talking about as San Elizario was much larger then Taos, and just the thought of another border war disturbed them greatly.

Now that I'd described the problem, it was time to explore the solution I'd come up with, and any others they could think of.

"Gentlemen, regardless of whether I'm right about a war between the North and South, in the next few years we all know that at some point, someone will figure out a way to buy the Salt Flats and the border war I described will happen. I've been thinking about this for over a year, ever since I learned about the salt flats and its history.

"The only real solution I have come up with

has two parts. The first part is the hardest, and that's to get the Texas State Legislature to pass a bill allowing the sale of mineral rights with any common use land bought *if* the buyer is a Public Trust. Then that Bill must be signed by the Governor. The terms of the bill would require the Public Trust to allow use of the land by everyone, and the land could only be resold to the State of Texas, and for no more than what it was originally purchased for.

"Once that becomes the law I want a Public Trust I set up and fund to buy the salt flats. The problem I'm seeking advice from you on, is how to make the first part of the plan happen in the next year. By all accounts Governor Elisha Pease is a solid forward-thinking man, but I don't know him. Nor do I know anyone who knows him. Likewise, I don't know any of the Texas Legislature, and even if I did I don't know how to get this started without raising suspicion. I could really use your advice on how to go about this, and whatever assistance you can provide, in making it happen."

I sat back and waited while they thought through everything I'd said. It didn't take long before the Judge and Tom were embroiled in a conversation dominated by legal jargon, and I was soon lost in the legalese.

I continued sipping my coffee and looked over

at Lucien. He held up his glass of whiskey in a toast saying, "Being around you is never boring."

He didn't have anything to add to the conversation, and we both sat quietly listening to the other two talk for almost an hour. Eventually, the Judge looked over at me. After a small nod from Tom, he told me they both thought that not only could what I'd described work from a legal standpoint, but that it was a good common-sense idea, and in keeping with the Treaty of Guadalupe-Hidalgo.

The only thing they would change to make the proposed law stronger was to require that the Public Trust be federally recognized. This would help keep the law intact if the civil war happened as I predicted, and a new constitution was written.

As far as assistance, he and Tom would write a draft of the law. They would share it with his friend the Federal Judge in Austin, as a proposed New Mexican law, and ask for his thoughts. The Federal Judge in Austin was not only a gregarious man with innumerable friends among the Texas legislature, but an influential businessman as well, and would assuredly talk about the proposed New Mexico law thereby starting the ball rolling. Tom broke in at this point telling us that he would write the same kind of letter to Governor Pease's secretary, who happened to be his old roommate when they were studying law together.

I sat there, stunned. It couldn't be this easy, could it? I just stared at both the Judge and Tom for a few minutes until finally Lucien started snorting and laughing.

I looked to the Judge who nodded his head. "There's no guarantee it will work, but it's a start. Once Tom and I get responses from our letters we'll be in a better position to determine what else might be required."

I looked at Tom. "Will you write up the trust for me, with yourself as administrator?"

Tom smiled and gave me a nod. "It will be a pleasure. I'll work with the Judge on getting it completed, and ready for your signature, and filed in Federal Court."

I thanked them both profusely. This issue had been a major focus for me for so long. In my original timeline, every school kid, from Van Horn to Deming, learned that the El Paso Salt War had indeed erupted in the 1870s, resulting in the only surrender by a troop of Texas Rangers ever recorded, and ultimately the use of US Army troops to put down wide-spread rioting along the border. The result had not only been death and destruction, but long-term mistrust between Anglos and Hispanos that still hadn't healed in 2016.

With business over, we adjourned to the game room where we found Hiram waiting for us wondering where we were. I apologized for delaying the game, and made a note to myself to have the warehouse owner split one of my next cases of Scotch between Hiram, the Judge, and Tom.

We played poker for the next few hours, with the assistance of the liberal application of Scotch and Whiskey. Finally, just after 5PM, I told everyone I needed to go rescue the merchants of Santa Fe from the depredations of Anna in clothes hunting mode for the kids. Hiram also said it was time for him to go, as he expected he and Helen would be eating supper with us tonight. I raised a questioning eyebrow, and he said he'd been told by Helen not to make any plans for supper tonight.

We made our goodbyes and walked together down to the hotel to meet Helen, Anna, and the kids. We sat in the lobby of the hotel for fifteen minutes before they all arrived in a good mood with the kids wearing new clothes.

I hugged Anna giving her a kiss, before looking at the kids and complimenting them on their new clothes. Anna put her arm around my waist, and gave me an arm hug as they told us all about their shopping expedition. When that was over, Anna announced we were eating at the club this evening. She took my arm, and we followed Helen and Hiram to the club, herding the kids in front of us.

At supper, Helen doted on Rose; with the able assistance of Anna, Sierra, and Beth. Manuel and Mike looked uncomfortable and out of place with all the females, so Hiram and I made a conscious effort to include them in our conversation.

Over our after-supper coffee I asked, "What's the plan for tomorrow, my love?"

She replied with a shrug and said, "The only thing that's firm is a visit to the seamstress after breakfast for a fitting of the riding outfits being tailored for Beth and Sierra."

"Perfect!" I said with a broad smile. "We all have an appointment tomorrow morning to see about horses for the kids."

That got the kids excited and I held up my hands. I told them that nothing was for certain yet, as much depended on what their abilities were, and how they matched to the available horses. Meanwhile, Anna was beaming a huge super megawatt Anna smile!

It was good to be me!

As we were leaving the dining room the manager was coming out of the large ball room. Anna looked at me, and at my nod, stopped him asking if we could use the piano for a little while. He smiled and told her we could, and asked if we'd like something to drink. Anna thought for a second and then asked for coffee for the adults and Beth and milk for the kids.

The manager hurried off to see to the drinks, and Anna led us into the ballroom with Hiram and Helen following curiously. It dawned on me that in all the times we'd had supper with them, they were never with us when we'd stopped to play and sing in the ballroom.

Anna got the kids seated and went to sit down with them, but I told her she had to join me at the piano for a few songs. She beamed me an Anna smile, and joined me at the piano bringing coffee that had just been delivered for both of us. Hiram and Helen joined the kids and made sure everyone had their drinks.

When I started playing, Anna and I sang the songs that had come to have the most meaning to us as duets. We started with "10 Minutes Ago", then did "Keeper of the Stars", followed by "If Tomorrow Never Comes", and finished with "Impossible Dream".

When we were done I looked over at the table

where everyone was sitting, and found them all staring at Anna and me in wonder.

I turned to Anna. "I think our audience liked the songs."

She giggled, gave me a light arm slap, and got up. "Play a couple for the kids and then it's time to get them to bed."

I sang "Puff the Magic Dragon" and "The Unicorn Song" both of which the kids, really liked. Anna started to get up, and I shook my head at her.

"You should know better by now my love."

When she had reseated herself, looking at me expectantly, I sang her "If I Could Save Time in a Bottle" earning me a really nice Anna smile. When I was done, I looked at Anna with all the love I had. She had to know it was coming, but she still broke into a huge super megawatt Anna smile when I started singing "Anna's Song".

It was definitely good to me tonight!

We bid goodnight to Hiram and Helen outside the club, and walked back to the hotel where Anna and Beth put the younger ones to bed, while I went to the restaurant and bought a bottle of cabernet and three wine glasses for Anna, Beth and me. When I got to the room,

Anna and Beth had the kids already in bed and were talking in the living room.

Anna was explaining what a quinceañera was. From what I could gather, as I opened the wine and poured, Beth had asked Anna how we met, leading to more questions about the celebration. Before the wine was gone, Anna had told Beth about both of our histories. Beth was quite surprised to learn that not only were both of us orphans, but were informally related through my adoption by the Apache.

The kids were up early the next morning, frothing with anticipation at getting a horse. Even Beth was excited, although she did her best to hide it from the others.

A quick breakfast was followed with a fast visit to the seamstress, as the girls simply tried on the clothes that had been tailored for them. When the fit was pronounced acceptable, each girl selected their favorite one and wore it when we left.

In no time at all we were all loaded into the buggy I'd rented and a few minutes later we pulled into the stables. I helped the ladies down, while the boys jumped from their seats eager to get to the horses. I had to settle them down a little when the owner walked out. I introduced everyone and asked the owner to start with Mike as the youngest. This thrilled

Mike to no end, as he was used to being the last when it came to clothes or anything else.

The owner smiled, put his hand on Mike's shoulder, and told him to come with him. We watched as the owner led Mike into the stables, talking to him about horses. I led the others over to a small corral where we watched several young horses playing and running.

The owner came out of the stable fifteen minutes later, leading Mike on a small pinto. The owner led him over to a large empty corral. He talked quietly to Mike for a minute or two, then opened the gate and let Mike into the corral. With the gate closed behind him, Mike walked the horse around the corral a couple of times, before moving into a cantor, then a trot, and finally a light gallop.

At the owner's signal Mike brought the horse to a stop and backed him up, before moving into a walk again. We all watched as the impromptu class was going on. The owner turned, smiled, and asked who was next.

Sierra was next. He led her into the stable as he had Mike. That set the tone for the rest of the morning. Sierra came out riding a nice chestnut mare. Manuel came out of the stable riding a bay mare, while Beth ended up with a buckskin mare.

Anna and I were standing outside the corral watching all four kids ride their horses, when the owner came up and asked me what I thought.

"We couldn't be more satisfied, but I'm not the important one here," I replied with a smile and pointed a thumb at Anna. "She's the granddaughter of Jose Mendoza, and grew up in his livery and freight yard. She knows more about horses than I could ever hope to know. I know how to ride them, she knows how to evaluate and price them."

I moved out of the way and let the two talk about the horses and negotiate the prices, while I watched the kids riding. By the time they were done, I'd decided that Sierra was the best of the group on a horse while Manuel was a close second. Mike was too young yet to get an accurate impression, while Beth was adequate at best. She seemed to like horses, but didn't seem to have a feel for them. That could change over time, of course, but for now she would be fine riding to the Hacienda.

I paid the owner what he and Anna had agreed upon for the horses and all the tack. We gave him our thanks and left, with Anna and I riding in the buggy, and the kids riding their horses behind us.

As we rode back to the hotel I took the opportunity to bring Anna up to speed on the Salt Flats discussion I'd had over lunch yesterday. She gave me one of her special Anna smiles, and a squeeze of my arm, while telling me that it sounded promising. I nodded, but cautioned her that the Judge said nothing was guaranteed in politics.

We stabled the horses at the hotel, much to the kids' chagrin, but they brightened back up when I told them we'd go riding every morning, while we were in Santa Fe. Anna loaded them all back up into the buggy, while I went inside and retrieved her shotgun and sling. We rode over to the gunsmith I'd dealt with on my last visit. He greeted me warmly, and asked how the shotguns were working out. I told him they were fine as far as they went, but I needed more of the 20-gauge breechloaders with the metal cased shells.

He grinned and proudly said, "I just received three dozen more of them. How many do you want?"

"I'll take all of them, and 300 more if the price is right," I replied.

"Well, I can certainly order that many, but I don't know how long an order that large will take to come in from back east," he said with a gulp.

I shrugged. "It will take as long as it takes, but if it will help you could break it into smaller orders, say in lots of fifty, and send them along to us as they come in."

He thought for a moment and then said he could do that. We discussed how many rounds of ammunition he had available and what he should order for each shotgun. When we were done with that, we discussed shipping everything to the Hacienda via the warehouse consigned to Mendoza Freight.

I paid for the large order, as well as the three dozen he had in stock and more ammunition. When we were done I showed him Anna's shotgun, and told him I'd take three of the shotguns with us, but I wanted them cut down like Anna's. He looked it over, and asked when I wanted them. I grinned and told him there was no hurry, tomorrow morning right after breakfast would be fine.

He laughed saying, "It's a good thing business is a little slow, right now."

The rest of the day was spent ordering the slings and eye bolts for the shotguns, followed by lunch, and then playing 'pack horse', as we stopped at all the stores picking up the various items Anna had bought for the kids. Anna had purchased items in stores from one side of Santa Fe to the other. How they had covered all that ground as they did their shopping is beyond me.

The first thing after breakfast the next morning we all rode to the gunsmith's store to pick up the three shotguns. I had the gunsmith screw in the eyebolts, and I added the slings before fitting them to Beth, Sierra, and Manuel.

Mike was feeling a little left out but perked up when I promised that he would eventually get one when his body had grown enough to be able to handle it. We all rode out of Santa Fe on our morning ride heading west in search of a suitable place to teach the older kids about their shotguns.

We found a nice spot with prickly pear cactus carpeting the side of a steep hill, an hour out of town. It was perfect for shotgun practice. We all sat down in a circle and I went through the now standard lecture on shotgun safety, use, and maintenance. I was a little tougher during the lecture than normal, stressing the safety aspects to get through to them that guns weren't toys. If they used them incorrectly, or without thought, they could kill friends or family just as easily as enemies.

The lecture was just as much for Mike, as it was for the others. When I was done, Anna showed them the proper grip and fired both barrels into the mass of cactus on the hillside. Seeing how big an area of cactus was hit, the kids began to understand the need for safety and caution.

One at a time, each of them took turns blasting the hillside, while learning how to hold the shotgun to get the most control. While we were watching them, I told Anna I wanted her to take Beth aside tomorrow, and teach her the basics of the rifle. I wanted to get her comfortable with loading the magazines and firing it, in case she ever needed to use it.

CHAPTER 3

W e left Santa Fe for the Estancia three days later. Anna spent those three days shopping for the kids, and rebuilding our supplies. I'd spent my time with the Judge, Lucien, Tom, and Hiram, reviewing information on 'the Boss', which remained slim to none.

Between the four of them, and Kit's friends and trusted contacts, there were over forty people reporting anything they heard about the mysterious 'Boss'. Unfortunately, none of the friends and contacts had heard a word. It was frustrating to say the least.

It was Lucien who opined that it was almost like 'the Boss' didn't even live in Santa Fe. Now that was something we'd never thought of. It was also something we currently had no way of proving or disproving. All we could do for the time being, was continue as we had been.

Anna and I had been discussing our plans whenever possible, both during the ride after rescuing the kids, as well as daily after we arrived in Santa Fe. Originally, we'd planned on a three or four week visit with Josefa and Kit in Taos before the last leg of our trip. The kids changed those plans significantly.

We'd decided before ever reaching town, that we would limit our stay to just Santa Fe, and leave for home as soon as possible. We were extremely worried about 'the Boss' coming after the kids, to get to us, while we were in Santa Fe. We were just as concerned about being ambushed or attacked, during the trip home.

Anna mailed a long letter to Josefa, giving her the details and our apologies, shortly after we arrived in Santa Fe.

We left Santa Fe at three in the morning. As far as we could tell, no one saw us leave. We were ten miles out of town riding south down the Camino Real, when the first light of dawn broke over the mountains.

Five miles later we left the road, heading east for a mile, before turning south again. I'd left my horse with Anna when we left the trail and while she led everyone away, I worked on hiding the trail we'd left leaving the road and the tracks heading east.

I caught up to them just after they stopped for a quick lunch of sausage dogs and tea. Anna and Beth had found and bought preserved soft foods like creamed corn and applesauce for Rose to eat during our lunch breaks, which was the real reason for the stop. Riding a horse while trying to spoon feed a baby was a losing proposition.

While we were eating, Manuel asked why we'd left the road, since it was the fastest way to get where we were going. I explained about roads being magnets for raiding parties and bandits looking to ambush travelers. Our goal was to avoid as much trouble as we could while we traveled. We'd ride parallel to the road and the river, at a distance of anywhere from one to two miles. Close enough to the river to get water when we needed it, but far enough away to keep out of sight from most troublemakers.

Anna and I had decided to use this opportunity to begin familiarizing the kids with the kinds of things they'd see, living on the Estancia in general and the Hacienda in particular. We started teaching them Apache as we rode. We explained that everyone on the Estancia was required to be fluent in English, Spanish, and Apache as well as learn Latin in school. They would spend their afternoons as we rode, learning Apache. The mornings would be spent learning about the desert, the plants that could be eaten, or used for medicine, the animals that were around us and their behavior.

We made camp early that night, and began teaching the kids Aikido. We'd started teaching them Tai Chi shortly after we'd rescued them, and they'd watched us do our katas, so it was a natural progression to them to learn what we were doing and why. They had fun learning to fall correctly. Watching them learn the throws was often hilarious, especially little Mike, who insisted on practicing each throw until he got it right, and succeeded in throwing Manuel.

Traveling much slower, with frequent side trips to explore whatever caught the kids' interest, along with making early camps; meant that our normal two and a half week trip turned into a five week trip. During that five weeks, the kids absorbed everything we taught them like the little sponges they were.

Mike proved to be the best of the group when it came to languages, picking up Apache far faster than the other three, and radically improving his previously limited Spanish. Manuel picked up everything dealing with survival in the desert, and tracking, at an equally astonishing rate; while Sierra proved to be a fearless fighter, picking up Aikido much quicker than the others. She was also much quicker in learning anything dealing with medicine. Beth spent most of her time with Anna, and caring for Rose, so I wasn't really sure where her talents or interests lie.

We stopped in Socorro for two days as planned, to introduce myself as the US Marshal. Socorro was another small village with pretentions of grandeur by calling itself a town. In the future, I knew it would become an important town in the area, but for now there wasn't much to it.

Our visit to Fort Craig, nine miles downriver, was a little better but like Fort Thorn, it was a dismal place for a fort. The commander readily agreed to a monthly delivery of cattle, and quickly signed the contract, telling us he was starting to get desperate for both meat and produce.

I made a mental note of the need for produce, and decided Tomas needed to visit Fort Fillmore, Fort Thorn, and Fort Craig to get a feel for what quantities they would be willing to buy. We stayed only a few hours at Fort Craig before resuming our trip home.

For once we were successful in avoiding confrontations and gunfights, as we saw no one during the entire trip, outside of our two day stop in Socorro, and the short stop at Fort Craig. We did come across two or three week old tracks left by groups of unshod horses numerous times, indicating that some raiding parties were active, but we never saw them or came across the remains of their handiwork.

It was mid-morning on the last day of the trip when we got the first indication that things on the Estancia had progressed at a rapid rate while we were gone. We weren't in sight of the levees yet, when I caught a flash of light coming from the Robledo Mountains.

I'd been talking to Anna and stopped mid-sentence to look at the flashing light. A moment later I was grinning, and Anna was trying to figure out why I'd stopped talking, and why I was grinning.

"We've been seen by a Scout/Sniper Team. The Hacienda now knows we're almost home," I said.

"How do you know that?" she asked in a slightly exasperated voice.

"Watch the Robledo Mountains," I said pointing with my chin.

Looking over there, she was just in time to see the flashes of the last word of an acknowledgement.

She turned back to me, grinning. "If they've started the lookout posts and signaling already, I wonder what else has changed. I have to say it's good to be home."

We had talked about the changes that were planned, and what we hoped to see when we were finally back on the Estancia. Even though we thought we were mentally prepared for the changes, we found we were emotionally unprepared.

Our first sight of the river, with levees down both sides as far as we could see, produced a lump in my throat almost as big as the one I got the first time I saw the Hacienda. I looked over at Anna, and saw tears in her eyes at the sight of the levees.

She grabbed my hand, gave it a squeeze, and in a croaking voice full of emotion said, "It's really happening!"

I could do nothing but nod as I didn't trust my voice just then. Beth could tell something unusual was happening and rode up next to us on Anna's side to find out what it was. That caused the other three to ride up next to us with the twins on my side and Mike pulling in between us.

Anna recovered a little quicker than I did. She pointed to the river and explained what the levees were and that it meant we were almost home. It didn't mean much to them as they had no basis from which to understand the planning and hard work that had been involved.

We continued riding six abreast for another hour before stopping for lunch. None of us really wanted to stop; but the baby needed to be fed, and that just wasn't happening while we were moving. So, we might as well all eat.

We were done eating a nice venison stew and were packing everything we'd used up, when a loud muffled explosion came from across the river followed closely by the eruption of a large dark cloud of dust.

I'd lost track of the days again, and had been about to ask Anna what day it was. Instead, I turned to her with a grin on my face, and told her it was either Saturday or Sunday. She smiled at me with a tolerant look, and told me it was Saturday.

The kids had all gathered around us, wanting to know what the explosion was. I explained that it was caused by blasting rocks loose from the mountain's side, so they could be used in building things like the levee. That reassured them, and we mounted our horses for the final ride of the trip.

Just under two hours later, we got our next completely unexpected surprise when we saw a stone bridge spanning the river, with a macadam paved road leading from the other side of the bridge to the slope up to the Hacienda.

I didn't know why Tom had decided to change the original timber bridge to stone, but I was sure he had a good reason and that I'd find out in due time. The bridge was much wider than I'd originally envisioned, but as long as the design work was solid, I was fine with that.

At the bridge, we discovered it was only partially complete, with three of the five concrete spans yet to be laid. At its highest point, the center of the bridge was less than eight feet above the river. It was gently sloped to tightly packed earth and rock covered slopes ending about twenty yards beyond the levees.

All in all, it looked to be a good well thought out design and implementation. We rode back to the river bank, through an opening in the levee, across the river through the opposite opening. Finally, we went up the slope to the Hacienda.

As we crested the slope, Anna and I both turned in our saddle to watch the kid's reactions to their first sight of the Hacienda. The look of wonder and disbelief on their faces, confirmed yet again that I would never get bored watching anyone's first reaction to the Hacienda.

Before turning back around Anna told the kids, "Welcome home!"

We dismounted to a welcoming party, as Alejandro and Izabella came running out jumping in my and Anna's arms for hugs, followed by all the adults. We happily greeted everyone and introduced the five new arrivals. The women quickly rounded up Anna and the kids leaving me with the men as they disappeared into the Hacienda.

I looked at the five men standing there along with the four young cousins who'd come up to get the horses and shook my head as I said, "We all now know where I stand in order of importance!"

They all laughed as we started unloading the panniers, and pulling off the saddlebags and scabbards, before turning the animals over to the cousins.

With six of us, it was a matter of minutes. We were soon done hauling everything into the office, where it was all stacked against the wall for later unpacking. I poured scotch for everyone, including the Padre, and handed them out.

Raising my glass, I toasted babies, which got a grin from three of the five other men in the room. Lorena, Sofia, and Esperanza were all in various stages of pregnancy, with Lorena due anytime. Sofia was due sometime in September, and Esperanza in October.

We talked about babies for a few minutes, before the obvious questions about the five new kids started the conversation in a whole new direction. I told the story of the rescue, and our travels home. Everyone had grim looks on their faces, and Tom started to say something, when Carla came into the room announcing supper was ready.

Supper was both crowded, and a riot of conversations; as you'd expect after a four-month absence, and the addition of five new people. I looked out over the table and realized we needed a bigger table if we were going to continue to all eat together. As it was, the four ladies of the housekeeping staff weren't eating with us tonight, as there was no room! We had twenty-one people seated around a table designed for twenty-two!

I mentioned it to Anna, and she said she knew just the one we needed. We would get it the next time we went to El Paso.

Supper was Christmas enchiladas, with all the sides. Yolanda told us Martina had changed the menu from pizza as soon as she got the word this morning that we would arrive tonight.

Beth looked up with a perplexed expression on her face at the references to Christmas enchiladas, pizza, and Martina knowing we would be here for supper tonight. Anna explained that Christmas enchiladas referred to the red and green sauces and that pizza was a favorite lunch and supper food she'd get to try in a few days.

Yolanda then explained that there were security teams out all around the edges of the Estancia. They sent signals back to the Hacienda anytime they saw someone approaching, and we'd been seen this morning. Both explanations satisfied Beth, and she went back to talking to Izabella.

The two young ladies were thrilled to have someone their own age to talk to. As I glanced around the table, I noticed the kid's conversations were broken into the various age groups. Carlo, Consuelo, and Mike were deeply involved in a conversation, while Antonia, Angelina, and the twins were involved in a conversation of their own.

I ate my mix of red and green enchiladas with relish, enjoying both the food and the conversation of close friends. The major bit of gossip was the frequent visits by George while we'd been gone, and the relationship that appeared to be developing between him and Celia. I smiled to myself hoping that the relationship continued to flourish. Even if George decided to stay in the Army, he needed some love in his life.

As we finished eating, the ladies from the kitchen brought coffee out for everyone. Tom started to talk about the work that had been done on the Estancia while we were gone. I waved him off, telling him that I was sure we'd see some of it tomorrow, on our way to church. The rest could wait until the Monday morning meeting.

What I was really interested in, was how the people were doing. I asked him if we'd lost any of the new arrivals from either the farmers or vaqueros. Was there enough work to keep everyone busy? How were Heinrich's people holding up, and how was Raul's family doing?

We talked about the people of the Estancia for the next half hour or so. I learned that no one had left, and everyone that wanted to be, was gainfully employed. Everyone appeared to be happy and content, as reported by Jesus, Miguel, and Hector's foreman. Raul's family had settled in nicely, and no one had heard any complaints from them.

There were various relationships developing among the older kids of the farmers, vaqueros, cousins, and masons. I smiled as I heard more about the people, and the integration that was occurring.

As I listened, I finally noticed that Grandfather Garcia was missing. As the discussions about the people were winding down, I asked how long he'd stayed before returning to Las Cruces. The room got deathly quiet, and Yolanda suddenly had tears in her eyes.

I looked at Anna with a sense of dread, knowing someone at the table was about to give us some really terrible news. From the expression on her face, it was clear Anna didn't have a clue about what was wrong either.

Finally, Tom cleared his throat. In a hoarse voice, he said, "Grandfather Garcia and Yolanda's father are dead."

Anna let out a small sob, and I put my arm around her hugging her close. With a deep sense of foreboding I asked Tom what happened. He took a large drink of coffee before launching into the story.

"A few days after you left, the Scout/Sniper Team south of the Estancia noticed vultures circling near the Camino Real, about four miles from Las Cruces. It was outside their patrol area, but they went to investigate anyway. They discovered the bodies of Grandfather Garcia and Yolanda's father three hundred yards east of the road.

"One stayed with the bodies, while the other got close enough to send a signal to the lookout Yolanda and Miguel had just established on Robledo Mountain. He, in turn, signaled the cousins watching the horses on the upper plateau.

"I put the Estancia on alert, and had the Reserve force stay near the Village while the vaquero's patrolled the perimeter across the river. Yolanda and I took all the cousins that were close by, and two of the farmers driving wagons. We got to the bodies a few hours later.

"The Scout/Sniper Team told us they had back tracked a wagon to the road where the ambush had occurred, but there wasn't much to see as a late spring rain had obscured most of the details. Regardless, from what they could tell, a group of between eight and twelve riders on shod horses, had ambushed the two men in the wagon, killing them.

"That group had broken up, with two loading the bodies on the wagon and dumping them in the desert, before taking the wagon Southwest and rejoining the road headed towards Las Cruces. The other group of riders had also headed south on the road to Las Cruces.

"Both the wagon and the rider's tracks disappeared about a half mile before Las Cruces, mixed in with all the old tracks around the area, and muddled by the rain. There was no way to tell the old tracks from the new tracks.

"I couldn't think of what else to do, but to try and track the group, and neither could Miguel. So, I had the cousins load Grandfather Garcia into a wagon, and they headed towards the Robledo Mountains, where they said Grandfather Garcia had already picked out his burial ground.

"I loaded Yolanda's father into the other wagon, and Yolanda and I gave our horses to the farmers telling them to ride back to the Hacienda, and let them know we would be in Las Cruces for a few days.

"Yolanda and I drove the wagon to the Mendoza's, and spent a few days grieving with the family before returning to the Hacienda. I did ride over to Mesilla to let Esteban and Ed know what had happened."

By the time Tom was done talking, I had a death grip on the edge of the table. My vision had slowly narrowed. All I could see was a black tunnel, with a small bright red dot at the far end. I knew I was hyperventilating but it didn't matter.

My first instinct was one I hadn't felt in over

thirty years: to get up, get my guns, and immediately go hunting. A hunt with only one acceptable outcome; the execution of the man who'd ordered Grandfather Garcia's death, and led the group that made it happen.

I knew, deep down inside, that this was a different desert and a different time. The last time I'd felt this way, I'd gone 'berserker' for two weeks during Desert Storm. That was the only thing that stopped me. I was leaning forward in my chair, trying with everything I had to control the anger and rage I was feeling.

I felt Anna's hand on my shoulder, trying to pull me back. It took everything I had not to shake her off. If anybody could pull me out of this fugue of rage and anger, it was my indomitable Anna.

Eventually she got me to sit back in the chair and climbed into my lap with her arms around me and cuddling close. I could hear Anna's sobs and feel the tears she was crying seeping through my shirt both of which only increased my anger.

Anna and I stayed cuddled together in the chair at the dining room table for some unknown amount of time. It felt like hours, but I'm sure it was only minutes. When I finally got my breathing under control, and felt like I had sufficiently mastered my emotions, I stood up still holding Anna.

"Anna and I need some time alone. We'll see you all in the morning," I said through locked jaws.

I carried Anna upstairs laying her gently on the bed and laid down next to her. She rolled on to her side, facing me, and put her arms around me. She tucked her head onto my chest, underneath my chin. Neither one of us moved for over thirty minutes. Anna's breathing had evened out into a regular pattern and I thought she had fallen asleep.

I started to disentangle myself from our embrace when I looked down and found Anna staring at me with a calm expression but with that hard angry glint in her eye that I'd noticed earlier.

"What are you doing, Pablo?" she asked.

"I need to do something physical to burn off some of the rage I'm feeling, or I'll explode," I replied as I moved to the center of the room.

With a small sad smile she said, "I feel the same way."

I helped her out of bed, and we both stripped down to our underwear before moving to the center of the room, and beginning our katas.

She matched me move for move through three-fourths of the katas, which were the ones she knew. She sat, cross-legged, on the bed, to watch me finish. When I started the Krav Maga katas, she rejoined me and kept up through the first third.

Before I'd finished the next two katas, she had redressed and left the bedroom, coming back ten minutes later with a coffee service and a small glass of scotch from the office. She set everything down on the small table in front of the couch. She sat sipping coffee while I finished the katas. When I was done she handed me the scotch and poured me a cup of coffee after I'd thrown back the shot.

We sat quietly together, drinking our coffee for a while, before she started talking.

"Pablo, I know with all my heart that you feel responsible for what happened, and that buried in your anguish is a bitterness over the thought that you could have prevented it. I also know you will not let Great Grandfather's and Uncle Jim's death go unavenged.

"While I agree with avenging them, I do not and cannot let you carry the burden of responsibility for their deaths. We both know that their deaths were in retribution for rescuing the ranchers, and killing the comancheros.

"We also both know that Great Grandfather and Uncle Jim were already dead, by the time we found out about the threats from Esteban and Ed. Apart from not going after the comancheros in the first place, there is absolutely nothing we could have done to stop it from happening. Canceling our trip wouldn't have done anything except allowing us to find the bodies a few hours earlier.

"By all means, keep your anger, but keep it tight! Bank it like you would a fire, until you can unleash it in a positive way. More importantly, you need to let that bitterness out, before it festers and poisons your soul."

I sighed, and looked into Anna's expressive eyes.

"My love, my mind knows everything you have said is true. My heart, on the other hand, knows with absolute certainty that it's my fault. There was a time when my heart would have overruled my mind. I would have already left by now on a manhunt that would not have ended until I had succeeded or was dead.

"Except when it comes to you, my mind now rules, not my heart. It will take some time for me to come to terms emotionally, with their deaths. But eventually, it will happen. Through it all, I know just being close to you will keep me grounded, and when we get past this we'll find that we love each other deeper, hug each other tighter, and kiss each other more often."

She crawled back into my lap for a tight hug and long kiss, before settling in my arms. It had been a long day, compounded by the emotional toll of homecoming, learning of the deaths, and when combined with the physical exertions we'd just completed, served to leave us both extremely tired. We both eventually got up, undressed, and climbed into bed. There we fell into an exhausted sleep.

It seemed like I'd just closed my eyes, when I reopened them to discover it was morning already. While the curtains on the French doors blocked most of the sunlight, there were still stray rays of muted light creeping out from around the edges. Anna's head was on my shoulder. When I looked down at her, I once again found her eyes wide open, staring at me.

She gave me a smile and rose up to give me a small good morning kiss, before telling me it was time to get up. We'd both been looking forward to sharing a nice hot shower since we started back from the Colorado River. Deaths in the family notwithstanding, we were bound and determined to make it a reality this morning.

Our mutual morning shower wasn't the usual frolicsome fun we were used to having. It was a gentle sharing of our love, instead. We completed our morning preparations and dressed for a Sunday at home, before heading downstairs for breakfast.

We were a little early for breakfast. Anna went to check on Rose and the other kids, while I had my first cup of coffee for the day. She came back a few minutes later carrying Rose, with the other four kids following along behind her all dressed in their Sunday best. They were almost immediately followed by the rest of the Hacienda. Cristina, Celia, and Carla brought in breakfast, even before everyone had finished pouring their coffee.

The adults were subdued while eating, and were looking at Anna and I quizzically. Anna apparently had soon had enough and addressed the table.

"We're both fine after last night's episode. While we're both still upset, we are back to functioning as adults."

Slowly the table conversations returned, and before we'd finished our after-breakfast coffee we were talking about a visit to Las Cruces next week with all the kids. Anna said that the rest of the family needed to meet the newest members of the family, and I needed to check in with Esteban and Ed. Tom and Yolanda decided to go with us, while the other three families decided to stay at the Hacienda, given the late stages of pregnancy all three wives were in.

We finished up the coffee, rounded up the kids, and walked outside to find a nice six-person buggy with sunshade, a wagon painted in the Estancia colors, and seven saddled horses waiting for us.

I raised an eyebrow at the buggy, and Tom told me that Mr. Mendoza had given it to the Estancia to use, since he never used it and it was taking up room in his stable he needed for other things. The pregnant ladies with the house staff all shared the buggy while the rest of us loaded all the kids in the wagon and then mounted up for the short ride to the village with me and Anna in the lead.

Anna and I pulled up our horses as we reached the top of the hill overlooking the village. As the rest of the group rode on into the village we looked down on what to me seemed a much more complete village than when we'd left. The stable and wagon yard complex was complete and trees had been planted in the plaza; the church was almost done, lacking only a roof, stained glass windows, and a door; and the storehouses on the opposite side of the village had been started.

I couldn't help but wonder who had decided to tint the stucco on the church with what had become known locally as Dos Santos Rose. Don't get me wrong, it was really nice; but most churches in this part of the world were either white, or stone brown.

Anna, who was beaming me a big Anna smile, said that it was almost done. I looked out over the village again and told her all we needed to finish it, was paved streets, a rectory, and a large school house. She grinned, telling me that was for next year as she started her horse down to the plaza. I followed her a few seconds later.

With the sun beating down relentlessly on the crowd gathered in the plaza, the Padre decided discretion was the better part of valor and kept the service mercifully short. As had become the local practice, a small aisle was kept cleared in the middle of the plaza. The Padre walked down the aisle at the end of the service, and waited at the edge of the plaza for the parishioners to walk by, saying a few words to each of them.

Anna and I waited at the very back of the line, and were the last ones out of the plaza. We chatted with the Padre in our turn, and he told

P. C. Allen

us we'd see him back at the Hacienda for lunch. We loaded everyone back in the buggy and wagon and returned to the Hacienda.

Lunch was back to the riotous affairs that we were used to during mealtime, with too many conversations going on around the table, in a mix of too many different languages to follow. I smiled at Anna and told her I'd missed this.

When lunch was over Anna told the kids to stay at the table, and asked the Padre to stay as well. Although school was over for the summer, the Padre was running a modified summer school in the mornings, to help the new arrivals catch up as much as possible before school restarted as normal in late September, after the rainy season. Anna asked him if he had room for Beth, the twins, and Mike to attend so they could start getting caught up in the languages, if nothing else.

The Padre assured Anna that he had the room, and told the kids he was looking forward to working with them starting the next morning. Beth and Mike were thrilled with the thought of going to school. The twins, on the other hand, weren't happy about having to spend their mornings in school while the rest of the Hacienda kids were out having fun. We told them it was only for a few hours in the mornings, and their afternoons would be theirs to enjoy. They both settled down a bit on hearing our assurances.

We took a few minutes to unpack the panniers and saddlebags, before settling down in the shade of the terrace, to discuss our plans for the coming week with Tom and Yolanda. Just before supper, we all agreed that we would spend Monday through Thursday getting caught up on Estancia business. On Friday morning, we would leave on a week-long trip to Las Cruces, with all the kids as well as Tom and Yolanda.

The trip was needed for many reasons, with the most important being grieving with other family, introducing our new kids; and reviewing our trip with Esteban and Ed, while getting up to speed on their activities since we'd been gone.

After supper, Anna led us into the living room and asked mc for some songs. With the grief of losing great grandfather and Yolanda's father fresh in my mind, I found myself playing "Vaya Con Dios", "Holes in the Floor of Heaven", and "One More Day". There wasn't a dry eye in the room when I finished. I apologized for the selection, letting everyone know I just wasn't up to playing something romantic or fun this evening.

The next morning as breakfast was ending,

Tom gave me a thick stack of papers, telling me it was all the reports since I'd left, and it would be helpful to read as many of them as I could get through before the weekly meeting started in a couple of hours.

Taking the papers, I asked Anna to join me in the study, and we'd read them together. Anna said she'd join me in a few minutes and disappeared into the kitchen. I walked into the office, sat down on the couch to get comfortable, and started reading. I had finished the first two pages when Anna came in, carrying a coffee service which she put on the low table in front of us before pouring two cups and handing me one.

I handed her the two pages I'd finished, in exchange for the coffee. We settled back on the couch to read. A little over two hours later we'd managed to make our way through all the reports, which we found to be concise and well written.

With the exception of Giuseppe's facilities reports, there was a single page report for each major area of the Estancia for each month. Giuseppe's weekly reports were much more detailed, and included drawings of everything that changed, along with the why's. At the end of the two hours, we knew what the status was in each area of the Estancia, what changes had been made, and just as importantly, why they were made.

It was going to be a close run to finish the bridge before the rainy season; and, as we discovered from the reports, the bridge was going to be a key component in keeping both sides of the Estancia connected during the rainy season. I almost slapped myself on the forehead when I realized I'd completely overlooked how we were going to get across the river in both directions during the rainy season, with the levees in place.

The planned wooden bridge had been replaced by a stone bridge design, when Juan had told them he wouldn't be able to get the wood in time to get it built this year. Thankfully, Heinrich and Giuseppe had a lot of experience in bridge building in Europe, and quickly reverted to the stone and concrete design.

The levees on the other hand, were going better than expected, and would be completed in early July. The irrigation intake channels had been cast by Heinrich and his crew, and were placed every three hundred yards along both sides of the river under the levees. The control gates had all been built by Raphael to Giuseppe's design, as approved by Tomas. The excess drainage channels had been completed from the dams to the river, and were good for this rainy season.

Giuseppe was evaluating the possibilities of building partially buried water retention tanks near the last dam, to retain even more of the water from the rainy season. Heinrich estimated that all the work he'd been contracted for so far would be completed, just after the start of the new year. Now that got my attention. There was still too much masonry work to be done, to lose the masons at the beginning of the year. I made a note to talk about this during today's meeting.

Meanwhile, the church had also been slightly redesigned. There now was a masonry lower section and an adobe upper section, to alleviate the foundation settling problems caused by too much weight on adobe foundations. The church was also scheduled to be finished in mid-July although the pews, prayer books, hymnals, and other interior items wouldn't begin to arrive until after July.

The stables and wagon yard complex were complete, the livestock were in good shape, and all the wagons had been painted and numbered in the approved paint scheme. The wagon yard had a good supply of wood to make replacement spokes, tongues, axles, and wagon beds. Wagon maintenance was an ongoing activity, as rock hauling took a heavy toll on wagon beds and sides, as well as on axles and wheels.

The only shortage I could identify in this area, was the lack of a third forge and blacksmith. It wasn't critical yet, but Raul assured us that once we started farming full time, things would quickly bog down with just two black-smiths.

Tomas had been extremely busy. He had a rotating team picking up compost material from the village and ranch, and had started a large compost area near the river. After four months in the sweltering heat, the first load of compost had been delivered to an earth worm farm he'd set up.

After mixing the compost with dirt and sand, it had been put in wooden forms built from scraps of wood salvaged from old wagon bed planks. Finally, the earth worms he paid the kids to collect were added.

While that was going on he'd had six teams clearing farm land starting at the Northern end of the west side of the river. Three more teams followed behind them with wagon loads of dirt and sand, roughly leveling the cleared ground; while two more teams came behind them, spreading manure from the stables and corrals on the cleared and leveled fields.

He had also devoted one team to preparing, plowing, planting, maintaining, and harvesting the two large areas on the upper plateau I'd shown him. He'd planted potatoes, corn, squash, watermelon, lettuce, carrots, tomatoes, onions, chiles, cucumbers, peas, and beans.

The bulk of the effort after the planting, was keeping the areas weeded and watered. The watering necessitated hauling buckets of water up the cliff face on ropes, and carrying them to the garden area. So far, all the different crops were doing well in the garden. He'd also developed a schedule to rotate all the teams through the various tasks, so that none of them were stuck with boring, smelly, or arduous tasks for more than two weeks at a time.

Hector reported that initial deliveries to Forts Fillmore, Thorn, and McLane had been made, and regular follow-on deliveries scheduled. The delivery of 2,000 head to Dr. Steck had been made. He had also contacted the Indian Agent at Fort McLane, closing a deal for 2,000 head with him. The large herds had left the Estancia for Fort McLane a month ago, and the twenty-five vaqueros he'd sent with them should be returning in the next few days.

At the urging of Jesus, the villagers and ranch families had been offered cattle at the price of three dollars a head, and they were taking advantage of the offer at the rate of fifteen head a week. Additionally, Hector had contacted the butchers in Las Cruces and Mesilla, and was selling an average of ten head a week at five dollars a head.

To my dismay I learned that even after all the sales, the herd had remained near 13,000 head. Apparently, despite the long drive last year, the bulls had managed to do their job with a bumper crop of calves resulting, this spring. I was going to have to work on getting more contracts. A letter to Kit and Lucien, as well as a visit to Fort Bliss, certainly seemed the best bets for quick sales.

Jesus's report was upbeat, with few problems requiring him in his official role of Alcalde. The villagers' moral was high, now that the heavy work of building the levees was almost done, and the clearing and preparing of the fields had started. At a recent village meeting, the villagers had decided the most pressing need, was for a combined multiple room schoolhouse and community activity center. Tom had agreed with the request, and Jesus had contacted Jorge. He was scheduled to visit the village at the beginning of July to talk with the villagers and ranch families, and begin to draw up the building design.

Yolanda and Miguel's report proved to be the most fascinating to me. They had trained an additional four Scout/Sniper Teams while we were gone, with another three teams scheduled to start training after the next rainy period ended. We'd all agreed that eight teams were the minimum number required to support the Estancia, so I was happy with the progress so far.

A new refresher Apache training course had been designed and added. The new course was taught on a team basis to each team, as they were assigned to Reserve Force duty. It focused on emergency first aid and communications, using the small signaling mirrors I'd given Yolanda before we left.

The signaling mirrors had really caught on with everyone on the Estancia, when one of the wagons had tipped over coming out of an arroyo, trapping two of the wagon's team with broken legs under the wagon. A Scout/Sniper Team on the way out for a two-week patrol had found the wagon team, and signaled the Hacienda for assistance before helping dig out the two men and setting their broken legs. The Reserve Force and two wagon teams had arrived less than two hours later to hoist up the overturned wagon, and transport the two injured men back to the village.

Miguel had two new posts established for relaying signals. Teams of the cousins were assigned to man them, along with the back-door post, on a constant basis. The older boys, responsible for the livestock on the upper plateau, had also been taught Morse code. Added to their work was the job of alerting the Hacienda when a message was coming in. Yolanda mentioned that the armory was in desperate need of more shelves, and gun racks would also be appreciated.

Anna and I talked about what we'd read until people started filtering in for the weekly meeting. Celia appeared with a fresh coffee service, just as Jesus and Raul - the last to arrive - entered the office. When everyone had their coffee and was settled in, Tom looked at me. I indicated, with a wave of my hand, that it was his show to run.

Anna and I listened as each of the men, and Yolanda, talked about their work status, and any changes that had happened since last week. I was particularly interested in, and happy to hear of, the amount of coordination that was going on regarding the use of manpower and resources.

After the meeting had run its course Tom looked over at me and asked if I had any comments. I told him I did, and first congratulated them all on their efforts, particularly with regards to the bridge.

I went on from there, "My major comment this morning concerns sanitation in the village and ranch areas. In the village, there are almost three hundred outhouses in a fairly small area, and I'm sure as the summer progresses the smell will begin to make itself apparent to everyone.

"Not only is the smell bad but open waste pits breed disease and that's my major concern. I will provide a gallon of fifteen percent carbolic acid solution to each home every week to be dumped into the outhouses. The solution will not only kill most diseases, but will reduce the smell, also. I'd prefer to have a team assigned to that job, rather than rely on each individual household to do it, but I'll leave that up to you all to determine. On the same theme of sanitation, there are two other issues. The first is where are all the cattle for the villagers and ranch families killed and butchered?"

Jesus answered that most folks killed and butchered the cows in their backyards and disposed of anything they couldn't use out in the desert.

I thought for a moment before starting again, "I want that practice stopped, immediately. Disease breeds in the accumulated blood pools and waste that isn't immediately removed to a dump somewhere else. Tom, I want you, Giuseppe, Tomas, and Hector to identify five or six different spots as abattoirs, where all cattle, sheep, pigs, and whatever else, are to be killed and butchered.

"Each abattoir is to be used for six months before being moving to one of the other selected sites. While the site is being used it is to be covered in a fifteen percent solution of carbolic acid monthly, and once again after it's moved. It should not be used for any other purpose for at least two years.

"In close coordination with this I want the same number of sites identified as dumps for whatever refuse the Estancia generates. This includes whatever animal and plant products we *don't* use for other things such as compost. The refuse dumps will be for common household refuse that can't be reused. Make sure that any arroyo or small canyons you select as sites, *aren't* a water drainage route.

"One site at a time is to be used until it's full when it will be covered up and the next site will start being used. Again, I need a team to be responsible for spreading a fifteen percent solution of carbolic acid weekly, and adding a four to five-inch-thick layer of dirt over each week's accumulation.

"I know you don't believe me, but doing these things will lessen the spread of disease, and help everyone stay much healthier. I will find the things I need to prove what I'm telling you as soon as I can. It will make my explanations much more understandable. Until then, please make this a priority."

When I'd gotten frowning nods from everyone I continued, "The rest of what I have to say, are thoughts or questions I want you all to think about. Next week, Tom and I will be in Las Cruces, so Giuseppe will run the meeting. Please talk about what I'm about to say at that meeting, and be ready to give your consensus opinions at the following meeting.

"These are not in order of importance, as you will determine the priorities. First, we need at least two wells on the upper plateau. So, what would it take to build a temporary crane to raise and lower a drilling rig to the upper plateau, as well as two or three wagons that would remain on the upper plateau?

"Next, we have numerous projects that still require the masons to build. Among those projects are the Segundo's houses, the stables, store rooms on the upper plateau, and the rectory. A schoolhouse still needs to be designed. Numerous water retention buildings at sites that have yet to be determined, as well as miles and miles of four foot high walls surrounding the Estancia, and both plateaus. I want you to prioritize each of those. I can get Heinrich started thinking about his bid on each of them. We can't afford to lose the masons simply because we haven't given them work to do. As it stands right now, they have nothing firm to do after the beginning of the year. Let's not wait until the last minute to assure them we have more work for them.

"Thirdly, I'm starting to get concerned about finding appropriate rock for road building. If Giuseppe doesn't find a source on the Estancia soon, I'm going to have to go elsewhere to get it, and that will put a major crimp in our cash flow. Is there any way we can free up Giuseppe from some of the tasks he's handling now, to spend more time looking for accessible quarry locations?

"Related to the crushed rock issue, is the fact that I want the current Camino Real rerouted 1,000 yards east of its current location, for all the Estancia. There are many reasons for this, most importantly, I want more farm land available to us for future expansion. Moving the road gives us that land. Second, at some point in the future, the railroad will come in from the northern part of the state, and the easiest route is alongside the Camino Real. To accommodate the railroad and the road I want the fence on the west side of the road 200 yards from the center of the road, with the road running 200 yards from the east fence. I also want the road widened to handle two wagons passing each other; and the entire length of it, from one end of the Estancia to the other, and paved with macadam. Anna and I currently plan on giving the railroad the right of way along the east side of the road, in exchange for a siding here at the Estancia, and railcar privileges.

"The signaling posts is my next item. I like what you did, and I'd like to see the other four planned and completed. Miguel and his teams should be involved in the planning and building of these sites, as they will be the ones manning them.

"Next, I need to know of any pecan and fig trees that are for sale, as I'd like to start getting those planted as soon as possible. Related to that, I'd like to find and hire a small group of groundskeepers to handle ornamental flowers and shrubs to be planted on both plateaus and around the village and ranch areas. Where do I find these groundkeepers?

"Finally, it has always been Anna's and my intention to share the bounty of any harvest with the families on the Estancia. To that end, we want to give them all a small taste, a very small taste, of what they can expect in the years to come. If Tomas' estimates on what the Hacienda gardens will produce are correct, we will have enough for everyone to get something from the harvest. I need your thoughts and recommendations. We want to use this opportunity to strengthen the sense of community around the entire Estancia. Anna and I are initially thinking that we will guarantee everyone who helps harvest the gardens and preserve the excess, a small amount of each item that is harvested. That means fresh and preserved corn, potatoes, onions, chile, lettuce, tomatoes, cucumbers, and all the other vegetables.

"We know that most families have their own gardens but even with those gardens there never seems to be enough. We'd also like to include the honey harvest for the hives owned by the Estancia, but we need to make sure that doesn't put a crimp in Jesus' honey sales. So, Jesus, you need to factor that into your thoughts and recommendations in this area as well."

I looked at each of the men and women in the room, seeing nothing but glazed eyes. I guess I'd given them too much to think about. I looked over at Anna who just gave me a serene smile and nodded, telling me without words that I had covered everything we'd talked about, and done it well.

I told them that I was done, and unless there were any questions, Anna and I had some other things to do and would see them later. There were no questions, so we left them to their thoughts. We stopped in the kitchen, asking Martina to send a coffee service up the dumb waiter. We'd take it from there.

Over the next six hours we talked about the plans we'd made for the next eighteen months, most of which revolved around the single burning ambition of Anna having our first child, somewhere within that time. There would be no long trips to the Colorado River or Santa Fe together. Instead, we decided to focus on actually building the Estancia community we envisioned.

We both agreed that the physical building aspects needed to be left to Tom and Giuseppe, with just a little oversight from us. The advent of the letter writing plan by the Judge had put both of our minds at ease, and would hopefully negate the long trip to Austin we had once both dreaded having to make.

That left us with lots of time to learn the farming aspects of the Estancia, make periodic trips as US Marshal to the east and north of the Estancia. This was intended to remind everyone I was still here, and mask the real reason for the trips, which was to hit Union Gulch for two or three weeks at a time, collecting more gold. Of course, I would still need to make periodic trips to Las Cruces, Mesilla, and El Paso but unless Anna was with me, those trips would be as short as possible.

Supper that night was completely back to normal, with the twins talking a mile a minute about the amazing things they had learned during their morning at school. Carl, Alejandro, and Mike were talking in hushed voices at the end of the table. I glanced at Anna, and she was watching them with a secretive smile on her face. She looked over at me and told me she had Beth and Izabella watching them closely, to keep them out of too much mischief. While that was some relief, I was still worried about what they could get into, and made a note to myself to check on them more frequently than I had been the last few days.

After supper, the kids had decided it was a singing night, so we all went to the living room. They had a ball and of course the last song they insisted on singing was "The Lion Sleeps Tonight". Anna, Yolanda, and Tom helped the new ones learn the words, cadence, and signals. We practiced, and then sang the whole thing through twice. After the kids went off to bed, I finished up by singing our three songs, "Impossible Dream", Keeper of the Stars", and "Anna's

Song".

We called it a night at that point, with Anna and I retiring to our bedroom where, of course, we explored some new possibilities.

CHAPTER 4

W hen we left for Las Cruces Thursday morning, it was with the knowledge that Miguel had a team scouting either side of the road a mile ahead of us for the entire trip. That settled both Anna's and my nerves, significantly. Beth and Izabella opted to ride in the wagon with the baby while Celia drove. She had asked to go with us for reasons of her own, which I privately hoped included seeing George during the visit.

I still couldn't figure out the situation with Izabella and Alejandro. They were supposed to be living with their Aunt in the village, but somehow they seemed to spend all their non-school time at the Hacienda. Most evenings they showed up at the supper table, and then slept in the rooms they'd originally had, before moving in with their Aunt.

Anna seemed to take it all in stride and tried to

explain it to me, but I still couldn't understand the apparent indifference the Aunt was showing towards her niece and nephew. I finally just gave a mental shrug, and accepted the fact that both kids were going to be living and traveling with us, whenever they wished.

In any event, the trip was peaceful and pleasant.

We all rode to the courtyard where we unloaded baggage for the stay from the wagon, putting it in the house. The ladies and girls all disappeared into the restaurant kitchen through the back door, while Tom and I, with the boy's assistance, rode over to the stables. We turned everything over to stable boys, who were supervised now by Martin Amador. I led the boys through the stable and out the back, to the table where Mr. Mendoza was sitting in his usual spot, working on the never-ending task of harness and tack repair.

He looked up as we walked out of the stable, and with a big smile on his face got up meeting us with big hugs and back slaps for me, Tom, and Alejandro. I introduced him to Manuel and Mike as our newly adopted sons, and they got the same big smile and back slaps as he welcomed them to the family.

I had Alejandro take the others and show them around the stables, and warned all of them to stay out of the way of any work that was going on, and to obey Martin. They chorused their agreement and disappeared through the doorway before I could say anything else.

I smiled while shaking my head and looked over at Mr. Mendoza telling him, "There goes trouble."

Mr. Mendoza grinned and told me it was good to see the exuberance of youth, again.

Taking him by the shoulders I said, "Anna and I were very sorry to hear about Grandfather Garcia and Jim. We both mourn their passing, and already miss them terribly."

The look in his eyes told me he was also still grieving. He thanked me in a gruff voice then cleared his throat and said, "Grandfather Garcia prepared us for his death two days before he died, telling us he didn't have long left in this life and would be dead in a few weeks at most."

Mr. Mendoza looked thoughtful for a minute before continuing, "He gave me a letter just before he left that morning, and instructed me to give it to you and Anna when you got back from your trip. It's in the house. I'll get it for you after supper."

I had an unexpected lump in my throat and just nodded. I was certainly curious what the letter had to say, but it had waited this long so another few hours weren't going to matter much, one way or the other.

Tom and I lazed away the afternoon talking, as we watched Mr. Mendoza's skilled fingers work on the repairs. Our conversation was mostly about the trip west and how we'd come across the kids, made the rescue, and returned home.

I did check on the boys every hour or so, and found them the first time having a hay fight up in the hayloft. The other times I checked I found them brushing down horses, or hauling feed and water, all under the watchful of Martin. He just gave me a grin as if to say that it wasn't so long ago we were just like them.

As usual during our visits, Mr. Mendoza led us all over to the back door for supper at the appropriate time. We all stopped as we entered to watch a new version of the kitchen dance - with new dancers - for a few moments, before herding the boys into the family dining room. Anna and Yolanda followed right behind us with coffee for the adults, and cool tea for the boys, before returning to the kitchen. A few minutes later the ladies arrived, bearing the platters and bowls of food.

While we ate, I asked Mr. Mendoza how the rest of his drivers had handled the news of Jim and Great Grandfather Garcia's death, and if he'd recovered the wagon. He told me that all the drivers had finally paid attention to his advice about taking shotguns and revolvers with them, and were more heavily armed as a result.

The wagon hadn't been recovered and it, as well as its contents - a cargo of furniture headed for Fort Thorn - were long gone. I wanted to assure him that I would find whoever it was that did this, but I felt the anger building again. I struggled to tamp it back, afraid to lose myself within the burning berserker I could so easily become, if I let the anger grow too much more.

I was beginning to think I was going to lose the battle raging in my mind, when Anna placed her hand on my knee under the table. Looking into her eyes, I found the love and hope that I suddenly realized I'd begun to crave. The anger suddenly receded to a much more manageable level.

Tom took that opportunity to ask Mr. Mendoza if he had found a new driver, to take Jim's place.

With a sigh, Mr. Mendoza replied, "Martin has asked for the job, but both Mrs. Amador and I are very concerned about his safety, and his ability to protect himself on the road. He's gone on a few trips, but those were always large trains of well-guarded freight wagons, not driving a single freight wagon by himself."

I perked up on hearing this, knowing that Martin would eventually become a freighter anyway. It was something I could help with. I looked over at Anna who, as usual, seemed to know what I was thinking. She beamed me a large Anna smile with a small head nod.

I looked at Mr. Mendoza for a moment before saying, "Sir, I think we might we be able to help Martin gain some experience, and put you and Mrs. Amador's minds more at ease."

With a confused nod from him, I continued, "You know we run all the new arrivals at the Estancia through something we call the Apache Training Course. The Apache Training Course isn't what the name implies. We just couldn't come up with a better name for it. The first farmers who went through the course gave it that name, and it stuck.

"The course isn't designed to teach people to be Apaches. It's designed with three goals in mind. First, how to survive for a week or so in the desert with nothing but the clothes you're wearing and your wits. Second, what to do if you're injured, much like what I had you and Mrs. Mendoza do for me when I was shot. Third, and most important for Martin, how to recognize an ambush before you get to it, and how to respond if you are caught in one. Everyone on the Estancia has completed the course, and we've moved on to other courses including a two-week refresher course that changes every year."

About halfway through my description, Mr. Mendoza's face had undergone a transformation from confusion to enlightenment, and he was now wearing a smile. I looked over at Yolanda as I continued, "Yolanda, how difficult would it be to schedule the original course for one person to attend?"

Yolanda was grinning at me and said, "Not difficult at all. As a matter of fact, it would help solve one of the problems we've recently run in to. The old ones who taught most of the survival and ambush portions of the course are starting to feel worthless, since they don't have much to do. Running the course for Martin, and any of the other drivers, would help them feel much better about themselves and about living on the Estancia. It would be great if we could get a driver every other month or so, to keep them busy."

I looked back at Mr. Mendoza and said, "The course won't replace years of experience, but it will significantly improve any of your drivers', including Martin's, chances of staying alive. The offer is there for you, Sir. You could even make the successful completion of the course a condition of employment. Think it over. If you want to give it a try, then all you have to do is let Yolanda know. She is the one who sets the goals for each course, makes the training schedule, and coordinates with Miguel for the trainers."

Mr. Mendoza looked with pride at Yolanda as he realized for the first time that she had a purpose at the Estancia, beyond being Tom's wife and Anna's companion. He nodded and said he'd think about it, and perhaps he and Mrs. Amador could talk to Yolanda over the next few days. Yolanda quickly answered that she would make herself available to talk, anytime he wanted.

Our conversation done we all turned to finishing the fantastic meal the ladies had prepared. I realized with a slight start that the anger that had been building in my brain was gone. Not tamped down and smoldering, but gone. I decided I needed to think about it later in the evening as I desperately needed to know whatever had caused it to disappear, so I could use the same technique in the future.

When supper was over, and the table cleared, I expected everyone to remain as usual as we savored our after-supper coffee and talked. I was more than a little surprised when Mrs. Mendoza brought in a small coffee service and two cups, putting them down in front of Anna and me.

She looked at everyone in the room before turning to the two of us and saying, "We'll take care of the young ones tonight, and see you both in morning."

Turning, she started motioning everyone else out of the room, and across the courtyard to the house. Mr. Mendoza, the last one left in the dining room besides me and Anna, got up out of his chair. He pulled a small square envelope out of his coat and handed it to me.

With a sad expression in his eyes and voice, he said, "Take your time."

As he walked out of the room, I looked at the small envelope in my hand, turning it over and over. Finally, I turned it so I could see who it was addressed to. After a moment of puzzling out the shaky writing, I discerned it was addressed to 'Pablito and Anna'.

I looked at Anna, who took it from my hands telling me, "Great Grandfather never learned to write well, and as he got older it became harder and harder for him to hold a pen. It probably took him almost five minutes just to write our names on the outside of the envelope."

She started to hand the envelope back to me, but I stopped her. "You open and read it aloud, since you have more practice reading both Spanish and his handwriting."

We traded teary looks before she nodded, opened the envelope, smoothed the three small pages of cramped shaky writing, and began reading out loud in a firm clear voice:

> *My Anna and Pablito,*
>
> *As you sit in the family dining room of the restaurant in Las Cruces with Anna reading this aloud I will have been in the Land of Ever Summer for quite some time. Please grieve no longer as I am where I am supposed to be as is James.*
>
> *Since Pablito came into our lives my power and visions have gotten stronger and stronger. It was almost like I was a young man again the power was so strong. Soon after meeting Pablito I had a vision of my future for only the second time in my life. I knew I would live to see the two of you married as well as the marriage of Yolanda and Tom. I also knew that my time on this world would come to an end less than a year after Yolanda and Tom were married.*
>
> *That second vision happened over an entire night and was of such power that it was almost overwhelming. My*

vision showed me that both James and I were to be the targets of an attack with the wagon and its contents a mere bonus. Know that we were killed as an act of retribution and that even if I had decided to stay in Las Cruces, James would have been killed. It was his time and it was my time to return to the spirit world. I tell you this only so you will know that I went to my death knowingly, and without doubt.

Pablito, when I first met you I told you that you were a young man with an old soul and that there was much more that I couldn't see. I know now that you are not just a young man with an old soul, you are a walker between times, protected by a very old and very powerful spirit. The spirit is a woman, very strong and very mature, who has lived many lives. In her last life, she fell in love with you, Pablito, and continues to love you very much. You ask how I know this and I tell you she was the power behind my second vision. She showed me many of the things to come and she showed me her life with Pablito. At the end of her last life she was sick. Very sick. She showed me her death bed and you *were there Pablito. It was you, but it wasn't you. She showed me a sky sign Pablito and told me to tell you of it. It was a fire-bird, she called it a Phoenix, rising out of the ashes of a fire. I hope you understand this sign Pablito, she said you would.*

Pablito, the spirit woman told me to remind you that you are NOT a death dealer, you are a defender who kills to defend his home, the people he loves, and the innocent ones. In times of doubt look to Anna for the truth of this. You will find it in her love and unquestioning support.

The spirit woman also told me that Pablito has shared all his secrets with you, Anna. It heartens me to know of the trust he has given you. His secret of being a time walker and of the two caves must be maintained for your family's safety but there are two others who must be told. You have already shown great trust in Yolanda and Tom. It is time now to finish what you've started and trust them completely. While the spirit woman and I will protect you the best we can, there are powerful forces struggling against you. Yolanda and Tom need to know with certainty that you are a time walker, Pablito, for you will be asking many things of them in the future. Likewise, if we fail and you and Anna should fall, then Yolanda and Tom will need to know the secrets of the two caves to continue to carry out the vision for the Estancia and the people on it.

Anna, just as the spirit woman is Pablito's protector, so I am yours. Know that I am with you. You know what you have to do to learn the ways of the spirit world and increase the power of the protection I can provide. Your training will begin a few months after your return from your trip. Don't worry, it won't hurt the baby boy you are now carrying.

My mind and my hand are tired. In a few minutes, I will begin my last journey. My final words to you both are to continue to love, support, and defend each other, for together you are a light of hope shining into the dark of injustice.

My Love to you both,
Jaime

I sat stunned with my mind stuck in a negative feedback loop for several minutes after

Anna finished reading the letter. The scope of his revelations and advice was astounding. Finally, I looked over at Anna who still sat in her chair with the letter in hand.

She wore a stunned expression on her face as well, but she also had a small smile and joyous twinkle in her eye. It took a moment but then my brain exploded as it finally processed the last part of the letter. It was like a huge gong went off right behind me, and I jumped out of the chair, staring at Anna.

"A baby!? You're pregnant!?" I shouted.

Anna looked up at me, her small smile blossoming into a full huge super megawatt Anna smile as she said, "Apparently I am."

"That's fantastic my love! How far along are you? Why didn't you say anything?"

Anna continued beaming her special smile in my direction before answering me. "Not long as I only began to suspect last week. I didn't say anything because it was too soon to get our hopes up."

I nodded at her explanation and gave another whoop! I pulled her out of her chair into a big hug as I lifted her off her feet, and twirled her around the floor. When I finally put her down she cuddled into my chest, hugging me tightly. I set my chin on top of her head as we embraced. I stared off into the distance, filled with happy thoughts of raising another child.

I'm not sure how long we stood there with our arms wrapped around each other, thinking about the baby to come. Eventually, Anna squirmed out of my embrace and looked around. She walked over to the pages of the letter that lay scattered on the floor, where she'd dropped them during our celebration, and picked them up.

Turning back to me, she reminded me that the letter had many other things in it that we needed to talk about. I sighed heavily, and said there were many things in the letter that we needed to talk about tonight, while we were positive no one could overhear us. Before we made any decisions though, we needed to think about them for a few days, and then discuss everything again, somewhere we were sure we wouldn't be overheard.

We sat at the table talking about Great Grandfather Garcia's revelations and recommendation late into the night. We both agreed that there was too much information neither one of us had told him, to doubt the remainder of his visions. Telling Tom and Yolanda all of my secrets was a big step, but we'd decided during our honeymoon that they needed to know. We'd just been waiting for the right time to do it.

Shortly before midnight Anna carefully folded up the letter, putting it away in one of her pockets. We cleaned up the table, poured out the cold coffee from our untouched cups, locked up the restaurant, and crossed the courtyard to the house for bed.

The kids woke us up earlier than we wanted the next morning, telling us it was time for Tai Chi and katas. We groaned and struggled out of bed to join them in the courtyard. We cleaned up afterwards, and rejoined everyone in the restaurant for breakfast.

Anna, Yolanda, Maria, and Mrs. Mendoza were soon herding the kids out the door for a day of clothes shopping, leaving me and Tom to fend for ourselves for the rest of the day. Tom had nothing planned, and decided he would accompany me to Mesilla, to let Esteban and Ed know I was back and talk about the recent raids.

Martin had our horses saddled when Tom and I walked to the sables. The horses were full of energy this morning, so once we were through Las Cruces we alternated between a canter and a trot for the rest of the trip, letting them burn off some of the excess energy.

When we pulled up in front of the office and

dismounted, Tom rubbed his rear end and looked over at me, as he said, "It's been a while since we rode like that. We need to ride a bit slower going back to Las Cruces this evening."

We were both laughing as we walked into the office, where we found Esteban and Ed going through what looked like a new stack of wanted posters and warrants. They both hurried around their desks, to greet us with handshakes and welcomed me back.

We talked for a few minutes about my trip and the adventures Anna and I had along the way when Esteban decided it was too hot and stuffy in the office with four of us and led us out the back to the courtyard, where we sat at a table on the small covered porch. Esteban left us there, returning a few minutes later with coffee for all of us.

As he sat down, Esteban said, "I'm really sorry to hear about Mr. Garcia and Mr. Ramirez. Ed and I rode out to see if we could find the tracks the day after we heard about it. We thought we'd gotten lucky when we found some tracks heading east off the rode about halfway back to Las Cruces, but it was just the killers dumping off three dead bodies. Mr. Garcia and Mr. Ramirez put up one heck of fight to get three of them. Anyway, the tracks rejoined the road after they dumped the bodies, and we lost them completely as we got closer to town, just like your cousins said."

Ed added his condolences before saying, "A couple of days later, we got word that the big flat nosed guy was in a saloon, bragging about killing two men and stealing a wagon of furniture. By the time we got to the saloon, he'd already left. Seems the guy was bragging that it was only the first of the killings. He reportedly intends to bring 'the coward of a US Marshal' out of hiding. We also learned that his name is Fulgencio Madrid. We wrote a letter to the Judge letting him know about the murder, the bragging, and the rest of the information we gave you, before you and Anna left. If nothing else we expect to get a bench warrant for his arrest on murder, kidnapping, and robbery in the next batch of updates we get."

Fulgencio Madrid?

"Esteban, Ed, thank you both for everything you've done. Both men meant a lot to our wives, as well as Tom and me. I'm almost certain I've never heard that name before, and I'm very certain I've never met anyone who remotely looks like a six foot four-inch-tall bear masquerading as a man with a flat nose."

With a questioning look, I glanced over at Tom who just shook his no. I continued, "For some reason it seems like this man has a grudge against me, Tom, and the Mendozas. Has there been any other activity since Mr. Garcia and Mr. Ramirez were killed?"

Ed was nodding his head violently, while Esteban answered, "There's been a lot of raiding activity as well as road robberies. We've learned a lot over the last few months, about both the activity before we wiped out half of the gang, and since the return of the other half of the gang."

Ed took over at this point, having returned from inside with paper and a pencil. He put the paper in the center of small table so we all could see it and started marking the paper with dots and X's.

"This is Mesilla, here's Las Cruces, and here's El Paso. Before we killed what we thought was the gang that was doing the raiding, they had raided seventeen small ranches mostly between Mesilla and El Paso, with a few raids northwest of Mesilla. Since the other half of the gang has returned they've killed Mr. Garcia and Mr. Ramirez here, just north of Las Cruces, and raided fourteen small ranches that we know of.

"They've also started robbing small wagon trains and individual travelers, on the trail to California. They usually take the people as slaves to sell but sometimes kill those they rob. There's no way of telling how many they've taken though, because we simply don't know how many small wagon trains or small groups of travelers leave El Paso, Las Cruces, and Mesilla for California."

As he was talking he was busy marking all the locations that had been raided.

He continued, "Most of the raids since the killing of your wife's relatives have been west of Mesilla and most of those have been twenty to forty miles away. By the time they're discovered and we hear about them, it's a week or more after they happened.

"We've traveled to all of them, to see if we could find any tracks to follow, but with the spring winds and rain we got this year any tracks we find are muddled and we lose them before we can track them for more than a couple of hours. Whoever is leading them is smart and they stick almost exclusively to hardpan, bare rock, or loose sand when they travel, and there's an awful lot of all three in this part of the country.

"The best we can figure at this point is that they are operating from somewhere in the Gila River area as they need water, if nothing else, to survive. Still that's a lot of country, and rough country at that."

Esteban took over when Ed was finished. "We've been to all three forts, Fillmore, Thorn, and McLane, to see what help they could provide. Colonel Miles at Fort Thorn was the most helpful. The area covered by Fort Thorn hasn't been hit by the raiders, but he said he would extend his patrols a day or two west and south of the normal area they cover.

"The commanders at Fort Fillmore and Fort McLane were sympathetic, but less helpful. All the raids that have occurred since you left have been in the extreme edges of their patrol areas. Both commanders would like to help, but they have their hands full with guarding the California Trail.

"They did promise to increase the number of patrols when they could, but they weren't hopeful it would be anytime soon. When the raiders started hitting the wagon trains and individuals traveling the California Trail, the army responded by increasing the number of patrols on the trail, and reducing the patrols, everywhere else."

I sat looking at the piece of paper with all the marks Ed had made as I thought about what they had said.

Finally, I looked up from the paper, "That's quite a lot of activity. The questions I have are:

first, do we have a map we can do all this on? I think we can get a better idea of the distances involved that way. Second, do we have a list of everyplace that's been attacked, when they were attacked, and how many people were killed and/or captured? Third, when was the last raid that you are aware of?"

Esteban answered all three questions without hesitation. "We haven't been able to find a map here in Mesilla, or Las Cruces. The only map we've found is the one in the Land Office and they only have the one that they use. We did ask the Judge in our letter for maps, so maybe he'll send them in the next batch of information he sends. We do have a list of where, when, and how many. We've both looked at it so many times, we've almost got it memorized. There hasn't been a raid reported for almost three weeks now, and while that's a relief it's also a concern. They've stopped the raiding for a reason, we just don't know what the reason is."

Damnit, it's times like this that I miss having topographic maps and computers. There was nothing I could do here to help, at this point. So instead, I took the long view.

Pointing to the paper, I said, "Ed, please mark each dot with the town it represents, then mark each X with the name of the ranch, the date it was hit, how many people were killed and captured, and how far it is from Mesilla. I want to take that with me and look at it some more, while I give it more thought." I looked over at Esteban as Ed went back inside with the paper. "While he's doing that, tell me about what else has been going on."

Esteban leaned back in his chair, "Thankfully, there really isn't much else going on. Since our little set to with the Stevens Gang, the word has gone out that we're here and actively working. So, any fugitives that come to town keep quiet. They seem to come into town, get what they need and leave, before anyone can figure out who they are. Ed and I spend some time in the saloons and the rowdier cantinas in town every two or three days to check on the local gossip, but with the exception of 'Flat Nose' it's been quiet. Most of our time since you left has been spent riding to the raid sites, looking around, and riding back here."

Tom had been quiet up to this point. I looked over at him as he put his coffee cup down on the table and said, "This is even more serious than I thought it was, Paul. We need to get as much of this information to Miguel, Maco, and the rest of cousins, so they understand what's at stake. Maybe they can even spread the word to the cousins not living on the Estancia. They could help you guys find this gang quicker."

"Those are good points, Tom. We'll talk to Miguel and Maco as soon as we get back," I replied.

I continued while looking at Esteban, "In the meantime, let's put the southern circuit trips on hold, for now. There's not a whole lot of people west of here and most are living close to a fort, so the army is patrolling near them.

"My biggest concerns at this point, are the areas getting hit the hardest, followed closely by your safety. I want you both to stay together whenever you leave Mesilla. If these guys are after me and mine, then at some point they will try to use you two to draw me out. Apparently, they haven't figured out I don't live in Mesilla or Las Cruces yet. When they do figure out where I live, I think we'll see the raids shift closer to the Estancia."

Esteban nodded in agreement, "We had about reached the same conclusion, and were going to recommend holding off on the trips until we catch these guys."

Tom and I spent the rest of the day with Esteban and Ed in Mesilla, before returning to Las Cruces riding at a slow walk, arriving just in time to wash up for supper. Supper was the usual riot of conversations, with the kids talking mostly about their shopping adventures, their new clothes, and commiserating with the twins over having to spend the afternoon learning English.

We stayed at the table tonight with our after-supper coffee, and Anna handed me the guitar without a word. We spent the evening singing songs. Of course, I made sure that I started with "Keeper of the Stars", and ended with "Impossible Dream" and "Anna's Song". Yes, that meant I got my huge super megawatt Anna smile. I was a happy man!

The next morning after breakfast, all the kids decided to stay with the twins for a couple of hours of English lessons. Anna and I strolled over to Mrs. Delgado's leather store, carrying Rose with us. Mrs. Delgado spent the first ten minutes playing with the baby before turning to business.

We ordered saddlebags for the kids, with their initials on them. Anna had talked to the kids in some detail while they'd all been out shopping, and they had all decided they wanted to be formally adopted, and use McAllister as their last name. To solve the problem of having two sets of saddlebags with the same initials, we left Miguel's initials in the usual place below the brand; and then put Mike's outside the brand, with an M bracketing each side.

Anna and I split up once we got back to the

restaurant. She continued inside with Rose as I wandered over to the stable to join Mr. Mendoza and Tom. Tom and I spent the morning helping out around the stables until lunch, when we cleaned up and returned to the restaurant.

As we walked in it was like 'déjà vu all over again', as Yogi Bera used to say. Anna and Yolanda met us at the door with our hug and kiss all the while beaming their respective smiles. Anna pointed back to our old table while Yolanda disappeared into the back. Anna brought us coffee, telling us that lunch would be out in a few minutes before she too disappeared into the back.

They both reappeared a few minutes later with hamburgers, fries, and fresh coffee. They set everything on the table, seated themselves in their accustomed places and we all dug in to the food. As we were eating, I asked how the kids were doing.

"Beth and Izabella have them out in the courtyard playing bebeleche," Anna said with an accompanying laugh from Yolanda.

I tried to figure out what game she was talking about, but try as I might I just couldn't think what baby's milk or drinking milk had to do with a game. Seeing my confusion, Anna laughed and led me out the back door for a quick look.

A quick look was all it took, and we were back inside at the table finishing our lunch. Or trying to. I was laughing just hard enough that I couldn't chew. Finally, I told them I had grown up with the same game, but we called it hopscotch. I still couldn't figure out the name Anna had used, bebeleche.

Anna and Yolanda both gave me one of those long suffering looks that women the world over have perfected.

"The name refers to the shape of the court the game is played on," Anna said.

I laughed some more, holding up my hands saying, "That makes sense. I've just never heard it called that before."

I still got my after-lunch kiss, hug, and Anna smile when we left the restaurant, so I was happy.

Tom and I decided to catch up with Juan; and maybe Jorge, if he was in town this afternoon. So we headed towards the brick yard, stopping at Mrs. Amador's store on the way to pick up some chalk for the kids to use at the Hacienda or the school, to draw the hopscotch court.

CHAPTER 5

W e found Juan inventorying a large stack of adobe bricks on one side of the yard. His back was to us as we walked up, and we heard him mumbling something under his breath about crazy stupid Anglos. Tom and I grinned at each other. I cleared my throat, watching Juan jump and turn around with a startled look on his face.

"I hope it isn't us you're mad at, Juan. I just got back, so it can't be me."

He laughed and said, "No, it's those soldiers at the fort. They can't make up their minds whether they want stone or adobe bricks. Meanwhile, the adobe bricks I made for their last order are sitting here. If they don't decide soon, a lot of these will be lost during the rainy season."

Tom and I looked at Juan with puzzlement

clear on our faces, and Juan continued, "Some soldier came up from El Paso and told the fort commander that the army had decided that adobe was a substandard building material, and to delay all contracts until they came up with a replacement. Now they are looking at stone as a replacement, but they don't like that they'll have to pay more than triple what adobe costs."

"Did they say why they thought adobe was a substandard material?" I asked.

Juan snorted before replying, "They said the roofs leak after a couple of years. The damn gringos who designed the buildings in El Paso built flat roofs, with a six-inch-high ledge around the top and didn't put in any drainage holes. So, every time it rains, the water sits on the roof. After a year or two, the adobe gets saturated, and of course it starts to leak. The part that makes me so mad is that Jorge and I wrote them a report when we'd finished building the first group of buildings. It specifically talks about how the buildings are to be designed to prevent leaking, as well as how to maintain them so they'll provide many years of use."

Tom snorted and said, "Sounds about right for army thinking."

I ignored Tom's snort and asked, "Have you tried to talk to the commander about this

Juan?"

Juan got so mad he actually stomped his foot as he said, "I've been over there at least once a week for the last month, but I always get some excuse about the commander being away from the fort, in a meeting, or out on patrol. I know he's in his office! He just won't meet with me."

That sounded par for the course for a newly assigned eastern bred officer. I glanced over at Tom before telling Juan, "We were going to visit my cousin George at the fort, tomorrow. Do you think if we went with you this afternoon, it would help you see the commander?"

Juan gave me a careful look, "It sure couldn't hurt. If nothing else, I can tell George what the issue is and how to fix it, as well as tell him about the report that's in that office somewhere."

I nodded and told Juan that we'd be ready to go as soon as we got our horses from the stables. Juan told us he kept his horse stabled with Mr. Mendoza also, so we all walked over to the stables.

While Tom and Juan were taking care of getting the horses, I found Mr. Mendoza out back of the stables working on his leather repair tasks. I told him we would be at the fort for the afternoon, and that we'd try to get back in time for supper, but we might be a little late.

Tom groaned as we mounted up for the ride saying, "Another butt bouncing ride. I'm still not recovered from yesterday morning's ride."

Juan laughed and told Tom, "The ride will make a man of you, it'll put hair on your chest. At least that's what my papa used to say."

We were all laughing as we rode out of Las Cruces. We pulled up at the fort a quick ninety minutes after leaving the stable, and I was agreeing with Tom. Before going inside the headquarters building I took my badge out of my pocket, and pinned it to my coat, figuring the nice shiny star in a circle would get us into the commander's office that much quicker.

As we walked in, we were met by a Sergeant who eyed my badge and asked how he could help us.

I smiled at him replying, "I'm US Marshal Paul McAllister, here to make my manners to the new fort commander. I just returned from a swing through the southern Territory or I'd have been here earlier."

The Sergeant nodded, and said he was sure the commander would be available to see me and turned away to tell the commander I was here. Before he disappeared I hastily added that I needed to speak with Lieutenant George

Pickett as well, if he was available. The Sergeant nodded and dispatched a runner to find George, before disappearing into the commander's office.

The Sergeant came out less than a minute later, beckoning us into the office while holding the door open. As we walked in, the commander, a portly middle-aged man, was walking around from behind his desk. I introduced myself as we shook hands.

The commander released my hand saying, "I'm Colonel Ezra Watson. It's a pleasure to meet you Marshal. I've met your Deputies who both appear conscientious and capable."

"Thank you, Sir. It's good to hear they made a good impression. This is Tom Murphy, my brother in law, and this is Juan Ortega, a good friend of ours."

The colonel shook hands with both Tom and Juan before asking, "What brings you all to Fort Fillmore today?"

"Well, Colonel, there are a few reasons we're here. First, like I told your Sergeant, I just returned from a trip through the southern part of the Territory and this is the first opportunity I've had to make my manners. Second, I need to see Lieutenant Pickett on a personal matter. Finally, I understand the army is experiencing some problems with adobe buildings that I may be able to help you with."

Colonel Watson looked intrigued at my reply, and was just about to say something when the Sergeant came back in with coffee for everyone, followed closely by George. George greeted me and Tom in Apache, with a big hug and back slap, before turning to Juan and greeting him almost as effusively, in Spanish. Juan replied in clear English.

I looked at George's uniform, "Damn, cousin, you're moving up in the world. Congratulations on the promotion."

George grinned back, "Just goes to show they'll promote anybody if they're in the right place at the right time." His face went from a grin to a frown as he continued, "We lost Henry Stanton while you were gone, so we were down a Captain. I'm the replacement."

George and I sat down with the others as I told him, "I'm sorry to hear about Captain Stanton. He was a pretty good sort when he visited us."

George agreed saying, "That he was, Paul. The army has decided to name a new fort they're building up past the Tularosa basin after him."

I could tell from the twist in his jaw, and the glint in his eye, that he was just being nice while in public. We'd talk more about whatever was on his mind in private, later.

Turning back to the Colonel I said, "As you can tell, my visit with Captain Pickett is purely personal as we are cousins, and he is well acquainted with both Tom and Juan. The other reason I'm here, is the problem I mentioned earlier. Is the engineer from Fort Bliss still here by any chance?"

The Colonel gave me a hard look trying to figure out what I was up to, before reluctantly nodding his head saying, "He is. You think he should be here to discuss this issue?"

"I do, Colonel, as Juan and I can be of some assistance in providing building stone locally, if you should decide to go that route. But more importantly, you may want to reconsider once we have finished with our discussion."

The Colonel looked over at the Sergeant, and asked him to send a runner for Major Long. While we were waiting for the Major to arrive, we chatted with George and asked when we would see him at the Hacienda again.

George responded, "Anytime, Paul. My patrol is due two weeks of recuperation and recovery; but with all the activity lately, we just haven't been able to spend more than a few days at a time in garrison."

"I understand, George. On the plus side, the

raiding party activity will fall way off in six weeks or so for the rainy season, which will give the entire fort a reprieve. The comancheros, on the other hand, may not be smart enough to quit raiding during the rainy season; but we've had no word about them for more than three weeks now, so they may be working somewhere else or even be in the Comancheria for the rainy season."

I turned to the Colonel. "Sir, did Colonel Miles give you a report about the buildings here when you took over from him?"

The Colonel thought for a moment and then said, "Yes he did, Marshal. I have it here, somewhere. Why do you ask?"

"Well, Sir, if you have it handy, it will make our explanation go much quicker once the Major gets here. Then we'll be out of your hair that much faster."

The Colonel, clearly put out by my request, got up and went over to his desk, looking through the various drawers until he found the thick report Jorge and Juan had prepared shoved in the back of the bottom drawer. He brought it over and handed it to me, and I handed it to Juan who started looking through it.

The Sergeant came back just as Juan finished perusing the document. He walked in followed by a slim and fit Major, who was introduced as Major Robert Long. It was obvious he was full of curiosity at being invited to attend a sit down meeting with a US Marshal and two civilians, but he held his tongue and simply looked at the Colonel in expectation.

The Colonel gave a brief explanation about our claim we might be able to help him with the adobe problem; and if not, then we could help provide the stone they were looking for. The Major turned to me expectantly.

The entire time this was going on, I was trying to come up with the right way to go about this without making the two officers mad. Finally, after another moment's hesitation I plunged in.

"Major, if I may, I'd like to ask you a few questions before we explain, just to make sure my friends and I have a full and accurate understanding. Is that alright with you?"

The Major, now looking perplexed, nodded in agreement and I continued, "Thank you. Now, can you tell me if the problem you're having with adobe is army wide, or just this district?"

The Major thought for a minute before replying, "As far as I know it's just this district, Texas and New Mexico Territory. Of course, we don't use adobe in many other places, as wood or stone are much more available."

"And who designed the adobe buildings at the various forts in the district? Just for argument's sake, let's use Fort Bliss."

Again, after a moment's thought he said, "I'm not sure who designed the original adobe buildings. As far as I can tell the original design work was done in eastern Texas and reused as the army moved west."

"I see," I said. "So, the same design was used at all the forts that are having problems?" At his nod I continued, "Are there any forts in this district that aren't having the problems the others are having?"

He responded immediately with, "Yes, Fort Fillmore and Fort Thorn are not having that problem. That's one of the reasons I'm here, to see if I can find out why the roofs here aren't leaking like everyone else's. Of course, Fort Thorn is still almost brand new, but the buildings here are over two years old."

I considered his answer for another moment before saying, "Is it safe to say that the original design was done by someone from back east who was unfamiliar with both the use of adobe as a construction material, as well as the weather of the greater southwest?"

At this the Major hesitated, glancing quickly at

the Colonel, before replying, "Yes, that's probably true."

Now came the delicate part of the conversation. "Major, there really is a simple explanation for the roofs at the other forts leaking. But before we get to that, I need to preface it with some background so you'll understand that what we'll tell you isn't drivel."

Again, a nod, and I continued, "The reason the buildings at this fort aren't leaking like the others is that Colonel Miles used a different design. A local architect, Jorge Ortega, trained in Mexico City. He specializes in the use of adobe and stone. He designed the buildings in this Fort as well as Fort Thorn, most of Las Cruces, and all of the buildings on my Estancia. None of the buildings he designed, and his brother supervised the building of, have issues with leaks as long as appropriate maintenance is conducted."

I motioned to Juan at this point and said, "Juan Ortega, Jorge's brother, provided all the building material used in the construction of this fort, and supervised all the construction. Juan why don't you explain what the problem is with the buildings in the other forts."

As Juan started to talk I looked at the two officers. The Major was wearing an expression both curious and hopeful, while the Colonel was barely holding his temper in check.

'Oh, well,' I thought to myself, 'so much for being delicate and diplomatic.'

I listened as Juan explained. "There are really two problems at the other forts. The first problem is in the construction. The corners of the buildings aren't square. This is a common mistake as most people believe it's not necessary, since they can simply cut the adobe blocks for the roof to make up for the lack of the corners being square. The problem is that each cut compounds and exaggerates the complexity of sealing the roof. This alone will eventually cause leaky roofs."

Seeing the Major nod his head in agreement, Juan continued, "The second problem is in the design. The original design had a flat roof with no pitch, and a six-inch-high ledge around the top of the roof. Quite simply, there is no way for the rain water that collects on the roof to drain off. Eventually, the water saturates the adobe brick under the stucco. That, combined with the bad seal resulting from the corners not being square, causes the roof to leak. The fix - adding drain holes to the roof ledge, and replacing the roof bricks - is relatively easy, and much cheaper than completely rebuilding from scratch. With minimal annual maintenance and care the buildings will last for many years if not generations."

The Major sat quietly thinking about everything that Juan had said. The Colonel on the other hand, had finally lost his temper.

He looked at me with a red face and asked, "You expect us to believe that this man is an expert at building anything?" Before I could answer he turned to Juan asking him with a sneer, "Just how many buildings have you built that makes you the expert you claim to be?"

Juan looked over at me and at my nod responded, "I've built around a thousand adobe buildings in the last seven years."

The colonel snarled, "Just where are these buildings? You claim to have built most of this fort, but that's only thirty buildings. Where are the rest of the buildings you claim to have built?"

Somehow, Juan remained calm answering in an even voice, "Thirty here, thirty at Fort Thorn; and, as Pablo said, most of Las Cruces and a good part of everything between Las Cruces and Mesilla as well. That includes the Marshal's office. Oh, and all the adobe buildings on the Estancia as well."

Before the Colonel could fire back I said, "Juan is being modest. He's built over twelve hundred buildings, including all the adobe buildings on the Estancia."

The Colonel glared at me and asked in a disparaging tone, "How many buildings are on this Estancia of yours? Five, ten, maybe fifteen?"

I looked over at Tom raising an eyebrow in question, and he answered the Colonel with, "Currently there are over three hundred adobe houses on the Estancia. They are all large three-room houses. There is also the church which is almost complete and will hold eight hundred people for services. There's the six thousand square foot Hacienda, the stables and wagon complex for slightly more than five hundred horses and mules, and almost a hundred wagons, as well as the entire ranch operations area. That houses eighty vaqueros and their families."

Tom's answer surprised the Colonel into silence. I wasn't certain what had gotten the Colonel all riled up, but I was certain that something was going on we didn't know about.

I looked over at the Colonel, "Colonel, we're not trying to tell the army how to do anything. We simply offer an explanation. The choice of accepting or investigating that explanation is yours. Should you chose to ultimately not accept the explanation, and to pursue rebuilding everything with stone, then Juan can offer all the stone you will need at a fair price. It will be more expensive than adobe of course but it is available locally."

The Major recovered from his far-off thoughts at that and asked, "What do you mean by local, Marshal? I've scoured both Mesilla and Las Cruces and no one knows of any quarries in the vicinity."

I smiled at the Major and said, "No one knows about it, because it's my private quarry. All the stone used in the masonry buildings you have on this fort came from my quarry. Juan is the only one outside the Estancia who has access to it. Otherwise, everything from the quarry is used for various building projects on the Estancia."

The Major's eyes bulged out at my response. "Good lord, man, what on earth could you possibly be building that would require that much stone?"

I looked over at Tom who responded with a smile and another litany.

"Oh, well, there's sixteen miles of levees to start with, followed by the six thousand square foot Hacienda, a bridge over the Rio Grande, stables of various sizes for roughly five hundred horses, and mules, various store rooms and seed stores, the ranch operations area where eighty vaqueros and their families live, eight small dams, and of course, eventually, a four foot high rock wall around the entire Estancia, not to mention some unknown number of water retention buildings and additional dams."

Apparently, the Major hadn't heard it the first time. When Tom was done reciting the activities, he gasped out, "I'd really like to see that!"

"Major, you're welcome anytime. As a matter of fact, the next time George comes out for a visit, you should come with him." I looked over at the Colonel, "That offer includes you as well, Colonel."

The Major grinned excitedly while the Colonel barely nodded his head acknowledging the offer. A moment later the Major turned to Juan saying, "You mentioned annual maintenance, what did you mean?"

Juan replied, "When Jorge and I were done with the initial phase of the construction here at the fort, it was apparent to us that no one here was used to building or maintaining adobe buildings. To help, we put together a booklet with all the blueprints, design specifications, and maintenance requirements." He handed the book to the Major before adding, "The maintenance information starts on page thirty-five. Luckily, Colonel Miles remembered to give it to Colonel Watson before he left for Fort Thorn; although, if needed, I do have a couple more copies back in Las Cruces."

The Major shook his head, muttering to himself as he looked through the book.

By this time I'd figured out two things. First, the Major had more power regarding fort construction than the Colonel, and secondly, there was definitely something *off* about the Colonel. What that was, I had no idea, yet. I decided to make it one of my goals to find out. I'd just about decided we'd done what we came here to do, and was confident that the Major would get things moving one way or another, when a thought suddenly hit me.

I looked over at the Colonel. "Colonel, I've made my manners, and talked to my cousin, and I've given you some information you didn't have before that broadens the choices you have available to you, regarding the buildings here at the fort as well as other forts in the district. I know you're a busy man so we won't take up much more of your time. I have just one more question for you."

He had calmed slightly from his previous anger and at least made the attempt to reply in a civil tone.

"I thank you for the information, Marshal. I'm

sure it will prove most helpful to the Major when he makes his recommendations back at Fort Bliss. I'll be happy to answer any other questions you might have."

"Well, Colonel, I just want to make sure you're getting all your cattle delivered on time. With all the comanchero activity in the area the last six or seven months, it's only a matter of time before they start adding cattle to the list of things they steal."

The Colonel got another sour look on his face and responded. "Yes, we're getting the deliveries we contracted for, but the beef we're getting is overpriced and of the poorest sort, so I'm looking at other providers in the local area or perhaps even driving some up from Mexico where beef is much cheaper."

I looked over at Tom who had a puzzled look on his face and he gave me a brief head shake to let me know we culled the worst cattle out of any group we sold, just so we didn't get a bad reputation.

I noticed, as I turned back to the Colonel, that the Major, George, and the Sergeant all had perplexed looks on their faces.

"I'm real sorry to hear that, Colonel. I'll look into the quality situation and make every effort to correct it when I get back to the Estancia."

Now it was the Colonel's turn to look perplexed. "Marshal, why do you care about it, and how would you be able to the correct the problem?"

In a very serious tone I replied, "I care because it's my reputation on the line. Your cattle deliveries come from my herd on the Estancia. As a matter of fact, the Estancia also supplies the cattle for Forts Thorn, McLane, and Craig and I haven't heard anything but glowing reports from those commanders. We also supplied 2,000 head each to the Indian Agents at Fort Thorn and Fort McLane and they were happy with the beef as well. I'd hate to lose my closest customer, if the problem can be easily solved."

The Colonel's face had soured once again, while the Major and Sergeant's expressions were carefully neutral. Tom, Juan, and George all had smiles on their faces.

I looked at George, "Well, cousin, we've done what we came to do. Now, with the Colonel's permission, why don't you show us out? We can have a little family talk on the way."

George and I looked over at the Colonel who gave a brief nod as we stood up. "Colonel, it's been a pleasure talking to you and your men. Please seriously consider a visit to the Hacienda with Major Long the next time George comes out to see us."

The Colonel stood up and shook hands with us saying he'd definitely consider it. We all shook hands with the Major and Sergeant, and followed George out of the building into the late afternoon sun. We untied our horses from the hitching post and walked with George towards the fort's gates before stopping in the middle of the parade field, so we could talk without being overheard.

George gave a deep sigh before saying, "Every time that man opens his mouth, I lose more and more respect for him. I may have to respect his rank, and obey his orders, but damned if I can respect the man."

"I did get the impression that something else was going on here. Tell us about the man, George."

George rubbed his chin for a minute then said, "I don't really know all that much about him. He supposedly comes from a very well-connected family back in the northeast somewhere. I can tell you though, he's like a bull in a china shop.

"I was with Colonel Miles down at Fort Bliss when he was picking up the new troops for Fort Thorn. Colonel Watson barged into a meeting Colonel Miles was having with the district commander, yelling about the sorry state of the buildings at the forts in the district. He'd already negotiated a contract for delivery of stone to replace all the current adobe buildings, and demanded the district commander approve and sign it.

"The commander just looked at him, and told him that he had an engineer coming from the War Department to review the forts, and determine what the best course of action would be. Until he had the engineer's recommendations, he wasn't going to sign any contracts.

"Colonel Watson stewed and asked how much longer the men were going to have to live in hovels, and be expected to fight Indians as well. The commander threw him out of the office. Colonel Miles told the commander that Fort Fillmore wasn't having any problems with the buildings, and perhaps the engineer should start his investigation at Fort Fillmore and that's what happened.

"The engineer showed up about three weeks ago, and was getting ready to leave; but decided he needed to stay through the rainy season, to see for himself if the buildings leaked. Anyway, a month after the Fort Bliss meeting, Colonel Watson showed up here as the new Commander. I knew we were in for a hard time.

"The first thing he did was to put Juan's contracts for adobe on hold, using the excuse that the War Department will probably decide to build with stone instead of adobe. He wasn't going to waste funds on something that would be torn down four months after it was built. He did this, despite the fact that we have twice as many troops stationed here than we did a year ago, and all those new troops are living in tents that are going to be soaked as soon as the rainy season starts.

"The second thing he tried to do, was sign a contract for beef delivery from some ranch south of El Paso at ten dollars a head. When he was told that there was already a contract in place for seven dollars a head, and with a local rancher, he about blew his top. When he calmed down he tried to find some way to set that contract aside, but the legal officer saw no reason to have it set aside as the deliveries were being met as scheduled.

"Last but not least, the man has us on full patrols, with only forty-eight hours of rest here at the fort before riding back out on two weeks of patrol. The places he has us patrolling make absolutely no sense. Almost two thirds of all the patrols are out in the Tularosa Basin where very few raiding parties have been reported. Meanwhile, west of here, on the California

Trail, he sends a couple of light patrols a month, despite the fact that wagon trains and travelers have been lost. Forget about northwest of here where all the raids have been happening. He refuses to send anyone there. I'm not sure anymore if the man is incompetent, or working with whoever is leading the raids."

By the time George was done, Tom was looking at me with some concern. Juan was swearing under his breath in disgust.

"What are you going to do, George?"

My question brought him up short. He stared at me giving me a hard look before asking what I meant.

"If you really think he's either incompetent or working with the comancheros, then don't you have a duty to report it, or try to correct it somehow? There's the other added worry of the Major's report never getting to Fort Bliss if he sends it through the official courier system. For that matter, the Major himself might never get back to Fort Bliss. I'm not in the army and I don't understand how everything works, so I'm certainly not in a position to advise you; but something needs to be done, even if it's subtle and indirect."

George slowly nodded his head as he mulled over what I said, and the possibilities. I'd put the thought in his head which had been my intent, and I left it at that. George was a smart guy and I had no doubt he'd come up with something without my help. We told George goodbye, and I reminded him that he was always welcome when he could get away from his duties. He said he hoped to visit sooner, rather than later.

The trip back to Las Cruces was longer as we rode slowly, talking about our impressions of the meeting with the Colonel, and what George had said afterwards. I listened to what the other two were saying but remained quiet as my mind churned.

Nothing about the Colonel made sense to me. On the one hand, I was all for someone making a profit on a business transaction, it was what we were doing on the Estancia, after all. On the other hand, given the current economic climate, I just couldn't see either a quarry or a rancher charging what the Colonel had agreed to in the contracts he wanted the district commander to sign. Neither could I understand why he would want to replace a steady reliable delivery of beef, with a more expensive, less reliable source.

His reactions to being told no in both instances were also disconcerting, as was his reaction to our explanations of why the adobe buildings were leaking. Combine these things with his decision to focus most of his patrols in areas that weren't having any problems, while ignoring the areas where people were being killed or captured for slavery, and only two conclusions were possible.

As George had said, either the man was incompetent, or he was using his position to increase his wealth at the expense of others. In either instance, he was a threat to the Estancia, and I was starting to get angry. Part of the anger, I knew, was caused by the feeling of helplessness the whole thing brought about. I couldn't take any immediate, direct, physical action against the Colonel, even though every instinct was screaming at me to do just that. He wasn't a direct threat to my safety. Being incompetent wasn't against the law, nor was there any evidence of his complicity in the comanchero raids.

I was going to have a long talk with Anna about this, tonight. Maybe she could come up with something. Regardless, I knew I'd be back in Mesilla tomorrow morning to talk to Esteban and Ed about broadening their information network, and keeping an eye on the Colonel.

We arrived back at the stables a half hour after sundown. We turned our horses over to the stable boy, who was getting ready to go home for the night. Tom and I said our goodbyes to Juan, and trudged over to the restaurant for supper.

As we walked into the family dining room, we were greeted with the special smiles reserved for us by our respective wives, along with a hug and kiss. Suddenly the issues I'd been dealing with on the ride back didn't seem so large or threatening, and all was well with my world.

Supper was about halfway through when Anna and Yolanda sat us down at the table. We fixed our plates from what was in front of us, and dug into the food as we joined the conversations around the table.

Tom and I told everyone that George was fine, and was planning to visit as soon as the commander gave him some time away from patrolling. We also gave a brief rundown on what happened during the meeting. Anna and Yolanda knew we weren't saying everything, and the looks in their eyes told us we'd have a long talk tonight, which I would welcome.

After we were done with supper, it was another night of singing. Anna and Yolanda led them in most of the songs, saving my voice for another day. I did have to concentrate on the playing though, and that took my thoughts away from the threats of the day and improved my mood.

Eventually Anna told the kids it was time for bed, giving Beth and Izabella the task of getting them into bed. The rest of the adults called it a night also, and in short order only the four of us were left in the dining room.

It took Tom and I almost an hour to give them every detail of the meeting we could remember, and what George had to say afterwards, as well as my thoughts on the ride back to Las Cruces. Both Anna and Yolanda's faces reflected their growing concern as Tom and I revealed more and more about the meeting.

Like everyone else, sometimes I'm too close to a problem to clearly see the cause and effect. For me, delving into the weeds and seeds is rarely a good thing. I'm a big picture kind of guy, but this time I'd lost sight of that. Anna, with her logical mind and intuitive understanding of people, cut through the fog I'd created in my mind. Kipling once wrote, "A woman's guess is much more accurate than a man's certainty." Anna certainly proved him right.

"Pablo, from everything you and Tom have said, this appears to me to be an extension of our problems with 'the Boss'. The solution appears fairly simple as an idea, but the implementation will be difficult, as you and I have discussed on numerous occasions. It is also potentially deadly to those assisting us."

That simple statement was the equivalent of a psychic bomb. I couldn't figure out how she'd come to that conclusion.

"Anna, how in the world did you come up with that, and what solution are you talking about?" I asked as confused as everyone else at the table.

"Pablo, you said earlier that you couldn't figure out if Colonel Watson was trying to line his own pockets using inflated cost contracts, or if he was in league with the comancheros. You seem to think those are mutually exclusive activities. In fact, I not only think they are both true, I think 'the Boss' is behind the Colonel. Pulling his strings if you will."

Looking around the table, Anna saw the confusion still on our faces.

"Okay, let's look at the facts. We know 'the Boss' is behind the comancheros, from their attack when we first started building the Hacienda. We know the comancheros are raiding homesteads to the west and travelers along the California Trail. We know Colonel Watson is wearing out his patrols sending them on long patrols to the east with little rest, allowing the comancheros to raid at will. We know Colonel Watson has tried to get stone and cattle contracts signed with inflated costs. Does anyone dispute these facts?"

Those were the facts as we knew them, and we all told her so.

"With those facts agreed to, let's go to observations. First, and most important, is your observations about the character and intelligence of the Colonel. You both said, in different ways, that the Colonel was easy to frustrate and anger, and had great difficulty controlling and hiding those emotions. You also said that he knew next to nothing about either building with stone or ranching.

"If both of these observations are true, then we have to ask ourselves two questions. First, did he come up with the idea of working with the comancheros as well as the contracts on his own? Second, is he smart enough and physically tough enough to lead the comancheros into doing what he wants, when he wants, and where he wants?

"From what you two have told us, the answer to both questions is a resounding, *no!* Given that, then we have to ask ourselves two other questions.

"First who's giving him directions on where, when, and how often to send out patrols? Second, who gave him the contract ideas and how did he find the resources for the contracts he wanted signed, if he's new to the area?

"The only answer to those questions that fits with the facts we know is 'the Boss' is leading both activities from behind the scenes, just as he's been doing since his first try at getting your gold."

Finished, Anna looked around the table daring us with her eyes to find fault with her analysis. For the next twenty minutes we certainly tried, but she countered every attempt to punch holes in her conclusions.

"Okay, Anna. For now, let's agree that your analysis and conclusions are valid. What's the solution?" Tom asked.

"I must admit I'm curious about that as well," I chimed in.

"I'm not surprised that Tom and Yolanda don't see the solution. As a matter of fact, I'd be very surprised if they did. I am, however, very surprised you don't see it, Pablo. After all it was your idea in the first place."

Color me startled! "What are you talking about, Anna?"

"I'm talking about an information network, Pablo. How much time have we spent trying to figure out what businesses to set up, who to approach to lead those businesses, who to approach for pieces of information, where to set up those businesses, and in what order? Is Santa Fe more important that Mesilla? What specific information are we looking for?"

Anna gave an exasperated sigh. "Everything we've learned since we got back from the last trip leads me to believe 'the Boss' is all about power. Everything he's done, and is doing, is about gaining, consolidating, and holding power. Everything he sets in motion is done indirectly, and often very subtlety. We've already indirectly formed an information network in Santa Fe with the Judge, Tom, Hiram, Helen, and Lucien looking for and evaluating information. That's a good and necessary thing, but the direct threats aren't in Santa Fe."

I couldn't help but admire the fire in her eyes, and the passion in her voice as I continued to listen.

"The direct threat is in or near Mesilla. Mesilla is the county seat, and therefore the basis of power for our entire area. You can bet 'the Boss' is actively working on other plans in the county besides killing us, coordinating comanchero raids, and signing lucrative contracts. I don't know what those other things are, and I'm not saying that every illegal thing that's going on there is the result of plans set in motion by 'the Boss', but I am saying there is more going on than what we know."

"You two now know who the brain in this outfit is," I said approvingly to Tom and Yolanda. "I'd already decided to talk to Esteban and Ed in the morning, and have them expand their network to include keeping an eye on the Colonel. I can see now that it needs expanding even further, to include everything going on in Mesilla and Doña Ana County. What are your thoughts on how to set this up, Anna?"

The fire in Anna's eyes changed to the twinkle I loved to see, and the angry passion left her voice as she replied.

"That's the simplest part, mi Pablo. We need to bring them in on everything: the connections we see, the types of information we're looking for, how best to obtain that information, and how to get it to us. In short, we need to formalize and prioritize the Mesilla Valley information network."

After another hour we had a plan. The plan relied almost exclusively on Esteban and Ed having, or developing, the right contacts. Everyone agreed that I should spend tomorrow talking to them about everything we'd learned, and about their role in the bigger information network. We'd bring George in, the next time he visited the Hacienda.

After breakfast the next morning, Tom and I mounted up and rode for Mesilla. A long, slow, pleasant ride. Later we walked into the office in Mesilla where we found the two Deputies going over a new stack of paperwork.

Esteban looked up as we walked in, grinned, and threw me a package of papers wrapped in butcher paper. The bundle, densely packed, was rather heavy. I groaned, taking a step backward as I caught it.

I looked up at the still grinning face of Esteban, who said, "The latest love letter from the Judge had three packages, just like that. One for each of us, as well as the warrant for Flugencio Madrid, two maps of the territory, and this letter for you."

He handed me the letter, and I shook my head telling him, "When it rains, it pours. This is going to take a couple of days to go through, and even longer to really sink in. I'm glad he sent the warrant and maps, though."

Opening the letter, I found it was really just a note telling me that he'd received a letter from his friend in Texas. The letter informed him that Governor Pease had been quite intrigued by the law that the New Mexico Territory was considering, and not to be surprised if it surfaced in Texas. I smiled on reading that. I refolded the note and put it in my pocket to show to Anna, later.

I looked over at Esteban and Ed. "Gentleman, it's time to discuss some business. Tom and I were over at the fort yesterday visiting George, and making my manners to the commander. We found some information that we need to share and discuss, so how about we sit out back in the shade and talk for a while?"

Ed led us out the back door to the courtyard table. With coffee in hand we settled into the seats at the table. Tom and I began relating our conversation with Juan, the meeting with the Colonel, and George's comments afterwards.

When we were done, Esteban blew air out of his mouth heavily. "That explains a lot," he said.

Ed nodded his head, "When we visited him, the Colonel said all the right words, but his facial expressions and body language didn't match what he was saying. I thought maybe he just didn't like the idea of us trying to get him to search a large chunk of land. What are we going to do about it, though? There's no evidence he's broken any law, and as the commander he's well within his rights to send patrols wherever he wants."

"And those are the reasons we can't do anything in our official capacity as Marshals," I replied. That got their attention. "We'll talk about that in a few minutes, but first you need to understand the bigger picture. We think the problems we discovered yesterday are really part of a bigger set of activities, and are not just two unrelated events."

Both Esteban and Ed leaned forward in interest. They stayed that way for the next forty-five minutes, as I took them through last night's conversation and conclusions. With all the background information out in the open, it was time to talk about the solution.

"Our job as US Marshals, relies on information. It could be information like a description on a wanted poster or in a warrant, a tip from a concerned citizen on where a fugitive is hiding, or even the information that tracks give us, about condition of the horse a fugitive is riding, or how long ago they passed by. It's all information. Up until now it's been a formal activity, and we gathered information only when there was a warrant to arrest someone. From now on, we are going to expand our information gathering, through an informal network."

"I follow your words, Paul, but I'm not quite sure what they mean," Esteban said with an accompanying nod of agreement from Ed.

"Whatever we do, has to be done as ordinary

public citizens, not as US Marshals. Information has to be gathered as a structured part of your everyday activity. That information comes from not only talking to people; but paying attention to not only *what* they say, but *how* they say it as well. You need to keep notes on who tells you things, how accurate their information has been proven in the past, and does the information dovetail with something someone else said?

"You get that information from everyone you talk to. From the housekeeper here in the office, the barber, the bartenders you talk to, the counter clerk at the store where you buy coffee, the men you play your weekly poker game with, and even your girlfriends. Most of these people never know you're gathering information from them. To them it's just talking to be pleasant, pass the time, or make an observation.

"There are some folks though that are going to know you're gathering information. They'll know because you'll tell them specifically what information you're looking for, and why. Collecting the information you'll be asking for will place some, if not most, of these people in danger. It will most certainly put you and us in danger."

"Whoa there, Paul. I can understand how having someone collect information for us can put them in danger, but how will it put us in danger?" Ed asked concernedly.

"It will put you danger if and when you act on the information they give you," I said with certainty. "Here's an example. Let's say you get information from the Colonel's housekeeper that he's meeting with the leader of the comancheros at a certain place and time. You two decide to be there close enough to listen to what they're planning or to arrest them. What happens if the information is false, and it's a trap they laid to kill you? The information is false either because the Colonel figured out his housekeeper is providing you information, or because the housekeeper is really working for the Colonel instead of you."

"Wow!" Ed exclaimed. "There's more to this information gathering than it looks like at first glance."

The rest of the morning was spent going over information gathering, analyzing, collating, and reporting. The biggest concern was accurately rating the validity of the information being reported, how trustworthy the person providing the information was, and how valid the information that specific person had reported in the past was. We came up with a grading system for all three that we agreed to use. We also agreed they would send me a weekly information report through Mr. Mendoza.

Shortly before lunch, we returned to talking about the comanchero raids. We went back inside, and after hanging one copy of the map on the wall, Ed pointed out where all the raids had taken place. I suggested they get some stick pins and place them in the map with a piece of paper listing the name of the location and the date of the raid. They could also place stick pins without pieces of paper for places that hadn't been raided. Perhaps looking at the information presented in that way would give them some ideas.

We had lunch with the two Deputies at our favorite cantina before riding back to Las Cruces with the new package of papers from the Judge, and the second copy of the map. We got back to Las Cruces in late afternoon, and were more than ready for a relaxing hour or two sitting with Mr. Mendoza at the table behind the stable, before supper.

CHAPTER 6

W e left Las Cruces on our return trip home as scheduled, with a passel of kids dressed for the ride, and a wagon full of clothes for growing kids. Tom, Martin Amador, and I rode along behind the wagon, as the ladies rode near the front of the wagon on either side, talking to Celia, Beth, Izabella and the rest of the kids.

Celia hadn't had a chance to see George during the trip, as he was back out on patrol early the next morning after our visit with the Colonel.

Martin had reluctantly come with us. He had adamantly refused to attend the training at first, not seeing the need. But a stern talking to by his mother, and a warning from Mr. Mendoza that he wouldn't be hired as a driver unless he attended and passed, persuaded him to take us up on the offer.

The stone bridge coming into view was a welcome sight after a seven-day absence. What was even more impressive, was the fact that it had been completed, as evidenced by a group of wranglers coming across the bridge with a small herd of fifteen replacement horses for the ranch stables. As we crossed the bridge I couldn't help but be impressed by its sturdiness as well as its beauty. The masons had a done a really nice job.

Martin hadn't been north of town in quite a while, and was amazed at the changes he was seeing. His first glimpse of the Hacienda as we rode up the slope, produced the now expected jaw dropping expression. The amazement continued, as two of the cousins came up to help us unload everything, and then take the horses and wagon down to the corral.

We entered the Hacienda to find it strangely quiet for a weekday just after lunch. Anna and Yolanda disappeared into the kitchen, to find out what was going on as Celia, Tom, and I made sure each of the kids took their clothes up to their rooms. Beth and Izabella were tasked with making sure the younger kids put up their clothes properly, before having a late lunch.

As the kids disappeared upstairs with their first loads, we heard a whoop of excitement come from the kitchen. The ladies came out talking so fast we could barely understand a word they said. When they finally slowed down enough to understand we discovered that Lorena had delivered her baby in the wee hours of the morning.

Mother and son, Tomas Jerome Lopez, were doing fine, but everyone was exhausted and were in their rooms having an afternoon siesta.

We could hear the kids upstairs making noise, and Anna went up to quiet them down while Celia took Martin to show him his room, and explain the bathroom situation. Tom and I went upstairs after loading a coffee service in the dumb waiter. We retrieved the coffee, and went out to the terrace, sitting down in the shade waiting for the ladies to join us for lunch.

We passed a quiet afternoon in the shade of the terrace awning talking amongst the four of us about everything that had happened the last two weeks, and the plans we needed to finalize for the rest of the year.

Two of the things I was most interested in, were buying and setting up greenhouses, and building an ice making machine near the new school and community center. Tom and Yolanda had heard me talk about the greenhouses with Tomas, so they were at least familiar with the term and how I planned on using them.

The ice making machine caught them completely by surprise. I explained that a doctor in Florida had invented it in 1845. He received a patent for the process in 1851, but had died a short time later. I told them I'd show them the patent tomorrow morning after breakfast. Anna smiled at that, as we had decided that tomorrow morning was the best time to let them in on all our secrets.

I explained a little bit about how the machine operated, and my thoughts on using the ice-cold water that was a byproduct of the process, to cool the school and community center during the summer. I also explained that if we could build the machine, everyone on the Estancia would be able to use blocks of ice to keep meat, milk, eggs, butter, and the like longer before it spoiled.

We'd have to experiment building ice boxes, to see what worked the best, but eventually I was sure every family on the Estancia would have one. The biggest hurdle I could see at this point, was finding a small steam engine to run the machine, but Juan had assured me that he would be able to get us one, eventually.

Supper that night was an even more boisterous affair than usual, as we all celebrated the birth of Tomas Lopez. Hector was pleased as punch with his son's arrival, and Lorena was radiant. Martin didn't quite know what to make of such a large gathering at meal time, but he fell in to the spirit of things, and joined in on the conversations that interested him, at least the Spanish conversations. His English was still too poor to really understand what was being said, and he lacked any knowledge of Apache, so he missed those conversations completely.

At breakfast the next morning I asked Giuseppe to tell Miguel and Maco that I'd like them to come for lunch today, if he saw them. Giuseppe said there was a better way now, and he'd show me how to contact them before he left.

Tom, Yolanda, and the rest of the adults grinned, while Anna and I looked puzzled letting us know that we were the only adults at the table who didn't know what Giuseppe was talking about. A half hour later, Giuseppe led Anna and I into the office where he told me to write out the message and who it was for.

When I was done, he led us upstairs and out the upper courtyard to the corrals, where Giuseppe had me give the note to one of the young cousins on corral duty. The boy read the message, then turned towards the Robledo Mountains taking one of the small signaling mirrors from his pocket.

He flashed a quick signal towards the center of the mountain, and then waited until he got an answering ready signal from someone about three quarters of the way up the mountain.

My Morse code was a little rusty, but I think whoever was on the mountain sent back 'rdy', which I assumed meant ready. I stood next to the cousin as he sent a short message. I was sure the reply when it came was 'ack', which I knew meant acknowledged. I wasn't sure what message he actually sent but it wasn't a direct copy of what I'd written, as sending it was far too quick.

While we were waiting for a response I asked the cousin what message he had actually sent. He took a short stubby pencil from his pocket, and wrote what he'd sent on the paper I had given him: 'fm dp to mm lnch tdy hac'. I couldn't help but laugh after I read it. Just to be sure I asked him to translate it into English for me.

He smiled while telling me, "In English it says, From Don Pablo to Miguel and Maco, Lunch today at the Hacienda."

I nodded, clapped him on the shoulder, and looked over at Anna, "That's pretty much what I wrote out."

Less than a minute later we saw a flash from the mountain, and the cousin flashed back a 'rdy'. The signal was quickly sent, and I found I could decipher what it said, now that I knew the shorthand they were using.

I held up my hand just as the cousin began to tell me the message, and said, "Let me try. The message read, 'fm mm to dp lnch tdy hac ack, wbt'. Which means, from Miguel and Maco to Don Pablo, Lunch today at Hacienda acknowledged. Will be there."

An incongruous thought popped into my head as I found myself thinking these folks would have no problems texting in 2016. I looked at him expectantly, and he grinned, telling me that was exactly what it said. I thanked him for his help, and we all returned to the Hacienda to head our separate ways.

We made sure all the kids got off to school, and that Rose was being looked after in the kitchen, before Anna and I led Tom and Yolanda into the office. The last one in, I closed the door and dropped the bar across the back, before going over to the desk. I opened the top drawer and removed the letter from Mr. Garcia, and my old billfold, then joined the others on the couches.

Tom and Yolanda were looking at me expectantly with a slightly worried expression as Anna took Yolanda's hands and told them both, "Pablo has some things he needs to tell you about himself. You need to keep your minds clear, and not discount what he tells you, because it will be difficult to understand. I know, it was for me."

"Anna is right, but before I say anything else you need to read this letter from Mr. Garcia, first," I said as I handed Yolanda the letter.

Anna and I waited patiently, as first Yolanda and then Tom read the letter. When he was done reading, Tom refolded the letter and handed it back to me.

"So, you're going to tell us your secrets and let us know about the two caves because Mr. Garcia told you to in a letter he wrote before he died?"

I shook my head and replied, "No, Tom. We had already decided you and Yolanda needed to know my secrets and about the caves. We were just trying to figure out *when* to tell you. Mr. Garcia's letter helped us decide to tell you now, rather than later."

Tom and Yolanda were now staring at me intently with an almost eager expression on their faces waiting for me to start. I looked back at Anna. Seeing her calm and tender look settled me down enough to start talking again.

"Almost everything you think you know about me, except my name, is probably wrong. I am not twenty. As best as I can figure, I am about to turn seventy-one."

I stopped there, as Tom and Yolanda were both looking at each other with a half smirk on their face, telling me with their body language that they didn't believe a word I'd just said. I looked back over at Anna and resettled myself before taking a deep breath and starting again.

"Well, hell! You two need to understand that I'm not having fun with you, or telling you lies. I was born in El Paso in 1952. Yes, you heard me right. I was born in 1952, almost a hundred years from now." I spent the next forty-five minutes giving them the story of my twentieth and twenty-first century life. My parents teaching school at the reservation, being adopted by the Garcia's, joining the military, finding and marrying Laura, my education, my kids, my work in the service, my retirement, Laura's death, and finally waking up here, after driving into a low fog. As I talked, I watched their expressions change from disbelief to incredulity, and back to disbelief again with a touch of anger by the time I was done.

"I don't expect you take my word for a story like the one you just heard. I will try to prove it to you."

I reached down and picked up my wallet from where it was laying between Anna and me. I opened it up and dumped the coins I'd put in the bill compartment into my cupped palm. I handed the coins, a penny, nickel, dime, and quarter, to Yolanda. I pulled out a one-dollar bill, a five-dollar bill, a ten-dollar bill, and a twenty-dollar bill, handing them to Tom.

I let them examine them closely before saying, "Those are the most common coins and currency from the early twenty-first century. The dates they were minted or made are on them." I waited a few moments longer, before opening the billfold again as I said, "One of the common themes in the late twentieth century and early twenty-first century, is the fact that government issued identification is required to do almost anything. Here is my retired military identification card issued by the Federal government. This is my license to carry a concealed weapon, and here is my license to operate a motor vehicle, both of which are issued by the State of New Mexico. Again, they are all dated and have my picture on them."

They set the money coins and bills down on the table and took the ID's I gave them to look them over. Their faces had lost any trace of anger, but still maintained the look of disbelief. While they were examining the IDs, I looked at Anna, getting a nice tender loving Anna smile in return and a pat on my hands, as she told me without words that everything was going to be alright.

I was still staring into Anna's eye's when Tom looked up from the driver's license he was holding and asked me what else I had in the wallet. I picked the wallet back up and pulled out each item one by one, and handed them to him as I told him what they were. "My Veterans of Foreign Wars membership card, my American Express Card, my Visa Card, a picture of my wife and kids, and my business card."

Tom took each item as I handed them to him, giving them a quick glance before passing them on to Yolanda. They looked at them for a few minutes, before handing them all back to me. I put everything, including the coins and bills back in the billfold.

When I looked up from putting everything away, Tom and Yolanda were both looking at me expectantly.

"You have more to show us, Paul. Where is it and when will we go see it?" Tom asked.

"Tom, you've always been a skeptic. You're right, I do have more to show to you, and the time and place is here and now."

As I'd been talking, Anna had gotten up, retrieved the key to the cave door, and was standing near it. I asked Tom and Yolanda if they still had their key to the armory door, and they said they did. I nodded and told them Anna was holding a similar but much longer key, that would open the door to the caves in much the same manner as the armory was opened. I nodded to Anna, and she inserted the key, giving it a good push and the cave door swung open.

Tom and Yolanda stared in stunned disbelief at the opening. I cleared my throat, regaining their attention and told them, "Only two other people besides you two, Anna, and me know about this, and I expect it to remain that way. The caves are never discussed outside this room, and then only if the door is closed and barred. The two other people who know about the door and the caves are your grandparents, Yolanda."

That took them both by surprise, but they just nodded their heads still too stunned to talk. I waved at Anna and she beckoned them to follow her as she picked up the lamp off the desk that she'd lit while I was talking. She walked through the door, and into the cave. Tom and Yolanda hurriedly followed Anna through the door, while I followed more slowly, content to let them take their time exploring.

I watched from the doorway as Anna led them to the smaller cave to start their exploration. Just as when the Mendozas and Anna had first explored the cave, all I could see was the soft glow of the light and Anna's soft murmur in the distance, as she explained the water wheel and the pipes.

The glow from the lamp began to get stronger as she started back to the front. I stepped fully inside and joined them as they entered the larger cave. Both Tom and Yolanda stopped in their tracks when they realized the glint reflected from the light cast by the lamp was coming from stacks of gold bars. Anna had been expecting this of course. She stepped closer to the shelves, raising the lamp higher so they could better see the stacks of gold bars.

Tom looked over at me. "Good Lord! How much gold is there?"

I gave a shrug. "Based on the price we got for the last load we sold, that's about two-point-eight million dollars you're looking at."

Yolanda swung around and stared hard at Anna with bulging eyes, while Tom was giving me the same look.

Anna gave them both a small grin. "And now you know another secret."

Tom looked around the large cave, "So did you bring the gold with you, or was it already here?"

My reply startled him yet again. "No, Tom, I didn't bring it with me, and it didn't come from any cave. It came from a dry stream bed, where I dug it up and melted the nuggets down into the bars that you see."

"Okay. Where's the stream bed?"

"It's not on the Estancia, Tom. I promise I'll take you there and to other areas for more gold in the future. For now, I want to talk about these two caves. Right now, we, the four of us, are responsible for ensuring the welfare of over twelve hundred people. The gold you see on those shelves represents the future of the Estancia, and the people on it. Without that gold, there would be no Estancia. These two caves provide security for the gold reserves we will need in the hard times to come, as well as providing a safe refuge should it ever look like we will be overrun. So, the caves really serve two purposes.

"They also serve other purposes, which we'll get to in a few minutes; but, for now, those are the two reasons they are kept a secret. What you need to know right now is that Anna and I do not own the Estancia. When we were in

Santa Fe, after we got married, we placed all the land and the Estancia bank accounts into a trust, which she and I jointly manage. A lawyer in Santa Fe administers the trust for us. Anna and I are paid as employees of the Estancia, just like everyone else.

"Everything you see in these two caves belongs to the Estancia, as far as we are concerned. Which brings me to why I'm telling you this. If anything happens to Anna and me, you two will be the managers of the Estancia. Your pay will go up, of course, and the Hacienda becomes yours to live in; but more importantly, all the responsibility becomes yours as well. You are also named as the guardians of any surviving children we might have, and you will of course be expected to raise the children we've adopted. If we do have children that survive us, they will become the Estancia managers when they reach the age of twenty-five.

"Now you know why Anna and I had already decided to tell you the secrets, and why Mr. Garcia said what he did in his letter."

Anna and I stood patiently waiting side by side with our arms around each other, while Tom and Yolanda processed everything they'd seen and heard over the last hour. A short time later, Yolanda shook her head and muttered, "My God!" before looking over at Tom.

Tom looked at her for a moment before turning back to us, "Okay, so you've told us the secret that you're from the future, and shown us the caves. There's still the *proof* of you being from the future you promised us."

I gave a soft laugh saying, "Tom, you really have to quit being so shy, and tell us what you really mean."

Tom and Yolanda looked startled, and then grinned at each other. I went back over to the cave door and swung it shut, before returning to Anna's side. "The proof I promised you is on the other side of the shelves.

Anna led the way around the shelves followed by Tom and Yolanda, with me bringing up the rear.

Anna led them around the RV, so they could see what there was to see besides the RV and trailer. I heard Yolanda's gasp when she spotted the small mountain of gold nuggets piled on the cave floor near the front of the RV, and the gold bars stacked against the far wall. When they'd finished looking around they rejoined me near the door.

Tom said in a quick breath, "Two questions. First, how much gold do you have on this side of the shelves?"

I shrugged again, telling him, "What it's worth depends on the price we can get for it. If the last price holds then it's worth roughly six million dollars. Anna and I may be altruistic, Tom, but we aren't stupid. If anything happens to the Estancia, hopefully we can use what's here to start over somewhere else. What was the second question?"

Tom grinned at my reply, and then waved his arm towards the RV and trailer asking, "What the hell is this thing?"

I laughed again, telling Anna, "That's almost what you said the first time you saw it." She nodded with a grin, and I continued, "It's actually two things, Tom. The front part is called a Recreational Vehicle, or 'RV' for short. Think of it as a small house on wheels, that can travel long distances almost anywhere by means of an internal combustion engine. The second part is a trailer, used for hauling material or for storage. In this case, I used the trailer to carry and store my inventory. It's kind of like a tinker's wagon, but instead of being pulled by horses, it's pulled by the RV."

Anna let out a small giggle at the confused expressions on Tom and Yolanda's faces. "Don't think too much about it. It's all confusing at first, with the odd names he calls things. Just listen and look. It will become clear in time."

I turned and opened the rear doors on the trailer. Reaching inside, I flicked the light switch. Tom and Yolanda gasped at the sudden light, and looked inside to see what was on fire.

Seeing the panic on their faces, I hastily told them, "There's nothing to be concerned about. It's just an overhead light."

I stopped at that point, once again realizing that none of what I said made any sense to them. I thought for a minute and said, "It's an artificial light, created by applying the right type of power to an incandescent bulb. It's not dangerous, and it's not magic. In about twenty-five years a man named Thomas Edison, back East, will invent the first useable form of this technology. Nothing else I can tell you about it will help you understand it any better without a lot of discussion and explanations, which we don't have anywhere near enough time for right now."

They continued looking at the light inside the trailer for a moment, before tearing their eye's away and glancing at the work table, lathe, storage racks of rolled steel and bins of wood before looking back at me.

"We can talk about all the things inside the trailer at a later time but most of what I tell you will require much more time than we have, right now. Suffice it to say that what you see inside the trailer, are the tools and materials I use to build guns or pieces of guns."

They both nodded and pulled their heads out of the trailer. I closed up the trailer and beckoned them to follow me. I walked to the front of the RV, opened the door, and watched them file past as they followed Anna into the RV. I left the door open to get some fresh air inside.

I couldn't help but think that now the fun would begin, as I followed them inside. Anna had turned on the interior lights, and started up the air conditioner to get rid of the stuffy stale air. I moved up to the driver's area, and waved Tom and Yolanda up to stand behind me as I sat down in the driver's seat. Anna grabbed the coffee pot, and left us to get water from the small cave.

While she was gone I explained what I could about driving, steering, the gas pedal, the brake, and the gear shift. When I was done with that I reminded them that nothing could happen until the engine was on, and then I started the engine. I turned off the engine, and looked over at them. They were both shocked, and although they were still wearing slight looks of disbelief, I could see the dawning of understanding of what I'd been trying to tell them in their eyes.

Anna walked back in as I sat them down at the kitchen table. I took the coffee pot from her as she handed it to me. I pulled the coffee container out of the freezer and filled up the basket with grounds before putting it back. Pouring the water in, I placed the pot in position, and closed the lid on the water reservoir before telling them the coffee would be ready in a few minutes. The look of disbelief remained on their faces, although at this point I couldn't be sure if it was the technology, or the fact that Anna was letting me make coffee.

I went through the same routine I'd used with the Mendozas and Anna on their first visit, and explained all the appliances. We drank the coffee and ate microwaved popcorn. I answered all of their questions as fully as I could, given their limited knowledge of technology and the limited amount of time we had. Eventually I had to call an end to things.

"There's much more I could show you, but we're about out of time, and I need to do one more thing before we leave here. Please excuse me while I work for a few minutes."

I got up and went back to the bedroom, returning a moment later, carrying my laptop and charger. I hooked up the laptop to the outlet, finished my coffee, and turned on the computer. When it had booted I opened the hard drive, searching for my old senior mechanical engineering project folder. When I finally found it, I opened up the file for US Patent number 8080, and hit the print button.

The printer, sitting on a small table behind the kitchen area, started up. It began whirring as it prepared the paper to print. The sound of the printer starting up startled Tom and Yolanda, and they looked around trying to find where the noise was coming from. I smiled at them, and told them what it was.

My explanation made absolutely no sense to them of course, and with a chagrined look on my face I told them that was a subject for another day. When the printer was done printing the twelve-page patent document, I returned the laptop and my wallet to the bedroom. Picking up the papers, I led the way back into the office, before someone came looking for us.

With everything closed up and hidden away once again, the ladies went to the kitchen for coffee. While they were gone I gave Tom the papers. I told him to read them, as they represented our next major project.

The ladies returned a few minutes later with a coffee service, letting us know that lunch would be ready in an hour. I shook my head wondering where the morning had gone. It seemed like we'd only been in the cave for a half hour, yet almost four hours had flown by.

Tom's rustling of the papers as he shuffled them together focused my thoughts back on why we were here. He handed me the papers, and started to ask me a question. I asked him to hold his thought for a few minutes as I gave the papers to Anna.

As Anna was skimming the papers, I got up and barred the door. Sitting back down, I poured a cup of coffee. Anna quickly finished skimming the papers and handed them to Yolanda.

After reading the first paragraph, Yolanda mimicked Anna and quickly scanned the rest before handing the papers back to me.

Tom looked at me, and at my nod asked, "Paul, with everything we have going on why do you want to add this now? I mean, we have virtually everyone tied up on various construction projects, clearing land, driving cattle to the various forts, or planning the next phase projects. Why now, and why this? Do we even know if this contraption will work?"

Anna was smiling at me with an 'I told you so' look, while Yolanda was waiting for my answer with a curious look on her face.

"Those are all good questions, Tom. First, let me assure you the contraption works. I know it works, because I built one using this patent when I was in college as my senior project. The one I built was on a smaller scale, and compared to what is available in the twentieth century it was very inefficient, but it did work.

"Second, this is going to take a lot of planning to implement correctly, and even then, we are going to be using trial and error to get some things right. To build the system described in that patent, we will need Raphael to make most of the metal parts, the cooper to make the wooden parts, the masons to build the structure, Juan and Mrs. Amador to find and obtain the parts that we can't build, and Giuseppe working with you and me, to make it all work together correctly.

"Once it's built and working, everyone on the Estancia will have ice available to them. Think what that would mean to every family on the Estancia. Anna and Yolanda probably have a much better idea of what it would mean to the families, but suffice it to say having a reliable way to keep meat, milk, butter, eggs, and liquids cool, would greatly reduce the amount of spoilage.

"Part of the planning we have to do, is to figure out how the ice can be most efficiently stored in the home. Is an icebox the best answer? What should it be made of, and in what shape? Is there a way to make the ice last longer than just a day or two? There are a host of other questions as well I'm sure.

"If that was all that this machine did, I would say you're right that it could wait. However, one of the byproducts of making ice, is cold water. Very cold water. That cold water can be used to cool large buildings like the combined school and community center, if the ice making machine is close enough. That, in and of itself, is a major reason I want to go ahead with getting the planning started.

"The kids in school will learn much easier if the building isn't sweltering in the spring and fall. Meetings and celebrations in the community center will be much more comfortable. To make that work effectively, we need Jorge to include the pipes and vents into the design of the school and community center. We will also need to do some work experimenting with fans powered by windmills or steam engines, or both.

"Another reason I want to get started is because one of the major components of the machine is a mechanical water pump. I have some other ideas for cooling houses and buildings but they all require mechanical water pumps much smaller than what's available today. Over the next few years, I want to do some research on water pumps, and this gets us started in that direction.

"Everything I've talked about will take time, lots of time, but the crucial thing that must be done now, is making sure that Jorge and Heinrich both understand what we are trying to achieve, and for them to account for it in their building design and construction."

As I talked I could see Tom mentally trying to put the pieces together for what I was describing. By the time I was done, it was clear he hadn't been able to figure out how it would all work, but he was very interested in the challenge. I hoped Giuseppe, Raphael, and Jorge would also be intrigued when it was explained to them.

I continued, "Ultimately, what we'll be doing is proving the concepts of making ice, using it in the home, and cooling buildings with and without the use of very cold water. Once these are proven, we can duplicate them commercially in Las Cruces, Mesilla, or anywhere else in the territory. We will eventually make, sell, and deliver ice; make and sell ice boxes; and make, sell, and install building cooling systems. The commercial enterprises will employ people in the area, raising the standard of living, so they have more money to buy our beef and produce. Of course, it will also enrich the Estancia, which is a good thing, too."

By the time I was finished, both Tom and Yolanda were nodding their heads at the idea. I couldn't help but wonder what they would think in twenty-five years or so, when I started in on electricity and the telephone. A knock on the door interrupted any further questions, as it was Celia telling us that lunch would be ready in just a few minutes.

We walked into the dining room, finding both Miguel and Maco among those already at the table. We greeted them as we were sitting down, and talked pleasantries as we waited for the rest of the Hacienda to come in before lunch was served.

As we were eating I explained Martin's presence and asked Miguel and Maco when they could start a special Apache training course just for Martin, to be focused more on recognizing ambushes and avoiding them, or getting out of them, with less focus on survival. I added that Martin needed training on using and caring for a shotgun, as well as use of the medical kits, in addition to the other things he would learn; and that everything needed to be done, four weeks after he started.

Miguel looked at Maco for a few moments, and then turned back to give Martin a long look. Finally, he nodded his head and said he could start first thing Monday morning after

Tai Chi. He noticed Martin's confused look and explained that Tai Chi was a set of exercises everyone did in the mornings before breakfast. I told Martin I'd show him the basics tomorrow morning, and after breakfast we'd show him how to get to the village, where his training would start.

Lunch over, Maco motioned for Martin to follow him, as he walked upstairs and out to the upper courtyard. I walked Miguel out through the lower courtyard while telling him that I wanted him to be at the weekly meeting on Monday morning, to discuss some security concerns. He looked at me curiously, but told me he'd be there. As he walked off down the slope, I turned to go back inside and found Tom and Yolanda waiting for me.

As I walked up to them, Tom said, "Paul, if you don't mind, Yolanda and I would like to talk to you in the office, for a while."

"I don't mind, Tom. I sort of expected to spend the day at this. Let's find Anna and I'll join you in the study," I replied.

Yolanda spoke up at that point. "Anna will join us with coffee so we aren't disturbed for a while."

I nodded and led them to the study, where we found Anna already in her accustomed seat with a fresh coffee service on the table. Tom closed and barred the door before sitting down, and then the questions started.

For every question I answered, three or more follow-up questions were generated. At first, the questions were general in nature, but they quickly became more and more specific. Tom and Yolanda both were extremely disappointed and, in some cases, disturbed by my inability to give detailed answers. At one point, I stopped the questions for a few minutes, and tried to explain my inability to answer specifics.

"Look, I know you're both having problems with my inability to give detailed answers to most of your questions. You both need to understand a few things. Yes, I went to school from the age of six to eighteen. A total of twelve years of required education. That education covered reading, writing, math, a second language, the sciences, and history.

"It was very comprehensive, but it was also very broad. Let's take math as an example. In the first six years of school, I was taught the basics: the numbers, addition, subtraction, multiplication, division, fractions, and ratios. The next six years were a mix of algebra, geometry, introduction to trigonometry, and calculus. All that education was meant to provide a grounding in the basics.

"The same held true for the sciences. Basic science, including the scientific method, was taught the first six years while a grounding in the specific science fields like biology, chemistry, and physics were taught the last six years. No one was going to hire a high school graduate as a mathematician or scientist. A high school education simply doesn't give anyone enough knowledge in a specific field, to be of real value in the job market.

"A high school education does give you enough knowledge to function in a technological world, and more importantly it helps you determine where your interests lie, so you can chose a field of work or study in your adult years. Like most other kids, when I graduated high school, I still had no idea what I wanted to be when I grew up. I went into the military, where I was taught to be a police officer.

"In the course of my work, I discovered gunsmithing. Once I expressed an interest, the military gave me the training I needed to become a gunsmith. I went to college, when I discovered that a degree in mechanical engineering would help me do a better job as a gunsmith. I never took a single college course on how to be a gunsmith. Mechanical engineering is about building mechanical systems in general. Things like pumps, for example. What type of materials are best suited for different types of uses, and solving different types of problems.

"Mechanical engineering is a distinct field of study completely separate from civil engineering which is about building structures like houses, offices, dams, bridges, and the like. Civil engineering is completely separate from electrical engineering. All three are engineers but with completely different focuses.

"Despite having formal training as an engineer, I am not now, nor have I ever been, an engineer. It didn't take me long after starting college to figure out that I didn't have the mindset of an engineer. Engineers approach problems much differently than everyone else. I can't really explain it but look at Giuseppe and Heinrich. They are engineers. Watch them as they go about their work, and you'll see that problem solving to them, whether the problem is building a bridge, a road, or a house, is a methodical process that requires examining every facet of the problem.

"College taught me many things, but the most important one, was that trying to think like an engineer is exhausting and frustrating.

"To make matters more complicated, there are many engineering fields, and each has further specializations. The same holds true for scientists, which can be broken down into biologists, chemists, physicists, and so on. They are all scientists, but their fields of study are so focused, that about all they have in common is that basic education they were originally given.

"The other thing you need to remember is that knowledge doesn't stand still. For me, high school and college are forty years in the past. The sheer volume of what changed in that forty years is staggering, and unless I made a conscious effort to keep up with current knowledge, what I knew quickly became outdated.

"Suffice it to say that unless it was knowledge I felt was instrumental to my success as a gunsmith, I ignored it. You ask me how a water pump works, and I'll tell you what I remember learning in 1980, not how a water pump in 2016 works. It was knowledge I didn't need as a gunsmith, and it was knowledge I wasn't interested in.

"It's very similar to Tom not being able to tell me the best way to refine the impurities out of gold nuggets, or Anna and Yolanda not being able to tell me the best way to prepare a supper of octopus and eels. You might like to know; but you've never needed the knowledge, and you most likely never will."

When I was done with my explanation, even Anna seemed to have a better understanding of the problems I was having trying to answer their questions. We picked back up with the questions and answers but now their questions were better thought out, and more general in nature.

We spent the rest of the afternoon with them asking questions, and me answering them as best I could. Gradually they began to narrow down their questions to those about what things in the future I was trying to change, why I was trying to change them, how I was trying to change them, and the outcome I expected the changes to bring about.

I talked about the Salt War, and what I was doing to stop that from ever happening. I talked about Statehood and what Anna and I were planning on doing to help that along, including the need to stop Southern forces from occupying Mesilla at the start of the Civil War. We didn't spend much time on the Civil War itself. Yolanda's first question on the subject was why I didn't just stop the war from happening. My response of "How?" shut down all further discussion on that subject, and the questions switched almost immediately back to the Mesilla Valley.

They were quite surprised when I told them the most important thing we needed to do over the next few years, was cultivate Martin Amador. I believed he would be a key to getting the support of the Hispano community, in both Las Cruces and Mesilla.

Our talk came to end for the time being, when we were called to supper. As far as I was concerned the day had been a success, with Tom and Yolanda now in on all of our secrets. The price had been a couple of days of worry, and concern along with a day of mental and emotional stress.

It could have been worse, and I fully expected it would, in fact, get worse. Especially once they both realized that we hadn't talked about the role my first wife's spirit had in my being here in the first place, and who was continuing to play in the events that had occurred up until now.

I put those thoughts away as I sat down for supper. I listened to the kids tell us what they had done today, and all the exciting discoveries they had made.

Martin joined us for Tai Chi the next morning. We coached him through the exercises. He was a reluctant participant but we all knew he would become a convert over the next few weeks, as he began to see the benefits to both his physical and mental well-being.

After a quick breakfast, we took Martin, along with all the kids, for a morning ride. Martin had been on the Estancia for two days, but hadn't been anywhere except the Hacienda. He'd heard about the village and the ranch from the others, but what he saw during our ride was clearly much more than he expected.

When he finally worked out that there were almost as many people in our little village as there were in Las Cruces, and that our store was supplied by his mother, he finally began to understand the scope of the Estancia.

That understanding was further bolstered when we visited the ranch, and he saw Hector and his team working on plotting out where they thought fences should be. They were using the large wall mural and arguing their points of view. As we were riding back to the Hacienda, Martin asked why the farm area wasn't being discussed, as it seemed to him to have much more going on and more people to support.

I told him that the finca operations area was in the long building opposite the school rooms he'd seen. Much more complicated discussions were probably going on inside it this morning, than what he'd seen at the ranch. He was quiet the rest of the way back to the Hacienda as he thought about the complexity of managing such large operations. I took that for a good sign, and encouraged him to ask more questions about anything he didn't understand, whenever he had them.

The rest of the weekend was quiet and peaceful. On Monday morning, Martin rode over to the village after Tai Chi to start his training. I knew we would see little of him for the rest of his time here.

Our weekly operations meeting started immediately after breakfast, taking up most of the morning just to cover the normal items and the requests I had made before leaving for Las Cruces. It was a mixed bag of results. All of the important things were moving forward at a satisfactory rate. The purely ornamental activities were like a can being kicked down the road, though. I decided I was going to have to look elsewhere for assistance in finding pecan and fig trees, as well as finding groundskeepers to start making the Hacienda, village, ranch, and lakes a more pleasant place to live.

With an hour left before lunch, we finally disposed of existing and planned activities and moved on to new activities. One of the things we had decided yesterday afternoon, was that Tom would reveal the plan to build an ice maker in the village, and the potential for commercial development. We had decided not to discuss the swamp cooler aspects, until after the ice making plans were completed.

I gave a nod to Tom, who spent the next half hour showing everyone the patent and discussing the long-term plans, including using the cold water byproduct to cool the school/community building.

He closed by saying, "We hope to have this project completed and working by the time the combined school and community building is finished, but one is not dependent on the other. The timing of the ice making machine is fully dependent on Raphael having both the time and talent to make the necessary parts, as well as the arrival of the various pumps and small steam engines. Paul and I will be having discussions with Raphael, Giuseppe, and Juan on these items over the next few weeks, so there isn't anything you need to do, nor will these plans impact current operations as they are now set."

As far as I could tell, everyone accepted what Tom was saying at face value. Without exception, they seemed happy to support this particular project, as long as we didn't need a lot of people to build or run it. I was sure none of them were going to accept the final subject for today's meeting with such equanimity.

"That's it for me. Do you have anything else?" Tom asked me.

"Thanks, Tom. Yes, I have one final item to address at this meeting, and it's the most serious subject we'll talk about today."

That got everyone's attention.

"While we were visiting in Las Cruces, we learned a couple of things that have a direct bearing on everyone on the Estancia. First, Mr. Garcia and Yolanda's father were killed at the direction of the leader of the comancheros, who has started operating in this area again. Apparently, their deaths were in retribution for the attack on their camp, and the rescue of their captives. Their leader has decided this is personal and acted accordingly.

"Second, at the moment, there doesn't appear to any threat of a raid on the Estancia, as there hasn't been a raid anywhere in the county for the last four weeks. That could change without warning, however, so we need everyone to be aware of the potential danger.

"Given the size of the comanchero group, which we estimate to be somewhere around fifty men, we need to get more serious about our defenses, and our ability to rapidly respond to any threat. Miguel, we need the people who've volunteered to man the four new signal posts on duty, and watching the approaches to the Estancia as soon as possible. Don't wait for the signal posts to be completed, let's get them up there and working, now.

"I also want the response force increased from two teams to six teams, but broken into three groups. Group one will be assigned to duty at the south end of the Estancia. Group two will be assigned the north end, and Group three will be in the middle ready to support either of the other two groups."

I'd been watching Miguel the entire time I'd been talking, and was beginning to get worried at the stoic expression on his face. I stopped talking and continued to stare at him for a moment, before he suddenly broke into a grin and nodded.

Relieved, I turned saying, "Tomas and Hector, I want you both to add two more teams to the response force rotation, starting Monday."

They both nodded without protest, which was a little surprising given all the complaining they'd been doing about losing teams to other tasks. But, after a moment's thought, it was understandable given the nature of the threat.

"Miguel, are there enough cousins to handle

the normal security assignments, scout/sniper patrols, the new signal posts, lead each of the three response force teams, and still have a five-man auxiliary force?" I asked.

He thought for a moment before saying, "Yes, as long as you don't mind the old ones doing all the training for Martin, and for the refresher training already scheduled."

"I think having the old ones doing the training is a very good idea. Let's start that and the auxiliary force next Monday. In the meantime, I want you and Maco to work with Yolanda on building five or six different attack scenario's, which we can have the response forces practice reacting to. I want the scenario's to be as realistic as possible, and should include the best way to deploy the response forces for each specific threat."

Yolanda had known this was coming, and simply nodded her head. Miguel said he would be available whenever Yolanda wanted to start. I told everyone that unless there was anything else, the meeting was over. Within a few minutes everyone had left, and I was alone in the study with my thoughts.

I was thinking about everything we had done so far, what we were working on now, and what we could do better in the future, including security; when I heard that oh so familiar soft whisper from my first wife, Laura, in my left ear.

"Don't worry so, my love, you are doing fine. You will have one small problem this fall, and another bigger problem late next summer, but you will come through both just fine."

It had been months since I'd last heard that whisper in my ear, and I'd almost convinced myself it was wishful thinking. Here it was again, and it seemed so real.

I heard Laura's light giggle in my ear again, "Of course it's real, my love."

I sighed, and couldn't help thinking that this is how sane men went crazy. Laura's giggle sounded in my ear once again; and then, like the sound of the waves in a seashell, faded away into the distance.

I had started to get up to pour myself a scotch, when Anna came bustling in the door, closing and barring it before turning to me with excitement in her eyes. She took one look at my face, and came to me giving me a deep kiss and hug before nestling her head into my chest as I held her. We stayed cuddled together for a couple of minutes, before she pulled away and looked into my eyes.

"You had a visit, too, didn't you? Was it Grandfather Jaime, or Laura?"

I gave her a startled look, "It was Laura, but what do you mean, 'too?' Did you get a visit?"

"Yes. Grandfather Jaime visited me, and told me we were doing well. He also said we'd have a small problem later this year, and a larger one next summer; but we'd meet them head on, and come out fine in the end," she replied.

"Laura told me the same thing in almost the exact same words. Laura's visits always leave me a little unsettled. I was just going to pour a drink when you came in. Instead, how about we take a bottle of wine up to the terrace, and spend the afternoon there?"

She thought that was a wonderful idea, and beamed me one of her rare huge super mega-watt Anna smiles. We had a private lunch on the terrace with a bottle of wine, and whiled away the afternoon talking or just sitting holding each other's hand.

We rejoined everyone for supper and listened with interest as the kids regaled the table with stories about their day.

CHAPTER 7

Although they were always on our minds, we put the unsettling spirit visits behind us, and got on with our lives. I spent as much time as I could in the RV cave melting gold, but it was only a couple of hours most days, and the small mountain of gold seemed to defy my attempts to reduce its size.

Giuseppe returned from his short trip to the base of the Doña Ana Mountains late Wednesday afternoon in a jubilant mood. Over supper he informed us that he'd found the rock we needed to build the roads. The source was indeed at the base of the East side of the Doña Ana Mountains. He thought a wagon could make the trip, but we'd need to make a trail and smooth out the bumps and holes that would otherwise eventually tear up a wagon. Tom agreed to go with him to do a few test blasts, so he could get a better understanding of the extent of the rock.

It took them a couple of days of experimenting, but they finally settled on the best way to get the gravel they needed. With approval to start blasting, Giuseppe went into high gear. He spent the rest of the month out surveying the new portion of the Camino Real and the wagon trail to the gravel quarry. He left every morning right after Tai Chi, grabbing a quick breakfast sandwich to eat in the saddle, along with a lunch in his saddle bag. We wouldn't see him again until supper.

I started to worry about his health when he started missing Tai Chi. Just after my birthday, I finally had to sit him down and find out why he was pushing so hard.

Giuseppe gave a heavy sigh at my question. "Paul, Sofia is going to have the baby soon, and I need to get this done before then so I can spend some time with her."

"Giuseppe, when the time comes for the baby you can have all the time you and Sofia need, but you aren't going to be much help to her if you're exhausted or, even worse, sick. Yes, the roads are a priority, but nothing ranks higher than your health. Slow done a little. Work a normal day, not the extended days you've been working the last three or four weeks."

In the end, it took a combination of me, Tom, Anna, and Yolanda harassing and nagging him to get him to slow down. He finished surveying the new Camino Real road, and was about three-quarters of the way done with the wagon trail when the rains started. Now that we had the bridge in place, even the rains didn't hold him up much. He finished the quarry wagon trail well before the end of August.

Meanwhile, everything else continued along at a steady pace on the rest of the Estancia. Martin Amador finished the Apache Training course, and told me before he left that now that it was over he was thankful for what he'd learned. I gave him one of my sawed off semi-automatic shotguns with a sling after teaching him how to use and maintain it. I suggested he make sure he had one hundred of the brass shotgun shells with him on every trip, as well as two or three good muzzle loaders for longer distance shooting. I had hopes and plans for Martin, and wanted to make sure he stayed alive to achieve what I saw as his destiny as a major business and civic leader in Las Cruces.

Every week saw another one to two hundred yards of fields cleared and prepared, even though there were fewer teams working on them. We started harvesting the Hacienda vegetable gardens the third week in July, and continued through the end of September. Everyone on the Estancia spent at least a few hours in the garden during that time, and there were happy faces everywhere. Tomas was careful to pull one-third of the harvest as seed stock for the following year, while the other two-thirds were distributed fresh or canned according to plan.

Near the end of the first week in August, George rode in for an extended visit. I'm not sure if he was visiting Celia or us but it didn't really matter as we were all happy to see him. He brought news of the fort, Mesilla, and the country outside New Mexico, which was always welcome.

The news from the fort was of immediate interest, if for no other reason than the apparent tie-in between the commander and the comancheros. George gleefully told us that Colonel Watson had been recalled to Fort Bliss the last week in July, and Major Long had assumed temporary command until a replacement was assigned.

Major Long had written a long report about the meeting Tom, Juan, and I had with Colonel Watson, recounting everything that was said. He went further though and, in a thoroughly unmilitary move questioned the suitability of Colonel Watson to command, given his failure to patrol the areas under attack by comancheros, failure to give patrols sufficient recovery time between patrols, and his blatant attempts to cancel both construction and cattle contracts. He'd also included a copy of Juan and Jorge's adobe construction and maintenance manual.

As it turned out, Major Long was nobody's fool. He'd sent a copy through the military courier system, and a second copy through the US Mail from Mesilla. The District Commander received the report through the US Mail, but never received the copy sent through the courier system. After Major Long had assumed temporary command of Fort Fillmore he found the unopened copy he'd sent through the courier system shoved in the back of Colonel Watson's desk drawer.

On reaching Fort Bliss, Colonel Watson had been told he had two options: accept reassignment to Kansas, or resign. He immediately resigned. Although no one had seen him, it was thought he was still in Doña Ana County somewhere.

On the Mesilla front, everything remained quiet. There were no sightings of the comanchero leader, Fulgencio Madrid, or any of the suspected comancheros who rode with him. Likewise, there were no new reports of raids anywhere in the county.

Major Long had ridden into Mesilla two days earlier with George, and had met with Esteban and Ed telling them that after the men and horses had been rested and equipment repaired he would start patrolling any areas that were raided, regardless of whether it was thought to be the work of Indian raiding parties or comancheros. Esteban had thanked the Major, and agreed to work closely with him, keeping him advised of their investigations.

I surely welcomed this particular bit of news, and worried much less about Esteban and Ed as a result.

With regard to the country outside New Mexico the news was mostly about Kansas, and the two Territorial Legislatures currently in existence, one pro-slavery and the other anti-slavery. The rumors were that President Pierce would step in with Federal troops and recognize the pro-slavery group.

I knew that was exactly what would happen and that it would set Kansas up as a powder keg for pre-Civil War violence. As much as I'd have liked to stop all this from happening, there was nothing I could do.

We celebrated Anna's twentieth birthday the third week in August. The lower plateau had been set up just as it had when Tom and Yolanda were married, with almost everyone on the Estancia participating in one way or another.

It was a happy, song filled occasion, made even more joyous by Anna and Yolanda's announcement that they were both pregnant. Luckily, the rain that threatened all day moved east of us and about half the village ended up camped out overnight on the lower plateau. Anna and I were both surprised to find over two hundred men and women on the upper plateau the next morning to join us for Tai Chi and katas.

The next three weeks were filled with afternoons sitting on the terrace, or in the study, talking with George. He was full of questions about what I made of the activities in what was already becoming known as Bleeding Kansas and what they meant for the future. I talked in generalities about the coming Civil War while I focused on specifics for what the war would mean to New Mexico.

I knew that if I was going to be successful in keeping George out of the war, I had to paint a picture where he could see himself as a New Mexican, and not a Virginian. We talked about the probability of Texas sending forces to try and take New Mexico Territory for the Southern states. The loss of regular troops as they were pulled east, and their replacement by, at best, half trained militia from California or other states.

He did not question my assertion that the Indian population would all think they had driven the white men back east when the soldiers left, and what that would mean to the citizens of the territory for many years after the war was over. We spent almost an hour a day talking about the economics of warfare, and why it meant that the South would eventually lose the war even if they won most of the battles.

When George left the Estancia in the middle of September, his heart was filled with love and his head was filled with the potential for life outside the Army as a New Mexican. It was apparent to any who saw them together that George and Celia were deeply in love.

The question in my mind was not whether he and Celia would get married, but whether he would stay in the army and take Celia with him to his next assignment or leave the army and stay here. I was no closer to determining that than I had been before his visit. I could only hope for the best.

Two days after George returned to Fort Fillmore, we had two reasons to celebrate. First, just after breakfast, Donatello Gambino came into the world kicking and screaming. Mother and son, while noisy, were doing well. Second, we were alerted by the Northern scout/sniper team that a large family group of Apache's were traveling south down the Camino Real towards us. Apaches actually using the road was unusual in itself, especially a large family group. We were even more surprised to find it was Cousin Alvaro's family group coming over the bridge.

I sent Tom to the upper plateau to send a signal to Miguel that Alvaro's group was at the Hacienda, and asked him to come for supper. Anna, Yolanda, and I walked down and waited for the group to arrive at the base of the slope. Tom arrived, after getting an acknowledgement signal from Miguel, leading all the kids who'd decided to join us in welcoming the group.

As they got close enough to make out individuals, we were dismayed to find no sign of Alvaro. Instead, they were being led by a man I vaguely recognized as one of Alvaro's immediate circle of advisors. Anna's frown turned to a smile and she took a couple of steps forward as the group stopped in front of us.

Anna formally welcomed the visitors to the Estancia before giving a big smile to the leader saying, "Welcome home, Tio Nantan, we've been expecting you."

Nantan looked startled at Anna's statement but just nodded his head before saying, "We thank you for your welcome, and will obey the rule of no raiding while we are here. Much has changed in the last year. We need to talk, but first we need to set up a camp. Where would you like us to set up?"

Anna waved her arm around her while saying, "The entire Estancia, with a few exceptions, is available to you. Set up wherever you like, for as long as you want. You can set up right over there for now, until you find something more to your liking. That will also allow us to talk more conveniently."

Nantan turned to the families, pointed off to the side, and told them to set up camp. I invited him, and any of the warriors he wanted to bring, up to the Hacienda for refreshments and talk. Apparently he was a man of few words. He simply nodded again, called out three names, and turned back to us.

While that was going on Anna asked Yolanda, Beth, and Izabella to find out if any of the families needed any supplies. They walked over to where the camp was already being set up, and began talking to the ladies as they worked. Alejandro joined them, followed by the rest of the Hacienda kids. Alejandro made sure to introduce everyone he talked to. As Anna, Tom, and

I led Nantan and his three companions up the slope, the kids were already off to the side of the camp playing and talking.

Once inside the courtyard, Tom and I led the guests up the outside stairs to the terrace while Anna continued inside to arrange for refreshments. Once on the terrace, our visitors went to the railing to look East out over the Estancia, towards the Doña Ana Mountains.

They stood silently for a few minutes only breaking their reverie when Anna arrived with Cristina, both carrying a coffee service and a platter of biscochitos. The combined smell of fresh coffee, mixed with the cinnamon and anise of the freshly made biscochitos, worked its magic. We could visibly see our guests relax for the first time since they'd arrived. We sat silently for several minutes in no great hurry as they savored the refreshments.

With a final sip of coffee, Nantan began talking. "Alvaro went to the Land of Ever Summer almost three months ago. He was an old man but in good health, or so we all thought. He died peacefully in his sleep one night after telling us he was feeling his age for the first time. I am now leader of the Northern Garcia families."

He stopped for a sip of fresh coffee Anna had poured for him before continuing. "We were all saddened when I felt your Grandfather

Jaime's spirit join those in the Land of Ever Summer. These are trying times for the Apache, and his counsel will be greatly missed."

Anna thanked him for the condolences and congratulated him on being named the new leader. He accepted the congratulations with equanimity, which was shattered into surprise at her next words. "Grandfather Jaime told me you would come, after he died. He also told me he is my spirit protector, and that you would teach me how to make that bond stronger."

Nantan sat staring at Anna with mouth agape for a few moments, before recovering enough to close his mouth and look at her closely. "With him as your spirit protector, you will be a powerful shaman. I will be proud to teach you everything a Shaman needs to know."

Anna was shaking her head with a frown when Nantan finished talking. "Tio, I am no shaman. Grandfather made this very clear to me. I need to learn how to strengthen the tie between me and him, and no more. I will never be able to use the spirit magic of healing or have visions of my own. Even if I did have the ability to be a shaman, I would still have to turn you down. I have too much to do here with the five children we've adopted, and one of my own on the way, not to mention looking after the Hacienda and supporting Pablo as he builds the

Estancia."

Anna's statement appeared to unsettle Nantan. He picked up his coffee taking another couple of sips before nodding his head. "I don't agree with you, but it will be as you and your grandfather wish it. Your training will start after we have settled on where we will be living."

Anna gave him a gentle smile. "It doesn't matter where the families live. If they stay on the Estancia you will be living here in the Hacienda. In a few weeks I won't be traveling until after the baby is born. If the families don't stay on the Estancia, then grandfather was wrong about you, and I will find someone else to teach me what I need to know."

Throughout this exchange Tom and I had been silent observers, biting our cheeks to keep from laughing, as it was clear that Nantan was not used to being thwarted, and by a young lady at that.

The three warriors Nantan had brought were not as circumspect, and were grinning broadly throughout the exchange. At Anna's last comment one of them snickered, and another gave Nantan the equivalent Apache gesture for, 'I guess she told you!'

For the next several minutes the three warriors kidded Nantan, who took it stoically while quietly drinking his coffee and eating biscochitos. The warriors finally had their fill of the fun, and Nantan resumed talking.

"Please tell me more about the Estancia and its limits. When we were here over a year ago Alvaro met with Miguel for a few hours. When he came back he told us we would rest for a couple of weeks, but we weren't staying. We stayed separate from the other cousins, and didn't really venture out of the camp except to cross the river and hunt, up in the mountains. We don't know much about the Estancia."

This was news to Anna and me, and I could tell it was news to Tom. I put my questions aside for now and answered Nantan.

"The Estancia runs four miles in each direction along the river. Where the levee stops at the north and south ends of the river is where the Estancia ends. Going east and west it runs from the other side of the Robledo Mountains behind us, to the other side of the Doña Ana Mountains. You are all welcome to stay anywhere within those boundaries you like except for the quarry areas, the farmland along the river which we are clearing for planting, and along the Camino Real, which we are moving and widening."

Nantan thought for a few moments before saying, "That's a lot of land but it seems too small to support so many Apache families."

My reply startled him a little, but he listened without interrupting.

"You're right, it *is* too small to support all the Garcia families, if they are living in the traditional way. However, a little over half the Garcia families already here have decided to live in the village and work full time for the Estancia. The remainder seem happy with what they have available and most of them also work for the Estancia. Where you and those with you choose to live is up to you, but you will be welcome here whether you work for the Estancia or not. Nothing has changed in that regard."

"What 'jobs' do the Apache do here?" he asked. Showing a little emotion for the first time he continued. "Farming? Ranching? These are jobs for white men! Apache are warriors!"

"Farming, ranching, and warrior are all jobs that are, and will be, needed on the Estancia. You are wrong about the Apache, though. They are warriors when they need to be, but they are farmers, ranchers, and hunters when they aren't being threatened. You know this. Most of the people here are the same in that regard. They are all warriors when threatened.

"The difference is they are not warriors on the

attack unless they are chasing someone who has threatened them. I don't offer you any jobs you don't generally already know how to do. If some of your people want to be farmers, then the jobs are available to them. The same holds true for any that want to be ranchers or hunters. For those that want to be full time warriors, I offer that as well.

"Again, the Estancia warriors provide security for the Estancia. They are defensive warriors until the threat comes onto the Estancia. Then they fight! There will be times when we take the fight to the enemy, no matter where they are; but most of the time we fight on the Estancia, or nearby. We have accomplished much on the Estancia already. We will accomplish more in the future, but we will only be successful and grow if Anglos, Hispanos, and Apache continue to work together as we have been. Not as individual tribes or groups, but as a united people helping each other to succeed."

When I'd finished my little speech Nantan looked at the three warriors with him before turning back to me, and telling me what I already knew he was going say.

"You have given us much to think about. We will consider all you have said."

I nodded saying, "Please join us for supper tonight, and bring whoever you wish. Miguel will be here, and you can talk to him about his experiences on the Estancia, and the jobs the families that follow him have."

"Tell me, Thundercloud, where does Miguel live? In the village or somewhere on the Estancia."

I shrugged. "Miguel lives somewhere on the Estancia. I'm not sure where. Maco represents Miguel to the group that lives in the village."

Nantan looked interested now and asked, "Does Miguel come to supper often?"

"Miguel and Maco have a standing invitation to supper whenever they want to come. Neither comes often, unless I send them a specific invitation as I did when we found out you were coming here," I explained.

"I don't understand, Thundercloud. If you don't know where Miguel lives how did you send him a message when I arrived, and yet already know he will arrive in time for supper?"

"First off, Nantan, please call me Paul or Pablo. Second, we have a way of sending and receiving messages from anywhere on the Estancia. Would you like to send a message to Miguel to see how it works?"

Intrigued now, Nantan said, "I would send greetings to Miguel telling him I look forward to seeing him at supper."

I stood up and beckoned them to come with me. As we walked through the Hacienda, Anna detoured downstairs telling us she would have more refreshments waiting for us on the terrace when we got back. I led our visitors out to the corral on the upper plateau where I told one of the young cousins that Nantan would like to send a message to Miguel. The young man looked at Nantan expectantly.

"I, Nantan, would like to send greetings to Miguel, leader of the Southern Garcia Apache, and tell him I look forward to seeing him at supper tonight," Nantan told him.

The boy nodded, taking out his signal mirror, and flashed it towards the Robledo Mountains. He waited until he got a flash indicating the relay was ready to receive and then sent the message.

The young man told Nantan it could be a few minutes before we got a reply. Nantan turned to me, but I stopped him as he started to ask me how the system worked.

"Ask your questions to the warrior to be," I said. "Sending and receiving messages is part of a warrior's training on the Hacienda, and he can answer *all* your questions about it."

The young man visibly puffed out his chest

at this, and turned to Nantan. They talked for a few minutes as he explained the system to Nantan. The young man stopped talking mid-sentence as a ready flash came from the mountain. He sent an acknowledgement before pulling out a paper and pencil and writing the message as it was received.

When the message was done he looked it over to see if it made sense, before sending acknowledgement and turning to Nantan.

"Miguel acknowledges your message and sends, Welcome to Estancia Dos Santos, brother. I look forward to supper with you, also. I will join you within the hour. We have much to talk about."

Brother? Now that was an interesting development. I'd have to get the full story from Miguel, later.

Nantan thanked the young man, and we all walked back to the terrace where Anna and Yolanda were waiting with fresh coffee.

As promised, Miguel arrived less than an hour later. Anna, Tom, Yolanda and I left the five cousins together on the terrace to talk privately, telling them we would let them know when supper was ready. I took Tom into the study, telling Anna and Yolanda we were going to be working, and needed privacy until supper. This was our code for 'we will be working in the cave'.

While I was opening the RV cave I said, "Giuseppe said that almost half the time to build the road, was going to be used doing nothing but sorting rocks into the two sizes he needs. We're going to build some sizing screens to help speed up the sorting. I think I have enough small steel rods to build five sets of five foot by three-foot screens."

I had Tom help me take one of the folding merchandise tables out of the trailer, and set it up as a work table. Using the radial arm saw built along the trailer wall I cut quarter inch rods into five foot and three-foot segments. We spent the next three hours weaving the rods into five sets of three-inch screens, and five sets of three-quarter inch screens. As we finished weaving each screen I spot welded each of the rods into place with the welding torch.

When we were done, Tom looked at the screens and asked, "What's the plan now?"

As I coiled the gas hoses back up to put them away, I responded, "Tomorrow we take these down to the village and have the wagon shop make frames to hold them. Then we have rockers made to mount them in. Once that's done the work crews can shovel rock onto the top three-inch screen and use the rocker.

All the gravel smaller than three inches will fall through to the bottom three-quarter inch screen. They'll continue rocking and everything smaller than three quarters of an inch, will fall through to the bottom. The rocks are then moved into three separate size-sorted piles, and they start over again."

We moved the screens into the study and closed up the cave, before going into the dining room where we joined the cousins waiting for supper. I was surprised to see Giuseppe come in and sit down for supper.

At my raised eyebrow, he said, "Sofia and Don are sleeping so I decided to have supper. Besides, I may be too tired to eat supper for the next few weeks."

We laughed at his droll statement, and kidded him about midnight feedings, burping, and rocking the baby to sleep for a little while. The kids all trooped in along with the adults and started telling us about their day at school and playing with the cousins. It finally dawned on Nantan that Izabella and Alejandro where eating with us as if family, and he asked why their parents weren't here if we were including the kids for supper.

Izabella gave him a look full of sorrow and said, "Mama, Papa, and the baby are in the Land of Ever Summer. They were killed in a rock slide on the way here. We live in the village with our Aunt, but our best friends are here at the Hacienda, so we are usually here when we're not in school."

The rest of the adult supper conversation was dominated by a retelling of the story of how we found the two kids, the condition they were in, and what they'd been doing since then. Nantan and the warriors listened with interest as the kids talked about school, their friends in the village and ranch, and riding their horses.

Miguel ended up staying the night at the Hacienda, while Nantan and his warriors returned to the camp at the foot of the slopes. Early the next morning, none of us were surprised to see Miguel leading Nantan and his advisors into the upper courtyard for Tai Chi and katas. Afterwards, they disappeared with Miguel telling us that he was going to be showing them around the Estancia.

Tom and I loaded up a wagon with the screens after breakfast, and took them to the village. There we turned them over to the cooper at the wagon yard, along with the plans for the rocker that I'd drawn up. We saw Miguel leading about half of the Northern cousins and their families around the village explaining things to them, while Maco was doing the same thing with the other half.

The next four days were extremely busy. Tom and I divided our workload so that he could replace Giuseppe on the road crews, working on clearing and leveling the new Camino Real road; while I handled the blasting every morning, before the teams arrived to load and haul the crushed stone to the road bed.

We got two surprise guests at supper that night. The first was Nantan, who told us that he liked what he had seen of the Estancia so far and would be staying until Anna had been trained to his satisfaction. He had told his families that if they decided to leave, he would not be going with them. He wasn't sure how many would be staying, but there were some who had been as impressed as he was, and were likely to stay.

The second surprise was Maco walking into the dining room for supper with Beth. He seated her, and then sat down next to her, all the while continuing their conversation as if it was the most natural thing in the world. Anna told me with nothing more than her smile, that this was something she had expected. It also told me that she expected Maco to become a regular visitor.

Anna and I retired to the bedroom shortly after supper to talk and cuddle. At her request, I grabbed a bottle of wine and two glasses on the way up to the bedroom. I lit a small fire, more for the ambiance than heat, and we cuddled on the couch with a glass of wine.

For the next three hours we talked. Most of the time was spent talking about the visits she was getting from her great grandfather's spirit. They were frequent, almost daily, but most of the time she just heard his voice, and couldn't make out what he was saying.

The latest visit was earlier this afternoon, when she heard his voice clearly telling her that Nantan would be staying to train her. He also said we needed to nurture Maco as the future leader of the combined Northern and Southern Garcia family groups. I suggested we each start a journal to write down what the spirit protectors told us, so we'd have something to help us remember.

The last hour or so we talked about the relationship blooming between Maco and Beth, as well as a trip to Las Cruces and El Paso. Both Anna and Yolanda were concerned about traveling while they were pregnant and they wanted to see their family in Las Cruces before they got too far along in their pregnancies. They both also wanted to go to El Paso to buy what they needed, for after the babies were born.

I couldn't help but think that after Anna's baby was born there would be five babies under nine months old, plus Rose who would be almost two, living at the Hacienda. I'm not sure what Yolanda and Anna thought they would need that wasn't already available at the Hacienda, but I kept that to myself. If Anna wanted a shopping trip to El Paso, then that was what she would get.

We announced our trip the next morning at breakfast. I'd talked to Giuseppe while we were cooling down after the morning Tai Chi and katas, and he assured me he intended on being back to work in another week.

While I was talking to Giuseppe, Anna was talking to the ladies of the Hacienda, trying to figure out if it would be better to take the kids with us or leave them at the Hacienda. The kids - with the exception of Beth and Izabella - were all in favor of going with us, just for the adventure. Anna, Miranda, Cristina, Celia, and Carla were in hushed conversation throughout breakfast. Finally, just before the kids left for school, Anna told them they wouldn't be going this time. They were disappointed, but didn't make too much of an issue about it, soon turning their attention to school and their friends.

Tom and I rode over to the village to check on the rock sorters, and found the coopers team in the wagon yard finishing up the last of the five. We inspected the other four that were waiting and found them solid so we got a couple of wagons from Raul and loaded three of them up to take out to the road.

While we waited for the last one we talked to Raphael who had a couple of surprises for us. First, the steel roller that Giuseppe had ordered was done. I grinned, knowing Giuseppe was sure to get back to work when he heard the news, if for no other reason than to test out his design. The second surprise was his request to make the trip to El Paso with us. He wanted to see if he could find another blacksmith. He thought one of the men who'd apprenticed with him was back in El Paso, and might be talked into coming to work on the Estancia.

I saw no reason he couldn't go with us and told him so. We talked for a few minutes about the timing of the trip and the stop in Las Cruces, before loading up the last rock sorter with the other one, and taking them both out to the road.

The rock sorters where a hit with the work teams, and we left them to their work. Giuseppe was a happy man at supper, and couldn't wait to get back to work to see the rock sorters in action and to test the new roller he'd designed.

CHAPTER 8

We pulled out of the Hacienda bright and early on Thursday, the 11th of October, 1855, right on schedule. By we, I mean Tom, Yolanda, Anna and me along with Raphael, who was driving the wagon we were taking with us, and a team of vaqueros who were going along for security.

The wagon Raphael was driving was one of the original wagons, with the steel box bolted behind the driver's seat. Tom and I had loaded the box with 2000 gold bars late the night before. The Estancia was getting low on money, so we were taking advantage of the trip to sell some more gold and bring back enough money to last us another year.

The trip was almost delayed a few days, as Esperanza started having contractions Monday evening. After fifteen hours of hard labor, she gave birth to Mercedes Guadalupe Salazar, late

Tuesday morning. We were all concerned as Esperanza was not recovering as quickly as the other two ladies had. Tomas assured us that this was normal for Esperanza, as she had been the same way with her previous two kids. Reluctantly, we gave in to his assurances, and set off on the trip, as planned.

Everyone rode warily, all the way to Las Cruces. Our shotguns were in hand and rifles loose in their scabbards with the scabbard tops off. We pulled into Mr. Mendoza's stable shortly after lunch and turned all the animals over to the stable boys. The ladies walked over to the restaurant while the vaquero's discussed whether to get rooms at the hotel, or stay in the hayloft.

Tom, Raphael, and I wandered back through the stables and found Mr. Mendoza at his customary table, working on harnesses. He gave a big grin at our arrival and got up giving us big hugs and back slaps. Before we got settled in, I told him we were going over to the restaurant to get something to eat and asked him if the hayloft was still available.

He grinned and shook his finger at Tom and me, saying, "Already in trouble with your wives? What am I going to do with you two?"

We all laughed and I told him the hayloft was for the five vaqueros we had with us. Still grinning, he nodded and told us it was available. We left for the restaurant, taking the vaqueros with us and telling them along the way that the hayloft was available if they wanted to use it.

Inside the restaurant we were met with hugs and cheek kisses from Yolanda's mother, Maria, and Mrs. Mendoza, who were all at our usual table against the wall talking with Anna and Yolanda.

The ladies all left to go back to the kitchen when the coffee arrived, and Tom and I sat down with our wives. Lunch was delivered a few minutes later. I couldn't help but remark that it was almost like old times.

Anna laughed and said, "There are two major differences you must be forgetting about. First, we are now married and second, both of us are pregnant."

She said the last in a low whisper, as she and Yolanda had told us they were going to tell the family at supper and not before.

Tom and I grinned at each other and Tom said, "Those are both really good differences."

Tom, Raphael, and I spent the afternoon out at the table behind the stable with Mr. Mendoza, talking about all the changes happening both on the Estancia and in Las Cruces. Shortly before dark we all followed Mr. Mendoza over to the back door of the restaurant, where we watched the kitchen dance for a few moments before going into the family dining room. I couldn't help but glance at Jaime's old chair, and feel more than a little saddened by his death.

My mind had started working on how to get justice for Jaime and Mr. Ramirez, when I heard Laura's soft sweet whisper in my left ear. "Let it go for now, my love. Remember it's justice you seek not vengeance. It will happen in its own time, don't try to force it."

As I sat thinking about what Laura had said I looked up and found Anna sitting next me giving me one of her sweet smiles with a look of tender love in her eyes. "Listen to her my love, now is not the time to be tilting at windmills."

Her statement startled me, and damned if I didn't hear Laura's soft laugh. It quickly faded away into the background noise, as I glanced around the table to make sure no one was paying us any attention before turning back to Anna.

She saw the questioning look in my eyes and simply nodded her head confirming that she had heard Laura this time. I was about to ask her what she'd heard when the ladies arrived carrying supper into the room.

The table had been cleared and everyone was sipping their after-supper coffee, when Anna and Yolanda calmly dropped their bombshell about being pregnant. The room was quiet for a few seconds as everyone processed what Anna had said, before erupting into pandemonium as smiles and congratulations were given all around. Tom and I sat back in our chairs, sipping our coffee as we gave each other a grin now and then.

The after-supper coffee and conversations ran a little longer than normal, but both Anna and Yolanda were happy, so neither Tom nor I said anything about being tired or wanting to go to bed. Eventually, the ladies were all talked out and we escorted them over to our rooms in the house

Once in the room Anna and I did talk about Laura's spirit but only after we had explored some 'possibilities'. Anna had heard exactly the same thing I'd heard, and we were both left wondering if Laura was going to start talking to Anna, as well as to me.

Tom and I spent the next morning catching up with Juan and Jorge, before heading over to Mesilla for a quick visit with Esteban and Ed. All was quiet in the area with no raids, either Indian or comanchero reported anywhere near Las Cruces. There continued to be periodic rumors of raids in the Tularosa basin, but nothing had been confirmed. We reviewed the progress on the information front they had been working. Between them they now had eighteen people around town, including in the fort, who could be classified as at least acquaintances. I picked up a new set of warrants the Judge had sent which, interestingly enough, contained a wanted poster and warrant for our old friend, Colonel Ezra Watson.

Along with the package, there was a personal note letting me know that things continued to go well in Texas. Based on his correspondence with his friend in Austin, he expected the bill containing the mineral rights language to be presented for a vote early next year.

We spent the bulk of the afternoon at the fort, visiting cousin George who was getting ready for another patrol. George confirmed that everything had been quiet, and also told us that the patrol he was taking out in a few days was going to investigate the rumors of raids in the Tularosa basin.

Early the next morning we left for El Paso, joined by Martin Amador who was hauling freight to El Paso that he'd picked up in Santa Fe. With the vaqueros scattered out around us as scouts throughout the trip we had plenty of time to talk with Martin over the two-day journey without constantly worrying about ambushes or attacks.

I was interested to see that Martin had taken my suggestions on weapons to heart, as he had both the sawed-off shotgun I'd given him, on his lap, and another longer barreled shotgun on the floorboard of the wagon seat as well as two muzzle loading rifles. He'd also spent some money on a Colt Navy Revolver he carried in a cross-draw holster.

Martin told us about his experiences on his first solo trip to Santa Fe, making a point to thank us for the training he'd received. Because of the training, he had spotted an Indian ambush before he'd driven into it, and had stopped fifty yards away to fortify his wagon and prepare. As a result, he was ready for the battle when they finally lost patience and attacked him. He lost a few hours, but between his shotguns and muzzle loaders the Indians eventually suffered too many losses and gave up.

Martin left us on the outskirts of El Paso the next afternoon, as his delivery was on the Mexican side, close to where he forded the river. We waved him off, and once we were sure he'd crossed the river without difficulty, we resumed our ride into El Paso arriving at the hotel about a half hour later.

We ended up taking the entire top floor of the hotel, with Tom, Yolanda, Anna and I in the suite, and the vaqueros doubling up in the rest of the rooms. The vaqueros were excited to be back in a large town again, and all had lists of their own to fill for their families and friends while we were there. We released them, after reminding them we were leaving after breakfast in four days.

Raphael told us he would spend the next few days looking for his friend. He intended to stay with friends near where he used to live. We wished him good luck as he rode one of the vaquero's horses down the street.

While the ladies settled into the suite, I went over to the bank to arrange for the deposit, while Tom drove the wagon around to the back door of the bank in the alley. Levi greeted me with a smile which only got bigger when I told him I had a deposit to make and asked if he could open the back door. Tom was just pulling the wagon up when Levi opened the door, and the three of us immediately set to, hauling the bags from the wagon to the weighing room.

In less than two hours we had the gold inside, weighed, and sold and had deposited it all into the Estancia account. I let Levi know that I wanted to withdraw $60,000 in a mix of coins when we left in four days, and arranged for an early morning pickup just after breakfast.

The three of us sat in Levi's office sipping some of the good stuff. As usual, Tom was tolerant of the scotch, while Levi and I thoroughly enjoyed every single sip.

As we were getting ready to leave, Levi asked, "Paul do you have any cattle for sale?"

Tom laughed heartily, as I told Levi, "We are always looking to sell cattle. How many head are you thinking of buying?"

This time it was Levi who laughed, "I don't want to buy any cattle, but a rancher by the name of King from somewhere in Southeast Texas is in town looking for a cattle herd of at least 3,000 head."

"Well, Levi, we would certainly be interested in talking to him. Can you tell us where to find him?" I asked.

"I'm having supper over at the hotel with him tonight at eight. Why don't you join us and I'll introduce you?" he replied.

I looked at Tom who nodded. "We'll be happy to join you. Anna and Yolanda are with us so there'll be four of us. We'll see you then, and thanks in advance for the help."

Levi laughed saying, "It's all part of being a full-service banker my friend. What's good for you, is good for the bank."

We said our goodbyes and went back over to the hotel, letting the ladies know about supper. They had unpacked, had a bath, put on fresh clothes, and were waiting for us in the lobby. We told them about the cattle buyer and Levi's offer of supper and introductions.

Anna looked at me with an appraising eye and said, "You and Tom look like you are 'down on your luck' cowboys. You both need to go get a haircut and a bath if there's time before they close."

Yolanda was nodding her head in agreement with Anna. I looked askance at Tom who just shrugged his shoulders. We both gave the droll, "yes, dear", response before heading upstairs to get some clean clothes. I looked back as we climbed the steps to see Anna and Yolanda both quietly giggling to each other.

Tom and I managed to get to the barbershop thirty minutes before they closed. For an extra dime each, the barber agreed to stay open long enough for us to get a bath and haircut. Clean, shaved, and shorn, we walked back into the hotel feeling like new men.

Anna and Yolanda were waiting for us up in the room with a fresh hot coffee service. We cuddled on the couches, sipping coffee until it was time to go downstairs for supper.

Downstairs, we found Levi waiting for us, with a man not much older than we were. As we walked up, Levi turned and welcomed the ladies by name, and then introduced us all to the cattle buyer, Captain Richard King.

As Levi was making the introductions I looked Mr. King over, liking what I saw. He was of medium height with a very full head of dark brown wavy hair and sported a chin beard, no sideburns or mustache just the chin whiskers. His dark eyes were clear and very focused on whomever he was being introduced to, although I was quite sure he didn't miss much that went on around him either.

By common agreement we let Tom answer most of the questions Captain King asked about the cattle we had for sale, while the rest of us just listened. Tom, in his turn, asked numerous questions about the ranch Captain King was buying for and where it was located.

Early in the conversation, we learned that Captain King was, in fact, a river boat Captain who had recently bought some land in the Nueces Strip between Brownsville and Corpus Christi and was turning it into a ranch. He had purchased an entire village's cattle in Mexico, and hired the villagers as his vaqueros last year.

Now he wanted another 3,000 head of cattle if he could find them at a good price.

I fought to keep a startled look off my face, as I realized that Captain King was none other than the founder of the King Ranch, a Texas legend. The King Ranch with the Running W brand would become the largest ranching operation in the United States.

I decided then and there that Anna was going to conduct any negotiations for the cattle because I knew for a fact that King was a prototypical nineteenth century business-man, whose primary goal was always to maxi-mize profits, regardless of any personal feel-ings he might have for those he dealt with.

I leaned over and whispered as much to Anna, while Captain King's head was turned towards Tom. She beamed me one of her smiles and I knew she understood that this was a time to maximize our own profits.

Negotiations for the cattle began in earnest, with our after-supper coffee. Captain King was more than a little surprised when it was Anna who, smiling sweetly, answered his initial question on a price for the cattle.

"Captain King, the asking price will vary, de-pending on whether or not you expect us to deliver the cattle to your ranch, meet us part way, or will trail the herd from the Estancia with your own resources. The lowest price will be if you trail the herd yourself. If you want us to trail it part way, the price will be higher and if you expect us to deliver the herd all the way to your ranch, then the price will be even higher yet. So, before we can set a price, we must know your intentions in this regard."

Captain King swallowed his surprise, and looked at Anna with a little more respect before addressing her.

"Mrs. McAllister, I have fifteen vaqueros with me, and we will drive the herd ourselves."

Anna gave him another sweet smile. "In that case Captain King the price is ten dollars a head for up to five thousand head. If you want more than five thousand head, the price will come down a little."

Tom, Yolanda, and I were all using the coffee cups to hide the smiles on our faces at Anna's starting price. I didn't know what figure she had decided on, so we all waited with amusement as the conversation continued on.

"Mrs. McAllister, you can't be serious. That's much too high a price for cattle in today's market. I can pay much lower prices here, and even lower prices in Mexico if I should go there."

"Captain, you are correct that you can get lower prices both here and in Mexico, but not much lower. The price of range cattle, both here and in Mexico, is currently just over seven dollars a head and going up after the kill off caused by the glut of the past few years.

"What you will *not* get, is a lower price for all the cattle you want to buy at one time and in one place. You will spend at least two months buying a hundred head here, fifty head there, and you'll have to find somewhere to gather, hold, and feed all the individual purchases you make, until you get a herd large enough to trail them home. Our price takes that into consideration, and therefore includes a premium for a single buy, from a single source."

The negotiations took off in earnest from there, and forty-five minutes later the deal was struck for four thousand head of cattle at eight dollars and seventy-five cents a head. The Captain and his vaqueros would accompany us back to the Estancia. The rest of us could only marvel at what Anna had just accomplished.

We all toasted the completed deal with wine, scotch, - or, in Tom's case, beer - before calling it a night.

Back up in the suite, I congratulated Anna on her masterful negotiations with a big hug and a long kiss. The four of us settled in with coffee, and I told them what I could remember of Captain King, the King Ranch, the litigation against King by his late partner's estate, and their impact on Texas and US history.

When I was done talking, Anna got a speculative look on her face and asked, "Is that what we're going to build? A ranch large enough to compete with the King Ranch?"

I shrugged. "Not really. Captain King will build the King Ranch into the third largest ranch in the world, that's true - the others will be huge multimillion acre spreads in the outback of Australia. But along the way, he will own and control every aspect of the delivery infrastructure. His intent was always to maximize his profits. It won't be until after he dies, that his wife and son-in-law start looking at the bigger picture of social responsibility, but even then, it will be within the context of business profits.

"Our goals turn that around, with our businesses existing to gather the funds necessary to improve society in the Mesilla Valley, New Mexico, and the United States in that order. Of course, we'll make money and live comfortably in the process; but that's a byproduct, not our primary goal.

"We've worked on defining the goals for the

last couple of years and built tentative plans. We'll buy the Salt Flats to prevent the Salt War from happening, we'll hopefully limit the battles in New Mexico when the Civil War starts, we'll fight for public education, woman's suffrage, and Statehood in the next few years all while providing a place of refuge and peace for the people of the Estancia and the Apache.

"We'll build a university in Las Cruces, pave the roads, develop the ice and cooling industries, and encourage conservation of resources. All of these things will require money. More money than we currently have. So, we will end up buying land in the Texas panhandle, where huge petroleum and natural gas reserves are located. Eventually, in forty years or so, we will form a company to drill, produce, refine, and market gasoline and natural gas to the US and world markets. That will bring in even more money to use, as our children and grandchildren fight to make additional improvements to the Mesilla Valley, New Mexico, and the US."

Anna beamed me one of her huge super megawatt Anna smiles.

"We've never talked to Tom and Yolanda about the plans we've made," Anna said, "nor the reasons behind them. I wanted to make sure they understood we were different from Captain King as our goals are completely different."

I looked over at Tom and Yolanda, who were sitting with slightly stunned expressions on their faces and realized Anna was right. We'd never followed up the initial disclosure of my secret with a discussion about our goals and plans.

"We'll have to fix that when we get back to the Estancia. As I said, Anna and I have a list of goals with plans on how to achieve those goals. Most of the plans are tentative but they are a start, nonetheless. It'll take a few days of talking and explaining, because I'll have to give you some of the history behind the goals and plans but when we're done you'll have a better understanding of what we're trying to do and why."

Yolanda gave us a saucy grin saying, "Good! I was starting to get bored anyway."

Tom groaned before saying, "My head already hurts thinking about what you just told us. I don't think I'll be ready for another *talk* for at least two more weeks."

We all laughed and talked for a few more minutes, as we finished our coffee. Then we headed to our separate rooms in the suite. Anna was ready to explore some more possibilities, which interested me, too!

Our first stop after breakfast the next morning was the jewelry store where we were greeted like family by Mr. and Mrs. Greenburg. Anna's necklace, earrings, and ring were exquisite as were the pendants, all of which were ready to take with us. Tom and Yolanda were amazed at the craftsmanship of the jewelry even though they wore two of the pendants themselves.

The rest of that day and the next, Tom and I struggled to keep up with the ladies as we escorted them from store to store on their shopping expedition. I was never really sure what they were buying or why. You can bet that neither Tom nor I were going to voice that question within hearing of the ladies, and risk getting put in the dog house.

Tom and I did take a couple of hours away from the ladies to visit the water driller, John Gillespie. He was tickled to get our business, and promised to be at the Hacienda between the 5th and 7th of January to start drilling. He also agreed to bring as much pipe, connectors, and valves as he could spare from his inventory when he came.

At lunch on our last day in town, the vaqueros came into the hotel restaurant and asked for Anna and Yolanda's help in finding some of the items on their lists. Smiling, both women agreed to help. Tom and I gamely escorted them out the door, down the street, and into a store followed by the vaqueros.

As we entered the store I saw the Town Marshal walking up the sidewalk on the opposite side of the street. I told a slightly distracted Anna, that Tom and I would meet them outside when they were done. With her nod, Tom and I walked across the street to talk to the Marshal.

As we approached him, he put a glum look on his face saying, "There haven't been any gunfights in the last few days, so you haven't been in town long."

Both Tom and I laughed. I couldn't help but tell him, "The day is young yet, Marshal. No telling what's going to happen before it's over."

We all laughed, and the Marshal greeted us with a handshake. We talked about the travails of escorting wives on a shopping mission for a few minutes, and were about to take our leave when a very thinned down Ezra Watson stepped out of a saloon two doors down from where we stood talking.

As Ezra walked towards us I quietly told the Marshal I had some Marshal business of my own to conduct, as I took my badge out of my pocket and pinned it on my coat. His eyes widened at the sight of the badge, and he simply did as I asked when I asked him to step off to the side and act as a witness.

Ezra was twenty feet away when I started talking to him. "Ezra Watson, I'm US Marshal Paul McAllister. I have a warrant for your arrest on the charges of Murder, Kidnapping, and Theft."

Ezra was slightly inebriated but not staggering drunk. He looked at me calmly for a few moments before saying, "You aren't arresting me for anything, because you'll be dead."

As he finished talking, he smoothly drew a Colt Dragoon, cocking it as it cleared his holster. Without another word, I drew and fired two rounds hitting him with both shots in the upper chest. He looked down at the two holes in his chest in surprise before collapsing onto the sidewalk with his unfired gun still in his hand.

I started walking towards him to make sure he was dead, when a commotion broke out across the street. I turned, seeing Anna and Yolanda come out of the store and started to wave to Anna that I was alright when she snarled, pulled her pistol, and fired two shots at the saloon.

Puzzled, I turned, flinching as a pistol went off. I watched a smoking handgun, followed by the man who'd been holding it, fall out of the saloon doorway and onto the sidewalk.

I turned back to tell Anna and Yolanda to go back into the store, but they had been surrounded in a protective shield by the vaqueros, who had their guns drawn. I walked over to Ezra and knelt down next to him. He wasn't dead yet, but it wouldn't be long.

"Ezra, why did you try and fight? You could've probably beat the charges, as there wasn't any real evidence that I'm aware of."

In a coughing gasp, he looked up at me with hate in eyes, saying, "My brother in Santa Fe has made arrangements for you. I was going to save him the trouble and expense."

With a final cough, he died, leaving me wondering. Wondering what the hell was going on, who his brother was, why he wanted me dead, and who the hell was the guy who'd tried to shoot me from the saloon?

I walked over to the second man and rolled him over. I didn't recognize him. I turned as Tom and the Marshal walked up, followed by Anna and Yolanda still surrounded by the vaqueros. I gave Anna a quick hug and kiss thanking her for looking out for me, and complimented her shooting. She gave me a small smile and asked me who the men were, and why they wanted me dead.

"My love, I have no idea who this man was, nor why he would want me dead. The other man is Ezra Watson, late Colonel in the US Army, forced to resign his commission a few months ago. I think he blamed me for being forced to resign but I have no idea why he wanted me dead. He said something about his brother in Santa Fe just before he died," I replied.

I turned to the Marshal. "Do you know this man, Marshal?"

The Marshal took a good look and said he didn't know him, but had seen him in town a few times. I scratched my head, both literally and figuratively, before deciding to do a little investigation of my own.

I walked into the saloon and found the barkeep behind the bar holding a sawed-off shotgun. When he saw my badge, he visibly relaxed and put the shotgun away under the counter. The saloon was empty except for the barkeep. I waved away his offer of a drink and asked him if he knew the man who'd been shot in his doorway.

His reply wasn't helpful. He shrugged his shoulders and said, "He was just a customer. He's been in a few times over the last month always with that other man. They'd buy a bottle and sit at a table near the back of the room sharing it until it was gone and then they'd leave. They didn't talk much, and then only to each other, so there isn't really anything else I can tell you Marshal."

I turned to go back outside, and found Anna and Yolanda in the doorway with their guns out acting as my backup, while Tom and the vaqueros were spread out behind them watching the street for any other threats.

I smiled to myself when my first thought was: 'what a woman!' My smile grew when my second thought was 'what friends!'

I walked up to Anna and Yolanda and gave them both a small hug, and kissed Anna again.

"I think it's over for now, so you two go back to getting those lists filled for the vaqueros. I need to spend some time with the Marshal writing up a report on this for the Judge. I'll meet everyone back at the hotel, this evening."

Anna gave me one of her smiles, intertwined her arm with Yolanda's, and the two of them walked regally back across the street followed by the still watchful vaqueros. Tom stayed where he was, telling me he'd just as soon be bored in the Marshal's office as in the stores. I laughed, and we turned to find the Marshal going through the pockets of the man Anna had shot.

Finished with his search he said, "They weren't carrying much. Besides their guns, which are relatively new, they had less than twenty dollars between them."

"Were they carrying any papers?" I asked curiously.

"Nope. Nothing in their pockets but coins, and neither was wearing a money belt," the Marshal answered.

He started to hand me the pistol belts and money, but I stopped him telling him to use it to cover the costs of burials. He grinned and turned to arrange for the undertaker when I stopped him again, and told him I'd meet him at his office when he was done, as we had to write up a report about what happened for the Federal Judge back in Santa Fe. He nodded, telling us as he left that he'd see us in about fifteen minutes.

Tom and I watched him walk halfway down the block, where he paid a young boy a nickel to go fetch the undertaker and then walked back to stand over Ezra's body. We both turned and walked away. We made a quick stop at the hotel to pick up the latest package of wants and warrants I'd picked up in Mesilla, before walking over to the Marshal's office.

We spent the afternoon in the Marshal's office,

as both the Marshal and I wrote up a separate report. While the Marshal could technically read and write, he struggled with both to the point where Tom finally wrote the report the Marshal dictated to him. When Tom was done, he handed it to the Marshal who spent almost an hour reviewing it to make sure Tom had written exactly what he said.

My report was finished in less than thirty minutes, and I added both the wanted poster and warrant for Ezra Watson with 'Killed Resisting Arrest in El Paso' with the date written across them. I spent the rest of the time going through the stack of wanted posters to see if I could find the second dead man.

It was slow going, as most of the wanted posters didn't have pictures, just descriptions. Each one had to be read carefully. Those with actual pictures I could discard easily, but they were few and far between. Of those with pictures, over eighty percent were hand drawn, and very poorly at that, so it was back to reading the descriptions.

I finally found him at the bottom of the stack, or at least I thought I found him. The picture was hand drawn and the likeness to the dead man was almost nonexistent. The description on the other hand was spot on. Two things nailed it for me.

First, the man was described as a known associate of, and a Lieutenant in, the Fulgencia Madrid gang, with which we suspected Ezra was working. Second, and more importantly to me, was Laura's soft voice in my left ear whispering, "Well done, my love, well done. Justice has been served on this one."

I handed the poster and warrant to Tom, who looked it over. His eyes hardened when he read the part about known associates which convinced him as well. He turned to hand the papers to the Marshal before stopping and reading the description out loud.

When he was done reading, he handed the papers to the Marshal who said, "The description is an exact match, but you'd never know it from the drawing."

I took the papers from the Marshal and wrote 'Killed during Attempted Murder of US Marshal Paul McAllister in El Paso,' and added the date on both the poster and the warrant. I added the two sets of posters and warrants to the Marshal's and my signed reports, and got up from the chair.

"Marshal, I thank you for your help today and I'm sorry about the inconvenience. I was here on personal business, not on Marshal business. But, ever since I took this job, it seems to follow me wherever I go. I've got to get these into the mail to the Judge. We're leaving in the morning, so hopefully things will be quieter around here."

The Marshal smiled and said, "You weren't lying when you said the day was young. Don't worry about it. I was more surprised to find out you were a US Marshal than anything else. Next time you're in town, you'll have to give me the full story on how that happened."

"That's a deal, Marshal. Until my next visit, stay safe."

Tom and I walked over to the post office and mailed off the reports to the Judge, then returned to the hotel where we found the ladies waiting for us. As we were walking through the lobby towards them I saw Anna lift a finger at the counter man, who nodded and disappeared down the hall behind the counter. I gave Anna a questioning look. She just shot me one of those infuriating enigmatic female looks, and gave me a hug and kiss.

She broke the embrace, placed her arm in mine and said, "Let's go upstairs to the room, where we can talk."

Tom and I obediently escorted the two ladies upstairs to our suite. Once inside Anna grinned at me and said, "The coffee service should be here any moment, and then we can get down to talking about this afternoon."

I shook my head with a wry grin on my face, just as there was a knock on the door. Tom opened the door and a maid entered the room setting a coffee service for four on the table before leaving. We all poured our coffee and sat down to talk about the gunfight. An hour later, the ladies knew everything we did, the coffee was gone, and we were all ready for supper.

Raphael was waiting in the lobby for us, with another young man he introduced as Frank Lucero. Frank was the long-time friend he had gone looking for and obviously found. We invited both of them to join us for supper. Over supper, we discovered that Frank and Raphael had been friends ever since they could remember, and had apprenticed together.

Frank was single and much preferred making and repairing mechanical parts, but was also more than adequate at the more common tasks of shoeing as well as making and repairing farm tools. He was fluent in Spanish, and could struggle through a conversation in English if he had to. He could read and write Spanish, but not English.

Raphael told us he had explained to Frank that he would have to take the Apache Training Course, and learn to speak Apache and English, as well as read and write English.

I asked Frank if he understood everything Raphael had told him. When he said that he did, I turned to Anna, Tom, and Yolanda getting a brief nod from all of them. I turned back to Frank and told him the job was his, if he still wanted it. He was overjoyed and said he would be ready to leave in the morning.

Back up in our room in the suite, Anna and I told each other the parts we'd both left out of the story about the gunfight.

Anna said she had come out of the store at her Great Grandfather Jaime's insistence. He'd told her that I needed her help. I told her about Laura telling me justice had been done. We both agreed that having whispering voices in your head in public was still unsettling, but we were both glad that we had them looking out for us.

CHAPTER 9

T he next morning, bright and early, Tom and I loaded up the wagon and drove it over to the back door of the bank, where Levi was waiting for us. I signed the withdrawal receipt and accepted a deposit receipt of $35,000 for the sale of 4,000 head of cattle to Richard King. We loaded the bags of money into the steel wagon box, locked it up, and drove it back over to the hotel.

In the hotel restaurant, we found the ladies waiting for us, along with Richard King, a total of twenty vaqueros, and Raphael with Frank. After a quick breakfast, we mounted up and rode for home, with Raphael and Frank driving the wagon and everyone else on horseback.

With such a large party, no one was really worried about being attacked, but without being told the Estancia vaqueros disappeared once we were out of town to perform screening and scouting duty. The Captain was a little confused by the departure of the vaqueros until we explained what they were doing.

We pulled into Mr. Mendoza's stable late the next afternoon, tired and hungry. Anna and Yolanda left their horses with us, and walked over to the restaurant. We got all the horses taken care of and introduced Mr. Mendoza to Captain King. Captain King's vaqueros were invited to spend the night in the hayloft with the Estancia vaqueros, and they rapidly accepted the offer after being told about the abysmal accommodations offered by the hotel.

The vaqueros all disappeared into the restaurant for their supper, while the rest of us joined Mr. Mendoza at his work table behind the stable. There we all relaxed and brought Mr. Mendoza up to date on the cattle sale and gun fight. Captain King seemed to enjoy the relaxing atmosphere. He listened attentively to everything that was being said, including the hiring of Frank. I made a mental note to myself to be careful about what I said around this man.

Captain King and Frank were apparently invited to supper, as Mr. Mendoza made sure to include them in our walk over to the restaurant. We stopped just inside the back door as usual to watch the kitchen dance for a few moments, before going into the dining room. Captain King looked around at the huge table with all the place settings and asked if this was a special function room.

"Well, in a way it is," I replied. "This is the Mendoza family dining room. Mrs. Mendoza owns the restaurant and most of the family works either here or hauling freight for Mr. Mendoza, so the entire extended family eats their meals here."

He was about to ask more questions when the ladies came in bearing the platters and bowls filled with our supper. The kids all trailed in behind them, and we all dug in. Captain King listened with fascination to the various discussions going on around the table. I told Anna in Apache that I couldn't wait to see his reaction to meal time at the Hacienda, if supper here fascinated him so much. She beamed me one of her special smiles and agreed that it would be interesting to watch.

After supper, with the table cleared and the after-supper coffee served, Anna picked up the guitar from behind the chair. She handed it to me without a word. I tuned the guitar and sang what had become my standard opening song, "Keeper of the Stars". When I was done, Mrs. Mendoza said that she'd heard that the visit to El Paso was interesting. I grinned at her and sang "Mi Vida Loca", which had everyone including Frank and the Captain grinning.

I played a few more requests, before the kids started begging tio Pablo to play the lion song. Anna threw me a huge super megawatt Anna smile as I started the introduction of "The Lion Sleeps Tonight". Anna and Yolanda got all the kids and most of the adult's ready and I started singing. Everyone came in on que, and we went through the song twice before I brought it a close. The second time around, even the Captain had joined in and was smiling.

The kids were happy, and they all thanked me as they filed out to get ready for bed. I mixed things up after that, singing "Do You Know Where You're Going To", "I Have a Dream", and "Hooked on a Feeling", before finishing up with "Anna's Song".

We talked for a while longer enjoying the coffee, before everyone headed across the courtyard to bed. Anna and I escorted the Captain to the guest bedroom in the house where his saddlebags were laying on the bed, and bid him a good night telling him we'd see him at breakfast in the restaurant.

With a good night's sleep and a filling breakfast under our belts, we left Las Cruces the next morning right on time. The vaqueros, very aware of the danger that could be waiting anywhere between Las Cruces and the Estancia, pulled their disappearing act as soon as we were out of Las Cruces. They rejoined us once we were on the Estancia, knowing that the Scout/Sniper teams had already spotted us and alerted everyone on the Estancia.

We stopped just inside the Estancia for the ladies to relieve themselves, and I took the opportunity to send a message to Hector, asking him to meet us at the Hacienda for lunch with a cattle buyer, and to start rounding up 4,000 head of cattle.

The captain watched curiously as I sent the message with the little mirror we all carried, and was surprised to see an acknowledging flash from the mountains. I explained that I had sent a message to the Ranch Segundo, asking him to start rounding up 4,000 head of cattle and meet us for lunch at the Hacienda.

We had resumed our ride when the message came back from Hector telling us he would get the roundup started, and would meet us at the Hacienda. I acknowledged the message as we rode and returned to talking with the Captain who was full of the usual questions. I explained about the annual flooding and the need for the levees as well as the road work he could see going on in the distance.

A few minutes before we reached the bridge,

the lead vaquero came up beside me and told us he was taking the Captain's vaqueros to the Ranch where they would stay until they left. I nodded and told him to draw any additional supplies needed for the extra vaqueros from the store. He nodded and spurred his horse off towards the Ranch operations area, waving for the other vaqueros to follow him.

Captain King was again full of questions about why the vaqueros were riding away and I explained that they all lived at the Ranch operations area, while we lived at the Hacienda. I laughed, telling him he would understand better after tomorrow morning's ride. In the meantime, we would spend the afternoon unpacking and relaxing at the Hacienda, where many of his questions could be answered much easier.

We'd just crossed the bridge when Captain King asked, "How much farther to the Hacienda?"

"It's just over the top of that slope," I replied, pointing at the slope where the top of the Hacienda was visible.

Anna rode up next to me to get a better look at Captain King's face as we crested the slope, and he got his first look at the Hacienda. She giggled a little as his eye's bulged out in shock at the size and the architecture.

He was just starting to get over his shock, when three of the young cousins came running out of the courtyard door to get our horses and take them down to the stable. We all laughed at his expression.

"You'll get used to it soon enough," I said congenially.

Anna and Yolanda took the Captain to the room he'd be using while he was here. I sent Raphael and Frank up to the terrace to relax for a few minutes, while Tom and I unloaded our part of the wagon and hauled the bags of coins into the study and then into the cave. When we got upstairs to the terrace, the ladies and the Captain were already there, enjoying coffee with Frank and Raphael.

Frank and Raphael left a few minutes later to deliver the vaqueros' packages to the ranch, before taking the wagon to the village. As they were leaving, the Captain got up. He walked to the railing and looked out over the river towards the Doña Ana Mountains.

The rest of us sat sipping our coffee with smiles on our faces, knowing that he was still trying to process what he had seen so far. Eventually, he turned around and rejoined us at the table telling us it was a magnificent view.

Hector arrived a few minutes later, and while

we were introducing him to the Captain, Cristina, Celia, and Carla brought out our lunch.

Over lunch we talked about the roundup, and I asked Hector how long it would take to roundup 4,000 head with the extra fifteen vaqueros the Captain had brought with him. His immediate reply of about five days surprised the Captain.

Seeing his surprise Hector elaborated. "Between you're fifteen vaqueros, and the forty or so vaqueros currently available we'll round up 5,000 head in the next three days, then spend two days culling that down to 4,000 head your vaqueros find acceptable."

With a surprised look on his face the Captain asked, "How many vaqueros do you have?"

"The Estancia currently has eighty vaqueros." Hector replied. "At any given time twenty are on security duty patrolling the Estancia, and ten are working on the roads or loading and hauling stones for the masons. The other ten are getting ready to deliver the monthly beef quotas to the forts we currently supply."

Miranda made a rare appearance outside the kitchen, bringing us a plate of biscochitos to snack on shortly after lunch. We spent the rest of the afternoon on the terrace drinking coffee, snacking on biscochitos, and answering the

Captain's questions about the Estancia.

The Captain was again surprised when Beth and Izabella came out on the terrace, leading the rest of the kids to welcome us home. After a round of hugs for everybody we introduced all the kids to the Captain and explained which ones were ours, and which ones were Tomas and Giuseppe's. As the kids were leaving, chatting away to each other, the Captain asked how many languages they were speaking.

I listened for a moment and told him, "Sounds like four at the moment." I listened for another moment and smiled. "Nope, it's five languages. English, Spanish, Apache, Italian, and German."

"Good lord man! How do they understand each other?" he asked.

Anna laughed and explained, "Everyone on the Estancia is required to be fluent in English, Spanish, and Apache. The kids also learn Latin in school, but since Giuseppe's kids are Italian they are teaching the other Hacienda kids that language also. The German was picked up informally, from the mason's kids at school."

"School? What school? Why Apache?" he asked.

We all laughed at his confused look. Anna and Yolanda answered all his questions about the school, as well as the relationship to the Apache and their security work on the Estancia. They finished up just as Cristina announced that supper would be ready in a few minutes.

We all walked into the dining room, to find everyone already seated at a much bigger table. Seeing my puzzled look Anna told me that it had been delivered yesterday and set up this morning before we arrived. With that puzzle solved, I introduced the Captain to everyone, including the three babies lying in basinets next to their mothers.

Supper was the usual riot of conversations in multiple languages with the kids constantly shifting between languages depending on who they were talking to. The Captain ate supper with a look of amazement on his face, as he tried to follow along while the kids told us about school, riding their horses, and the new friends they'd made while we'd been gone.

When the younger kids started yawning after supper, Beth and Izabella got up from the table telling the kids it was time to start getting ready for bed. The kids all went to their parents, gave them a hug, and wished them good night, before being led out of the dining room by Izabella, with Beth the last to leave behind the rest of them.

I cocked a questioning eyebrow at Anna, who

gave me a small shoulder shrug. Sofia laughed at our exchange, and told us that she had asked Beth and Izabella to mind the kids until the babies were a little older.

Anna and I retired ourselves shortly thereafter, telling everyone we were tired from the trip and would see them all the next morning. In reality, of course, we were both simply craving a nice warm shower followed by exploring some more possibilities.

The next morning, we had our normal Monday morning staff meeting, which didn't last long as things were progressing better than we'd hoped on all fronts. Especially good were the road building activities, due to a combination of the rock sorters Tom and I had built, and the effectiveness of the steel roller Raphael had built. The rest of the morning was spent riding the Estancia, accompanied by Tom, Giuseppe, and the Captain.

The Captain expressed the expected wonder at everything he saw; from the village to the dams, to the quarry, to the Ranch operations area. His biggest excitement was reserved for the stable and wagon yard operations, where he saw row after row of wagons painted in the Estancia colors undergoing maintenance. As a river boat captain, he was interested in all things dealing with transporting and hauling goods, so his interest shouldn't have surprised us, but it did.

He was curious about everything, and spent more than a few minutes talking to Lupe in the store as well as Jesus when I introduced him as the Village Alcalde. He was interested to learn about the elections, and what Jesus did as the Alcalde. When he was done talking to them, we pointed out the school rooms just as two of the rooms opened up, and a horde of kids came boiling out for a recess. Four village ladies and the Padre walked out behind them. We waved at them before showing the Captain into the Finca operations center.

We found Tomas standing with his back to us, deep in thought as he stared at the mural. He started a little when I cleared my throat, to let him know he had company. He turned around and smiled when he saw us, and walked over to greet us.

I asked him if he had time to answer any questions the Captain might have, and he grinned telling us he always had time to talk about Finca operations. The Captain's first question dealt with the mural. Tomas took him over to stand in front of it as he explained why it was there, and how it was used. A half hour later we were in the saddle again.

We had lunch with the ladies at the Hacienda after visiting the dams and the quarry. Captain King was amazed at the organization and efficiency of everything he'd seen so far, and couldn't stop asking questions especially about my and Tom's involvement in day to day operations.

When I said I had little day to day involvement, and left Tom to run most things he turned to Tom to get his answer. Tom told him that Giuseppe, Tomas, and Hector ran the day to day operations all by themselves. He provided oversight and brokered resources if necessary, but other than that, most everything was worked out at the weekly staff meetings.

It was easy to tell from his facial expressions that the Captain was still skeptical of everything he'd been told. It was equally obvious that he was having a hard time reconciling his belief that Anglos were inherently more capable than any other race, with what he'd seen during his visit so far.

The afternoon was spent at the ranch, where Hector gave the Captain a tour of the entire ranching operations starting in the operations center. The cattle pens already held over a thousand head, with more being brought in as we watched. The Captain wanted to see the round up in progress, so we headed to the north end of the Ranch.

We found a small group of cattle being watched over by one vaquero, and watched individual vaqueros bringing in one or two head of cattle at a time increasing the size of the group until there were twenty-five head. The four vaqueros decided that was enough, and started driving them towards the operations center and the holding pens.

The Captain couldn't understand why the vaqueros were taking such a small herd back to the holding pens, instead of building up a larger herd and then taking them back. Hector smiled and tried to explain about individual cows out on the range, versus a large herd of cows on a cattle drive, and the toll a roundup had on the horses; but the Captain couldn't quite seem to grasp what Hector was trying to tell him.

Hector looked over at me and Tom for help, and I grinned telling them it looked like we going to learn to be vaqueros. Hector laughed as we all pulled gloves from our saddlebags and put them on.

Hector noticed that the Captain wasn't wearing gloves, and he reached back into his saddlebags pulling out another pair and throwing them to the Captain.

"Make sure you wear those, or you'll have blisters on your palms inside of two hours," he said.

The Captain looked at the gloves with apparent confusion. "Why do I need gloves, and why would I have blisters on my palms?" he asked.

Hector gave a deep laugh. "A roundup is all about the horses. A well-trained cow horse knows what to do, and the rider simply points the horse at a cow and then holds on. Tight! You'll get the hang of it soon enough, but until you do you're going to be spending most of your time just trying to stay in the saddle. The horse will be moving around stopping the cow from running off, instead of heading to where we're forming up the herd."

We rode east a half mile or so until we found a group of five steers. We watched as Hector and Tom gave a demonstration on cutting and herding them towards a staging area. We found a small grassy bowl and decided to use it as our staging area. The cows Hector and Tom were herding seemed content to stay in the bowl, so we all rode off in a different direction to start rounding up more.

The first couple of cows I found were pretty easy to herd towards the bowl, as they were nearby with nowhere to hide. After that, things got much harder. The horse really seemed to enjoy this, and as Hector had said, anytime I found a cow I simply pointed the horse at the cow, and then held on.

It was late afternoon before we'd managed to gather thirty head, and both the horses and riders were tired. Hector rode trail behind the herd as we started them moving towards the cattle pens. Once we'd closed the gate on the cattle pens, we all gave a wave to a small group of vaqueros who'd been watching us and rode back to the Hacienda.

We got back to the Hacienda in time to clean up for supper. Over our after-supper coffee, the Captain said, "It's obvious I need to learn more about the work the vaqueros do. So, with your permission, I'm going to spend the next few days over at the ranch working with them."

I looked at Tom and Hector, getting small nods from both. "Captain, I need to learn what they do myself, so I'll join you and we'll have Tom and Hector teach us."

The next morning the four of us left the Hacienda after an early breakfast, arriving at the ranch in time to have coffee in the courtyard with the rest of the vaqueros before they headed out in their work teams to start the day. Coffee in hand, Hector took us into the operations center, and over to the mural.

He showed the Captain where we'd been working yesterday and then said, "Today, we'll move a little further north than we were yesterday, to the edge of the Estancia, and start there. There'll be teams of vaqueros working the areas both east and west of us so don't be surprised if you see them out there."

We finished our coffee, mounted up and rode at a canter for the northern boundary of the Estancia. When we reached the boundary, we looked around until we found a small narrow draw with grass along the floor, and decided to use that as the gathering point.

This area hadn't been worked yet, so rounding up forty head was relatively quick. We headed back to the cattle pens with the forty head, arriving just in time for a quick lunch of hamburgers and fries, with cool mint tea to wash it all down. The Captain made no comment about the food, other than it was good and filling. We headed back out to round up more cattle.

By the end of the next day, our little group had contributed over two hundred head of cattle to the five thousand head in the cattle pens and corrals at the ranch operations area. The next two days were spent culling the herd. Hector and the Captain's lead vaquero quickly culled out any bulls, and all but ten of the steers leaving nothing but cows and heifers in the pens and corrals.

The serious culling then began, and ran through lunch of the second day. Everything that was judged to be too young or too old was culled. Any animal with a serious wound was also culled. After lunch on the second day the cattle were herded out of their pen, one pen at a time, and then let back in as they were counted. When the count reached 4,000 near the end of the day, the remaining cattle left outside the pens were all herded back out onto the Estancia range.

At supper that night, Captain King thanked us for the education and the cattle before telling us he would start herding the cattle after taking a day of rest. I started to tell him he was working his horses too hard, but stopped myself, as I knew it wouldn't be appreciated. From the expressions on Hector and Tom's faces I knew they felt the same way, but I gave them a small head shake before they could comment, either.

Hector, Tom, and I sat our saddles two mornings later, watching the herd led by Captain King and his lead vaquero disappear towards Las Cruces and El Paso. "There goes one very focused and driven man," I said.

Hector snorted saying, "If he doesn't learn to take advice and slow down on working his men and animals, he'll be too focused to see he's driving them to death."

"He's a very smart and capable man, Hector. He just doesn't believe that others can be as smart or capable as he is. He'll learn as he goes, though; and, as he's learning, his attitude will change as well. As a matter of fact, he learned quite a lot while he was with us, and his attitude is already starting to change. Whether he learns, and changes quick enough, is anybody's guess."

Hector headed back to the Ranch operations center, while Tom and I took the opportunity to tour the southern end of the ranch area before heading back to the Hacienda and recuperating for the rest of the weekend, from the strenuous past few days.

CHAPTER 10

A fter the Monday morning staff meeting, I holed up in the study with Tom and Yolanda. I'd been wrong in El Paso. It didn't take two days to give them the background and go over the tentative plans Anna and I had been working on. It took all week, and even then I'd just scratched the surface of the background.

The major problem, as always, was trying to figure out how to answer their questions in terms they could understand. I tried to stay away from things they didn't need to know about. Things like specific battles in the Civil War, the names of the Generals involved, and the locations. We couldn't affect any of these things, so I didn't want to get involved with them and further muddy the waters. Instead, I did my best to focus on those events and personalities that would affect the local area and territory, over the next twenty-five years.

While I was with Tom and Yolanda, Anna began her training with Nantan in earnest. She tried to explain what she was learning but it sounded like a meditation based self-induced trance state. I knew that she needed to learn this so I supported her as best I could. She joined us in the afternoons, and added her perspective to whatever topic we were discussing.

In the evenings after we turned in, I told her what the three of us had covered during the morning, and what I planned on covering the next morning, while she was practicing with Nantan. Anna provided some key input on the sequence and specific discussion items that eased the explanations.

We talked at length about the Texans crossing into New Mexico Territory once the war started, and what we could do to limit, if not prevent, it. I emphasized the role the Confederate sympathizers in Mesilla and Tucson would play and that we needed to come up with a way to neutralize them.

They were surprised to hear me say that the real issue was the relationship between Hispanos and Anglos. I reminded them that until recently, Mesilla had been in Mexico and was mostly populated with people who had moved from the US to Mesilla, so they would be Mexican instead of US citizens. They viewed Anglos with deep suspicion, especially easterners, and felt they would be treated much better by the Confederacy. They wouldn't be, of course, but they would only learn that the hard way if we couldn't come up with some way to influence them.

We talked about the Salt Wars, and what Anna and I had come up with to prevent it from happening; as well as the continued relationship problems, once easterners started moving into the area in large numbers after the war. From there we turned to accelerating statehood, compulsory education, the railroad, and starting a university in the area with specific colleges focused on agriculture, engineering, medicine, law, and business.

Each of those issues took half a day of discussion at a minimum and by the time we were done, they began to see that all the issues were interrelated and couldn't be addressed in isolation.

The need for more money was very apparent, and we spent Friday afternoon talking about the need to continue recovering the gold at both the Caballo Mountain and Colorado River sites. I also reminded them that we had other, even longer-term plans regarding land in the Texas panhandle, that would require funds. So it was critical we continue recovering gold from the La Paz site, before it was "discovered" in early 1862. Tom suggested we get the cousins to help. He was quite surprised to learn that trying to get the cousins to help would be worse than getting the gold in the first place.

To the Apache, gold was the color claimed by the creator, Ussen, and the metal was exclusively his. There was no other reason for gold as far as they were concerned. After all, unlike silver, it was too soft for decorative use, couldn't be used as arrowheads, and wouldn't hold an edge. Finally, the Apache believed that the various earthquakes, tremors, and cave ins, were all caused by white men digging in the ground for metals, instead of using what was provided by Ussen on the surface.

I did let them know that Anna and I had a few other ideas we were working on to get limited help, but they needed time to develop. In the meantime, we could only rely on ourselves.

The last thing we did Friday afternoon, was come up with a schedule for gold trips Tom and I would take. The trips to the Caballo Mountain site were relatively easy to schedule and we all agreed one trip a quarter for no more than thirty days, with the first trip to start in two weeks.

The trips to the La Paz site were much tougher. Neither Tom nor I wanted to leave Anna and Yolanda behind for three to five months at a time; at least, not for the next few years. After much heated discussion, Anna and Yolanda's view finally won out, and Tom and I resigned ourselves to taking an annual trip starting in mid to late April returning before mid-August.

We also discussed the need to make an annual trip to Santa Fe to make substantial deposits, and to hold discussions with the Judge and Tom Stevenson. We decided that those trips would be made every October by the four of us, all the kids under five, and at least two teams with us, for security.

The next two weeks were busy for everyone. Tom and I took our morning rides over the Estancia, and we spent the afternoons in the caves melting gold nuggets into bars. Anna spent her time with Nantan learning what he could teach her while Yolanda started developing the new refresher course for next year built on the evasion and hiding portions of the Scout/Sniper training.

Tom and I left as scheduled using the excuse that we were going on an eastern swing of the Territory. I'd sworn Tom in as one of my part-time Deputies, so both of us wore badges as we left the Hacienda. We would go to Socorro first, and spend a day or two to show the flag, so to speak, before going to the Caballo Mountains for the remainder of the thirty days.

Nothing had changed in Socorro, and all was quiet with no reported raids of any kind since August. We spent the night, leaving for the Caballo Mountains early the next morning having done our duty.

My camp site in the little bowl was undisturbed, with no evidence of anyone having been there since Anna and I had last been there. We spent the next two and a half weeks digging up and melting enough gold to fill the panniers of the four pack mules we'd brought with us. When we finally returned to the Hacienda the mules were fully loaded with nuggets and bars, so we both considered it a good trip.

Tom and I rode up to the Hacienda, and with the help of the cousins manning the lower corral we lugged all the panniers into the study. That major task done, we went in search of our ladies and found them in the kitchen. Both struggled to get up as we walked in, with Anna beaming me one of her super megawatt Anna smiles. I couldn't believe how beautiful and radiant she was. I told her so as we hugged and kissed. The hugs were light, and the kisses were short as we were separated by pregnant bellies.

The four of us adjourned to the study, where Tom and I gave them the short version of our trip, while we moved the burlap bags of gold nuggets and bars from the panniers into the RV cave. We spent the afternoon cuddled up with our ladies on the couches, just talking to each other and snuggling.

With the start of December, I began to get more serious about the greenhouses. I had Tom help me pull the boxes for two plastic greenhouses out of the trailer in the cave and into the study. While everything was made entirely of plastic they were far from the flimsy temporary things I'd expected.

Each greenhouse consisted of a heavy-duty PVC type of frame, that when assembled measured fifty feet long and twenty feet wide. The sides and roof were one-foot by one-foot squares of individual clear plastic panels, that snapped into the frame. For the most part, the panels were interchangeable, with only the door and venting panels going into specific locations. Once both Tom and I understood the instructions thoroughly, we put both sets into burlap bags and hauled them up to the upper courtyard.

Everyone seemed to want to help with the preparation for building the greenhouses. Even with all the help, it still took three weeks to get everything ready to actually put up the greenhouses. Giuseppe laid out the two greenhouses on the North side of the Hacienda on the upper plateau. Tomas had the ground inside the two areas prepared for planting.

Tom and I spent two days with one of the teams, moving two stoves from the village storehouses to the upper plateau using the lifting rigs Giuseppe had designed and built. The week before Christmas, we were finally ready to build the greenhouses. Tom, Giuseppe, Tomas, and I put up the greenhouse frames in less than five hours and started snapping the side panels into place. At that point we realized we'd overlooked not having ladders to stand on to put the upper wall panels and roof panels in place.

We solved that by using one of the wagons as our platform, and moving it around both inside and outside the greenhouses by hand as we went. When we were done at the end of the day we were all proud of the work, but very tired from the effort. At supper that night I turned the greenhouses over to Tomas, and told everyone that we needed to come up with a list of what we wanted planted in the greenhouses for Tomas to use as a guide.

The rest of the evening we listened as the ladies discussed the list they wanted, and Tomas either agreeing with an item or rejecting it for various reasons. By the time we all retired, the list stood at lettuce, tomatoes, onions, carrots, potatoes, beans of various types, cantaloupe, watermelon, and various cooking herbs.

Early the next afternoon we received three expected and welcome visitors. Cousin George rode in with Esteban and Ed. They'd all been invited to spend the holidays with us on the Estancia. I had ulterior motives for all three of course, but spending time with these three men was always a pleasure. We got a quick greeting from George, who then disappeared looking for Celia. I raised an eyebrow at Anna and asked if I needed to have 'the talk' with him. Anna laughed radiantly, and said the time was soon coming, and Cristina would appreciate it.

With George out 'heing and sheing', the rest of us moved to the lower living room where we were met by Cristina and Carla with coffee and biscochitos. Once we were all settled, Esteban began talking.

"Pablo, a few days ago we received word from one of our friends that a group of suspected comancheros were in one of the saloons, in Mesilla. When we got there, we found eight men drinking at the bar. We had warrants for two of the eight, and when we tried to arrest them all eight went for their guns. We killed three of them, wounded two others, and captured the other three. The two with arrest warrants were unharmed. All five are being held in the county jail for now. The Doc expects the two wounded men to recover sufficiently enough to travel by the middle of January. We wrote up a report and sent it to the Judge in Santa Fe, but based on his previous letters to us he will expect us to bring the prisoners to Santa Fe. How do you want to handle transporting them?"

This was good news. In fact, it was great news! The information network was finally beginning to pay off.

After a moment's thought, I replied, "Well done, you two! The Judge will be very happy to have prisoners to bring to trial. When you go back to Mesilla, stop by Mr. Mendoza's stable in Las Cruces and see if he has a freight wagon we can rent or buy, as well as a driver to transport the prisoners. I'll pay for any modifications you'll need to have made to it, to secure the prisoners and stop them from reaching the driver. If he doesn't have anything, check with the other freight haulers in Mesilla; and, if necessary, El Paso. Once you have a suitable wagon and a driver, I want both of you to escort the prisoners to Santa Fe."

The always irrepressible Ed grinned. "I figured that's what you were going to say. Mr. Mendoza has a wagon and driver for us to use, and he's already making the modifications to the wagon I asked for. It should be ready for us by the time the holidays are over. Mr. Mendoza said to tell you he'd put it on your bill."

Anna, Yolanda, Tom, and I all laughed at the standing joke between Mr. Mendoza and me.

"There you have it. Take a few days to enjoy Santa Fe after you've delivered the prisoners. I'll give you enough money before you leave for a week at the best hotel in Santa Fe, as well as a temporary club membership. You've both certainly earned it."

George joined us in the living room just as I was finishing, and asked about the shootout with Colonel Watson in El Paso. We spent a few minutes describing what happened, and his last words.

"I'm still not sure what he meant or who his brother is, but I can't remember ever meeting anyone in Santa Fe or elsewhere with the last name of Watson." I said. "I wrote the usual report to the Judge and in a separate note asked him to look into it for me, but so far I haven't gotten any word back from him. I have a suspicion that there is much more going on here than meets the eye, but I have no idea what it is. I guess time will tell but it's awful worrisome, nonetheless."

We spent the next three weeks relaxing as Christmas and New Year came and went. We celebrated at the Hacienda, instead of the village, as both Anna and Yolanda wanted nothing to do with riding horses or wagons for any distance. I was able to spend quite a bit of time with George, and it soon became apparent that something was on his mind. Two days after Christmas George finally broached the subject that was weighing on his mind.

We were out riding, touring the Estancia, when he suddenly started talking.

"Paul, I'm thinking about resigning my commission and staying here. I'm in love with Celia, and I believe she feels the same about me. I've come to believe that the Army and a family are incompatible, at least for me. If I decide to resign is that job we talked about still open?"

"George, you're not only family but you've become a close friend. There will always be a place here for you and yours, should you want it. To answer your question; yes, the job we discussed is still open, and I can't think of anyone better to fill it than you. However, there is one question you have to answer to yourself and to me before I'll offer it to you," I replied.

"What question is that?" he asked, visibly concerned.

"George, you know that I believe war between the North and South is coming in the next few years. The signs are getting stronger and stronger, every time I pick up a newspaper. The question you have to answer for yourself is, what are you going to do when that war starts? If you feel strongly about Virginia and the South, then you will ride for Richmond and get a commission in the Southern Army. If your feelings are stronger for your wife and family as well as New Mexico, you will stay here and protect them from the aggression of the Southern Army, as they try to take control of the Territory for a base to launch attacks against the Pacific states. "Until you can answer the question of what you will do with certainty, I can't offer you the job," I said.

George looked at me thoughtfully as we continued riding and I couldn't help but wonder what was going through his mind. Based on our conversations over the last couple of years, he knew where I stood on the issue of state's rights, and my belief that we were Americans first and foremost, owing our allegiance to the country and not to the state of our birth.

Finally, George broke his silence. "What if I

can't give you the assurance that I'll stay here and fight for the North?"

I smiled at him. "George, you will always be welcome here, regardless of what you choose to do when the war starts. If you can't give me your word, then I won't be able to offer you the job. What I will offer you instead, is the job of training the men of the Estancia in both offensive and defensive operations. You will not lead them, you will not be part of planning, or developing the strategy and tactics we will use, and you will have no responsibility to the Estancia nor any expectation of staying when the war breaks out."

George made a sour face at my statement and then broke into a grin. "I kind of thought that would be your feelings on the matter. I guess I have some serious thinking to do. Thank you for the straight talk, Paul."

I nodded, and we rode on finishing our ride back at the Hacienda. We didn't talk about the job or the war I predicted again during this visit. I made sure to discuss the conversation with Anna, Tom, and Yolanda so that they all knew where I stood, and which job to offer George if I was away when he came back.

All three of our visitors left to return to their duties on Thursday morning, the 3rd of January 1856. Anna and I watched from the terrace, with our arms around each other, as they rode away down the Camino Real.

As they disappeared from sight Anna turned to me, gave me a kiss, and said, "I know he doesn't know that much of our future is riding on him making the right decision. I hope for our sake as well as his and Celia's, that he comes to the same conclusion we have."

"We've given him the reasons and arguments for reaching the conclusion we want, my love. All we can do now, as with so many other things, is wait and see," I replied.

Things began to pick up once again, the following Monday. The annual reports were completed and the four of us spent two days reading and discussing the results of the previous year, and the plans the three Segundo's had come up with for 1856.

Thanks to all the cattle sales, the Ranch had covered its entire annual payroll, as well as the coming year's payroll, and even a few of the Finca's expenses. The Finca, of course, didn't have any income, so we were still investing in it. However, we all fully expected some small level of income this year.

None of us saw any issues with their planning, although I was a little concerned they were overestimating what they could get done this year. After a little discussion, I agreed that based on what we'd accomplished so far, their plans were valid. As none of them would interfere in our private plans, we gave the go ahead at the next weekly meeting.

The second week in January also saw Esteban and Ed escorting a freight wagon full of chained prisoners to Santa Fe. I met them as they passed by the bridge to the Hacienda and rode with them for the next mile. I gave Esteban two letters and asked him to make sure the Judge and Tom Stevenson got them.

The first letter let the Judge know that Tom and I were going to make a westward swing to the Colorado river starting in late April and asked him for any thoughts on recruiting a Deputy for either Colorado City, or Tucson.

The second letter asked Tom to set up the three specific Trusts we had discussed with him on our previous visit. Anna and I had talked to Tom about all three of these on our last visit to Santa Fe, although we didn't have names for them at the time. We had discussed in detail the specific purposes of each of them, how they were each to be structured, and who the initial officers were to be.

The first was the Mesilla Valley Community Association Trust, to fund community improvement activities in the Mesilla Valley. The second, was the Mesilla Valley Education Association Trust, to fund elementary and high schools in Las Cruces and Mesilla. The last, was the Rio Grande and New Mexico Land Corporation. Tom would know this as the business we would use to build and run a railroad that would eventually stretch from Yuma to the Texas panhandle, and from Las Cruces to Santa Fe. All three were to be funded at an initial level of $10,000 from our private account in Santa Fe.

Giuseppe became extremely busy as he monitored the masons starting on the School/Community Center building, the crushed stone quarry blasting, and the road building. This became worse when John Gillespie showed up with two rigs on the 7th of January, and began drilling new wells almost immediately with the first rig.

We hoisted the other rig to the upper plateau, and within two days of arrival that rig had started drilling more wells. The drilling was done by the middle of February and John took his rigs and people home, happy for the out of season work.

We welcomed George back to the Estancia less than thirty-six hours after John and his drilling crews left. George dismounted, grabbed me by the shoulders, and looked me straight in the eyes.

"I've resigned my commission, the answer to your question is yes, I can commit to remaining on the Estancia if war breaks out. We can talk later about this, right now I need to talk to Celia."

Laughing, I pointed inside. "She's most likely in the kitchen with the rest of the women and babies."

He was off in a flash. I shook my head in bemusement, grabbed his saddlebags, scabbard, and bedroll - which was apparently all he had of his own - and carried everything inside to the study. As I was setting everything down I heard a faint shout and a squeal from somewhere upstairs, and smiled to myself. I was walking out of the study when Anna came down the hall from the kitchen.

"Paul did you hear that shout? Do you know what's going on?"

I pulled her as close to me as I could get her, given the state of her belly, and gave her a hug and kiss.

"That was Celia, I believe. She was either overjoyed with happiness that Cousin George has resigned his commission and taken a job here, or more likely she was reacting to the news that she has a wedding to plan. I suspect we'll know for sure, either way, in a few minutes."

Anna beamed me a smile, pulled herself in for another hug and kiss, and left to go back to the kitchen and the other ladies. Celia and George were coming down the stairs arm in arm as Anna walked by and she stopped to wait for Celia. At the bottom of the stairs Celia gave George a kiss, and turned to walk with Anna into the kitchen.

Smiling, I waved George into the study and poured two glasses of scotch, handing him one as we sat down. Cristina came in with a coffee service before we could start talking. She set the coffee service on the small table between our chairs, leaned down and kissed George on the cheek, patted him on the shoulder and left, throwing a, "It's about time!" over her shoulder as she turned to walk down the hall.

"Well, George, it sounds like the ladies in the kitchen are planning a wedding. From that and the squeal I heard earlier I assume she said yes?" I asked.

A grinning George replied. "Yep, and hopefully it won't be too long either."

I sighed. "George, you know she's a devout Catholic. There's a specific set of procedures to follow, not to mention social decorum. I don't want to put a damper on things, but the timing may be more up to you, than her."

At his look of confusion, I continued. "You're not Catholic, are you?" He responded with a 'no' and I said, "The thing that may hold up this wedding longer than necessary is your conversion to the Catholic faith. How long that takes, is strictly up to you. Well, you and the Padre."

He smiled then, and said it would be as quick as he could make it. I raised my glass in a silent toast and we sat sipping our excellent scotch for a few minutes. When I was done with my glass I poured us both coffee, and we talked about his resignation.

Apparently, he'd returned from his last patrol late yesterday afternoon, and received an immediate summons to the commander's office even before he'd had a chance to clean up. When he walked in, the commander handed him new orders, reassigning him to Washington Territory with a report date of "immediately upon receipt".

George had read the orders, and then asked the commander for a sheet of paper. He sat down at the commander's desk and wrote out his resignation, effective immediately. He'd cleaned out his quarters, saddled his horse and spent the night in Mesilla, before riding to the Hacienda today. Tom joined us halfway through George's story, and we caught him up on all the events since George's arrival.

We were joined for breakfast the next morning by Miguel and Maco who added their congratulations to the couple. Afterwards, they joined the rest of the executive staff and George, in the study. I wasted no time as everyone knew that we had hoped that George would join us, and we had talked at length with everyone about what would and would not change if that happened.

"George, you've taken on the role of Estancia Militia Commander. We've talked about this at length, but now it's time to formalize the position and responsibilities. You will be responsible for organizing and training all the men of the Estancia into an effective fighting force capable of conducting both defensive and, when necessary, offensive military operations.

"Miguel, Maco and Yolanda are your staff officers, and your primary Lieutenants. Miguel and Maco are responsible for Estancia security and early warning. Their people identify incoming threats and provide us a warning as well as initial counters to those threats once they are on the Estancia.

"Yolanda develops and plans all the security and training plans, as well as building and maintaining intelligence files on known threats. You'll work closely with all three of

335

them. You'll also work closely with Tomas, Hector, Giuseppe, and Raul, in scheduling activities so as to limit the impact to Finca and Ranching operations. I don't have to remind you that everyone in your militia is a part-time soldier, and a full-time farmer or vaquero."

At his nod of understanding I continued, "Based on the recent events in Mesilla with the group of comancheros, as well as our shootout in El Paso with your old commander, I have a bad feeling that we're going to be raided by Flat Nose and his gang, sometime in the next few months.

"Tom and I need to make a swing west to fulfill my US Marshal responsibilities but given the pending births, we won't be leaving until May at the earliest. Between now and then your primary responsibility is to develop a plan of defense for the Estancia against a force of up to a hundred raiders.

"Flat Nose and his men have shown themselves to be very inexperienced in military matters, and seem to rely almost exclusively on raw strength, numbers, surprise, and overwhelming brutality. Based on past raids I expect them to come in a single group from either the South up the Camino Real, or from the East around the Doña Ana Mountains."

I looked around the room before adding, "That's all I have, for now. Are there any questions?"

When no one voiced a question or had anything to add I turned to Miguel.

"The three of you take George upstairs, and familiarize him with the war room and the full extent of our security operations. I'll meet with the four of you after lunch, should he have any questions that you three can't answer."

After everyone had filed out of the room to start their day's activities I turned to Anna and hugged her close. "It's starting, my love. I hope and pray none of these men die because of this, but even their deaths fighting these raiders, would be preferable to having them give up without a fight."

Anna hugged me tight telling me without words that what we were doing was the right thing.

There were no questions after lunch, so Tom, Giuseppe, and I spent the afternoon with Raul at the blacksmith shop, looking over the plans and the parts Frank had been working on for the ice making machine.

Frank had built most of the parts shown in

the patent plans, and he'd done a fantastic job on them. All we needed now was the pump, a power source, and a building in which we could start building and testing both the ice making and building cooling functions.

Juan had sent Giuseppe a lead on water pumps. The United States Wind Engine and Pump Company in Chicago was a new concern manufacturing pumps and windmills of various sizes. Giuseppe had written them, asking for information giving them our size and volume requirements for two different size pumps, with windmills to drive them.

We all preferred a steam engine to drive the ice making machine; but until we could get a line on one that met our needs, and was cheap enough to ship here from the northeast, we would work with what was available.

While we were waiting for information on pumps and windmills to arrive, I asked Frank and Giuseppe to start work on a prototype swamp cooler. I drew them a sketch of what it would look like, and described how it operated. They were excited about the concept, and wandered off to look at the metal stock Frank had, to determine what they had and could use.

Tom and I left the two alone, and stopped by the School/Community Center building site to see how Heinrich and the masons were doing. We didn't see Heinrich, so we just watched from a distance for a few minutes. All the footers had been dug, poured, and cured. The masons were laying the first rows of stone down, so from what we could see things were going well.

Back at the Hacienda we found Yolanda had started labor an hour earlier, but the contractions were still over twenty minutes apart, so supper went on as usual with Yolanda insisting that she sit at the table and eat with the rest of us. Tom, concerned about Yolanda and the baby, was so tense with worry that I don't think he tasted a bit of the food he ate, or could even tell us what he'd had for supper.

Periodically, throughout supper, Yolanda would tense up for a few seconds then relax and pat Tom's hand telling him to relax, she was the one doing all the work. Eventually, Tom settled down and, at one point, even gave Yolanda a droll, "Yes, Dear."

Late in the evening, when it became clear that the baby wasn't coming anytime soon, the ladies of the Hacienda - including Beth and Izabella - broke up the rest of the night into two hour shifts. Two of them were sitting with Yolanda at all times until the baby was born. When that had been organized, everyone but

Tom, Yolanda, and the first shift, turned in.

It wasn't until almost ten the next morning, Thursday, the 21st of February, that Joseph Murphy entered the world, kicking and screaming for all he was worth. An exhausted Yolanda and Tom finally fell asleep with the baby at about noon, and the rest of the Hacienda went back to their normal activities.

Yolanda quickly recovered and it became common to see her around the Hacienda in the company of George, Miguel, and Maco as they worked on whatever plans they were coming up with.

CHAPTER 11

T om and I were becoming bored. The Segundo's were all doing their jobs well. Cattle were being delivered on time, and the herd continued to grow. The land along the river was being cleared and prepared for planting, while early harvesting in the greenhouses had already started for some of the crops, like tomatoes.

Building activities were continuing at a furious pace; with the fences, roads, water retention buildings, and School/Community Center all in different stages. We spent quite a bit of time on the terrace or in the study drinking coffee, talking, adding details to our initial plans, and fine tuning them where we could.

At one point, in midafternoon two weeks after Joseph's birth, Tom gave a sigh, and looked up from his writing.

"You know Paul, after everything that's happened over the last couple of years it's getting downright boring around here. It would be nice to have a little excitement again."

I looked at him in mock horror. "Bite your tongue, Tom! The last thing we need around here is excitement. At least until after Anna has had the baby and recovered."

Tom laughed and, putting a droll look on his face, responded with, "Yes, dear."

We were still laughing over the exchange when Celia came out on the terrace and said, "Paul, Anna would like to see you in the bedroom, the baby is coming."

I looked over at Tom with a grin, "You wanted some excitement? Well, here it is."

I hurried into the bedroom through the terrace doors and found Anna laying on the bed surrounded by all the ladies. I squeezed through them and sat on the side of the bed at Anna's side.

She beamed one of her Anna smiles. "It won't be long now."

"Anna, my love, don't be in a hurry. It will happen when your body is ready for it, not before," I replied.

Anna laughed and with a giggle said, "The contractions started this morning as we were getting ready for breakfast. It's not me who's in a hurry, it's our son. He's in a hurry to greet the world, my love."

Anna was hit with a strong contraction just as she finished talking and gripped my hand. Hard. The contraction went on for what felt like forever. When it was over Anna released my hand and relaxed.

"Now give me a kiss my love and go back to what you were doing. You'll know when it's time to greet your son."

Obediently, I gave her a deep kiss, packed with all the love I felt for her, and stood up from the bed. I returned to the terrace to wait, just like all the anxious fathers before me. Time seemed to slow to a crawl.

Over the next hour we were joined by Giuseppe, Tomas, Hector, Miguel and Maco. Izabella ensured fresh coffee was available for all of us as we waited, and she did it with a smile.

My nerves were worn thin and I was about ready to head down to the study for a large scotch, when the clear wail of a newborn came from the bedroom.

We all smiled at each other for a moment. I gave a fist pump, walked through the French doors into the bedroom, and watched as Anna received our son in her arms while beaming me a huge super megawatt Anna smile.

I sat down beside her, giving her a brief hug while I kissed her head and looked down at our son. Anna held him up for me to take. "Jaime Jose McAllister meet your father."

Taking him in my arms, I gently rocked him back and forth before telling him, "JJ, I've been looking forward to meeting you for quite a while. Welcome to the Hacienda son. I hope you are as happy here as your mother and I are."

Naturally, being a McAllister, he broke the mood by peeing all over me. I just laughed, handed him to Beth who was waiting to clean him up a little more, and went to take a shower after giving Anna another kiss.

The smile never left my face the whole time I was showering. Not even when I heard Laura's soft voice in my left ear.

"I'm proud of you. You're well on the way to becoming the man you were always meant to be."

I was still smiling when I came out of the bathroom, and found both Anna and JJ asleep. Beth sat rocking in a chair near the bed watching over them. I gave Anna and JJ a light kiss and told Beth to join everyone else for supper as I was going to stay in the room. After Beth left, I lay down on the bed next to Anna, and snuggled both her and JJ in my arm before falling into a light sleep.

I awoke in the wee hours of the morning to find Anna feeding JJ, and silently lay there watching her for a few minutes before falling back to sleep. When I woke up for the day, just before daybreak, I found Anna feeding JJ again. I smiled at them, gave her a quick kiss, and headed downstairs. I was hoping the coffee was ready.

I found all the ladies doing the kitchen dance, and asked Izabella for a coffee service upstairs and to send up breakfast for two, when it was ready. She flashed me a huge smile, and said it was on its way.

I checked the dumb waiter upstairs, and true to her word the coffee service was there. Anna looked more than ready for some coffee, and after her first cup told me she was famished. I laughed and told her breakfast would be up in a few minutes. I went in to take a quick shower and put on clean clothes.

JJ was fast asleep in the middle of the bed when

I came out. Anna had opened the curtains and the French doors, and was standing just inside watching the sunrise over the Doña Ana Mountains. I walked up behind her and put my arms around her. She leaned back into me with a light sigh.

"It's nice to feel your holding me again, my love. I've missed that," she said.

"No more than I have," I replied as I pulled her in closer, and settled my chin on her head.

Our reverie was broken a few minutes later when Beth came in, carrying a large tray with two large plates full of eggs, bacon, potatoes, and toast along with fresh coffee. Beth looked over at JJ sleeping on the bed and smiled as she set the tray down on the breakfast table in the corner of the room.

"Since you both missed supper last night we figured you'd be really hungry so Miranda fixed you both large plates. How's JJ this morning? We didn't hear anything out of him all night, and we were beginning to get worried."

"Thank you, Beth and thank the other ladies as well. Pablo and I are both famished. JJ slept most of the night, only waking up once to be fed, so he's doing fine," Anna replied.

As Anna and I dug into our breakfast Beth sat down on the bed and gazed at JJ with a wistful expression on her face. I glanced at Anna and in between mouthfuls nodded at Beth saying, "Maco's going to have his hands full with that one."

Beth overhead my quiet comment and snorted saying, "Maco is moving so slow, I don't know if one of these will ever be in our future."

Anna and I both laughed at her comment. "Beth don't be in such a hurry. Pablo and I waited over three years before we were married, and we were just a little younger than you when we met. Maco is still unsure of our way of doing things. Things like courting and proposing. If it's meant to be, it will be."

Beth looked over at us and nodded, but I'm sure she wasn't convinced by Anna's reassurance. I decided I needed to have 'the talk' with Maco sometime soon.

Anna and I finished our breakfast and were talking over our coffee, when JJ woke up. Beth cooed over him for a few minutes before Anna got up, asking me to take the tray back downstairs on my way out. I raised an eyebrow at her, and she giggled.

"You'll not be hovering over me all day, getting in our way, my love. Go pretend like you are responsible for the Estancia, and everyone on it for a while," she said with a grin and the devil dancing in her eyes.

I harrumphed with a mock scowl on my face, muttering about not getting any respect, leaving the room with the tray to the sound of Anna and Beth's laughter.

Izabella was waiting for me at the bottom of the steps and took the tray from my hands, telling me to join the others in the dining room. My arrival seemed to be some sort of signal, as all the ladies except Yolanda got up telling the kids it was time to leave for school.

When the ladies and kids had all left, I looked around the room before raising my arm to sniff my armpit saying in a concerned voice, "I took a shower, this morning. Was it something I said?"

Everyone in the room had a good laugh at my antics as I poured myself a cup of coffee and sat down.

George looked around the table before looking at me.

"Paul, for the last two weeks I've been learning about the land in and around the Estancia as well as reviewing the threats you've faced in the past. I've reviewed the reports that were written in each case and I think you're right about the comancheros raiding the Estancia. But, I haven't been able to get a feel from the reports about how soon that might be. Regardless, we've come up with some detailed plans. If you have time, we'd like to go over them with you to see what you think."

"Well, since Anna kicked me out of the bedroom for getting in the way of 'woman's work', I'm all yours today, George," I replied.

Yolanda gave Tom an arm slap and said, "See? Pablo can take a hint."

Tom delivered the by now expected response of, "Yes, dear."

As muted grins broke out around the table I laughed. "Yolanda, you know good and well that Anna doesn't give hints. She specifically told me to leave, because I was getting in the way of woman's work."

Tom reached over and lightly tapped Yolanda's arm imitating an arm slap. "See? Anna knows how to say what she means."

Yolanda looked a little startled, but recovered quickly. Imitating Tom perfectly, she gave him a droll, "Yes, dear."

The physical and verbal exchange was so unexpected that by the time they were done we were all laughing loud and hard.

When we'd all recovered we followed George's

lead, and refreshed our coffee before following him upstairs to the war room. I hadn't been in the room in a few months, so I was surprised to see what looked like a completed model of the Estancia and the surrounding land sitting on a plank table taking up the center of the room.

The far end of the room had two roll top desks separated by two wooden three drawer filing cabinets. Framed and wood mounted maps of Doña Ana County, New Mexico Territory, and the United States had been hung on the wall opposite the door. I nodded approvingly at what I saw, and started to ask questions; but stopped myself before saying anything, realizing my questions could wait until later.

It was a tight fit, but all ten of us crowded around the model. Up close, it was readily apparent that the model was still a work in progress, but it had progressed past the point of being nothing more than a papier-mache outline.

George cleared his throat, and in a lecturing voice I was sure he'd learned at West Point, began talking. As he started, I wondered if he would follow the centuries old three-part military briefing practice of: 1) Tell them the information you'll be telling them; 2) Tell them the information; and 3) Tell them the information you told them.

I'll be damned if that isn't exactly what he did.

"Paul, you told us that you were most concerned with attacks from the south and the east, so that's where we concentrated our efforts. We'll look at the current resource and communication situation on the Estancia and the surrounding area before turning to specific plans we've developed to counter raids from those two directions. Finally, I'll talk about the changes we want to make to better support those plans."

George stopped there to take a sip of coffee and look around to make sure we were all following along without questions.

Satisfied, he put his cup down and continued. "Miguel and the cousins did a fantastic job of siting the observation and signaling posts. Because of their work, we have what amounts to a three hundred sixty degree coverage of the approaches to the Estancia.

"Likewise, the use of Morse Code and the signaling mirrors gives us rapid and continual communications ability during daylight hours, except during the rainy season when it becomes dependent on the cloud cover. Unfortunately, we have no rapid long-distance communication capability during the hours of darkness.

"Additionally, enough Scout/Sniper teams have been trained to provide continual coverage with two teams on each side of the Estancia at any given time. These teams are usually anywhere from three to five miles outside the boundaries of the Estancia, and provide excellent early warning information.

"All the men of the Estancia are well trained with their firearms, and will ride to the sound of gunfire without a moment's hesitation. On the negative side, they haven't been trained to fight in anything larger than five or ten man teams. That alone could cause unnecessary deaths from friendly fire, or from inaction. That will have to be addressed in the near term."

He paused for a sip of coffee before continuing. "With these factors in mind we've come up with two different plans for attacks from the south, and two plans for attacks from the east, for a total of four plans. Which plan we use will depend on which direction the attack comes from, and how much warning we get.

"All four plans have three key common elements. The first is that three teams each, are designated as being responsible for defense of each of the living areas. That means that three teams will immediately report to the Hacienda, three teams will report to the village plaza, and three teams will report to the ranch building.

"In the village, the three teams will spread the alarm and enclose the open areas of the plaza using wagons from the wagon yard.

"The second common element, is that the teams assigned to stone quarry duty will immediately form up as a rapid response force, and report to the Hacienda for dispatch as the attack evolves.

"The third common element is that all the other teams will report to one of two staging areas. Which staging area, will depend on where the attack is coming from."

At this point he stopped for more coffee, and picked up a long wooden dowel. Using the dowel as a pointer he continued. "If the attack is from the south, then they will report to the staging area here. If it's from the east, the staging area is here. When everyone has gathered at the appropriate staging area, we will move together to one of two ambush sites which Maco and his team have selected.

"In each case there is an ambush site less than a mile off the Estancia and another just inside the Estancia. For lack of better names, and to keep it simple, we are calling the four plans S1, S2, and E1, and E2. The letter tells everyone which staging area to use, and the number indicates which ambush site we plan on using.

"Our hope is that we can move fast enough to ambush the attackers, well off of the Estancia. If the attackers are moving faster than we hope, then we'll use the ambush sites on the Estancia, instead."

George asked if there were any questions so far. Neither Tom nor I had any at this point and George continued. "So far everything I've talked about assumes that the comancheros make their attack in broad daylight, sometime after all the men are at work.

"Miguel, Maco, Yolanda and I have talked about this at length and based on the reports from the group you rescued last year, none of us think this is the way it's going to happen. Instead, we expect them to follow the same pattern they've used successfully so far.

"They will ride in, in small groups, to a meeting place somewhere within five miles of the Estancia. They will make a cold camp for the night. While the bulk of them are sleeping, they will send a few scouts in during the night to see what the situation is, and try to identify where they can expect resistance.

"Most likely those scouts won't be expected to report back, but instead will take up positions where they can observe and shoot from concealment, to cover the main body during the raid. If we're right, and this is what happens, then our plans remain the same except we will also make a cold camp at our ambush point, and the Scout/Sniper teams will be responsible for taking out any scouts the comancheros send in.

"That summarizes the plans we've made, so far. We want to start practicing, next week. We can go into details and visit the staging and ambush sites later today or tomorrow, if you'd like. But before we do that, there are some changes that need to be made to the Finca and Ranch operations, to make this work. I'd like to cover those, now."

George stopped and waited for me to agree or disagree. At my head nod, he moved right into the changes they were recommending.

"The first change is the work locations. Starting Monday, and continuing until the attack, the bulk of the farmers and vaqueros will work south of the Hacienda and the Ranch Operations Building.

"Additionally, the three closest teams to the Hacienda, Village, and Ranch Buildings, along with two of the off duty Sniper/Scout teams will be specifically identified. They will be told every Monday, which areas they will support, in case of an attack. The stone quarry teams and any vaqueros working north of the Hacienda will specifically be told to report to the Hacienda, regardless of where they happen to be, if an attack occurs. This includes the masons.

"The second change is that starting Monday, everyone will need to carry enough food and water to remain comfortable if they have to stay out, overnight.

"The third change is the distribution of horses. The farm teams and road teams working the farthest away from the south boundary, need to have saddled horses with them in addition to the normal wagon horses. A wagon is simply too slow to get the teams furthest away to the rally point in time.

"The Estancia has plenty of horses. What we don't have enough of, is saddles! So, we'll need to experiment a little to see how many teams we can support with saddled horses. In addition, we also need to have twenty horses and saddles moved to the Hacienda corral for use by the rapid response teams that will be forming up here.

"Finally, we need to explain all this to everyone! Monday morning, we'll begin practicing. We don't believe we'll need more than three or four practice runs, but we could need more.

Our recommendation is that we spend all day Monday on this, and then have at least one practice drill every week, on different days and times."

George looked around the room before beginning his conclusion. "I've talked about the current resource and communication situation on the Estancia and the surrounding area. That was followed by specific plans we've developed to counter raids from those two directions, and finally, the changes we want to make to better support those plans. If everyone agrees we can return to the dining room and get fresh coffee before getting into questions and details."

As I looked around the room, it was clear that the three Segundo's and Jesus had already heard this pitch, and had agreed, which meant that Tom and I were the only ones who hadn't heard it before and we would be the ones asking most of the questions.

By Tom's body language, I could tell that he was impressed but I didn't know how many questions he would have. I was greatly impressed with what George and his group had come up with, and only had a few questions at the moment.

I turned to George and the other three. "George, you four have done a lot of work and I'm very impressed and pleased with what you've come up with. By all means, let's head downstairs where we can discuss things in comfort."

Cristina, Celia, and Carla followed us into the dining room carrying fresh coffee services for everyone. We all settled in after pouring ourselves more coffee, and the discussions began in earnest.

My first set of questions was directed not at George and his team, but at the three Segundo's and Jesus. They all said that they knew about the plans and agreed with both them and the changes George was proposing.

My second set of questions was about the rally and ambush sites, which Maco answered in detail and we agreed that Tom, George, Miguel, Maco, and I would ride out and look at the sites after lunch.

My last set of questions dealt with communications procedures for anything dealing with an attack, or exercises practicing for an attack. To my surprise Miguel answered my questions in detail. All attack or exercise messages would be in Apache, and only Apache. Exercise messages were preceded and ended with three X's.

I raised my eyebrows in surprise. "Miguel, how

can the messages be in Apache? There's no Apache alphabet or written language."

"Simple, Paul. We use the Spanish alphabet and rules. It took a little bit of work but we've got it figured out and have practiced it so we know it works," he replied with a grin.

Done with my questions, I turned to Tom, who asked how the teams working the crushed rock quarry would be notified, and what their responsibilities would be. George finished answering his questions just as everyone began arriving for lunch.

I again complemented them on their planning and gave them the go ahead to start all the changes on Monday. I also told Miguel that I wanted to see all the off-duty Scout/Sniper teams - including him and Maco - tomorrow, after lunch.

Anna brought JJ down with her for lunch where he was, of course, the center of attention. Eventually, she put JJ in the big enclosed play pen in the corner of the dining room, with the other four newborns, while we ate lunch.

After lunch I told George, Miguel, and Maco that Tom and I would meet them outside in a few minutes and asked them to get the horses ready. I took Tom into the study, barred the door, and opened up the cave door telling him that we needed to get something I wanted to demonstrate, and hand out, once we got to the first rally point.

I handed Tom two silencers, forestalling his question on what they were, telling him to put them in his saddlebags and I would explain what they were for, later. I put nine more in a burlap bag, and we rejoined the others who were waiting for us, outside.

The southern rally point turned out to be a large arroyo just off the road about a half mile from the Estancia boundary. It was a good location, close enough to quickly move the men into position once everybody had arrived, and more than large enough to hold everyone. I dismounted still carrying the burlap bag, and at my request the others joined me.

"Gentleman, what I'm about to show you is a special tool that I don't want to ever hear talked about. You will all receive two of these special tools, as will all the Scout/Snipers. No one else on the Estancia except Anna, Yolanda, Tom, and me will have, or even know about, these tools. One of the purposes of the Scout/Sniper teams is to unsettle our enemies through long-distance shooting. Another way to increase the enemies fear, is to take out their guards and scouts quietly from close range."

I reached into the bag and pulled out a silencer

before putting the bag down. I held up the silencer so that they all could see it.

"This is a silencer and allows us to use our pistols without a lot of noise. There are two major drawbacks to using this tool. The first drawback is accuracy. You all know that I'm extremely good using a pistol."

While I was talking I'd screwed the silencer on to the end of my pistol. I pointed at a small barrel cactus growing on a ledge halfway up the arroyo wall about twenty feet from where we were standing.

"Please watch and listen closely."

I aimed and fired three rounds at the cactus. The only sounds from the gun were three soft muted pops and the mechanical sound of the pistol ejecting and reloading rounds. I hit the cactus with one shot, while the other two just missed to the left of the cactus.

I'm not sure whether they were more surprised by the lack of noise, or the fact that I missed two of three aimed shots at such close range.

"As you can see, twenty feet is about the maximum range when the silencer is being used. Closer is definitely better. It would be nice if we could practice for accuracy, but we can't. Which brings us to the second drawback."

I turned and fired ten more rounds at the cactus. After the fifth or sixth round the noise level from each round went up until by the tenth round the sound was almost as loud as not having a silencer.

I turned back to them and wryly finished my demonstration and lecture. "Each time a round is fired the silencer becomes less and less effective. Each of these are only good for five or six rounds, before they are no longer effective which is why everyone will get two. If you have to use one, please don't throw it away. Bring it back to me so I can salvage parts and make new ones."

All of them started firing questions at me, and I held up my hand. "These are simple to make although it is time consuming detail intensive work. When I say simple to make I mean they are simple if you have the right material. The material to make these came from back East just like the guns we all use. Just like the guns, the knowledge of how to make the material has been lost. I have a very limited amount of material to make these, so when the material is gone I won't be able to make any more silencers."

They all stared in wonder at the two silencers I'd given to each of them as I talked. I put the now empty burlap bag in my saddlebag,

very little knowledge about. I don't know how most of the materials on any of the things I surprise you guys with are made, and I have no clue even to where they come from and that's frustrating in and of itself.

"Third, I don't like waiting for something to happen. I much prefer to be active rather than reactive, and waiting for Flat Nose and his gang is starting to wear on my nerves. No matter how often I remind myself to keep calm, my temper is getting shorter and shorter the longer we have to wait."

Tom looked at me for a few moments, then sat back in his chair. "Shortly after we met, you gave me one of the greatest pieces of advice anyone has ever given me, and a tool to help me through tough times. I suggest you follow that piece of advice and use the tool more often before you lose your temper with the wrong person."

'Wow! Where did that come from?' I wondered to myself. I sat thinking about what advice I'd given him that was so profound and what the tool he was talking about was. I couldn't for the life of me think of what he was talking about. Finally, I asked him to remind me.

Tom gave a short chuckle and said, "We were on our way back to El Paso and I was worrying about telling my father about Yolanda. The piece of advice you gave me after listening to my story, was not to borrow trouble. The tool was The Serenity Prayer."

I chuckled remembering that trip and the fireside conversation we'd had. "Thanks for reminding me, Tom. Somehow, I'd forgotten all about that."

Laura's soft voice whispered in my left ear as I finished and took a sip of coffee.

"He is a good friend, Paul, and his advice is sound. Remember it and use it in the days to come."

I sat in deep thought thinking about what Laura had said. My reverie was broken by the arrival of Izabella, telling us that supper was ready. As we walked downstairs I made a promise to myself to follow my own advice.

Monday morning found the plaza packed with every man on the Estancia, except those at the Observation/Signal posts. Many of the village and ranch women were there as well, to listen to what I would say. I intentionally kept my remarks short. I introduced George, and reminded everyone that he was my cousin and was engaged to Celia, before telling them that he had left the Army and was now in charge of Estancia defenses.

I finished up by saying, "You all know that

comancheros have been active in the valley for the last year. We have reason to believe that they will attack the Estancia, soon. George, Miguel, Maco, and Yolanda have come up with a plan to stop any attack they try to make, at or near the boundary of the Estancia, rather than letting them get close to our families.

"Today, with the full support of mc and the Segundos, he will tell you of those plans, and your role in them. You will spend the day walking through the plans. Over the next few weeks we will practice those plans, so that everyone knows where to go and what to do, should the attack come. Please give him your utmost attention, and do what he tells you to do."

I turned it over to George, and while he was beginning his talk, Tom and I left the village returning to the Hacienda. At the Hacienda, we gathered our things from the study and moved upstairs to the terrace, where we returned to trying to find the flaws in our plans and come up with work arounds and additional options.

We stopped a little later to watch the parade of men on horseback, and in wagons, as they crossed the bridge and moved down the road towards the first rally point. Seeing almost five hundred men in a single long group, drove home the point about how far we had come, and how many people were unknowingly relying on us to get our plans right.

Shortly after lunch, one of Mr. Mendoza's freight wagons came across the bridge and up the slope to the Hacienda. The driver was shown up to the terrace, where he accepted our invitation to have a cup of coffee and rest for a few minutes. As he sat down, he handed me a thick letter from the Judge. I glanced at it, and put it on the table as he filled us in on the news from Las Cruces and Mesilla.

After he left, I opened the letter and began reading, curious about what the Judge might have to say. The first part of the letter praised Esteban and Ed for the prisoners they'd brought in to him. The second part of the letter was the news we'd been hoping and praying for.

The Texas Legislature had passed a bill with the exact wording the Judge had sent his friend, and the Governor had immediately signed it. Unfortunately, the new law also contained a couple of provisions that were going to make it a little harder than we hoped.

The law stipulated that only the Governor's office could sell public use land covered under the Treaty of Guadalupe-Hidalgo. It required that the Public Trust documents be presented in person, to the Governor's office, by an officer of the Trust at the time of purchase.

I sighed on reading this knowing a long trip to Austin was in my immediate future. As I continued to read, I couldn't help but smile as I got another big surprise. The Judge had reached the conclusion that I was too important to the peace and stability of the Territory to leave anytime soon, and had therefore asked Tom Stevenson to make the trip on my behalf, in his role as an officer of the Trust. Tom had agreed, and was scheduled to have left Santa Fe late last week. If that was so then he was already on his way here, before going on to Austin.

I finished reading the letter and handed it to Tom to read. I was deep in thought about what the Judge's news could do to our plans when Anna and Yolanda walked out of the bedroom. The babies had just fallen asleep after being fed, and both ladies needed a small break from them. Tom handed the letter to Yolanda to read who in turn handed it to Anna when she was done.

When Anna had finished reading the letter, Tom said, "I've seen that look on your face too many times over the last two years, Paul, as you mull over changing the plans. How do you see this affecting our plans?"

I snorted and replied, "I'm not exactly sure yet, Tom. It certainly gives us an opportunity to possibly buy as much of the land as we can get, much earlier, and therefore much cheaper than waiting a few years. But we need to look at the ripple effects doing that will cause. We won't be able to hide behind some obscure corporation for very long, so if we buy early that means our plans become public knowledge that much sooner, for anyone who cares to look. We need to work on the railroad plans, with an eye towards starting sooner than we anticipated. I think this news will have the biggest impact on that set of plans, as well as the subsequent petroleum plans."

Tom nodded his head in agreement, but it was Anna who said, "We need to have as much of this worked out as possible, before Tom Stevenson arrives. We need to understand the full set of plans to get his help, and his help is essential in making it all work. He has too much influence with the Judge, Kit, Hiram, and Lucien Maxwell among others in Santa Fe. If we can gain his trust, he will do his best to deliver the others we need to make this happen."

Tom and I both groaned at the thought of spending the next two weeks bent over papers, as we changed the plans yet again.

I said, "It's uncanny how this is happening. It's almost like we were getting divine help."

As I finished the statement I heard Laura's

laugh in my left ear, followed by her whisper of, " You are, my love, you are."

Startled, I looked over at Anna who had whipped her head around to look at me. It was clear to me that she had heard Laura's voice again. I gave Anna a shaky smile, and took a sip of coffee whispering to Anna, "That answers that question."

It began to get a little chilly as we lost direct sunlight. The ladies returned to the babies as Tom and I went back to the study, to review our original railroad plans and start changing them.

Over the next two weeks Tom and I worked in the study on our plans, joined by the ladies for a few hours every day when the babies were asleep. George kept us advised on how the defensive planning was progressing, and both Tom and I were on hand for both the weekly exercises that George and his team pulled.

Two and half weeks after the Judge's letter arrived we were informed that a small single horse buggy was coming south down the Camino Real. The four of us in the study looked at each other in amazement.

Yolanda wondered out loud, "Who on earth would ride a buggy down the Camino Real?"

Three hours later, just before supper, we got

our answer. It was Tom Stevenson. Tom and I helped a very stiff Tom Stevenson out of his buggy and grabbed his luggage before leading him into the Hacienda. We parked him in the dining room with fresh coffee delivered by Beth, and took his things to the room Anna said would be his during his stay.

As we walked back into the dining room I said, "Welcome to Hacienda Dos Santos Tom. How was your trip? Oh! Before I forget, Tom meet Tom."

Tom gave a long melodramatic groan as we sat down and replied. "It was the worst trip I've ever been on." Then he brightened before saying, "But forget about the trip we can talk about that anytime. Tell me about this marvelous Hacienda you have here. It's quite unexpected and spectacular."

Anna and Yolanda walked in carrying the babies with Beth following along behind carrying Rose. Anna spoke up as she set JJ down. "Welcome to the Hacienda Tom. This is Yolanda, Tom's wife. Oh dear! This is going to get confusing, isn't it?"

Before anyone else could say anything, Tom Stevenson spoke up. "My friends in school used to call me Steve. If it helps stop the confusion you can all call me that."

Anna nodded and said. "In that case, Steve this is Yolanda, our daughter Beth is carrying her sister Rose, and the two babies are our son JJ and Yolanda and Tom's son Joseph. How was your trip? I can't imagine it was very comfortable in that little buggy you arrived in."

Steve groaned again. "I should never have let that lout at the stables talk me into using that buggy and I definitely should have turned around and taken it back after the first five miles."

We all laughed in sympathy and lightly chided him for such a tenderfoot mistake. He sighed again and shrugged his shoulders. "I don't ride well, and the only other option was a wagon that I knew would be a hard ride so I figured I'd give it a try. It broke down twice on the way here. It's very clear that it isn't made for long distance travel. But enough about the trip. Tell me about the Hacienda."

Anna gave me a nudge and I got up telling Steve, "Come on. I'll give you a quick tour. Supper won't be ready for another half hour or so anyway and walking around a little will help loosen up some of those sore muscles."

I gave him a full tour of the upper and lower plateaus as well as the house answering all his questions as we went. We walked back into a full dining room just as supper was being brought out. I introduced him to everyone after we'd seated ourselves.

When I'd finished the introductions, I asked him with a grin if he was ready to take the test now. He laughed and said he was hungry so the test could wait until after supper. At that point, the normal mix of supper table conversations broke out. Steve looked a little startled when he realized that the conversations around him were being held in a mix of at least four different languages.

The Padre gave him a pitying look. "You'll get used to it Steve. Everyone on the Estancia speaks English, Spanish, and Apache so you'll hear those three everywhere you go. The kids at the Hacienda are also learning Italian from Giuseppe and Sofia's kids and are picking up a smattering of German from the mason's kids at school."

That started a conversation between the two that lasted through supper. I wasn't really paying attention to their conversation as I was absorbed in listening to the kids tell us about their day.

When supper was over we all went to the living room for after-supper coffee and of course Anna asked me to play. For the kids I sang "Bless the Beasts and the Children". For Tom I sang "Pretty Woman". For Anna I sang "Where Do I Begin", and "Can't Help Falling Love", before ending with "Anna's Song".

CHAPTER 12

"**D**amn Paul! None of this was here two years ago! How many people live in this village?" The questions were coming rapid fire from Steve, as we sat on our horses looking out over the village from the hills.

We'd insisted that Steve spend his first day on the Estancia recovering from his trip. The only thing remotely resembling a discussion of our plans, was getting him to accept that he would need to ride a horse to Austin and back. Well, that and convincing him that his chances of surviving the trip alone, were slim to none. He'd finally given in, and agreed to have ten of the Estancia vaqueros accompany him when he left for Austin.

This morning, after breakfast, we had started his regimen of slowly lengthening morning rides to toughen him up for his trip. This morning's ride was limited to two hours, which was almost perfect for a slow trip to the village and back. On the ride out from the Hacienda, I'd told him that when he first met Anna and I, the only thing that existed on the Estancia was the Hacienda which was only completed a couple of days before we were married.

At Steve's outburst, I turned towards him and answered his questions, and then gave him the short version of the Estancia story, as we walked our horses down the hill to the plaza. Like all visitors, he was amazed at the number of the people living on the Estancia, the size of the stables and wagon yards, and all the activity that was going on around us.

We dismounted, and Tom and I gave him a tour of the buildings surrounding the plaza. I let Tom do most of the talking as we walked around. When he'd seen everything, and all of his questions had been answered, we returned to our horses and rode back to the Hacienda.

Ensconced back on the terrace with fresh coffee Steve asked, "So what's on the agenda for tomorrow's ride?"

I pointed out over the river and replied, "I thought we'd ride to the Ranch tomorrow, and you can see where most of the rest of the

people on the Estancia live and the Ranch operations."

"More people?" he asked incredulously. "How
many more people? What do you mean most of
the rest?"

Tom laughed at his rapid-fire questions and
the look on his face as I answered. "There's
just short of five hundred more people at the
Ranch. By the rest, I mean the cousins who decided to live a more traditional lifestyle for
them. That's another thirty or forty families
living around the Estancia in small groups,
mostly in and near the mountains."

"How far is the Ranch from here?" Steve asked
after a few moments of thought.

I stood up and motioned him to join me at
the terrace rail. When he'd joined me, I took
out my monocular and handed it to him, as I
pointed towards the Ranch buildings.

"Look through this almost due east of us and
you'll get a taste of what you'll be seeing, tomorrow."

When he'd seen what there was to see of the
Ranch at this distance he handed me the monocular and we returned to the table. As I
was pouring myself some more coffee he said,
"This is so much more than we expected. None
of us had any idea of the scope of what you

were doing. No wonder you turned down the Marshal's job the first time the Judge offered it to you or that you put the limitations on it that you did."

I shrugged. "How do you tell people about something like the Estancia if they haven't ever seen it?" I asked.

"You did try, that's true enough. I'm not sure I could have done any better but I'm sure going to try when I get back. So, what's the plan for the rest of the day? Are we just going to sit here and relax or actually do some work?"

I couldn't help but laugh. For such a focused disciplined mind Steve bounced from topic to topic without any apparent thought or focus.

"We're going to try and get some much needed work done, Steve. But, before we do, there's some background we need to give you and some things we need to discuss."

He cocked an eyebrow in question.

"Did you bring the paperwork for the various projects we asked for in the letter Esteban brought you?" I asked.

"Of course, I did. I figured you'd want to see them," he replied.

Anna and Yolanda came out on the terrace and

joined us at the table.

"Your timing couldn't be any better, my love. We were just about to start talking business and I wanted you both here for this," I said.

Anna grinned as Yolanda replied, "It's not our timing anymore Pablo. It's the boys."

We grinned at her remarks and I resumed the conversation. "Steve, we'll want to go over each of the three documents in detail with you, to make sure we all understand them. The Land Corporation document may have to have some changes made to it, but we haven't reached a decision on that yet. Before we get to those though, we have some serious questions for you."

Steve nodded and said, "Ask away."

"The first question is how much do we need to pay you to make us and our businesses your primary, if not only, clients?" Anna asked him.

Steve sat back in his chair looking stunned at her question for a few moments before replying, "Anna, you all have given me quite a bit of business, but I just don't see enough work to justify that."

"What my wife is trying to tell you, Steve, is that we want to hire you as the full-time Legal Counsel and Comptroller for the Rio Grande and New Mexico Land Corporation. That position, combined with the other work the family will be giving you, will occupy all your time for the foreseeable future," I told him.

Anna grinned at Steve's expression. "Steve, there's lots of things going on here that you don't know anything about yet. Paul and Tom will talk you through everything, but suffice it to say for the time being, that Estancia Dos Santos will be opening many businesses over the next few years.

"The railroad is the first, the largest, and the most expensive. Hiring you full time just makes sense. You know the law, you've a well-deserved reputation for being as honest as the day is long, you're well respected in Santa Fe, and you have innumerable contacts in the North and East.

"We need all those things and we need them now. If we can get it all worked out you'll be traveling north and east to find us the right people to build this railroad and to coordinate our orders for three steam engines with Baldwin in Philadelphia, not to mention arranging for purchase and delivery of the rails, spikes, freight cars, and passenger cars."

Anna stopped talking, and I was just about to start explaining a little more when she piped back in with, "Oh, and yes, we will need you to set up some unrelated businesses for us as well."

We could all see that Steve was having problems processing everything Anna had told him, so we sat and quietly talked among ourselves as we enjoyed the morning sunshine and drank our coffee.

After a long twenty minutes or so Steve finally spoke up. "When do you expect to start working on this railroad? There's a lot to do besides what you mentioned, first and foremost is getting a charter so that you can have the land you need to build it."

I gave a slight shrug, and said, "Steve, we are starting now with trying to hire you. We won't be applying for a charter as we don't want the government involved if at all possible. Not because we don't appreciate the free land a charter would mean, but because it would take years to get it approved.

"By my estimate we will be done with construction and will start full-time operations by the time Congress even brought it to a floor vote, and that's only if something more politically important, which is almost everything, doesn't come to the floor and take their attention.

"No, we will buy the land we want outright,

once you've agreed to join the team. Our goal is to start construction early next year, and have the Las Cruces to Santa Fe portion operational with stops in Fort Thorn, Fort Craig, Socorro, and Albuquerque, by the end of 1860. When that's a reality we'll look at extending the line from Santa Fe to Raton Pass on Lucien's land and perhaps beyond to someplace in Kansas. We'll also look at expanding east and west to other parts of the Territory from Las Cruces."

He looked at all four of us and asked, "Do you have investors already lined up for this? If so, what level of funding do you have?"

Anna smile sweetly at him. "You're looking at all the investors Steve. Between the four of us we have ten million dollars which should cover everything from the land, to the construction, to the operations for the initial Las Cruces to Santa Fe route that Pablo talked about. It should also be enough to cover extending the line to Raton, but that will depend on Lucien. Extending the line east and west from Las Cruces will have to be evaluated after the Raton decision is made."

Steve looked at each of us, one after the other, with cold unblinking eyes for a moment. "The four of you have ten million dollars?" he asked.

In a serious and quiet voice, I replied. "No, Steve. Between us we have more than that. Not a whole lot more, but we won't be destitute if we lose the ten million we are investing in the railroad."

Steve gave an explosive sigh before asking, "Why in the world would you want to invest that much money in such a risky venture?" He gave a brief pause shaking his head and continued, "There must be other things you could do with that money."

Tom got up from his chair and walked towards the railing, saying, "Steve, come over to the railing for a minute, and I can help you answer that question."

When Steve had joined Tom at the railing Tom swept his hand out over the Estancia. "Steve, when you look out over the Estancia you probably only see the river, the desert, and the mountains. The four of us, and the rest of the people who live and work on the Estancia, see something quite different.

"We see more than 10,000 head of cattle that need a market. We see over 10,000 acres of the world's most productive farmland we will plant and harvest every year. We can sell some of the cattle and produce here in Mesilla, and Las Cruces, as well as to Fort Fillmore, and Fort Thorn. We can, perhaps, sell some to the people of El Paso, and Fort Bliss. What we can sell in the surrounding area will be a small fraction of what we produce.

"A railroad would expand our market significantly! Imagine being able to harvest fresh produce here one day, and having it available for sale in Santa Fe the next day! Imagine loading two or three thousand head of cattle here one day, and unloading them four hundred miles to the north in Raton before driving them up to Pueblo or Denver to feed the miners there.

"We can't afford to wait another twenty or thirty years if we want to survive. That's what the railroad means to us, and that's why we'll build it. Imagine the people around Socorro, Albuquerque, and Santa Fe having the opportunity to buy fresh produce and meat almost all year round or moving the products they've grown or made to other markets.

"Once the main line is in operation we can extend that reach even further inside the Territory, so that everyone benefits. Will we carry a lot of passengers? Probably not. Will we carry a lot of freight in both directions? We certainly hope so, but even if we don't, the benefits of a railroad to the Estancia are critical to our future plans and even if we are the only ones who ship our freight on the railroad it will be worth it to us."

When Tom finished talking, he turned and came back to the table. Steve stood there, by himself, looking out over the Estancia for another few minutes before he too rejoined us at the table.

Yolanda poured him a fresh cup of coffee telling him, "It's a lot to take in, I know; but, just like the Estancia, this too will happen."

Steve looked at Yolanda for a moment and then turned to Anna. "To answer your original question, I average about six hundred dollars a year, most years. Some years I make much more and some years much less but that's the average over the last five years. At the moment, I have no work pending and no active accounts besides the Estancia Trust which is why I agreed to make the trip to Austin when the Judge asked me. I know you'll be good for the expenses and my fee which isn't cheap."

Anna gave him a small smile and said, "So a salary of one hundred dollars a month, and a share of any annual profits the railroad makes, would be acceptable?"

Anna's question startled Steve and he took a moment to recover before nodding his head saying, "Yes, what you offer would be most acceptable."

"Good! Over the next two weeks we'll fill you in on all the plans and the things you'll be doing to help make those plans a reality in the next few years. I'd like to spend the rest of the day going through the two sets of Valley Trust documents we asked you for, and getting those finalized," I said.

Steve got up and went to his room to get the documents I asked for. While we were waiting for him I said, "I'll leave for El Paso Monday morning after the meeting."

With concern in his voice Tom said, "With the comancheros still out there I hope you're not thinking of going alone."

Anna was vigorously nodding her head in agreement with Tom.

"No, I'll take a wagon and twelve men. A driver, rider, and ten vaqueros. It's time to quit hiding who and what we are! I want to arrive in El Paso before mid-day, make the deposit, get the bank drafts, and start home before nightfall."

Anna smiled at me saying, "It's about time, my love, but please be careful."

Steve rejoined us just as she finished and we turned to reviewing the documents. We took a break for lunch, after we'd finished reviewing the Mesilla Valley Community Association Trust and continued with reviewing the Mesilla Valley Education Association Trust afterwards.

With his usual thoroughness and foresight, Steve had done exactly as we'd asked, and had then improved the language to make them unassailable, should they ever be questioned in court. The Judge had approved and registered them, so we were ready to start on both fronts.

Tom and I continued our morning rides with Steve through the weekend and began filling him in on our goal of Statehood, the impediments we saw that would delay us from reaching that goal, and the various plans we had designed to overcome a large number of those. We also talked about our ice making plans, and the building cooling plans.

Sunday afternoon I gave Steve the year-end report for 1855, telling him to read it so he would be better prepared for the Monday morning meeting he would be attending. Tom and I left him on the terrace and locked ourselves in the study. We opened the cave door, and spent a couple of hours filling up burlap bags with gold bars and hauling the bags out to the study, so we were ready to load the wagon Monday morning before breakfast.

Between the year-end report, and the meeting, Steve got quite an education on the Estancia and our future plans as well as the planning it took to get this far. When the meeting was over, I talked with him for a couple of minutes to get his reactions.

To say he was impressed with all three of the Segundo's was an understatement. He also realized the full scope of the threats we faced on a daily basis as well as the comanchero threat when George and Miguel gave us their updates on the attack defense plans and the observation/signaling posts.

I walked out of the courtyard to find Anna, Tom, and Yolanda waiting for me at the wagon to say goodbye. I gave Anna a big hug and long kiss, promised them all to be careful, and mounted my horse. Giving the lead vaquero a head nod I followed them and the wagon down the slope, over the bridge, and down the road towards El Paso.

Tom and the ladies must have talked to the vaqueros while they were waiting to say good-bye because as soon as we turned South off the bridge four of the vaqueros rode off. One rode ahead, one far out to each side and one staying well behind us. The rest of the vaqueros rode alongside the wagon three to a side leaving me just behind the wagon.

We pushed hard and even with the heavily loaded wagon arrived just outside El Paso in the early evening two days after leaving the Estancia. During the trip we had passed numerous travelers and wagon trains heading North who looked at the guards curiously but otherwise the trip was non-eventful. We camped in the arroyo Anna had used on our first trip here after being married and remained until mid-morning letting the mule team rest and recover a little before traveling the last five miles into El Paso.

None of the men with me knew what was in the wagon and were quite surprised when I lead them straight to the bank. As I dismounted I told them to spread out a little and guard the wagon until I returned when I would need seven of them to help me unload it.

Inside the bank I found Levi hard at work at his desk. I knocked on his door and he greeted me with the usual good cheer I'd come to expect from any of the Greenburg's. I told him I had a deposit to make and needed several bank drafts in return. He got serious for a moment and as he walked out of his office asked me how long I was staying in El Paso.

"I'm leaving as soon as you give me the bank drafts. No, not the back door, Levi. From now on we'll be using the front door," I said as he turned to go down the hall towards the back of the bank.

He turned and followed me curiously to the front door and out of the bank. When he saw the twelve men with shotguns guarding the wagon he looked a little alarmed. When seven of them started grabbing bags out of the wagon he realized they were my guards and relaxed.

With all the extra help, it was a matter of only a few minutes to unload the one hundred twenty-five bags of gold bars from the wagon and move them to the weighing room. As planned, the lead vaquero then took the men to get lunch.

Back in the weighing room, Levi quickly stacked and weighed the bars in groups of 100. When he was done weighing, he told me the price was still $12 an ounce and the total for all 10,000 bars was $600,000. I nodded and handed him the sheet of paper I'd written up while he was weighing.

He looked at it for a moment and then asked in disbelief, "You want all this right now?"

"Yes, please. I'd like to leave in the next half hour. I really need to get back to the Estancia as soon as possible."

He shrugged and said it would take about twenty minutes to write up the bank drafts, and count the money I wanted. True to his word, twenty minutes later, he handed me a leather folio with the bank drafts tucked inside. I quickly looked through them and saw that he'd written them up in the amounts I'd asked for.

He came back a few minutes later, carrying two of the large coin bags accompanied by a teller carrying another. Putting them on the desk, he asked if I wanted to count it. I told him I trusted him, there was no time, and I thanked him for his help and speed.

While I signed the withdrawal slip I asked, "Levi, are you so important to the bank that you can't take a few weeks off around the end of the year?"

He snorted. "Not really, Paul, I just don't have anywhere else to go or much else that interests me at the moment," he replied.

"In that case you and your parents are invited up to the Estancia for the holidays. I won't take no for an answer. I'll send ten vaqueros down to escort you and your parents to the Estancia. Be ready to leave the morning of the 15th of December and plan on staying until at least the 5th of January. I'll make the same invitation to your brother when I see him later this year in Santa Fe," I said handing him the withdrawal slip.

He looked a little startled for a moment and then said, "Why not? I'll let my parents know, although I'm not sure they'll want to make the trip."

"Remind them that Hiram and his family are getting the same invitation," I said.

I'd been standing in the doorway to his office as we'd talked, and saw that the vaqueros were back from lunch. I put the three bags of money into separate burlap bags, picked two of them up and asked two of the vaqueros to bring the other bag and the bags full of now empty burlap bags.

Levi followed me outside and as I put everything in the wagon. I thanked him for all his help yet again, and told him I'd see him in another couple of weeks.

I mounted up, nodded to the lead vaquero, and followed them at a walk out of town. About an hour out of town I stopped and called everyone to me.

"I just a made a large deposit at the bank, and I'm now carrying papers worth a lot of money as well as a large amount of coins in the wagon. Our goal is to get home as quickly as possible without trouble finding us, so we will push the animals hard for the rest of the trip and we will all stay together. I'll set the pace," I told them.

When I got a nod or yes from everyone I spurred the horse forward to a canter and stayed there until we lost the last bit of daylight. We made dry camp and rested for the night leaving as soon as there was enough light to see by and continued the grueling travel pace I'd set the previous day.

We almost made it home that day, but lost daylight just before getting to the Estancia boundary, So, again, we made a dry camp and spent a restless night before riding the last five miles to the Hacienda, as soon as we had enough daylight to see.

Unsurprisingly, Anna met us outside the courtyard. After a hug and kiss, she told us all to come inside for breakfast. We gathered the bags of coins and empty burlap bags out of the wagon, putting them in the study on our way to the dining room.

Everyone else had already finished breakfast and were about their daily activities so the twelve men and I were left alone to eat a very large breakfast in peace. When we were done, I walked them out and thanked them for making sure I got to El Paso and returned home safe.

The lead vaquero asked what was so urgent about the trip. I told them we'd just brought back the payroll for the rest of the year. With smiles, laughs, and back slaps they all rode off tiredly down the slope, but in a good mood.

Anna was waiting for me as I walked back in to

the courtyard, and gave me a little longer hug and kiss before saying, "You smell like horse and sweat! Go shower and change clothes. The rest of us will meet you in the study when you're done."

I smiled, gave her a nice long bear hug, and escorted her inside. As I started up the stairs, I handed her the leather wallet with the bank drafts inside. She took the wallet and turned into the study.

I luxuriated in the shower, washed off the dust and sweat from the trail, and used the hot water to relieve some of the strain and pain the last few days of hard riding had caused. I walked in to the study a half hour later, and found Anna, Tom, Yolanda, and Steve seated in the conversation area. Anna poured a cup of coffee and handed it to me as I sat down next to her.

Yolanda asked about the trip and I told them there wasn't much to tell. It was quick, and we didn't have a single problem, probably because no one knew we were making the trip in advance, and we were moving so fast that by the time anyone discovered we were on the move we were so far ahead of them they couldn't catch us.

In turn, I asked how things were going with the planning. Tom said we'd be ready in a couple of days, but Steve would need another seven or eight days of riding to be ready. Steve was up to four hours a day and he and Tom were going to do today's daily ride when we finished up our meeting.

I told them to get going then because I didn't have anything else to add or any other questions at the moment. Everyone but Anna left the study to go about their day. Anna and I remained cuddled together on the couch for another fifteen minutes as we talked and had another cup of coffee.

Done with my second cup I asked Anna to stay and help me for a few minutes. She followed me into the RV cave, and asked what I was looking for, as I was rummaging through the plastic bin of maps. I told her I was looking for a map we were going to use to plan the general route for the railroad. I finally found the Exxon New Mexico Roadmap I'd used for years, before getting a navigation system.

We returned to the study where I got out the Territorial Map the Judge had sent us. The Judge had mentioned it was the same map that the Land Offices were required to use, so that was one less issue we had to worry about.

As I spread the map of the territory out on the top of the desk, I asked Anna if we had any really thin paper we could use to trace the route we wanted. She giggled and said we did and left to go get it. When she came back she handed me several thin sheets of paper that I had grown up calling 'onion skin.'

It was a little thicker than tracing paper, and more translucent rather than transparent, but we could still see through it. It took four pieces of paper to cover the Rio Grande from Las Cruces to Santa Fe on the territorial map. I traced the city locations and at least two other major bends of the Rio Grande on each piece of paper, as reference marks. Then the hard work started.

I folded the road map to show only Interstate-25, from Las Cruces to Santa Fe, with five inches on either side. Anna marveled at the detail of the roadmap and then got caught up in the mental gymnastics required to translate the route of I-25 from the road map to the territorial map which was a smaller scale, yet much less detailed map.

With Anna's help, I drew the general route of I-25 onto the paper using straight lines from point to point. The paper was just thick enough that it was hard to see the map underneath and we kept having to remove the paper to check the map and make sure we were in the right area. When we were done the paper showed a series of over thirty short straight connected lines from Las Cruces to Santa Fe.

Anna looked dubiously at the paper and asked, "Is that what the railroad is going to look like?"

I couldn't help but laugh and told her, "No, my love. We're not done yet, and by the end of the day what we have, will help us decide what land to buy and help the surveyor lay out the railroad."

Using a wooden ruler, we measured a mile, and drew that on the map with each of the original lines as the center point. When we were done I put the territorial map away and using my pocket knife, the ruler, and small cutting board from the kitchen, cut the mile-wide lines out of the paper.

We put the territorial map back on the desk, and after we aligned the four pieces of paper I said, "The part of the map you can see through the areas we cut out is the land we will buy and build the railroad on. Where, exactly, in that swath of land, will be up to the surveyor."

I quickly put the map away back in the plastic bin underneath the RV, and then we walked out of the study to find that lunch was ready. Yolanda joined us, and agreed to Anna's suggestion that we have lunch on the terrace. They went off to feed the babies and I arranged for lunch and coffee on the terrace. I was sitting on the terrace gazing out over the river deep in thought about the things we were putting in motion when Anna and Yolanda joined me. They were followed almost immediately by Carla who'd been waiting for them to arrive before bringing lunch out.

Over lunch, I remembered to tell the ladies that I had invited Levi and his parents to spend the holidays with us, and that I wanted to extend the same invitation to Hiram and Helen. Anna said she would write Helen extending the invitation and let her know that Levi and Mr. and Mrs. Greenburg would be here as well. She agreed that it was a perfect time to talk to all of them at the same time about opening a branch of the bank in Las Cruces.

Anna reminded me that Josefa and Kit along with the extended Taos family were joining us in Santa Fe on our next trip and would be coming back to the Estancia with us for an extended visit. She gave a little giggle and said the Hacienda would be full again if everyone we invited actually came.

I also told them I had decided to order two private coaches, when Tom and I escorted Steve down to El Paso. Yolanda quickly told me I needed to talk to Raul and her grandfather to get the names of the best coach wainwrights in El Paso del Norte. She stressed, with Anna's confirmation, that the wainwrights in the American El Paso were fine for farm and freight wagons, but they just couldn't deliver a fine well-built coach.

The next seven days quickly became monotonous as I settled into four-hour morning rides with Tom and Steve followed by working on details of the plans during the afternoon hours. I did manage to spend quite a bit of time with Anna and JJ though, and that made up for the monotony.

CHAPTER 13

I was on the terrace on a fine bright sunny afternoon, staring in horror at the list of things I'd come up with for Steve to do when he got back from Austin. No matter how I looked at it, I just couldn't see how he would ever get everything on the list done, in the time-frame we wanted.

I was seriously starting to think that maybe we'd over extended ourselves this time, and we would have to push the time-frame out another year, when something in my brain sparked. I suddenly remembered a conversation I'd overheard just after I'd been promoted to Staff Sergeant and joined the NCO ranks.

A crusty old Chief Master Sergeant was lecturing a new Second Lieutenant in his office. As usual, the Chief had left the door open. I was walking by on some errand or another. Everyone in the hallway clearly heard the Chief talking.

"Remember, LT, your job is to know the details of what needs to be done and when. It's the NCO's job to get those details done. If you learn nothing else, here; learn this, and learn it well. **Never, ever,** try to tell an NCO how to do something. You tell an NCO what needs to be done and when it needs to be done by. If the NCO needs help or additional resources to get something done, they'll let you know."

I was smiling to myself at the memory, when I heard Laura soft laugh in my left ear. Then I knew that I'd just gotten my answer to the problem.

I decided that I was done for the day and I was due for some Anna and JJ time, when George came up the outside steps and sat down at the table across from me. He looked a little wan and I asked what he'd been up to all day that had worn him down so much.

He barked a quick laugh and said, "I've been reminding myself why I left the Army, Paul. I've been in the saddle since just after breakfast riding the east side of the Doña Ana's with Maco trying to get as familiar with that area of the Estancia as I am with the west side."

I commiserated with him for a few minutes before turning to the subject of his impending wedding, and asked him how things were going with the Padre. He assured me things were going well, but Celia still hadn't set a date yet.

She was close to choosing the date, but there were a couple of things getting in the way that she needed to work out. She wouldn't tell him what those things were, so he had no idea how to help her. I shrugged and agreed that there wasn't much he could do.

We were talking about how the militia was shaping up, when one of the young cousins from the corrals on the upper plateau came running down the steps and handed George a message. George glanced at it, sat up straight, and read it more closely before handing it to me.

It took me a few moments to puzzle out the shorthand, but when I did I looked in alarm at George. The message read:

From: SS 2 South
To: SG

Message: lge nmbr (70+) men in sml grps mvng north cnvrg nr pt bravo

"Well, George, it looks like you were right," I said.

He nodded, and with a grim face turned to the young man.

"Send a message from me to the entire Estancia. Message to read, Alert, Alert, Alert. Execute Alpha One Alpha, immediately. Alert, Alert, Alert."

The boy looked at him for a moment, nodded his head, repeated the message verbatim, and ran off the terrace up the steps.

I was ready to run downstairs and ride out, but George hadn't moved yet. "What are you thinking so hard about, George?" I asked.

He gave a deep sigh before replying. "A lot of men are going to die sometime in the next twelve hours. I just hope I've trained them well enough that it's ours that do the killing not the dying."

"Me, too, George! Me, too. Let's go find our ladies, let them know what's happening. Then we'll head for the rally point."

He nodded, and we went off in search of Celia and Anna. We found them together in the dining room. George told them what was happening, and we each hugged and kissed our lady goodbye before grabbing our weapons from the study. One of the cousins came riding up leading our saddled horses behind him as we walked out the courtyard door onto the lower plateau.

We mounted and began the long ride to the rally point, with George setting a steady but unhurried pace. As we rode, I asked George what the second Alpha in the message meant.

Still with a grim face he said, "That's a small refinement we came up with a couple of weeks back. It means the enemy is converging and settling in for the night three to five miles outside the Estancia. A Bravo instead of an Alpha would have meant one to three miles. In either of those two cases everyone was to go to the rally point without raising any dust. If the message had just read Alpha One that meant a full attack was on its way and to make all possible speed to the rally point."

I could see horses and wagons moving all around us heading in the same direction we were going and thought to ask him about food and water for the men and horses.

As it turned out the feed and water for the horses were staged at the rally point a few weeks ago. A wagon from the village and the ranch were sent out to both rally points every morning and brought back in every night. The food was used for lunch the next day. I couldn't help but laugh and agree when he said the ladies of the Estancia would make fine logistics and supply NCOs.

When we finally reached the rally point we found two hundred of the expected three hundred men already there. I followed George's lead again and we rode to a makeshift corral deep inside the arroyo. We unsaddled our horses, turned them loose inside the corral, and threw our saddles on one of the wagons lined up outside the corral.

As we walked back to where the men were gathering I asked George what Point Bravo was. It turned out that it was one of three places the Scout/Sniper teams had found within five miles of the Estancia where a large group of men could hole up and camp for the night.

We found Tom talking to a couple of men just outside the main gathering of men. He turned as we walked up and said, "The last message came in fifteen minutes ago and said that Point Bravo was confirmed. There are over seventy men preparing a full camp with small cooking fires and horse picket lines."

George nodded, thanked him, and turned to look out over the men when one of the cousins appeared at his side out of nowhere. George acknowledged his presence with a short nod but otherwise ignored him for the time being. He walked out to the middle of the arroyo and stood there looking at the men milling around. Without a word, men started coming forward and forming up into ranks of five.

George patiently waited until there were sixty full ranks of five men then turned to the cousin.

"Send all present and accounted for. Expect attack during early morning hours near first light. God bless and good luck," he said.

The cousin climbed out of the arroyo, took out his mirror, and began signaling.

"That was well done, George. Well done, indeed. The training you've given them has paid off very well so far," I told him.

Deep in thought he nevertheless acknowledged the compliment and again voiced his hope that it was good enough.

I turned towards Tom and saw Steve standing next to him. To say I was startled was an understatement.

"Steve, what the hell are you doing here? You're supposed to be at the Hacienda."

Steve shrugged. "Tom and I were spending a couple of extra hours in the saddle when the message was flashed and since this was closer than the Hacienda I just came with him," he replied.

"It's too late to send you to the Hacienda now,"

I groaned with dismay. "You haven't trained for this and you don't have a weapon so I want you to stay close to George until this is over. You do what he tells you to do, when he tells you to do it. Got it?"

George had heard the exchange and was shaking his head in disgust. I took the opportunity to change subjects.

"Tom, George, both of you raise your right hands and repeat after me." They looked at me curiously but raised their right hands. "I, state your name, do hereby faithfully swear to execute the duties of the office I am about to enter and enforce the laws of the United States."

When they completed the oath, I threw both a badge and said, "Congratulations. You are both now Acting Deputy US Marshals. I need you two to gather all the men, and administer the same oath to them. I'm a little short of badges so we'll have to make do with the two you have."

While I was talking, I had pinned my badge on my coat, and they followed suit before walking to the center of the arroyo together. George waved his arm around his head and less than a minute later sixty men were gathered around him and Tom. He talked quietly for a few minutes and the group broke up.

George stood on one side of the arroyo while Tom stood on the other as men began to line up in groups of five in front of the two men. Each team took the oath, were congratulated, and went back to whatever they were doing. In less than ten minutes after I'd given them the task, it was done.

They both walked back to me and George looked at me. "Now what, Paul?" he asked.

I shrugged and said, "It's your show, George. I do need to talk to you a little later, when you have time, about how you see this unfolding so that we're both working from the same plan."

George looked at me skeptically and asked, "What do you mean, 'working from the same plan'?"

I pointed to the badge on my chest. "We have to obey the law, too, George. So far, those men out there haven't broken any laws that I'm aware of. None of us even know who they are for sure. Tomorrow morning when they get close enough I have to be standing where we can see each other. If they are who we think they are, then I will identify myself and let them know they are under arrest. If any one of them goes for a gun, I expect you and the rest of the men to put holes, lots of holes, into every single one of them. But I have to give them the chance to surrender."

George gave a deep sigh. "I know you're right, Paul, but it makes me mad to think of the extremes we go to just to make sure the criminals are offered the chance to surrender."

Having had his say he turned around and walked off.

Tom cleared his throat to get my attention and said, "Come on. Let's get our saddles and some blankets so we can set up our area of the camp."

Steve and I followed Tom back to the corrals, where he showed us a wagon half full of blankets. We each grabbed a couple of blankets, found our saddles, and followed Tom over to an area against the arroyo wall where we set up our sleeping areas. We were losing daylight fast, so we walked over to the food wagons, and each grabbed a sandwich.

Leaning against our saddles, we ate the sandwiches and washed them down with water. George showed up carrying blankets and his saddle just as the last of the light faded away. When he sat down I handed him a sandwich and told him to eat, as he was going to need the energy later. He thanked me and quickly ate.

When George was done eating he leaned back against the saddle and gave a long sigh. "I wish I could figure these guys out."

"What's troubling you, George?" Tom asked.

"Well, either these guys are much better led and trained than we thought or they're being led by idiots. In either case I'm worried that something we haven't accounted for is going to happen and we won't be in the position to stop them," George said with an explosive breath.

We were all silent for a moment.

"Run it down for us, George," I said quietly. "Give us specifics of what has you spooked and then tell us how you see it playing out in the morning."

George sat quietly for a moment and then started talking. "What's bothering me is that, with one major exception, they did everything we expected all the way up until they got to the rally point. From there they haven't done anything I expected.

"From everything we know about them and the tactics they've used in the past, they shouldn't be here tonight. There's no moon for the next two nights. In less than a half hour no one out here will be able to see their hand in front of their face.

"Then there's their rally point. With no moon tonight they should have rallied much closer to the Hacienda. Instead, they rallied almost ten miles away and rather than moving closer as a group they pitched camp.

"When they did that I began to get really worried that something else is going on and they are just a distraction. However, the last report we got from the Scout/Sniper teams and observation posts, just before we lost the sun, reported no activity at all to the west, north, or east."

He gave another worried sigh, going quiet for a minute before continuing.

"The success these guys have had over the months clearly tells me they aren't being led by a complete idiot, and that someone in their leadership group has had some kind of training. This just doesn't make sense.

"As far as how I see it happening tomorrow there's not much to say. Given the lack of moonlight to see by, I don't expect them to send out their normal scouts. Also, with the lack of moonlight they won't be able to move towards the Hacienda until the false dawn gives them some light to see by.

"They really only have two options in the morning, if they are really going to attack us. The first option is that they ride out from their camp and up the road to get closer to the

Hacienda and Ranch figuring that everyone is going to be at breakfast and they won't be noticed until it's too late. In that case, we ambush them as planned.

"The other, much more worrisome option, is that they move out from their camp in small groups to another rally point much closer to the Hacienda. We didn't plan for anything like that, and it becomes much harder to stop them. We'll have to break the men up into their smaller teams and send one or two teams after each group. It's very likely that a lot more of our men are going to die if we end up doing that."

Tom interrupted George at that point. "Is it possible that there's a much simpler explanation for how their acting, George? Maybe something as simple as they think they are already close, within a mile or two of the Hacienda? Would that explain what they've done so far?"

I've always been a big fan of 'Occam's Razor', and Tom had used it to nail this problem down as far as I was concerned. I didn't say anything though as I wanted to hear how George would respond.

Time seemed to stretch out and slow to a crawl, as we sat quietly waiting for George's response. It seemed as if we'd been waiting thirty minutes, but I was sure it was less than two minutes when we heard George mutter something about 'Occam's Razor' under his breath. I smiled in the dark, knowing that George was upset that he hadn't thought of a simpler explanation.

It was quiet again for a moment and then we heard George say, "Tom, that would certainly fit the facts we have, and you're probably right. You'll excuse me, though, if I continue to try to come up with other reasons, just in case."

We heard Tom snort just before he said, "George, you're the expert. I'd be very worried if you weren't trying to come up with other reasons."

For the next hour, we talked quietly among ourselves about other things. Mostly George's forthcoming wedding, and his conversion to Catholicism. There was little to do besides talk and with no light there was absolutely nothing to see except the stars. Eventually, we all drifted off to sleep.

I don't know about everyone else, but despite the tension that had been building inside of me since we got the alarm, I slept extremely well. Perhaps it was exhaustion from all the worrying I'd been doing for the last few months or the stress of re-planning everything since word had come that Steve would be visiting us.

Whatever the reason, I slept soundly through the night, and didn't wake up until I felt someone nudging my arm. I opened my eyes, and saw a vague human shaped gray outline against the dark night sky. It was George telling me we were moving to the ambush site in fifteen minutes.

I must not have moved at all while I slept, because as I got up I discovered I was extremely stiff. As far as I could tell with the limited light I had plenty of room so I closed my eyes and concentrated as I began doing Tai Chi exercises. I stopped after ten minutes, feeling much looser and ready for what lay ahead.

Although a long way from daylight, there was enough light to see by now. I picked up the blankets and my saddle, and returned them to the wagons grabbing another couple of sandwiches from the food wagon as I passed it. With my shotgun hanging on my left side from its sling, and my rifle slung over my right shoulder, I walked around the arroyo looking for George, Tom, and Steve as I ate my sandwiches.

I finally saw them up near the road, and walked over giving them a quiet good morning. We stood quietly for the next five minutes and watched the activity as the men prepared to leave. Eventually, the men, all three hundred of them, were gathered around us and quiet expectation filled the morning air.

George broke the silence and in a calm normal talking voice said, "You all know where to go and what to do. We've practiced it enough times that there shouldn't be any surprises. We are using ambush point one. That's three quarters of a mile from here, and we don't know yet what the enemy is doing or if they've started moving towards us, so let's get there as quickly as we can. Team leaders, take your men out and get into position."

As the men started to move off, George spoke up in a little louder voice. "Oh, and remember that Paul is going to be standing in the middle of the road, so make sure you don't shoot him by mistake."

"I'd appreciate that, and so would Anna!" I added.

That got the nervous laughter that George was expecting, and he waved everyone forward. It was a far cry from a military formation, but as the men passed us they broke into a trot with each team staying together. The four of us joined in at about the middle of the pack, and ran forward as well.

It was immediately apparent that Steve was

struggling to keep up with us, so we slowed a little and let the rest of the men pass us. It was a good thing we didn't have to go farther than we did, because he wouldn't have made it. He was gasping for breath when George slowed to a walk, near the ambush point. He led us over to an arroyo heading east off the road and sat down with his back against the arroyo wall with a good view of the Doña Ana Mountains where he was expecting to get the signal updates from.

When Steve quit gasping for air George clapped him on the back, and with a smile said, "We'll work on your running when you get back from Austin."

Steve groaned and just shook his head, still too out of breath to talk. George stood up and motioned for me to join him. I joined him on the road and we walked fifteen yards further down the road. He stopped next to a four-foot-tall boulder standing just off the left side of the road.

"If you insist on standing and meeting them on the road this is the best place to do it. The boulder will give you some protection it you need it and somehow I think you will," he said.

I nodded, liking his thinking and then turned back to look towards the arroyo. "Remind me how the men are deployed," I said.

He turned and swept his arm along the length of the arroyo. "There are two hundred men in the arroyo waiting for the first shot to be fired. If they do what they've been told, then they won't be seen until then."

He turned to the west and swept his arm out towards the river. "There's a draw about fifty feet from the road that roughly parallels it. There are a hundred men in that draw with the same instructions as the ones in the arroyo."

He turned north and pointed to four separate small hills about three hundred yards behind the arroyo.

"There's a Scout/Sniper team on each of those four hills. At the first sign of someone pulling a gun or making any other threatening move they will fire. That is the signal for everyone else to rise up and start firing."

Something was off here but I couldn't put my finger on it. I turned around a full 360 degrees, looking at everything before it dawned on me.

I turned to George and asked, "What happened to all the brush?"

George laughed heartily for the first time since yesterday afternoon and said, "I had anything taller than a small barrel cactus cleared out for a hundred yards from the arroyo and the draw.

I left the mesquite and creosote growing along the edges of the arroyo and draw to give our men some extra concealment but the comancheros won't have anything to hide behind. It's now a classic killing field. If it comes to gun play this morning, the raiders will be wiped out in less than thirty seconds. Let's hope it takes them longer to wonder about that than it did you."

"George, I meant what I said yesterday evening. You've done a hell of a job, here. Let's get this done and then hopefully we can rest for a few years," I said in a very sincere voice.

As he was about to reply we both caught a flash from the Doña Anas. George turned and made a big wave, signaling a 'ready to receive' acknowledgement with a torch since direct sunlight hadn't reached us here yet. The message said that the raiders had broken camp. I raised an eyebrow when the message said the raiders were less than two miles away and coming up the road at a canter. They were much closer than I'd expected.

George waved another acknowledgement before turning to me. "I'd still like to know why they are doing it this way instead of how they usually do it, but at this point it's curiosity, not worry, that makes me wonder. Hopefully one of them will survive long enough to tell us."

While George had been talking I'd been watching the growing dust cloud to the south. "We can always hope George, but it really doesn't matter, anymore." I pointed to the south with my chin. "Whatever reason they have for doing it this way, they are doing it in a hurry. You best get along back to the men and let them know the raiders are almost here."

George turned and looked at the dust cloud with me for a moment before wishing me good luck and walked back to the arroyo. About halfway there he stopped and turned to look at me.

"None of us want to be the one to tell Anna you died from stupidity, Paul. Don't take any chances. You get your ass behind that boulder at the first sign of gunplay and stay there. Let us do what we trained to do."

Done, he turned and disappeared into the arroyo with the men.

I stood gazing at the dust cloud as it grew before walking back to the boulder. I unslung my rifle leaning it against the backside of the boulder and walked around to the side of the boulder nearest the road. I checked that the safety was off on the shotgun and that it was fully loaded before leaning it back against the boulder. I began clearing my mind using the calming breathing exercises, I'd been taught so long ago, as I waited.

Less than ten minutes later, I could clearly see the dark mass of riders below the dust cloud. After another five minutes and I could see the individual riders. I pushed myself away from the boulder, grabbed the shotgun and took two steps onto the road where I stood with the shotgun cradled in my arm.

The lead riders finally saw me when they were less than a hundred yards away. As they passed the last of the mesquite and creosote bushes entering the clearing George had made, the riders began to move out to the sides of the two lead riders before slowing to a walk. They all came to a complete stop when they were ten yards away from me.

There was no question about it any longer. It was indeed Flat Nose and his gang of comancheros. Flat Nose looked just as he'd been described.

A big burly man with thick, long, greasy, hair and a full beard that was just as long and greasy as his hair. His nose was indeed flat and spread out over much of his face. The hair, beard, nose, and beady deep-set eyes all combined to give him the look of an angry bear.

His looks and body language, even from the saddle, conveyed the impression that he was going to get what he wanted, and nothing was going to stand in his way. In short it screamed mean, sadistic, brutal, bully.

I calmly looked over both him and his men before saying, "Good morning, Flat Nose. I'd welcome you to Estancia Dos Santos. Sadly, though, you're not there yet. But where are my manners? Let me introduce myself, I am US Marshal Paul McAllister. You and all your men are under arrest for murder, theft, rape, and kidnapping. If you throw down your guns and surrender peacefully I can guarantee you a fair trial."

There were a few snickers from among his men, but Flat Nose just glared at me with those dark beads of coal where his eyes should be. When he started talking it was in a surprisingly smooth mellow voice not the deep gravelly growl I expected.

"Good morning, Marshal. I want to thank you making my day complete. Not only do I get the riches, women, and cattle of the ranch behind you, I also get you. You've caused me and the organization I work for much grief in the last few years, and today I have the pleasure of putting an end to it."

I smiled to myself. The man had a certain swagger to him, but he had no real clue of what he was facing. "Flat Nose, the ranch and everyone else on the Estancia has known you were coming since yesterday afternoon when you all met up at your campsite. They've had plenty of time to prepare. You aren't facing a single family living in a jacal, or badly built adobe home getting caught in a surprise raid. You're facing hardened farmers and vaqueros fighting from a large stone building. And they are expecting you. A few of your men may be able to make off with a few head of cattle but you, and the rest of your men, will be lying dead. I encourage you to make this easy on yourself, and surrender now."

Flat Nose gave me a sadistic smile. "Marshal, my name is Fulgencia Madrid not Flat Nose. You will die in just a few minutes, just for addressing me in such a manner. Not once, but twice. As for the ranch, I have eyes and can see the building from here so I know it's less than a mile away. The boss in Santa Fe wants you dead, and the ranch wiped out, as a lesson to everyone else in the valley. By the time we are done today the ranch building and the bunk house behind it will be destroyed. There won't be a building left standing at the ranch."

This time I couldn't help but give a loud laugh.

"Flat Nose, you are one stupid son of a bitch. I really expected more from a man who could lead as large a group of cutthroats as you've got here. Let me give you a little hint about what you face at the ranch, if you should get by me. The building you see is two stories tall and easily fifty times larger than any building you have ever raided.

"It looks so close because it's so big. It was built to house eighty vaqueros and their families. There are only two ways in, and both have long since been barricaded. Yes, there is a bunk house behind the ranch building. It has apartments for twenty single vaqueros. You are welcome to try and take it but you won't find anything there, as the single vaqueros moved into the ranch building last night. But enough of this chit chat. This is the last time I'm going to say it. Either surrender, or go for your guns."

I think I touched a raw nerve calling him Flat Nose publicly for the third time. He glared at me for another couple of moments then, keeping both hands on his saddle horn, he stood and swept his gaze in a 180-degree arc from the end of his line of men on the left past me, to the end of his men on the right. I knew he was playing for a little time to look things over and make sure he hadn't missed something obviously wrong.

When he was done he turned back to me. "Marshal, I told you when we started talking that you are a dead man. I don't listen to dead men. Even if you weren't dead, you are still lying to me so either way I'm not going to listen you. It's time to end this little game you've been playing. It's time for you to die."

I'd been halfway expecting him to have a saddle gun but the sight of him raising his hand from the saddle with a gun already in it still surprised me more than a little. It didn't slow me down any, though. I pulled the trigger on the shotgun three times as fast as I could get the barrel on target while taking two steps to my left to get what little protection the boulder could provide.

After the first blast of my shotgun bullets started flying from behind me and to my right as the men of the Estancia opened fire. I knew I'd hit Flat Nose with at least one of the shotgun blasts, as he was lifted off his horse and thrown backwards. His horse ran past me down the road and that probably saved my life as I saw it shudder from getting hit with at least three shots as it passed between me and the right side of Flat Nose's men.

By the time the horse passed me the fighting was over. All of the raiders were down on the ground along with several horses. Riderless horses were running off into the desert in every direction and those that weren't, were ground hitched and trembling.

I stepped out from behind the boulder and cussed as my right leg almost gave out from under me. Looking down I realized that either a lucky shot or a ricochet had torn most of the heel of my desert boot off. Grumbling to myself, I carefully stepped from behind the boulder and into the field.

After almost a full minute of looking at all the bodies I yelled back over my shoulder, "Tom, bring me two teams. George, check the men. I need a list of casualties and wounded. Everyone else stay ready. This may not be over, yet."

Tom came out from the arroyo leading the ten men I'd asked for. "Work in teams of two and check all the raiders. Be very careful, as some aren't dead and may be playing possum. One man checks, while the other guards him. Search each body for weapons, don't forget to check the boots. Throw any you find in piles well away from the bodies. Start a new pile after every five men."

They broke up into two-man teams, and started the grisly task I'd given them. When they were gone I turned my back to Tom and lifted my leg at the knee. "Do me a favor Tom. Use that pig sticker you carry and cut off what's left of my boot heel so I can walk without looking like I'm drunk."

Tom looked down at my heel, smiled, reached behind his back, and pulled out what to my way of thinking was a ridiculously large Bowie knife. When he'd finished carving the heel off my boot I thanked him and looked up to see George standing in front of me, holding my rifle out to me, and smiling.

"There are no fatal casualties to report, but there are five minor grazing wounds. Three arms, one shoulder, and one head. The head wound is bleeding a lot, of course, but it's just a graze," he said.

"That's great news, George. I'll say it again, you've done a hell of a job so far, and you were right! This was, indeed, a perfect killing field." I sighed at the thought of what was to come. "The fight may be over for now, but we have a lot of work to do. First thing first, though. Please get your signaler over here."

George turned and looked at the arroyo before putting his left hand in the air and pumping it twice. Before he'd turned back around to face me, the cousin who was his assigned signaler came running out of the arroyo.

He came to a stop next to George, and I told him, "Send the following signal. Battle over. No fatal casualties. Five lightly wounded, none serious. Wounded returning to Hacienda. Names to follow."

When it was clear I was done he turned towards the Robledo's and started sending the message after receiving the ready signal.

While he was sending I told George, "Give him the names to send when he's done, then get all the wagons and horses up here from the rally point. Use the first empty wagon that pulls up to send the wounded to the Hacienda."

George stayed with the signaler while Tom and I walked over to Flat Nose. He'd landed on his ass and was in a slouched sitting position. Using my foot, I gave his shoulder a small shove that sent him backward so that he was lying flat on his back. I'd hit him in the chest with at least two shotgun shots, as there wasn't much left between his neck and his waist. I don't know how long it took him to die, but he'd died too quickly as far as I was concerned.

George walked up telling us the messages had been sent. I nodded and thought for a minute. Sweeping my hand around in front of us I said, "This is a big mess, George. What do you intend to do about all the horses? Especially the dead horses."

George gave me another small grin. "I'm going to have the vaqueros round up all the horses they can find and bring them here for some of the men to ride back. I'll also have some of them drag the dead horses out to an arroyo or wash, push them over the side and cave the walls in on them."

I rubbed my jaw in thought for a moment and then gave him his new orders. "Good. After you've got that started I want you to send three Scout/Sniper teams out to back track the raiders and find out where they came from. When they find the main camp, I want two teams to remain and observe, while the third team comes back to lead you and eight teams to the camp. When you get there, I want you to end this once and for all. Arrest those you can, kill those who resist. I'm tired of people like these taking advantage of honest working people. Bring the bodies and prisoners to the office at Mesilla when you're done."

I turned to give Tom some tasks, and found two of the young cousins standing behind us. I gave them a curious look and started to ask George why they were here, when he said with a grin, "These are yours and Tom's signalers. I'm tired of you stealing mine."

He turned then, and walked off to start the tasks I'd given him.

I smiled at the two young men, clapped them on the back, and told them to stick close. "Tom, when the wagons start arriving, I want you to load the raiders in three groups of wagons. I want the dead loaded in one group of wagons, the dying in another group of wagons, and the wounded who will recover along with any unwounded in a third group of wagons.

"I want that third group well trussed up, hog tied would be nice, before they are loaded in the wagons. Make sure all the bodies are searched for papers and valuables before they're loaded. I want Flat Nose loaded on the lead wagon at the very top of the pile so he's easily seen. Pick out the drivers and shotgun guards for each wagon as well as eight teams to act as my escort to Mesilla."

Tom looked at me curiously for a second and then asked, "Eight teams? That's a little much, isn't it?"

Grinning, I replied, "It's time people saw just what we are capable of when pressed. Between the wagons loaded with dead bodies and the escorts I think they'll get the message I'm trying to send."

Tom grinned, nodded his head, and walked off with his signaler beside him.

It took fifteen more minutes for all the wagons

and horses to arrive and then the work really started. Tom and George rejoined me a few minutes later and we watched the activities for a couple of minutes.

Tom eventually broke the silence. "Paul, there are seventy-nine dead or dying and seven lightly wounded. The lightly wounded are tied up and sitting over by the road out of the way."

"Thanks, Tom," I replied. "Bring me the lightly wounded one at a time with a couple of guards."

The first prisoner was a surly young man who would only tell me his name. I made a big fuss smiling continuously at him, clapping him enthusiastically on the shoulder, and laughing like he'd said something funny. Finally, I told Tom to take him over to the boulder, and sit him down under guard before bringing me the next prisoner.

The next prisoner Tom brought me was a little older, and answered my questions readily enough.

When he said his name was Bernardo I acted quite surprised. "I'm surprised at how young you are Bernardo. Your friend Estefan over there told me you were one of Flat Nose's Lieutenants and knew where the camp was, who in Santa Fe was telling Flat Nose what to do, and what the future plans were. Yes, sir, I'm real surprised at how young you are."

Bernardo was visibly upset and angrily replied, "Estefan is an idiot. I'm the same as him. As far as Flat Nose was concerned we were both peons. We did what we were told to do, when we were told to do it, and were never told anything. Our job was to hold the horses when the men attacked. The only one left who might know the answers to any of your questions is Scar Face. He's the only one of Flat Nose's Lieutenants left alive."

I told the two guards to take Bernardo over to the other side of the boulder from his friend, and not to let them talk. When they walked away with Bernardo I turned to Tom.

"Tom, bring me the rest of the prisoners, one at a time. Save Scar Face for last."

Tom grinned at me, and walked back over to get another prisoner.

While we were waiting George said, "Well played, cousin. I'm impressed."

I must admit I was enjoying the little game I was playing and hoped that it would pay some dividends.

"It's a start, George. Hopefully by the time I'm done with Scar Face we'll learn something of value. Is Miguel here?"

George said he was, and I asked my new signaler to go find Miguel and ask him to come see me with two of his fiercest looking warriors. The signaler ran past Tom as he was arriving with the next prisoner.

Three of the next four prisoners talked willingly enough but they didn't provide much in the way of additional information. Apparently Flat Nose didn't give out much information to anyone outside his closest circle of Lieutenants, and they only talked to the rank and file to give orders. The fourth prisoner never said a word, and I felt like I was talking to myself. In disgust, I sent him over to the boulder with the others and told Tom to bring me Scar Face.

Miguel walked up with two of the cousins and we all greeted each other warmly. The two cousins he'd brought were middle aged, and their bodies bore scars from the tough life they'd lead before coming to the Estancia. The combination of their age, the scars, and the way they held themselves, screamed that they were highly capable warriors.

I explained why I'd asked for them to join me. "Gentlemen, the prisoner Tom is bringing over here has information I want. When they get here speak only Apache, and follow my lead. I'm going to try and scare him into giving me the information. Do whatever you think might help me get that information short of killing him."

Miguel grinned and said, "This sounds like it will be much more fun than loading dead bodies." The other two nodded, and the three of them laughed.

While we were waiting for Tom and Scar Face to join us, I asked them what they'd been doing since yesterday afternoon. It turned out that they had each been with one of the Scout/Sniper teams on the hills behind the arroyo. The hills were close enough that they used their rifles when the shooting started. We were laughing about Flat Nose and the certainty he had about succeeding on the raid when Tom came walking up leading Scar Face with his two escorts.

I stopped talking to the cousins and addressed Scar Face. "Ah, Scar Face, or do you prefer to be addressed as Rueben Rodriquez?" I stopped and waited for a response from the scowling man. When I didn't get one I continued unperturbed. "Well, since it doesn't matter to you, I'll just continue to call you Scar Face. Now, your friends over there by the boulder all tell me that you were Flat Nose's right-hand man, and his main Lieutenant. They also assured me you could tell me where the main camp is, who the leader in Santa Fe is, and what the leader's plans are. So, please, I'm all ears and ready to hear what you have to say."

When he remained silent I gave him a gloomy look. "You might as well start talking Scar Face because if you don't, then my friends here..." I stopped abruptly putting a startled look on my face and then continued a moment later. "Oh! Where are my manners? I haven't introduced my friends. This is Kills Slowly, the leader of the local Apache. The men with him are his Lieutenants. The man on his right is Knife Killer and the man on his left is Kills While Talking. Well, that's what their Apache names translate to anyway. I can't wrap my tongue around their Apache names, so please excuse me for not trying. Now, where was I? Oh yes, if you refuse to answer my questions, or can't answer them, then my friends here will take you off my hands. They assure me that I will have all the answers I need long before this time tomorrow. It seems the three of them have a contest. They compete against each other when they have a prisoner. Well, it's really two contests rolled into one. It tests their skills at skinning, and it tests the bravery of their prisoner as a warrior."

Miguel broke in at that point. "Does this man know anything about the Apache?"

I shrugged my shoulder and looked over my shoulder at Miguel. "I don't know. I don't think he understands the Apache language and if he's like most of these comancheros he doesn't think you're very bright. Is he acting like he understands what we are saying, or like he knows anything about the Apache?"

Miguel grunted and shook his head no.

I turned back to Scar Face. "Please excuse the interruption. They are getting a little impatient with all the talking. They're a little put out because they got here late this morning and missed their chance at having fun during the gun fight. They are really looking forward to the entertainment you are going to provide. What entertainment you ask? Well, like all Apache, these three are really good with their knives. Now, I've never seen them do it myself, but from what I understand they skin the prisoner by peeling off a one-inch wide strip of skin at a time. They start just under the chin and go all the way down to the toes before turning and going back up to the chin. The contest for them is how long those inch-wide strips are. I'm told that Kills While Talking is the current champion having peeled a 22-foot-long strip of skin before it broke the last time they played this game."

The scowl never left Scar Face's lips, but as I

talked his eyes began to take on a frightened wild look and his face began to pale. "So, what's it going to be Scar Face? Are you going to answer my questions or not?"

Scar Face remained silent although by this point I wasn't sure if it was from defiance or fright. I shrugged and waved the two cousins forward. They walked over to Scar Face and, each taking an arm, lifted him onto his toes walking him towards the arroyo.

They'd taken about ten steps when Scar Face started blabbering saying over and over that he'd tell me anything I wanted to know. After they'd taken three more steps I stopped the cousins and told them to bring him back to me. When he was back in front of me the cousins released his arms and walked back over to stand with Miguel.

Miguel said in Apache, "I think you have his attention now, Pablo. It will be interesting to see what he has to say."

"I think you're right. Look impatient and upset for the next few minutes if you would please. Maybe one of you can take out a knife and start sharpening it in a few minutes," I replied, also in Apache.

"My friends are more than a little upset with me now, Scar Face. I don't like to upset my friends. If you lie to me I will give you back to them, and I won't stop them again. This is the only chance you have so start talking," I said.

For the next half hour, we all listened as Scar Face answered my questions. Much of what he said was of no use, but we did learn a few things.

The main camp was a hard-three-day ride northwest of Mesilla in a large canyon on the Gila River. They'd left ten men to guard the camp and the seven prisoners they had. The camp wasn't expecting them back for another seven days.

Flat Nose had selected Scar Face as his main Lieutenant, because Scar Face could speak English, and the leader in Santa Fe didn't speak Spanish very well. Scar Face didn't know where the leader and Flat Nose had met, but Scar Face was introduced to him on a visit to the Comancheria last year.

His name was never spoken, and he was always addressed and referred to as Boss or the leader. He described the leader as about George's height, with short blond hair and blue eyes. Even in the Comancheria he wore a fancy suit and a funny little round hat. The leader had mentioned being from some place back east called Jersey and that his brother was the commander of one of the forts in the Mesilla Valley.

The leader's plan was to take over the Mesilla Valley. Using the valley as a base he intended to take control of all of Doña Ana County and eventually the entire Territory. How the leader was going to do this Scar Face didn't know.

The final thing Scar Face told us, was that there was a large network of people in Mesilla who were helping Flat Nose. He didn't know the names of everyone in the network, but he did give us a few names.

When I was sure that Scar Face had told us all he knew that was of value, I had the guards escort him over to the boulder. When they were out of earshot I turned to the others and asked for their thoughts.

Tom said, "We need to hit that camp, and free those prisoners like you talked about. The rest of the information is useful but besides the people who helped them in Mesilla, there's nothing there we can really act on for now."

Everyone agreed with Tom, so I turned to George, "Get what food is left from the food wagons and take six teams. Follow the Scout/Sniper teams you sent out. When you catch up to them, tell them what we learned and go hit that camp. Bring me back some prisoners if you can. Bring the bodies and any prisoners to

Esteban and Ed in Mesilla."

George nodded. "It'll be a pleasure!"

I turned to Tom. "Make sure the eight teams going with me are all vaqueros. Before you ask, it's because I don't want to be flashing our rifles around Mesilla and the vaqueros all have scabbards. The farm teams don't."

Tom grinned and said, "That's a good reason, and one everyone will understand."

He then left to get the drivers, riders, and eight teams organized.

I turned to Miguel. "You're in charge of Estancia defenses until George gets back. Please get everyone who isn't going with George or I, headed back home."

He smiled at me, clapped me on the shoulder, and said, "This was fun. The families will enjoy hearing the story of how you tricked the man into talking. Safe travels, Thundercloud."

Then they were gone and I was left standing alone in the middle of the killing field. The last few bodies were being loaded in a wagon and all the dead horses had been dragged away to an arroyo, somewhere. Except for some blood-stains that would soon disappear, there wasn't anything left to tell anyone about what happened here.

George walked over leading his horse and told me he and his teams were ready to go and were leaving, now. I gave him the same advice he'd given me about not being a hero as I didn't want to tell Celia her man was dead.

He laughed. "I'll try to remember that advice," he said as he mounted up.

"George, one final caution," I said seriously. "Someone once said, 'Whoever fights monsters should see to it that in the process he docs not become a monster.' Please remember that out there."

When he was settled in his saddle, he gave me a nod. He looked back over his shoulder, gave a shrill whistle to get his teams attention, and waved his arm forward spurring his horse as he rode into the desert followed a few seconds later by the eight teams going with him.

Tom walked up with Steve just as the last of the George's teams passed by. "The bodies and prisoners are all loaded, Paul, and the teams are ready to go."

"Thanks, Tom, I'll be leaving as soon as I send a message," I told him.

Turning to my signaler, I asked him if he was ready to send a message for me. When he grinned and said he was, I started giving him the message.

"To the Estancia from me. George leading eight teams to main comanchero camp to rescue prisoners. Expect them back in ten days. I am taking bodies and prisoners to Mesilla with eight teams. Will return tomorrow. Tom is returning to the Estancia with the rest of the teams. My love to Anna and the family."

When I was done he repeated the message verbatim and at my nod started signaling with his mirror.

Tom and I walked over to the road where our saddled horses were waiting for us. While we waited for the signaler to complete his message and get an acknowledgement back, I put my rifle in its scabbard, and checked the cinches on my horse. We were both mounted in our saddles when the signaler ran up and said that the message was sent and acknowledged. I thanked him before turning to Tom.

"Make sure this young man gets back please, Tom. Give everyone the rest of the day off, they've certainly earned it. They'll probably want to do a little celebrating, too. I should be back tomorrow afternoon, sometime."

I had just finished talking when I caught a signal flash from the mountains. My signaler flashed a ready to receive acknowledgment, and the flashes from the mountain started in. The cousins were getting really good at sending signals. The flashes were so fast I was having a hard time keeping up.

A few moments later the signaler turned to me and said, "Message to you from Doña Anna. She will meet you in Las Cruces tomorrow, with Yolanda, Tom and the kids. Stay safe until then. All her love until she sees you again."

I grinned at the signaler and told him to acknowledge, which he quickly did. I shook Tom's hand, telling him 'the ladies have spoken!' I'd keep his chair out back of the stable warm until he got to Las Cruces. I could hear him laughing as I rode to the front of the wagons and waved them forward.

CHAPTER 14

I led a procession of four teams, the wagons, and the final four teams down the road. Instead of staying on the Camino Real to Mesilla, I detoured to Las Cruces, rode down the middle of Main Street and then on to Mesilla. By the time the day was done, everyone in Las Cruces and Mesilla was going to know who I was and that neither I nor the Estancia Dos Santos was to be trifled with.

Entering Mesilla, I slowed my horse until I was beside the lead vaquero. "Rodrigo, when we get to the plaza, I want you to unload the bodies from the wagons and lay them out in neat rows. Leave the prisoners in their wagon for now but make sure they are well guarded. I'll join you after I've talked to my Deputies."

At his nod, I cantered off down the street to the office. Inside, I was greeted by Esteban and Ed. I told them I had some bodies and prisoners following me, and we needed to get some things done.

"Esteban, get the last full set of papers the Judge sent, and come over to the plaza with me. Ed, please go round up the Mayor, Town Marshal, Probate Judge, Justice of the Peace, Sheriff Bean if he's in town, and the bartenders from the saloons. Have them meet me in the plaza. Make it clear this is an order not a request. If they give you any gruff arrest them for impeding a federal investigation and bring them to the plaza at gun point."

That got them moving. Ed put on his hat and grabbed his shotgun as he went out the door. Esteban opened a drawer in his desk and pulled out a stack of paper almost twelve inches thick, before grabbing his hat and following me out the door.

We stopped just outside the door to watch as the four wagons full of bodies and the wagon of prisoners rolled by, followed by the four teams of vaqueros. We walked to the front of the plaza arriving just in time for the first of the bodies to be lifted out of the wagon.

"Esteban, we have seventy-eight bodies to identify, and hopefully there's some paper on more than a few of them. The first body they laid down is Flat Nose and I know we have paper on him." I said.

Esteban gave a low whistle of surprise at the number of bodies. "You're going to have to tell us how this happened Paul. It should prove to be an interesting story."

"I'll let you read the report later tonight. You and Ed are invited to supper at the restaurant in Las Cruces."

While the vaqueros started laying a second row of bodies Esteban, and I began trying to identify the bodies in the first row. It took us fifteen minutes to complete the first row and we were able to identify five of the twelve bodies. We were about to start on the second row, when Ed walked up herding all the people I'd asked him to bring. He was pointing his shotgun at three of the bartenders, and telling them to get a move on.

They stopped in a group at the front of the plaza and stared at the bodies laid out by the vaqueros in neat orderly rows. I walked over and paced back forth in front of them for a minute.

"Gentlemen - and I use that term very loosely in your regard - you all know, or should know, who I am. Under normal circumstances, regardless of how I feel about you personally, I would greet you with a good day. However, these aren't normal circumstances, and it's definitely not a good day. It's not a good day for these men you see laid out in front of you, and it's not a good day for you unless some things change, and change quickly."

I stared each man in the eyes moving from one to the next before continuing. "This morning, just after sunrise, eighty-six comancheros led by Flat Nose attacked the Estancia Dos Santos. As you can see they didn't succeed. In fact, they failed, and failed miserably.

"Of the men who attacked the Estancia seventy-nine are dead and lay in front of you. The other seven men, including Flat Nose's chief Lieutenant, were lightly wounded and are now my prisoners. Those seven men will be kept in the county jail here for a few days, before being transported to Santa Fe for trial. Living on the frontier as we do, I expect raids by Indians or bandits at any moment, so I'm not too upset by that. I don't like it, but I'm not too upset by it."

I put my hands behind my back and paced in front of them for another minute appearing to be deep in thought before speaking again. "What I'm upset about, what I'm mad about, what I'm *damned angry* about, is the fact that for almost two years each of you, or the people in your employ, have lied multiple times directly to my Deputies and indirectly to me."

I stopped in front of the three bartenders and

stared at each of them. Sheriff Bean picked that moment to get huffy and try to throw his weight around.

"Marshal, I resent the insinuation that me or my Deputies have been lying to anyone," he said.

"Sheriff, I don't give a damn what you like or don't like. You have two full time Deputies, don't you?" When he acknowledged that he did I said, "And you hired those Deputies yourself didn't you?" He grudgingly acknowledged that he had hired them. "Where are those Deputies now, Sheriff?"

The Sheriff looked around and not seeing his Deputies gave a shrug and said, "They're probably in the office at the courthouse."

"That's a curious thing, don't you think, Sheriff? Four wagon loads of dead bodies roll into town, and yet twenty minutes later there's still not a sign of the Deputies who should care about something like that."

I turned to the Town Marshal. "The same thing can be said about your Deputy as well Marshal. Where can we find your Deputy?"

The Town Marshal glared at me for a moment before grudgingly saying, "He's probably with the Sheriff's Deputies in the Courthouse."

"Esteban, Ed, go over to the courthouse and arrest all three of them for aiding and abetting known felons both before and after the fact in the commission of the crimes of murder, kidnapping, rape, and theft. Don't take any chances with them, they probably know that you're coming."

When Esteban and Ed walked into the courthouse I continued with my little speech. "Now gentlemen like I was saying the next time you or one of your employees lies to my Deputies you and them will be arrested for making a false statement to a federal official and impeding a federal investigation. You will be sent to Santa Fe in chains and tried in federal court. Do you understand what I'm telling you? This ends now!"

I stopped talking just as a muffled shot rang out from inside the courthouse across the street. A moment later Esteban came out the door and waved, yelling that everything was fine before disappearing back inside.

I called Rodrigo over and asked him, in Apache, if he had paper and pencil with him. When he said that he did I told him what I wanted him to do. He grinned in reply, and walked over to stand at the head of Flat Nose.

I turned to the town leaders and had them follow me over to stand at the feet of Flat Nose. "Now gentlemen, I have seventy-nine bodies to identify and you're going to help me do it. If you lie and say you don't know who someone was, you will be arrested and sent to Santa Fe with the others. All of you look at this body and someone tell me who it is."

The Mayor, the Town Marshal, and two of the bartenders all identified him as Fulgencio Madrid, also known as Flat Nose.

Rodrigo asked the two bartenders for their names and wrote them down in his little book.

"See, gentlemen, that wasn't so hard now, was it? Only seventy-eight more bodies to go."

We were halfway done with the first row, when Esteban and Ed came out the courthouse door pushing two men with their hands tied in front of them. Two other men followed them carrying another body.

Esteban told the men to stop in front of me. "Sorry it took so long, Paul. These two and the other Sheriff's Deputy over there decided to rob the county clerk and the land office before leaving out the back door. We caught them coming out of the Land Office and that one pulled a gun on us. Ed got him as you can see, and we arrested the other two. We had to find and untie the county clerk and the land office clerk, before we could bring these three out."

"Good job guys, and well done. Put the dead one in the last row, and then start trying to find paper on the rest of these guys where we left off earlier," I directed.

I returned to the town leaders, and we continued our efforts while Esteban and Ed checked each body against the wanted posters and warrants.

Two hours later we were done. Of the eighty bodies laid out on the plaza, we'd identified all but four and had paper on twenty-six of them. I had Scar Face brought over and he identified the four unknown bodies telling us what he could about them before I sent him back to the wagon.

I told the town leaders to stay where they were until I got back and then led Esteban, Ed, and Rodrigo a few yards away where Rodrigo gave me the note pad he'd been writing in, and I gave them instructions.

Rodrigo had the prisoners brought down off the wagon, and then led the vaqueros and wagons out of Mesilla to Las Cruces where I'd rejoin them at Mr. Mendoza's stable. Esteban guarded the prisoners while Ed went over to the office, to write up the report on the Deputies robbing the county clerk and land office clerk.

I returned to the town leaders. "Gentlemen, I hope you take the lesson from today's activity to heart. I won't be so lenient the next time. Mayor, unless you want the plaza to stink to high heaven, I suggest you get the undertaker and arrange for immediate burial of these men. Since the three Deputies you recommended have been arrested on federal charges, I'm confiscating their possessions and turning them over to you, to use for the burials. If their possessions don't cover the cost, then you'll just have to cover it out of your budget. I'd like the Judge, Justice of the Peace, and Sheriff to stay for a few more minutes but the rest of you can go on about your business."

When everyone else was out of earshot I gave the three men a hard stare. "I don't like the things I'm hearing about the way you three have been operating. The rumors about you all handing out light fines to your friends, while sentencing those you don't like to maximum prison lengths are rampant. The next time I hear a rumor of that sort, I'm going to have to investigate, and I *will* find the truth, gentleman. If even part of that rumor is true, you will be looking at a trip to Santa Fe, a trial in federal court, and probably jail time in the territorial prison. That's all I wanted to say. You other two can go but I still need a few words with the

Sheriff."

When the others had left I said, "Sheriff, I believe you're an honest and fair man but unfortunately you tend to listen to the wrong people. People like the Mayor and your brother Roy. I suggest you seriously consider doing the exact opposite of anything the Mayor advises, and get your brother under control.

"Now, you have nine prisoners who are going to be in your jail cells for the next ten days or so before my Deputies take them to Santa Fe. Unless you want to live in the courthouse until then, and guard those prisoners yourself, I suggest you find new trustworthy Deputies immediately. My Deputies and I will guard the prisoners until five this evening, when I expect you back."

Sheriff Bean clearly didn't like being talked to like I'd been talking to him especially by a much younger man, but he nodded his head and started to turn away.

"Sheriff, one final word of caution for you and your new Deputies. Those prisoners will be in your care. If they escape I will arrest you and the Deputies for aiding and abetting. Likewise, if any of them die, I will arrest you and your Deputies for murder."

With a clenched jaw, he hurried away to find his new Deputies.

Esteban and I led the prisoners into the jail cells in the courthouse and locked them up, before sitting down at the desks in the Sheriff's office. I rummaged around in the Sheriff's desk, until I found paper and a pencil. When I had everything I needed I told Esteban I would watch the prisoners, if he would be good enough to track down some coffee and sandwiches for us. He laughed and walked out the door, saying he'd be back in a few minutes.

I was hard at work on my report when Esteban returned with a large pot of coffee. Ed followed him in, carrying a plate of sandwiches, his report, and the papers on the dead comancheros. I thanked them and grabbed a sandwich with a cup of coffee before returning to my report. Esteban and Ed talked quietly and took turns checking the prisoners frequently while I wrote.

I finally finished and signed the report. I added the wanted posters and warrants with deceased written across them, and also Ed's report signed by Esteban and Ed. We hunted around the office until we found a large sheet of brown wrapping paper and twine to wrap everything in.

The Sheriff and his two new Deputies showed up while we were waiting for Ed to return from putting the package to the Judge in the mail. I gave the new Deputies the same warning I'd given the sheriff about the prisoners, and Esteban and I walked outside to wait for Ed. Ed came around the corner less than a minute later, and we all walked down to the stable, saddled our horses and rode to Las Cruces.

By the time we got to Las Cruces I was bone tired. We turned our horses over to the stable boys, and talked to the vaqueros who were lounging around the stables, most with a beer. Eventually we made our way out behind the stables, and found Mr. Mendoza sitting at the table working on harnesses as expected. He greeted us with a smile, and told us he'd heard from the vaqueros that we'd had a busy day. I snorted, and told him that was an understatement.

I sat and vegetated for what remained of the afternoon and listened to Esteban and Ed talking with Mr. Mendoza, until he said it was time for supper. We walked in the back door, watched the kitchen dance for a few moments, and went to the family dining room.

Mrs. Mendoza followed us in with coffee, and gave me a hug and cheek kiss before disappearing back into the kitchen. Over the next several minutes all the ladies of the Mendoza clan came in and gave me a hug and cheek kiss as well.

Supper was the normal affair much like supper at the Hacienda only a little tamer with only one language being spoken. The vaqueros had spread the word of what happened this morning, and this afternoon, so I didn't get many questions about those activities. When Mrs. Mendoza asked how Anna and Yolanda were doing, I suddenly realized everyone was waiting for news about the Estancia.

I grinned at Mrs. Mendoza. "Anna and Yolanda are fine as is everyone on the Estancia. You'll be able to talk to Anna, Yolanda, and Tom tomorrow at lunch, as they're bringing your two great grandsons for a visit." When the table had settled back down I continued. "Cousin George has left the Army, and now leads the Estancia Militia. It was his plan that allowed us to beat the comancheros this morning. He also proposed to Celia, so you can expect to get invitations as soon as the date is set."

I gave them any other news I thought was worthy of their attention, and everyone appeared pleased with my efforts. There were going to be a lot more surprises over the next few days, but those would be revealed in private discussions with the appropriate people.

I drank a couple of cups of coffee after supper, just to be sociable, and turned in early. I was as mentally exhausted as I ever remembered being. Just before I drifted off to sleep I heard Laura's soft sweet voice in my left ear.

"You did extremely well, today. I'm very proud of you, and the man you're becoming."

After breakfast the next morning, I sent the vaqueros and wagons home with a message I'd written to Hector. I told Esteban and Ed to be ready to leave for Santa Fe with the prisoners in ten days, and that I would send twenty men to them as escorts for the trip.

As they were mounting their horses for the trip back to Mesilla Esteban asked me to bring Anna for a visit, as he had something he wanted both of us to see. Curious at what he wanted to show us I told him we'd stop by sometime tomorrow afternoon.

With business over for the time being, I paid a quick visit to Mrs. Amador's store and picked up a new pair of boots, so I could quit limping around. Boots in hand, I walked over to the barbers and had a quick bath, before settling in for a much-needed haircut and shave. When I walked out an hour later, I was looking good. Even my clothes didn't look too bad as I'd had them brushed out while I was bathing.

I stopped by my favorite store on the way back to the stable, and said hello to Dolores Delgado, letting her know that Anna and Yolanda should be in town this afternoon for a visit. As I was leaving, Dolores told me she was looking forward to negotiating with Anna, as it was boring since she'd married me and left to live on the Estancia. I laughed as I walked out, thinking she was certainly going to be surprised the next time she met with us.

Back at the stables I found Mr. Mendoza at his usual spot, and spent the rest of the morning picking his brain about the best place in El Paso to get luxurious and comfortable travel coaches made. It was his opinion that the only place to get a coach like I'd described, was the Rodriquez Brothers in El Paso Del Norte.

From there we turned to talking about a wagon for transporting prisoners to Santa Fe. I told him I'd decided that Esteban and Ed needed a purpose-built wagon, that would keep the prisoners secured and the Deputies safe while they traveled.

He shrugged, and after a moment of thought said almost any wainwright could build what I needed. From his point of the view, the problem was going to be specifying exactly what I wanted built into the wagon to secure the prisoners. I was mulling over his comments, when we heard horses and a wagon coming into the stable yard along with Tom's voice.

Mr. Mendoza and I hurried out to the stable yard, arriving just in time for me to catch Anna in my arms as she dropped down from her horse. I hugged her tightly, and swung her around in a circle a couple of times. She giggled delightedly before I set her down, and gave her a big hug and long kiss. When we were done we turned and found Mr. Mendoza, a baby in each arm, walking towards the restaurant with Yolanda following behind him. I smiled at Anna as she hurried after Yolanda, catching up to her just outside the door.

I looked at the heavily loaded wagons with water pipes sticking out of the back from under the end of a tied down canvas and wondered why they'd brought that from the Hacienda. I turned to ask Tom and realized that Steve was standing next to Tom. My mind clicked, and I looked at Tom with a questioning look. He gave a brief nod, and I knew that hidden under the canvas sheet and pipes were 10,000 pounds of gold bars in burlap bags. I clapped both men on the shoulders, as I walked by telling them it was good to see them again, and it was time for lunch.

Tom led us back to our normal table in the restaurant, and one of Anna and Yolanda's younger cousins brought us our lunch and coffee almost immediately. The three of us ate our lunch and quietly talked about the timing of our plans for the next few days.

When I mentioned that Esteban wanted us to meet him in Mesilla tomorrow afternoon, it was decided that Steve and Tom would go with us. While Anna and I were with Esteban, Tom, and Steve would go on a buying spree. That decision allowed us to make another quick timing decision.

We would hold the meeting we needed to have with a few selected guests the day after the buying spree. That was as far as we could go with the timing, as everything else would depend on the reaction we got during our meeting.

Anna and Yolanda periodically came out to check on us while we were eating and talking. I let her know that we needed to be in Mesilla tomorrow afternoon, to meet with Esteban. At her curious look, I told her I didn't know why, just that Esteban had requested it. She nodded and asked about our plans for the rest of the day.

I laughed and told her unless she'd brought me some clean clothes, I was going to spend the bulk of the afternoon getting some new clothes. If she had brought clean clothes we were going to be in our usual spot, at the stables. She laughed delightedly at the thought of me shopping for clothes, before telling me she'd brought me a week's worth of clean clothes.

Tom and I left Steve sitting with Mr. Mendoza at the table behind the stables, telling them we were going to see if we could find Juan and Jorge. We found Juan out in his yard with two workers, doing an inventory of his building supplies. He turned as we walked up and gave us a big smile.

"Los hombres malos! You honor my humble establishment with this visit." he said.

I looked at Tom in confusion. "What the hell are you going on about Juan?"

Juan was laughing hard by this point. Tom was just as confused as I was, and we stood there for almost a minute, while Juan tried to get himself under control. Almost a full minute later he finally had enough control to tell us to come inside, and we'd have some coffee while we talked. He turned and led us inside still laughing.

Tom and I sat down at a small table in the back corner of the room, as Juan poured three cups of coffee from the stove behind the counter and brought them over. Juan sat down taking a drink of his coffee, and then sat back smacking his lips, and giving a deep sigh of appreciation. He looked at us with a smile still on his lips.

"So, los hombres malos, not that I don't appreciate seeing you, but what brings you to my little corner of Las Cruces?" he asked.

With confusion still on my face I replied. "Juan, we just stopped by to visit an old friend while we're in town. What the hell is going on, and why are you calling us bad men?"

Juan laughed lightly. "That is what everyone is calling anyone from the Estancia. I've heard many things since you rode through the middle of town, yesterday. You were leading a private army with five wagons full of dead and captured comancheros.

"Both Las Cruces and Mesilla are abuzz with talk about los hombres malos who wiped out a gang of cut throat comancheros that had been terrorizing the entire valley for almost two years. When they were done wiping out the gang, they brought the bodies to Mesilla, and laid them out in the plaza where the leader publicly chewed out the appointed and elected county and town officials along with a few prominent businessmen.

"Yes, he chewed them out for not doing their jobs, told them they were liars, and then threatened to arrest them and take them to prison if it happened again. But it didn't stop there. He killed a corrupt Deputy Sheriff, arrested another Deputy Sheriff, and a Deputy Town Marshal for robbing the county clerk and land office, threw them in jail with a handful of comancheros and then told the Sheriff that if any of the prisoners escaped or were killed he would take the Sheriff to prison in their place. Did I miss anything?"

I groaned and before I could stop myself said, "Oh, shit!"

Now Tom was laughing with Juan. "You didn't tell us any of that, Paul. You really are an hombre malo," he said.

Juan looked over at Tom. "You weren't paying attention, Tom. That name is being applied to anyone from the Estancia. Paul is the leader, true, and everyone knows that; but they also know it took the entire Estancia to kill the comancheros! Then they saw the little army he brought with him to the plaza. So, my friend, you too are an hombre malo, and not to be trifled with."

Juan shifted his gaze to me. "You made a few enemies yesterday, my friend, but you made many more friends. Especially in Mesilla, where you aren't as well-known as you are here."

I shook my head feeling a little dismayed. "Some of that was supposed to be private. I did expect some reaction, but this is much more than I expected," I said.

Juan shrugged. "People talk, Paul. And the talk among the people so far is all positive. The fact that everyone you threatened - except the Mayor - was an Anglo, did not go unnoticed, my friend. It meant far more to the people of Mesilla than it would have if it had happened here."

I rubbed my hand over my face. "Well, I guess I'll just have to live with it, for now. What's done is done," I replied. "So how have things been going with you, Juan? How's Jorge doing?"

"Things are going well, Paul. Between the construction business and the fees I charge for finding things no one else seems to be able to find, I manage to keep everyone employed and paid, and still have a little profit. I'd like to have more work and employ a lot more workers, but I can't really complain. Jorge is doing well although he'd like a little more work, too. Right now, he's down in El Paso delivering a set of drawings to Fort Bliss, but he should be back late today or tomorrow," he answered.

We talked about his business for a few more minutes. He got up and refilled our cups before sitting back down with a large grin on his face.

"I was going to send you this next bit of news in a short letter with Mrs. Amador's next delivery, but since you're here, I'll tell you now."

He took a sip of coffee prolonging my wait and anticipation. I knew that if he was this excited it must be good news indeed. Finally, I couldn't wait any longer.

"Out with it, Juan! What news?"

Juan's grin got even bigger. "Sometime in the next two or three weeks you will be receiving a thousand young pecan trees. You owe me a hundred and ten dollars, and you will owe the freight driver another thirty on delivery."

Both Tom and I were speechless.

Tom recovered first. "Where in the world did you find a thousand pecan trees for that kind of price?"

With a laugh in his voice, Juan told us the story.

"A farmer in Chihuahua ordered and paid for them, but he died before delivery. The freight company hadn't been paid for hauling them, so they were selling them to recover the freight cost. I offered ten cents a tree as an opening offer, and was completely surprised when it was accepted without a counter. The extra ten dollars is my finder's fee."

I laughed and told him, "Your fee is well worth it. Jesus and Tomas will be ecstatic when we tell them."

As Tom and I walked back to the stables a couple of hours later he said, "Juan and Jorge are really going to appreciate the extra work, if we can pull off the buying spree and the meeting."

I grinned at Tom. "Yep, it'll be our turn to surprise him, for a change."

Anna and I talked in bed that night and I filled her in on our visit with Juan. She laughed when I told her about Juan's greeting and the gossip was all about the comancheros, and my plaza performance in Mesilla. She was really excited though when I gave her the news about the pecan trees.

"Mi, Pablo, that's great news! It will be nice to see the Estancia at least partially planted this year and the addition of all those pecan trees will make it all that much more real," she said.

I agreed with her and then told her about the plans for tomorrow and our decision to hold the meeting the day after.

She was quiet for a moment. "That fits nicely with what Yolanda and I decided. I'll give grandmother the list of people we want invited to the meeting. I'll tell her that the invitation must come from her and grandfather, and that the meeting will last at least four hours. We can deliver Esteban's invitation when we go see him, tomorrow. Let's plan on leaving for Mesilla at ten, and having lunch at that little cantina."

I looked down at the top of her head laying on my chest. "That sounds like a plan, my love. Now tell me about the decisions that you and Yolanda have made."

Anna sighed heavily. A moment later she lifted her head from my shoulder and looked me in the eye.

"I'm not looking forward to being separated from you for the next few months, mi Pablo. Yolanda isn't looking forward to being separated from Tom any more than I am. Please don't take this as us trying to push you two away," she said with teary eyes.

I gently reached down and thumbed away the tears from eyes before leaning down and giving her a soft kiss. "I won't, my love, now tell me what decisions you've made, that make you think I'll take them as being pushed away," I said tenderly.

She gave another softer sigh and gave me a

small trembling smile.

"With our plans being accelerated, the gold trips have become much more critical. We can't afford to miss a single trip. Between the comanchero threat and working on changing the plans, we're pushing being able to get a trip in this year and still get back before the rainy season.

"Neither Yolanda nor I want you or Tom anywhere near the mountains during the rainy season. We decided that you and Tom would leave on your trip nine days from today. During those nine days we need to get the land bought for the various plans, convince the people in the meeting to participate in our plans, take Steve to El Paso with a wagon load of gold, get him the bank drafts to cover the purchase of the salt flats, and get back here to say goodbye.

"Before we left the Hacienda, I told Hector to send four teams here to provide escort duty. They will arrive in three days. You, Tom, and Steve will leave for El Paso the next morning. Two teams will escort Steve from El Paso to Austin and back to the Hacienda as planned. The other two teams will escort you and Tom back here before they go back to the Estancia.

"You will have a night to rest, and the next morning you and Tom will leave to mine gold. I've already talked to grandfather and he will have a good freight wagon ready for you with a six-mule team and enough feed for three months. He will also have two mules with panniers full of supplies. If you and Tom push the mules hard, you should be able to make Arroyo La Paz on the river in less than three weeks.

"That gives you six weeks to mine as much gold as you can, and eight weeks to get back to the Hacienda with a quick stop in Santa Fe. The last week of your trip will be the normal start of the rainy season; so please, my love, be careful."

Finished, she laid her head back down on my shoulder and gave me a long hug.

This time it was my turn to let out a small sigh. "As usual, your logic is unassailable, my love. We can't wait any longer to start our trip. Either Tom or I need to make a quick trip back to the Hacienda, though. We need the metal detector, shovels, molds, gas canisters, and heating head nozzles, if we're going to make this work."

I felt Anna lips smile against my chest as I heard her say, "In the front of the wagon just behind the drivers box you'll find a large rough built but sturdy box. In that box is everything you just said you needed, plus three complete sets of travel clothes and a pair of boots for both you and Tom."

I smiled at that, gave her a quick hug and kissed the top of her head. "Excellent planning. What would I do without you, mi querida?"

"You would have realized the same thing in a couple of days and then scrambled to come up with a different plan to make it happen my love. I've seen you do it before so I'm sure that's what would happen," she replied sleepily.

Comfortably cuddled, we both drifted off to sleep.

CHAPTER 15

"**W**hat do you mean something funny is going on in the land office, Paul?" Steve asked.

Tom, Steve, and I were in the family dining room going over our land plans one last time, after finishing a large breakfast. Anna, Yolanda, and the boys were with Mrs. Mendoza over in the house writing up the invitations after she agreed to host the meeting tomorrow.

"I'm not sure what, but something just wasn't right about the map in the land office when we were there the other day. In all the excitement at the time I didn't stop to take a closer look at it, and then I forgot all about it until I woke up this morning." I explained.

It had been Laura's sweet voice whispering in my ear as I was waking up this morning, as she told me something wasn't right with the map in the land office. When I'd opened my eyes, the first thing I saw was Anna's eye's staring back at me. Her first words were that Great Grandfather Jaime said there was something wrong with the way the land office was selling land.

Anna wasn't the least bit surprised when I told her that Laura had whispered the same thing to me. We talked for a few minutes, and concluded that I would have to do some investigating before Steve and Tom bought any land.

I continued trying to explain my thoughts to Tom and Steve. "Look, guys, I'm not saying we won't buy any land. I'm just saying I want an hour or two to see if I can figure out what's going on in that land office, before you two go in and start buying land."

They were both silent for a moment before nodding in agreement. We turned back to reviewing the town maps. That's how Anna found us when she walked in a half hour later.

"I'm ready whenever you all are," she said as she poured a half cup of coffee. "Yolanda will be here in just a minute. Joseph decided his breakfast looked better on her than in his stomach." She took a sip of coffee, sat down in my lap and with a small giggle said, "Grandmother is getting really curious about tomorrow's meeting. We finally told her it would ruin the surprise, and she agreed to not ask any more questions."

I grabbed a quick kiss between her sipping coffee and talking. She beamed me one of her smiles and started to take another sip of coffee when Yolanda came through the door mumbling. She gave Tom a quick kiss, stuck her finger in his face, and started shaking it back and forth.

"You need to teach that boy better manners, and quick, Tom! I'm running out of clothes! Then again, if you don't teach him, I'll just have to get more new clothes when we go to Santa Fe. Hmmmm, never mind, Tom, the boy's manners are just fine."

We were all still laughing at Yolanda and the look on Tom's face as we mounted up and left the stables. With the comanchero threat over, our ride to Mesilla was much more pleasant than it had been for a long time.

We decided to stable our horses rather than leave them tied up in front of the Marshal's office. Anna and I walked arm in arm from the stables to the office, with me carrying our two scabbards. Tom, carrying his and Yolanda 's scabbards followed along, arm in arm; while Steve trailed behind trying to get his bearings. Esteban got up from his chair to greet us as soon as we walked in.

"Glad you could make it," he said after greeting everyone. "Ed has the courtyard set up with coffee, so let's go back there and talk for a little while before I show you what I wanted you to see."

We followed Esteban out to the courtyard and sat down at the table where Ed was waiting for us.

Anna looked around the courtyard and said, "This is absolutely lovely, guys. You've done a marvelous job adding plants and color, back here."

I had to agree with her. Everywhere we looked was a small tree, shrub, or flower. Sitting in the courtyard with all the greenery made you forget you were in the middle of Mesilla.

Ed grinned, and Esteban said, "This has all been done in the last couple of weeks; and, in a way, it's what I wanted to talk to you about."

I swallowed my coffee and told him to go on. Esteban started telling us how the courtyard had come to look so beautiful.

"A couple of weeks ago a man came into the office and asked if we wanted our courtyard landscaped. I asked him how much something like that would cost, and he shrugged telling us it would depend on how big the courtyard was, what kind of shape it was in, and what kind as well as how many trees, shrubs, and flowers we wanted.

"Curious, I brought him out here, and he looked around with pleasure in his eyes as he saw the roses. He told me that we'd made a good start, and that he could not only complete it, but also maintain it for us. He went on to describe what he thought should be done going on at great length about where he would put different kinds of flowers, shrubs and small trees.

"He named plants I'd never heard of before and to tell you the truth I was lost before he'd finished two sentences. When he was done talking I said it all sounded very grand, but I just couldn't see what he was talking about in my mind's eye.

"He laughed, telling me he sometimes got carried away. Then he asked me to take a walk so I could see what he meant. I was really curious, so I agreed. He took me to a house a few blocks away that's about three times as large as this one.

"There were pots of flowers, shrubs, and small trees all over everywhere inside the house. I mean it all looked nice but they were everywhere. Then he took me out to the courtyard and it was like walking into paradise. He swept his arms around telling me he could make our courtyard look like his courtyard if I wanted, or he could just make it a little more appealing. It all depended on how much I wanted to spend."

Esteban paused to drink some coffee and Ed picked up the story.

"What you see costs us two dollars a month. The plants belong to Mr. Rivera and we had to pay five dollars for the pots that they're in. The two dollars covers the cost of his family coming by twice a week to water, feed, prune, and weed them. It's so pleasant now that we usually take our meals out here, if the weather is nice enough."

"I don't blame you. We do the same at the Hacienda, as you know, but this is a lot nicer," Anna said.

"So," Esteban said. "To make a long story short, for many years the Rivera family provided the landscapers and grounds men for the Maes family; first in Santa Fe, and then here. When Mrs. Maes, well, um, fell ill? Yes, fell ill, Mr. Maes, closed up the house here, paid the Rivera's what little wages he owed them, and told them their services were no longer required.

"Anyone in Mesilla who needed landscapers or

grounds men, and there aren't many, already had them, so the Riveras turned to farm work to survive. All the men, which is Mr. Rivera and his seven sons, all work as farm hands when they can find the work, and fill in the gaps by finding courtyard work like ours.

"I haven't mentioned anything to him about the Estancia, and I'm not sure he would want to move, but you may be able to hire some of them or perhaps, the entire family to work the Estancia. I'd like to take you to meet them, see their house and courtyard, and you can decide what you want to do from there."

The smile on Anna's face was all I needed to see to know she was very excited by this development, and was ready to go visit the Rivera's. The gleam in her eye and the small nod of her chin confirmed it. Yolanda gave me a very similar smile, gleam and chin nod, while Tom, the always frugal engineer, simply gave me a small shrug.

"Esteban, I really like what I see here and what we've heard. I think it's definitely worth exploring. Please escort Anna and Yolanda to the Riveras and introduce them. The decision is theirs to make, and I will support whatever they decide. If the Riveras want to meet with me then by all means invite them to lunch at our favorite cantina."

Smiling, Esteban said, "It will be a pleasure, Paul."

I turned to Ed as Anna, Yolanda, and Esteban left the courtyard. "I need you to come with me to the courthouse please, Ed. In all the excitement the other day we forgot to get statements from the two clerks, and I want to get that out of the way so we can get them in the mail. Tom, Steve, I'll see you back here as soon as I'm done."

Ed and I were greeted so effusively by the land office clerk it was almost embarrassing. He thanked us over and over again for saving him, and returning everything the Deputies had stolen from the safe. When I could finally get a word in edgewise I told him that we needed a written statement from him about what happened that day so we could send it to Santa Fe.

I walked him through what the statement needed to say, and he sat down to write it out. Ed sat with him and helped him at his request.

While they were busy with that, I went over to the map of the Territory hanging on the wall and examined it. It only took me a few seconds to realize why Laura had directed me to the map. A large part of the northern half of Doña Ana County, including the northern half of Estancia Dos Santos, was cross-hatched with a deep red marker of some kind.

The cross-hatching was centered on the Rio Grande, extending twenty miles on either side from roughly where the Hacienda was all the way to Socorro. There were various parts of the map shaded a light red and a small number of blocks around Las Cruces, Mesilla, the Gila River and the Organ Mountains shaded the much darker red of the cross-hatching, but they weren't cross-hatched. I stood staring at the map rubbing my chin thoughtfully for the next fifteen minutes trying to figure what it meant.

I still hadn't figured it out, when Ed brought me the statement to read. I reviewed it, and told the clerk it was well written and covered all the facts. He was still smiling when I turned back to the wall asking him to come over as I had some questions about the map.

When both he and Ed were standing next to me I asked, "Did the map look like this when it arrived from Santa Fe?" At his look of confusion, I clarified my question for him. "I mean was it all marked up like this?"

The confused look left his face. "No, Sir, Marshal. When it arrived the only marks on it were the light red shading. That indicates land that was sold by the land office in Santa Fe before the land offices opened in each county. The heavy red shading indicates land sold at this office." He stopped at that point to see if he'd answered my question.

"I see," I said and then pointed at the cross hatched area. "What does this mean then?"

"That's disputed land," he said and then expanded his answer when he saw the look of confusion on my face. "Uncle Mi...er, the Mayor has a land grant from the Spanish King giving all that land to his family. The Mayor was ecstatic the day the Probate Judge walked in and gave him the letter from Mexico City with the land grant in it, let me tell you.

"The only problem the Mayor has right now is that no one seems to know who bought the land shaded in light red from the land office in Santa Fe. Those records didn't come with the map and other stuff we got. I sent off a letter a while back asking Santa Fe for the name of the person who bought it, but we haven't heard anything back, yet. The Probate Judge has all the legal papers ready to serve on the owner once they know who it is."

When he started to talk about a land grant dispute I started to get alarmed. Then I heard Laura's soft voice whispering in my left ear again.

"Don't worry, the land grant isn't valid. You

need to learn more about this, though."

Almost without pause I turned to the clerk. "So, what happens when they find out who owns the land?" I asked curiously.

"Well, I overheard the Mayor and Judge talking about that, and from what they said the Judge serves the owner the legal papers and tells them nothing can be done with the land until the courts resolve the dispute. That could take years of course, so the Mayor will make the owner an offer to sell him clear title to that part of the land grant for five dollars an acre," he said innocently.

"That sounds like a fair deal, if the grant is valid," I said. "But why don't they just ride up there and see if they can find the owner?"

He snorted in derision. "That's rough land up there and neither the Mayor nor the Judge ride well, so they'd have to take a wagon which is really uncomfortable in rough country, as you know. There's a lot of land to cover trying to find someone who might not even be there. No, it's much easier for them to wait for Santa Fe to answer the letter."

"Well, I wish him luck, then." I returned my attention to the statement he'd written and held it up saying, "We're just about done with this, but I need to clarify a few things with you.

Now, you say here that the Deputies tied you up after you opened the safe at gunpoint, and then cleaned out the safe putting everything in a carpetbag they'd brought with them is that right?"

The clerk was nodding his head vigorously and said, "Yes, Sir, Marshal, that's exactly what happened."

"So, they left absolutely nothing in the safe, and when Deputy Montoya here brought you back the bag you took everything out of it and put it back in the safe. You're sure everything was returned?" I asked.

"Oh, yes, Sir. I accounted for all the land office material, as well as the items that the Mayor and Judge store in there as well. It was all there, no doubt about it. As a matter of fact, both the Mayor and the Judge came in and looked everything over to make sure it was all there," he responded.

I looked at Ed and gave the clerk a theatrical sigh. "Looks like we got a little more to do, then. We need to write up an inventory of everything that was stolen, and its value, to attach to your statement. The Judge in Santa Fe will need that to figure out which level of crime was committed. The larger the value of the items stolen the more serious the crime and the more prison time." After a short pause

I told the clerk, "Open the safe, pull everything out, and set it on the counter here so we can write up the inventory."

Eager to assist us, the clerk hurried over to the safe and opened it up. He came back with an arm load of documents, a small money box, and an obviously heavy burlap bag. Placing everything on the counter he said that was all there was. I asked the clerk to pick things up one at a time and tell us what it was and how much it was worth.

The clerk did as I asked. While Ed wrote down what the clerk said, I examined each item to confirm what it was. The various forms, stamps, and ledgers had no real intrinsic value of their own and were kept in the safe simply to prevent their theft and use in making false titles. I assured the clerk that the Judge in Santa Fe would understand that.

The small money box contained the $100 'starting bank' the clerk used to make change, as well as the money he collected for the land sold during the quarter. As this was near the end of the quarter there was almost $300 total in the money box. Finished counting the money in the money box, the clerk looked up and said that was everything. I looked at the burlap bag and told him we still had that to go through it, item by item, and assign a value.

He fidgeted for a moment before giving me a sheepish look. "Marshal, I was given strict instructions by the Mayor and the Judge to stay out of that bag and never look inside it. I don't know what's in there, so I'm not sure I can help you much."

"Does anyone else have the combination to the safe besides you?" I asked.

He looked around carefully, leaned forward, and whispered, "The land office clerk in Socorro has it. We give each other the combinations, to make sure someone can get into the safe if something happens to one of us."

"That makes sense. Excellent thinking. But what I'm trying to determine is if anyone could have taken anything out of the bag since you put it back in the safe and the Mayor and Judge verified it was all there."

"Oh, well, no, Sir. If I'm not here, the safe is locked and no one has put anything in or taken anything out but me," he said with certainty.

I smiled broadly at the clerk and said, "Good! To keep you out of trouble I will look in the bag and pull out each item one by one and describe it to Ed. You will witness everything and sign the inventory sheet when we're done."

The first thing I pulled out of the bag was a

large opened envelope addressed to the Judge from a Ramon Gutierrez in Mexico City. I described it to Ed and reached inside pulling out a thick fold of heavy parchment. As I unfolded it a small note fell to the floor. I picked it up, giving it a quick glance, as I stood up.

I couldn't help smiling to myself as I realized this was proof positive that the land grant was a forgery. I continued unperturbed, and simply told Ed to write down that the envelope contained a Royal Land Grant signed by one of the Kings of Spain and a note addressed to the Mayor and Judge regarding its provenance. I opened out the land grant and whistled in surprise.

It was a thing of rare beauty, more a work of art than an official document. We all stared at it for a moment before I asked the clerk for an estimate of how many acres the document covered and how much it was worth at today's price. Without a thought, he said it covered just over 600,000 acres and was worth just a little under $1 Million. This time it was Ed who whistled as he wrote the numbers down.

The second thing I pulled out of the bag was an accounting ledger. When I opened it, I found pages for each of the positions in the county funded by the Territory. What was interesting was that at the top of each page was either the

Mayor or the Judge's name. I flipped the pages quickly and set the ledger down telling Ed it was a payroll ledger. I knew it was something else entirely but didn't know exactly what, yet. I could wait until later to figure it out though, so I moved on.

The last items in the bag were two identical rather heavy locked money boxes. At my questioning look the clerk just shrugged and said the Mayor's initials were deeply scratched on the top of one box and the Judge's on the other. He also said that both men had keys to at least one of the boxes because he'd seen them open them and put money in or take money out at least once a month. I told Ed to write down that the contents and value of the money boxes were unknown as I was putting everything back in the bag.

While the clerk was reviewing and signing the inventory I said, "You know, you're a very lucky man."

He looked up from the inventory and grinned. "Yes, Sir! Why, I could have been killed!"

I gave him a very serious look. "That would have been the least of your worries if they'd gotten away with the robbery. Because you are a government official the government would have been forced to pay for everything in the safe, including the personal items the Mayor and Judge store in there. They would have paid out the claim, eventually and reluctantly, but they would have paid it. Of course, you would have been fired and put in jail, so it wouldn't matter to you. Unless, you had over $1 Million to pay the government back with."

The clerk blanched at what I'd just said. "I'm going to take this bag to the Mayor and Judge, and remind them what governmental regulations and the law says about storing personal items in government safes. You won't have to worry about this kind of thing, anymore."

Picking up the bag from the counter I looked at Ed. "Make sure you have the statement and inventory. We need to find the Mayor and Judge for a little chat before lunch."

As I walked out into the hallway I heard Ed tell the clerk that it didn't pay to bother me when I was in this kind of mood, as he hurriedly picked up the papers and followed me out. Once outside of the courthouse I turned with a huge smile, and waited for Ed to catch up.

"Ed go find the Mayor and the Judge. Tell them I want to talk to them in our office immediately, and that I sent you to escort them. If they give you any argument remind them again about the penalty for impeding a federal investigation. If they continue to argue with you, arrest them. Don't let them talk to that clerk for any reason."

Ed didn't really understand what was going on yet, since he hadn't read the note with the land grant, but he smiled broadly and hurried off to the offices across the plaza. I rapidly walked the short distance between the courthouse and the office. The office was empty and I walked out to the courtyard where Tom and Steve were drinking coffee at the table.

"Gentlemen, I need your help, quickly please, we only have a few minutes." I reached into the bag and handed Steve the ledger as I passed him on the way to a large potted plant ten feet behind the table and off to the side.

As I sat the bag down I said, "Steve, take a look at that and tell me what you think it is. Tom, help me move the table and chairs over here next to this plant please.

As Tom and I were moving the chairs and table over, Steve was flipping through the ledger. He looked up and started to say something, when he abruptly stopped himself and reopened the ledger. I passed by him and went back inside the office. I got two sets of manacles from the large cupboard we stored them in, and walked back out to the courtyard. After a quick glance at the table from the doorway I walked over to the corner and laid the manacles on the ground behind another plant.

Steve handed me the ledger on my way past him, back to the table. "At first, I thought it was a government payroll book, but the monthly pay isn't right for any of the positions that I'm familiar with which is most of them. Just as an example, a Justice of the Peace makes $30 a month, that ledger lists it at $10. A land office clerk makes $20 a month, the ledger lists $5. What's going on Paul?"

While Steve had been talking I'd put the ledger back in the bag and moved the bag back behind the planter where it couldn't be seen. I'd finally figured out what the ledger represented, and gave out a very loud guffaw as he finished.

I walked over to them, laughing at both the ledger and at their look of puzzlement. I put my arms around their shoulders and walked them over to the corner where I'd put the manacles.

"What's going on is that the ledger doesn't list what each position is getting paid, it lists how much pay from each position the Mayor and Judge are stealing. Ed is on his way over here with both of them right now. When they get here, I am going to arrest them. Which reminds me, Steve, raise your right hand, and say I do."

Steve did as I asked, and I tossed him a badge. "Put that on Steve, you're now an acting Dep-

uty US Marshal. I want both of you standing right here talking quietly, when Ed brings
our guests in. Tom, when I tell them they are
under arrest I want you to pull your gun and
cover the one closest to you. Steve, make sure
you're out of the line of fire if shooting starts.
Once I've had them empty their pockets on
the table, Tom, I want you to put the manacles
on them with their hands behind their backs.
When that's done, I'll start talking, and you'll
be able to make sense out of what is happening."

At their murmur of understanding, I went back
over to the table, poured a fresh cup of coffee,
and sat down to read the clerk's statement in
more detail. I was halfway through the statement when Ed came out into the courtyard.
I waved him over, quietly told him what I
wanted him to do, and sent him back inside to
get our guests.

I heard the courtyard door open as I pretended
to read the statement, and heard Ed tell the
pair that I was in the courtyard as they walked
out. I looked up from the statement and after
seeing the pair put a big smile on my face.

"Gentlemen, thank you for coming so quickly
at my call," I said pleasantly.

The Judge, completely misjudging the situation, said in a self-important tone, "It's hard

not to move quickly when your deputy is threatening to arrest me."

I looked over at Ed with a look of incredulity on my face. "Ed, you didn't, did you? You know better than that. Arresting people is my job, it's one of the few pleasures I get."

In a chagrined tone Ed replied, "I'll try to remember that, Marshal."

I looked back at the two men. "Well, since it's one of my hidden pleasures let's get right to it, shall we?" I was really enjoying the look of confusion on their faces. "Gentlemen, you are both under arrest for conspiracy to commit forgery, forgery, conspiracy to commit fraud, conspiracy to commit extortion, and theft of government payroll. When you leave here you will be taken to the county jail, where you'll be placed behind bars for a few days. You will then be transported to Santa Fe where you will be tried and, if found guilty, sentenced to hard time in the Territorial prison."

I paused to take a sip of coffee with my right hand, watching them carefully the entire time. What I'd said finally sank in as I put my cup back on the table.

"No sudden moves gentlemen or the guns trained at your backs might go off."

They both turned their heads to see Tom and

Ed pointing their guns at them. "Judge, step forward, and very carefully empty everything out of your pockets onto the table please. If you have any weapons please move very slowly when you pull them out," I said drawing my own pistol.

The Judge did as I instructed, leaving a small four shot pistol and a derringer on the table along with coins, a key ring, and a few scraps of paper. The Mayor followed suit leaving the same type of items on the table minus weapons. I raised an eyebrow in disbelief at him, when he said that was everything.

"Mayor, everyone in the county knows you carry a knife sewn into a sheath at the neck of your coat," I said, cocking the pistol to make my point.

He gulped and slowly reached behind his neck pulling out a throwing knife. He carefully placed it on the table, and then stood back. I waved to Tom, who brought the shackles over and cuffed the men's hands behind their backs.

Tom was finishing up the last bolt, when Esteban walked through the door into the courtyard. Seeing the two men shackled, he smiled, and leaned back against the door, with his arms crossed to watch.

"Gentlemen, I came back to Mesilla today, to

conduct a little personal business, as well as get statements from the clerk's about the robbery two days ago. Part of getting statements for a robbery includes an itemized list of what was stolen, each item's value, and whether or not it was recovered.

"Imagine, if you will, my surprise when I discovered that you two were storing personal items in the land office safe as the clerk so conveniently documented in his statement. He went on to say that every item was recovered, and the recovery of your personal items was later confirmed by both of you."

I set the statement down on the table, and looked at the two suddenly sweating and fidgeting men.

"When we were conducting the inventory of the burlap bag you two keep in the safe, we found a few more surprises. The first surprise was a thick opened envelope addressed to the Judge from a Ramon Gutierrez in Mexico City. The envelope contained a Royal Land Grant assigned to one of the Mayor's ancestors.

"Curious that it was the Mayor's land grant, but it was sent to you, Judge. Anyway, the document is a beautiful piece of work. More art than anything else, I must say. Unfortunately, the second item in the envelope was a note addressed to both of you from your dear friend

Ramon, telling you that the land grant is one of his better pieces of work, and well worth the two hundred dollars you paid him to make it. That covers the conspiracy to commit forgery and the forgery charges, don't you think?"

I paused to take a sip of coffee. "We were talking to the clerk about the land grant and I asked him what land it covered. He was nice enough to show us on the map where he had blocked it out with cross-hatches. Imagine our shock when he told us it covered 600,000 acres that, conservatively was worth a million dollars.

"Of course, that didn't count the 30,000 acres that someone else had already bought, and you planned to take to court. The clerk told us you had already prepared the legal papers to serve on the owner, once you found out who that was, but you were going to offer to clear the title of that land for the small payment of five dollars an acre. You are just too generous, I must say. That pretty much covers the conspiracy to commit fraud and conspiracy to commit extortion charges, I'd say.

"For the final charge of theft of government payroll you can thank the ledger you morons kept. It clearly documents how much of the monthly payroll you stole from each position and which one of you it went to. Not very bright of you to keep such detailed records of your theft, I must say."

I picked up the two rings of keys from the table. "As for where the money you stole is? I'm sure that one of the small keys on each of your key rings will prove to open the heavy money boxes that were also in the bag stored in the safe. How will I know which money box belongs to which of you? Why, you were nice enough to scratch your initials on the box you used. I'm sure when we open them, and count the contents, it will match almost exactly the amount in the ledgers."

I paused and glared at the two. Everyone else in the courtyard was staring in stunned disbelief at the scope of the planned activities, and the monumental stupidity the pair had displayed.

"Esteban, if you would, please escort the ladies, and any guests we may have, to the cantina. We'll meet you there in a few minutes. Please explain our delay."

Esteban gave me a big smile. "It will be my pleasure, Marshal. It's not often I get to escort two such beautiful and pleasant ladies to lunch."

I waited in silence for a full minute to make sure that everyone was out of the office before saying, "Let's go, gentlemen. You are more than familiar with the way to the Sheriff's office, I know."

Tom and Steve walked in front of the prisoners, while Ed and I followed along behind. We turned the two over to a very surprised Sheriff, reminding him that I expected them to remain behind bars and still be alive when we came to transport the prisoners to Santa Fe.

The Sheriff was a very confused and conflicted man at this point. "Marshal, you don't seem the least bit concerned that these men are my friends. Even if I really believe your threats, there's nothing stopping me from releasing these two and heading for Mexico. I don't understand how you can be so cavalier about this."

The three men with me gave a short chuckle and I gave the Sheriff a big smile. "Sheriff, I'm not worried about you releasing them. I'm more worried about you killing them. Tell me, Sheriff, how much do you get paid?"

"I get $20 a month just as advertised in the job description when I filed the election paperwork. The deputies get paid $15. That may go up when the county has to start paying our salary next year but that's what the Territory pays the first two years," the Sheriff replied.

"Sheriff Bean, these two men aren't your, or

anyone else's, friend. Between the two of them they were stealing wages from almost every Territorial and County official, including you. The Territory pays every Sheriff $30 a month. These two were paying you $20 and pocketing $10. No, they aren't your friends. They are smooth talking criminals masquerading as public servants and pillars of the community."

The confusion and conflict had disappeared from the Sheriff's face as I talked to be replaced by raw anger and conflict, as he realized how much money he'd lost over the last sixteen months.

I waved the others out the door and followed them. At the door, I stopped and turned back to the Sheriff giving him a very piercing stare. "One other thing you need to remember, Sheriff. I don't make threats lightly and, in my official capacity as Marshal, I don't make threats jokingly. If these men escape or are killed, you WILL take their place, or you'll be dead. You can run, you can hide, but I WILL find you. It may take a while but know that it WILL happen." I turned and walked out into the street rejoining the other three.

"Esteban told us you put on quite a performance, mi Pablo. Arresting the Mayor and Judge and then walking them down the street in manacles. It must have really been something to see."

Those were Anna's first words to me when the four us joined her, Yolanda and Esteban at the table in the Cantina.

I gave her a quick hug and kiss before sitting down. "It was … enjoyable," I said with a small grin. "Now tell us about your visit with the Rivera family."

Anna and Yolanda took turns telling us all about the Rivera's, their house and courtyard, and their perceived abilities with both landscape design and grounds keeping. It was clear to all of us that both ladies were very taken by the entire Rivera family, both personally and professionally.

"Did you hire them, my love?" I asked.

Anna gave me one of those looks all females seem to reserve for responding to questions from stupid men. "Of course not! I told them about the opportunity, and invited them to visit the Estancia so they could see it for themselves. They'll let Yolanda and me know in the next few days, if and when they'd like to visit."

After lunch, we all returned to the office. We quickly reviewed what we expected to do the rest of the afternoon. A short while later Steve and Ed left to visit the courthouse. Ed to get a statement, and an inventory of stolen items from the county clerk, and Steve to buy land.

Anna and Yolanda decided to take advantage of the merchants in Mesilla and went shopping. I sat down at Esteban's desk and started my report on the investigation and subsequent arrest of the Mayor and Probate Judge.

I was still hard at it when Steve came back, an hour later. I took a break from the report and joined him, Tom and the ladies in the courtyard, while Esteban and Ed decided to take a turn around town to make their afternoon saloon visits, hunting for gossip.

Steve had purchased most of the 192,000 acres of land we wanted for the railroad, save for a few acres near Socorro that had already been purchased, and some of the land near Santa Fe that we knew wasn't available. The average price per acre of two and a half dollars was a little better than we'd planned. The total cost coming in at $480,000.

Steve had also purchased plots in both Mesilla and Las Cruces for schools, a library and a large park. He hadn't been able to get the plots we wanted, so he bought what he could get close to our preferred locations.

The clerk was talkative about the arrest of the Mayor and Judge, and curious about the land Steve was buying. As planned, Steve told him he was buying land for a group of speculators. Steve told us that the clerk wouldn't have the land deeds ready to be picked up until tomorrow afternoon which meant another trip into Mesilla after the meeting.

Now it was Tom's turn to buy the land we needed around Las Cruces for the university and the railroad depot complex. As he walked out I wished him luck and returned to writing my report.

Tom was back less than a half hour later. He'd bought the parcels of land we wanted just outside of Las Cruces, on the South and West sides. He'd told the clerk the land was for the wife of the owner of the Estancia Dos Santos who wanted to build a house near town but couldn't decide whether she wanted a mountain view or a river view. The owner decided to buy both while he could, and he would sell the land she didn't want later. Tom was going to pick up the deeds just before five, that afternoon.

After he'd left to join the others in the courtyard I returned to the report, finally completing it a few minutes after four. I had Ed, Tom, and Steve read it and when they agreed with it I asked them to sign it. I bundled up the report, statements, inventories, ledger, and the land grant with its note into a large package, and mailed it off to Santa Fe.

Tom picked up the deeds as scheduled, and the five of us rode back to Las Cruces happy with our respective day's work.

CHAPTER 16

"What can I do to help?" I asked Anna after breakfast the next morning. The ladies were clearing the family table, to start getting the room ready for the meeting set to start in a couple of hours. Tom, Steve, and I were finishing the last of our coffee, and from the way the ladies were moving through the room, it was very apparent that we were in the way.

Anna beamed me one of her smiles and gave me a small kiss. "Take these other two, and go keep grandfather company. You three will only get in the way. We'll have everything ready a half hour before the meeting starts, so be back then."

I grinned, gave her a big hug and kiss, and waving the other two to come with me, I walked out of the dining room and out to the stables.

We found Mr. Mendoza out at one of the corrals looking at six coal black horses with John Benning, from the Bar J ranch. I introduced Steve and John to each other, and the five of us turned to watch the horses.

"They're fine looking animals, John, and they move real nice. What breed are they?" Tom asked.

"They're Tennessee Pacers. They have a nice easy gait and are almost as sure footed as mules. They were bred as all-purpose farm animals, but most of the time they're used for riding or for coach work. These are the best I've bred. They're young and need some work, but they'll do well at either task." John answered.

Mr. Mendoza looked over at me with a small grin. "John came by yesterday, asking if I knew anyone looking for prime horses, and I asked him to bring them by this morning for a look."

"Those damn comancheros really fouled things up for us last year." John said unexpectedly. "We were just starting to break even when they hit us. Between all the damage they did to the ranch buildings, the horses they stole that we never recovered, and the money we had saved up that they stole, we are falling a little behind. As much as I hate to sell these, they'll bring enough to set things right and get us back on track."

"They're good horses, Paul. Well configured and sound. If you're going to buy a coach you're going to need something to pull it with. These would make a fine team for you," Mr. Mendoza said.

I glanced over at Tom with a questioning look, and without hesitation he gave me a small nod of approval. I turned back to watch the horses and tried to visualize them in harness pulling a custom-made coach. I liked what I saw in my mind's eye, and turned to John.

"If you can get Mr. Mendoza and Tom to agree on a price with you I'll take all six of them," I said.

I backed out of the way of the three of them and knowing it would take a while for all three to agree on a price I walked around the corral looking at the horses from all angles. The more I saw of the horses, the more I liked them.

The three were still talking fifteen minutes later. From what I overhead it was pretty clear to me that the price would eventually be somewhere in the vicinity of $350 each. While they continued their negotiating, I went to the house and pulled $2400 from the bag of money Anna had brought for Tom to use to buy the land, but hadn't needed.

When I got back out to the corral they were

closing on a number they could all agree on. Still, none of them were going to be rushed, and it took another ten minutes for them to come to agreement on a price of three hundred and sixty dollars each.

I counted out the money with John watching, and gave it to him.

"John, I'm going to need another matched set of six horses for a second coach. Do you have any other horses that would meet that need?"

John rubbed his chin in thought for a few moments. "Well, Paul, I do have another set of Tennessee Pacer's like these, but they're brown with black markings. They're still a little young, so you wouldn't be able to use them, or even start training them for another six months."

"That's perfect, John. Bring them in to Mr. Mendoza at the beginning of October and let Mr. Mendoza look them over. If he approves of them, then I'll pay whatever price you and he agree on," I said with a smile.

John rode away a happy man, and I thanked both Tom and Mr. Mendoza for negotiating with John.

"Everyone knows how bad you are at negotiating, Paul," Mr. Mendoza said with a laugh. "It rivals your coffee making skills. It was the least I could do to save Anna the aggravation of you paying too much."

What could I say? It was all true, so I just nodded my head.

"Let's talk about how much you are going to charge us for training these beauties. I want to surprise Anna and Yolanda with these guys when we go to Santa Fe, later this year, so I don't want them at the Estancia until I bring the coach back from El Paso."

Mr. Mendoza shrugged his shoulders and said, "I'll just add it to your bill."

I gave my head a shake. "No, Sir. You've put too much on my bill already. If you're going to do the work, then I need to pay you for it. That's only fair."

He thought for a moment and gave me a number for stabling and training the horses for six months. I thought it was a little on the low side, but knew better than to argue with him so I simply said, "Done."

I paid him in full, from the money left over from buying the horses. We watched the horses for another few minutes before we walked behind the stables, and sat down at the mending table. We talked about the horses, the training Mr. Mendoza would put them through, and the harness gear they were going to need. Mr. Mendoza said the Delgados made the finest looking harnesses of any he had seen, and he would talk to them about making a couple of sets for us.

The four of us walked through the back door at the appointed time, and stood staring in surprise. The dining room was gone. In its place was a formal meeting room, with paper and pencils at each of the thirteen seats around the table. Coffee and cool tea were on the sideboards, along with some fresh baked cookies.

Anna walked up beside me putting her arm around my waist. "What do you think my love?" she asked with a grin and a twinkle in her eye.

"It looks amazing, Anna. There will be no doubt in their minds when they sit down that this is a serious meeting," I told her with a small squeeze of her waist.

Yolanda joined us a minute later and the five of us poured our coffee, and sat down on the far side of the table. We'd been talking for a few minutes when Mrs. Delgado arrived. She stood in the doorway scanning the room for a moment before walking in.

Anna welcomed her, pointed to the sideboards, and invited her to help herself. Within three minutes the rest of the invitees had arrived and were helping themselves to coffee or tea and cookies. When everyone was seated, and we'd spent a few minutes exchanging pleasantries, Anna stood up to get everyone's attention.

Once she had everyone's attention she addressed the room. "Thank you all for coming to this meeting, and thank you grandmother for allowing us to use this room. I know all of you are curious about why you're here. Let me assure you that the purpose of the meeting will become clear soon enough.

"I'd like to introduce our lawyer and close friend from Santa Fe, Tom Stevenson, who for obvious reasons we all call Steve. We've asked Steve here to talk to us about statehood. He'll tell us how it happens, the obstacles we'll have to overcome to become a state, and the changes we'll go through after we become a state."

Over the next hour Steve did a masterful job of explaining the process of becoming a state, how being a state differed from being a territory, and what it would mean to the citizens of New Mexico Territory to become citizens of the state of New Mexico.

He told them all the arguments that were currently being used to keep New Mexico a territory, and how they could be overcome. Finally, he told them that some very powerful Anglos were working hard to delay statehood as long as they could.

Mrs. Delgado asked why they would do such a thing. Steve replied with one word, and then explained.

"Power. As long as New Mexico is a territory, the Federal government makes the decisions. As soon as we became a state, the citizens will make the decisions locally for the state, through the state legislature, and nationally by their representatives in Congress."

The discussion with questions and answers went on a little longer. When there was a lull, Yolanda stood up.

"Steve, thank you for explaining all of that and for answering all the questions. If any of you have more questions for Steve, he'll be here a few more days before he leaves for Austin."

Yolanda paused to see if there were any questions. When there were none, she continued.

"We all know that the territory doesn't have the gold, silver or other minerals that territories like Colorado and Nevada have. If we do, then they haven't been discovered yet. We also don't have any other major resources such as the forests of Washington Territory. What we have is land, lots of land. Unfortunately, much of it is currently valueless. That may change over the years, but for now that's the way it stands.

"All of this means there is no compelling reason for Congress to vote for us becoming a state, or for the President to approve it. No, we won't become a state for our resources. Instead, we have to overcome the objections currently being used against us."

Again, she paused to allow anyone to comment and again, there were none.

"Pablo, Anna, Steve, Tom, and I along with a small group of influential like-minded men in Santa Fe, all want statehood, and we want it sooner, rather than later. All of the objections to statehood can be overcome. It will take some time, and it will take hard work, but they can be overcome.

"The objections over the size of the territory can be overcome, by advocating that it be split into two equal territories with the Eastern territory retaining the New Mexico Territory name and the new territory to the West being called something else. We know there is already some thought in Washington of doing this, and calling the new territory Arizona. We can get our territorial delegate in Washington to support this and not just because it will reduce the size of New Mexico Territory to something manageable. We need to encourage it, because it also helps us overcome two other objections at the same time.

"First, most of the Indian problems are happening in the Western half of the territory, what will become Arizona Territory. We do have some problems here of course, but if the Arizona Territory becomes a reality we can show that most of our problems are coming from it as well as Texas.

"The second objection is the lack of people. The majority of the people in the territory as it is now, live in the Eastern half not the Western half. Most of the population lives along or near the Rio Grande between Santa Fe and Mesilla. That includes Las Cruces, Socorro, and Albuquerque. There are, of course, people in Tucson and Colorado City, but as yet not in large numbers.

"The two objections we don't have to do anything about at all are the large numbers of Hispanos compared to Anglos, and the predominance of Catholicism. As Steve said, we simply point out that the same situations exists in Texas and California and neither have been a problem.

"That leaves us with two very real objections, illiteracy and civic status, that we can work to overcome locally. Both of these are in some sense perception issues, that we can address by encouraging visits by influential Easterners, after a little work. We all know that well over half of the Hispanos in this area can read and write Spanish, so they aren't really illiterate. Unfortunately, English is the language of the United States and that is the standard for judging literacy.

"Likewise, our villages and towns are large dust bowls. We all do the best we can, but there are few outward displays of civic pride in any of the towns in the territory. There are no public libraries, no parks, and the streets are all dirt.

"We believe we can change these things but the five of us and the group in Santa Fe that Steve represents can't do it alone. That is the reason we asked you to attend this meeting. We want you to join with us in this effort. We want you to lead the efforts in Las Cruces, and Mesilla."

The room erupted in voices as all the invitees started throwing questions at Yolanda at the same time. All but Mr. Mendoza, who sat quietly drinking his coffee with a small smile on his face. Yolanda looked around the room calmly, almost regally, and held up her hands.

When they had quieted she said, "The five of us will lead you through what we have planned so far, and answer all of your questions in the process. This will take a few hours and we have made arrangements for lunch to be served here so that we don't have to stop before we are done."

Finished, Yolanda sat down, and Anna stood back up.

"Before we go any further in our discussions and reveal the planning that has gone into this, I need your word that you will never reveal the source of the money that will allow us to make these plans a reality."

She looked at each one of the invitees and waited for them to give their promise. When she had obtained the solemn promise from all the invitees she waved her arm at Tom, Yolanda, me and herself.

"The four of us are the source of the funds for what we are proposing to do. There are, of course, some strings attached to the funds, and the funds will eventually be reduced but we will fund the initial activity. To do that we have created two Trusts.

"The Mesilla Valley Community Association Trust will initially be responsible for paving the roads, as well as building a library, and a park.

"The Mesilla Valley Education Association Trust will be responsible for building, maintaining, and staffing an elementary school and a high school.

"We expect all of these things to be a reality by the end of next year. To ensure that they become a reality each Trust has two Operating Committees, one for Las Cruces and one for Mesilla.

"Most of you are here today because we have selected you to be members of the Operating Committees.

"Specifically, grandmother, Mrs. Amador, and Tia Maria have been selected as the first three members of the Mesilla Valley Education Association Trust Operations Committee.

"Likewise, grandfather, Tia Dolores, and Esteban have been selected as the first three members of the Mesilla Valley Community Association Trust Operations Committee.

"You are each free to turn down the positions we're offering, and if you do all we ask is that you keep quiet about what you've learned so far.

"We'll take a few minutes now and let you think about everything you've heard, while we all refresh our drinks. When we start back up you'll each need to tell us whether you agree to serve on the committees or not. If not, you are free to leave.

"Jorge and Juan, although neither of you is on a committee you both are integral to what we are going to be doing and we ask you to remain for the rest of the meeting."

We were all seated at the table again, fifteen minutes later. I gave Anna's hand a small squeeze of reassurance as this was the part we had the most doubts about.

She stood up and asked each of the six invitees if they agreed to serve on the committees. When all six had agreed to serve, she beamed everyone in the room a smile and gave a brief nod to Yolanda who opened a cupboard under one of the sideboards removing a stack of papers.

Yolanda began handing out the papers to each invitee as Anna spoke.

"First we'll cover the Mesilla Valley Community Association Trust. Yolanda is handing out a copy of the trust documents in both Spanish and English along with our suggestions, recommendations, and the estimates we came up with, for constructing and maintaining the roads, buildings, and parks."

Anna took everyone through the trust document, taking great pains to emphasize that the committees were responsible for the detailed planning and scheduling of the actual work.

This included selecting a design for the buildings.

She also took great pains to make it very clear that the committees were free to choose any architect and design they wanted, and the construction could be done by anyone they wanted, but the trust would only pay for a design if it came from Jorge, and would only pay for roads and buildings built by Juan. Additionally, all the buildings the trust paid for, must clearly reflect the Spanish heritage of New Mexico while the primary building material must be either adobe or stone. Detailed planning must begin no later than the first of May and construction must begin no later than the first of October.

To say that Jorge and Juan were stunned would be an understatement. The committee members were surprised, but didn't voice any concerns. A few seconds later they were stunned as well when Anna told them that there was only one other string attached to the trust which would be covered later.

She then covered what we considered the committee's first task, finding two other residents of Las Cruces to become members of the committee. A secondary task was to identify three residents of Mesilla, to form the initial Mesilla Operations Committee. This was a secondary task because everything would be done in Las Cruces before work started in Mesilla.

When everything had been covered, we broke for a quick lunch and then resumed with Anna turning to the Mesilla Valley Education Association Trust. Again, Yolanda handed out copies of the trust document in Spanish and English, along with our suggestions, recommendations, and estimates.

She quickly covered the fact that the same strings from the other trust applied to this trust, as well. This trust also stipulated that the curriculum in all grade levels must include Language, History, Science, and Math and that all courses would be taught in both English and Spanish.

Yolanda pointed out that we had included the curriculum used on the Estancia, as a starting point for them to consider. She also told them that the four of us, with help from our friends in Santa Fe, would provide the initial cadre of six teachers, but it would be up to the committee to find any replacements or additional teachers.

Eventually, Anna finished covering what was in the document, and answered all the questions. She sat down with a soft sigh, and Steve stood up to speak.

"There is one other very important string that you need to be aware of and start planning for almost immediately. The trust will only be fully funded for the first five years. Starting the sixth year the trust switches to a system that will match dollar for dollar the money raised by the residents of Las Cruces up to an amount equal to half of the previous year's expenses.

"That system will remain in place for ten years after which time both Trusts will have served their purpose, and will be discontinued. How the money is raised and who authorizes the expenditure of money after the first five years will be up to you to determine.

"In your packages, we've included some suggestions for how the money might be raised, but one thing should be very clear. To succeed in the long-term, you are all going to have to enter the world of politics. You will do a lot of talking, persuading, and arm twisting to make whatever you come up with work. The earlier you start, the easier it will be to get what you want, especially after five years of visible and very public success."

It was my turn now, and I stood up as Steve sat down.

"We've given you a lot of information, and you all have much to think about; so I suggest we adjourn this meeting, and plan on meeting here again in seven days at the same time. Steve, Tom, and I won't be here but as should be obvious by now Anna and Yolanda are more than capable of answering any questions you might have, and providing any help you might need to get started. We thank you all for coming today, and for agreeing to serve on the committees."

Tom and I gave our respective ladies a hug and kiss, as everyone else filed out of the room. When everyone was gone, Tom and I joined Steve and Esteban for the ride to Mesilla.

We split up as we entered town. Steve continued on to the courthouse, while Tom and I stopped at the Marshal's office with Esteban. Steve joined us less than ten minutes later with the land deeds, telling us he'd also had them recorded at the county clerk's office, under the appropriate business or trust. After enjoying a cup of coffee, we bid Esteban and Ed goodbye and rode back to Las Cruces.

We arrived back at the stables and joined Mr. Mendoza at his usual afternoon spot, until supper was ready. We sat in silence for a while before Mr. Mendoza looked over at Tom and Steve.

"You two need to be careful about spending too much time with this one," he said waving in my direction. "If you're not careful you'll end up involved in his surprises."

Tom laughed. "Too late, Sir. We're already involved in them, and I'm sure there are a few more he hasn't told us about yet."

Steve gave Mr. Mendoza a very serious look. "Tom's right sir. It's much too late. I could have used that warning a couple of years ago. I'm not sure how he does it, but he has a habit of sucking innocent people into his surprises. I tell you, it's enough to set a man to drinking."

"It's my boyish good looks and charm, Steve," I replied with a grin.

The noise of many horses arriving out front interrupted our fun, and we went out to find Rodrigo leading the Estancia teams that had been sent as our escorts. We talked with Rodrigo and the men for a few minutes, and they assured us that things were back to normal on the Estancia. The wounded men were all on the mend, and most were back to work already. Eventually, they all drifted away to get supper and the rest of us returned to the table behind the stables.

Anna and I turned in early, as did Tom and Yolanda. We were all emotionally exhausted from the meeting and knowing the physical toll the trip to El Paso was going take on Tom and me. We were more than ready for bed. Of course, there was an hour or so of pillow talk, reviewing what we'd accomplished and our near-term plans to see if we could find anything we may have missed before we drifted off to sleep.

Morning seemed to come too early, and we were up and done with our morning routine shortly after first light. Tom and I unloaded all the drilling pipe from the back of the wagon leaving just the burlap bags of gold bars before we retied the canvas cover back down and headed inside to clean up a little and get breakfast.

An hour later we gave our ladies a long hug and kiss, and were on the road. Thankfully, two of the escort team took turns driving the wagon so Tom and I were spared that agony. This trip went much like the previous one. The only real difference was that we pushed a little harder and found ourselves pulling up in front of the bank late in the afternoon of the second day.

Rodrigo arranged half the escorts to guard the wagon while the rest followed me and Tom as we carried the gold bags into the bank. Levi was watching from his office doorway as we entered the door of the bank. He shook his head with a grin and led us back to the weighing room.

When all the bags were in the weighing room Tom left with Rodrigo to make sure we all had rooms in the hotel for the next two nights. I introduced Steve to Levi telling him that Steve was a good friend of his brothers, in Santa Fe. Levi knew about Steve from Hiram's letters, but this was the first time they had met.

Levi turned to weighing, while Steve and I talked quietly as we waited for him to finish.

Levi stood up from the scales, called two men into the room telling them to put everything in the safe, before leading me and Steve into his office. Once in the office with the door closed he poured us all a glass of scotch.

"Well, Paul, it's the same weight and price as your last visit. What do you want to do with the money this time?"

I handed him a piece of paper with various amounts written on it. "I want it all in bank drafts in those amounts," I said indicating the paper he held. "Steve here will pick them up two days from now after breakfast just before he rides out for Austin."

With a curious look Levi asked, "What are you going to be doing in Austin, Steve?"

I answered the question for Steve. "He's going

to be buying some land for me here in Texas, Levi."

"Branching out are you?" Levi asked idly taking a sip of his drink.

I took a drink before looking up at him. "In a manner of speaking I guess I am, Levi. When you come up for the holidays we'll talk about what's going on and the various activities I've got going between Santa Fe, the Mesilla Valley, and Texas. It's just too complicated to get into right now, and the plans aren't far enough along, yet."

"Now you've got me really curious but fair enough, Paul," Levi said as he finished his drink.

Steve and I finished our drinks, thanked Levi for the hospitality and turned to leave.

I stopped at the door and turned back to Levi. "I'm going to be buying a couple of coaches, tomorrow, over on the other side of the river. Hopefully from the Rodriquez Brothers, just so you know when the bills come in."

Levi gave a quick smile. "They are supposed to be the best around, Paul. I look forward to riding in one of their coaches."

Tom was waiting for us in the lobby of the hotel and handed us our keys as we walked up.

"I had your stuff put in your rooms. I'm off to see my father but I'll see you at breakfast, if not before."

I nodded. "I know he wasn't all that interested the last time Tom, but if he's not doing any better make sure to invite him to live on the Estancia. He might change his mind now that he has a grandson."

Tom grinned at the last part and walked out the door.

I turned to Steve and said, "I don't know about you, but I could sure use a bath and a shave."

Steve agreed and followed me up the stairs for a change of clothes before we got our bath and shave. Clean and freshly shaven we spent the rest of the evening in the hotel lobby relaxing, reading the various newspapers, and sipping a tolerable scotch, before joining Rodrigo and some of the vaqueros for supper in the dining room.

Tom joined us for breakfast the next morning in an ambivalent mood. He was concerned about his father's continued poor health. At the same time, he was extremely happy because his father had agreed to live on the Estancia. It would take some time to sell the business and house, but Tom figured that his father should be ready to move before the end of the year.

"I just hope he lives long enough to make the move," Tom said as we finished breakfast.

"We won't be leaving until tomorrow morning, Tom. Go back and spend all the time you can with him, until then," I said as we walked out front.

When Tom had gone, I told Steve I was going see about ordering some coaches, and unless he wanted to go with me I'd see him later. He declined, and I rode off for the river on my own. As I rode I realized that this was the first time I had ridden alone, in over two years.

That caused me to reflect on all the changes I had gone through in the last six years. How I'd managed to survive, find friends, and love again was a mystery to me. I heard Laura's soft laugh in my left ear and knew I had her to thank. Her and lady luck.

The Rodriquez Brothers turned out to be everything Mr. Mendoza had said. I spent most of the morning with them talking construction, wood types, finishes, and upholstery. By the time I was done, I had ordered two identical coaches. The brothers promised the first would be ready at the beginning of October, and the second would be ready at the beginning of December at the latest.

When all the paperwork had been signed and countersigned, I turned the subject to a wagon suitable for hauling prisoner's long distances. The countenance on both brothers underwent an immediate change from happy and smiling to frowning and grim. I was confused, and asked what was wrong.

"Señor, we do not build slave haulers. Slavery is not right, and we will not support it," the older brother said with disdain.

I held up my hands. "You misunderstand me, gentlemen. I'm not a slaver, I'm a Federal Marshal. My men haul criminals from all around New Mexico Territory to Santa Fe for trial," I said showing them my badge.

Their faces immediately switched back to happy and smiling again. We discussed various wagon and security designs. By the time we were done they had drawn out a design holding up to fourteen prisoners securely. Supplies for longer trips were stored underneath the wagon in compartments running the length and breadth of the bed.

They even agreed to provide fourteen sets of manacles for both the feet and hands to be permanently attached with strong chains to eye bolts in the floor of the wagon bed. After some back and forth they agreed to have the wagon ready to be picked up with the first coach at the beginning of October. We went through the paperwork, signing and countersigning quickly, and I rode back across the river quite satisfied with the morning's work.

Steve was nowhere to be found when I got back to the hotel, so I had a late lunch and spent the afternoon window shopping looking for something special for Anna. Nothing I saw struck my fancy, so it was back to the hotel, where I relaxed the rest of the afternoon in the room drinking coffee and thinking about the next set of plans we would need to start working on.

The growling and rumbling of my stomach interrupted my reverie some time later. Downstairs, in the restaurant, I found Steve ordering supper with the vaqueros he'd spent the day with. I joined them, and we ate supper, passing a pleasant evening talking about the Estancia and Steve's trip to Austin.

Tom joined us for breakfast the next morning in a much better mood, and less concerned about his father's health. We quickly ate and picked up the bank drafts from Levi, who had them ready for us as promised. Tom and I bid Steve and his escorts a safe journey and watched as they rode south down the street. When they were out of sight, we mounted up and joined the wagon and vaqueros for the trip back to Las Cruces.

With an empty wagon, we made much better time on the trip back arriving at Mr. Mendoza's stable just before lunch two days after leaving El Paso. The vaqueros quickly loaded the pipes Tom and I had removed, and left for home after a quick lunch. As they were riding out of Las Cruces, the two teams I requested to escort Esteban and Ed to Santa Fe with the prisoners arrived. They too had a quick lunch, before riding to Mesilla for the evening, taking the freight wagon they were going to use for the prisoners with them.

Tom and I found Anna and Yolanda in the house rocking the babies after their lunchtime feeding. Anna flashed me one of her smiles letting me know she was very happy to see me. She made the forefinger to the lips 'quiet gesture,' before I could say anything. I mouthed the word restaurant, before we quietly backed out of the room. We sat at our normal table against the back wall and drank coffee while we waited for the ladies.

Both ladies finally joined us, and after a long hug and kiss, we sat down with fresh coffee. We talked about the trip and the coaches I'd ordered which pleased both of them immensely. When I asked if there was any news from George the expressions on both their faces became somber.

"Yes, mi Pablo. George stopped by here two days ago, on his way back to the Estancia. They found the camp right where they'd been told it would be. As expected the comancheros guarding the camp put up a fight. Young Francisco Perez was killed during the fight.

"George was able to bring in three prisoners with minor wounds. He dropped them off at the jail in Mesilla, before stopping here. Like you did with the first set of captives you rescued, he let them split up the wagon load of stolen goods and horses between them. He said he wrote up a report that he left with Esteban."

I cursed under my breath. Francisco had just turned seventeen and was one of the Estancia's favorite young men. His parents would be devastated I knew, but at least he wasn't married or even engaged. I shook my head at the needless violence of it all.

Tom and I spent the rest of the afternoon and evening, holding and cuddling the boys with Anna and Yolanda.

CHAPTER 17

"**M**i Pablo, please get your work done quickly, and stay safe," Anna said quietly with tears in her eyes.

We were standing in front of the restaurant holding each other closely as we said our good-byes.

"My love, I promise not to fight any windmills on this trip, and I'll do my best to stay out of trouble. You take care of the kids, keep the Estancia running, and stay safe while I'm gone. I'll be home as soon as I can," I told her while thumbing the tears from her eyes.

She nodded, gave me a hard squeeze and a light kiss, before releasing me and backing up. I pulled her close for one more kiss, and then turned to join Tom walking to the stables.

Mr. Mendoza had two heavy freight wagons loaded with our supplies and ready for us. They each had a six-mule team. I tied my horse to the back of the wagon and climbed up into the seat taking up the reins. Mr. Mendoza wished us a safe trip, which Tom and I both acknowledged as we drove off down the street, heading West.

We made good time with the half empty wagons pulled by six mules. We pushed the animals hard the entire trip, knowing they could rest up while we were digging for gold. We skirted every village, fort, and town on the way and didn't see any sign of raiding parties or bandits the whole trip.

To make things even better, the weather cooperated, and it remained warm and dry with almost no wind. We made the five-hundred-miles to Colorado City in fifteen days before turning north. We traveled well north of Colorado City, following the rudimentary river road.

Three days later I found the landmarks I'd been looking for, and we turned off the road onto hardpan. A mile off the road I left Tom with the two wagons, and rode my horse back out to the road to hide the few tracks we'd made as best I could. When I caught up to Tom a couple of hours later, we resumed our trek. After a short ride, I led him down into the arroyo then up the sandy bed to the ramp up into the large grassy bowl.

Tom looked around in amazement. "How did you find this place Paul?"

I chuckled. "Mostly by accident, Tom but I'm thankful that we did. It protects us from discovery in all directions. Take care of the animals and start setting up camp if you would, please. I'm going to go back and hide the tracks from the last part of the ride in. When I get back we'll start digging."

Tom nodded and turned to do as I'd asked. I rode back to where we'd stopped the wagons, and did what I could to erase the tracks from there, to our camp in the bowl.

I topped the ramp on my return to find Tom had finished taking care of the animals, and was nearly finished setting up the camp. I unloaded the metal detector, two shovels, and four burlap bags from the wood box Anna had put them in.

I gave Tom a quick course on the metal detector and had him put the ear phones on and test it out. A minute later he gave me a skeptical look telling me it hadn't gone off at all.

Laughing, I told him, "It's not broken Tom, there's just nothing up here. Turn it off and follow me."

When we got to the area Anna and I had quit working on our last visit I had Tom turn the detector on with the volume on low.

Just like when Anna and I were here, as soon the metal detector was turned on a loud squelch came through the ear phones making Tom jump in surprise. I motioned him to swing it from side to side and the sound never lessened. I had Tom turn off the metal detector, set it aside, and move back a few feet so he could see better.

When he was in position I pulled up a shovel full of sand, and started the sifting action. Just like the first time, the sun caught the flakes as they fell from the shovel with the sand giving off a soft golden glow. Tom stared, entranced at the sight for a few moments, before picking up his shovel and joining me.

Tom was much bigger and stronger than Anna, and between the two of us we had twice what Anna and I had dug up in the same amount of time. We followed the same routine Anna and I had followed, and by the time we were ready to leave we had four hundred and fifteen bags of gold bars totaling ten thousand three hundred and seventy-five pounds, which we split between the two wagons.

Our final morning found us having a quick breakfast before striking camp and packing everything up in the wagons. We drove the wagons back near the road where I left Tom to guard the wagons as I spent an hour erasing the trail we'd made leaving the camp. Once we were back on the road, it was a few more minutes erasing the remaining tracks before we headed for Santa Fe.

We followed the same route Anna and I had followed last year, although it took us a little longer due to the heavily loaded wagons. We also lost at least four days from having to find suitable points to cross three large arroyos and a draw, all with high banks. Even after we'd found a place we could make work it still took some time to collapse both banks into ramps so we could cross. A couple of the crossings were a little perilous to my way of thinking but Tom confidently drove the wagon down, across, and up the other side without incident.

We were tired, dirty, and hungry, when we rode into Santa Fe late the morning on July 2nd. Just like in El Paso, I decided to do away with pretense. We rode right up to the bank. Tom stayed with the wagons as I entered the bank.

Hiram was putting on his coat with hat in hand, obviously getting ready to go out when he saw me walk in. He gave an overly dramatic sigh taking off his coat, hanging it and his hat back on the coat tree just inside his office. I laughed as I realized it was Wednesday, and we'd be cutting into his weekly card game.

Hiram waved and began to head towards the back door. I stopped him telling him we'd be using the front door from now on and asked to borrow one of his guards for a few minutes. He laughed and nodded waving one of the guards forward. I took the guard outside and told him to guard the wagons, while Tom and I hauled all the sacks into the weighing room where Hiram was waiting.

When all four hundred and fifteen bags were in the weighing room Tom left to get us a suite at the hotel. Hiram and I untied the bags and started stacking the gold bars next to the weighing table. I knew Hiram was in a hurry, so I remained quiet as he weighed out the gold.

When he was done he added up the weights and said, "This is your biggest load yet, Paul. I come up with 166,000 ounces." At my nod, he went on. "We're paying $14 an ounce for your stuff now, so that comes to a total of $2,324,000. What do you want to do with it?"

"Deposit it all in my private account, please, Hiram," I said.

He quickly wrote out and gave me a deposit

slip, before calling in one of the guards and telling him to watch the room. On our way to his office he called two tellers over and told them to move the gold from the weighing room to the vault. Once in his office I shook his hand and told him I was sorry for cutting into his card game. He laughed as he was putting on his coat and asked me how long I'd be staying in Santa Fe this trip.

"We'll probably stay four days Hiram. Tom and I need to spend a few days recovering from this trip before we head home, and the animals need at least that long. I'll see you over at the club a little later."

We parted ways outside the bank and I walked over to the hotel. Half an hour later both Tom and I were sitting in tubs in our suite drinking a really good pot of coffee as we turned hot, clean, clear water into mud.

When we were clean, dried, and dressed in our city clothes I took Tom over to the club, where I arranged a temporary membership for both of us for a week. With that done we visited the club barber for a haircut and shave, followed by lunch in the dining room. We joined Hiram and the Judge in the game room for an afternoon of cards. Both were happy to see us, as Lucien hadn't been in town for a few months and there was only one other player at the table, one of the ranchers from South of town, who'd come in for supplies.

We caught up on events while we were playing and learned that all the comancheros we'd sent up had been tried, found guilty, and hung. The lives of the two youngest comancheros had been spared. They joined the ex-Mayor and ex-Probate Judge who'd also been found guilty, in prison, turning big rocks into little rocks.

The Judge was full of praise for the way we'd handled the comanchero attack, the investigation into the land fraud, and the prisoners we'd sent up. I did remember to ask about the land grant itself and when the Judge said it was in his office, I quickly asked for it before it disappeared.

"What in the world do you want with that worthless thing?" he asked.

"Judge, it's worthless as a land grant, but it's a work of art in its own right, and it's a piece of Estancia Dos Santos history. I'm going to frame it and hang it my study," I replied.

He gave a shrug and then smiled. "As long you're not going to try and use it to get more land, I don't see why not. I'll bring it with me to lunch, tomorrow."

Tom and I laughed heartily at his reply. "Judge, that document wouldn't stand up long in court. It might fool someone who didn't know Spanish history but as soon as someone bothered to check the signature and year they'd know it was a forgery."

When I got a curious look from the Judge and Hiram I explained. "The grant is dated 1701 and signed by King Carlos III. He was a pretender to the throne supported by the English, Dutch, and others. Even as a pretender he wasn't declared King until 1703 and never had the power to grant land in New Spain to anyone. The rightful King, King Felipe V, fought a 12-year war against the pretender and his foreign allies which he eventually won."

"Where in the world did you learn that?" Hiram asked in amazement.

I chuckled replying, "Before Anna and I got married we spent time after supper looking at various books she'd bring over to the restaurant from her grandfather's library. We'd spend the evening together at the dining room table, well chaperoned, and discuss whatever book she'd brought. One of her favorite books and the second one she brought, was a history of the Spanish Kings through 1800."

"If that was the second book what was the first?" the Judge asked curiously.

Tom quickly replied with a laugh, "That would

be Paul and Anna's favorite book, *Don Quixote*."

The other three men at the table looked at each other perplexed. "I've never heard of it," the rancher said before asking, "Why is that your favorite book?"

"It's a timeless well-known classic. It was written 250 years ago by a Spaniard. The characters are both amusing and tragic, but the underlying story is about daring to reach for the impossible in all that you do, while remaining on the side of the good and righteous. The priests use it to teach students ethics and morals, as well as how to write Spanish properly," I replied.

"Huh!" was all the rancher said.

While we were on the subject of books, I took the opportunity to ask Hiram and the Judge for assistance in finding books for a school and a library, as well as six qualified teachers. At their request, I expanded on what we were looking for.

"We are starting both an elementary school, and a high school in Las Cruces. We need to know who publishes the various textbooks for all levels of school, so that we can write them and arrange to purchase what we need.

"Related to that we also need six teachers to start with. We'll probably need more than that, but six should do to start with.

"Finally, we are building a public library and need books for it. I'm hoping between you two and Steve that you'll be able to find various people to act as our agents at estate sales with large numbers of quality books suitable for a library.

"Steve will be able to provide a lot more details when he gets back which should be soon. I was hoping he would be back already, but he had as far to go on his trip as Tom and I did on ours and he may have stopped at the Estancia to rest for a while on his way back," I said.

We talked about schools, libraries, books, and teachers for the next couple of hours as we played cards. Eventually, the rancher called it a day, and left to take his supplies back to his ranch. When he was gone I casually told Hiram and the Judge that they were invited to the Estancia for the holidays.

Both men scoffed, and the Judge asked, "Why in the world would Hiram and I want to make that trip?"

Hiram nodded his head vigorously as he was raking in the pot he'd just won.

I shuffled the cards and quietly said, "You'll make the trip so that you have an opportunity to talk with Tom, Steve, Kit, and me about statehood, schools, libraries, and the railroad we're going to build." I turned to Hiram and addressed him. "You'll come to see your brother and parents, who will be visiting, and we'll talk about opening a branch of the bank in Las Cruces with a guaranteed initial deposit of $5 million."

When I looked up from shuffling Tom had a grin on his face but the other two were stupefied at what I'd said.

I dealt the cards in silence. The Judge picked up his hand before putting it back down and glancing quickly around the room to make sure we were still the only ones in the room.

"Paul, the rest of it I can understand, but building a railroad takes millions of dollars and a lot of time to get the land grants for eminent domain through congress."

I looked the Judge directly in the eye. "Judge, we have millions of dollars and we already own all but a few acres of the land we will use for the line between here and Las Cruces."

Hiram said with exasperation, "Paul, you have a few million in my bank but you don't have anywhere near enough to start up a railroad."

"Hiram, I've been using your bank as well as your brother's in El Paso for the last six years. The first four years of that time I was mining gold almost full time. Do you really think what I've deposited is all that I've mined or all that there is? I just told you I was going to deposit five million in a bank in Las Cruces. Hopefully that will be a branch of your bank. If not, I'll find someone else to open a bank in Las Cruces," I said in an even no-nonsense tone.

Hiram was about to respond when three men walked into the room. I held up my hand stopping him from speaking and said, "Steve knows everything about what we're planning both for statehood, and the business we were just discussing. I've asked him to hold a private meeting with both of you in his office when he returns. Please wait until then for the details. It should go without saying that what we just discussed, and what Steve tells you, should be held in the strictest confidence and not be repeated where it can be overheard."

Both men looked at each other, then at Tom and I, before nodding. I went on, "Tom, Yolanda, Anna and I will return here the first week in November with our three babies. Kit, Josefa, and their kids are meeting us here for a two week stay, and then traveling south to the Estancia for an extended visit.

"If you should decide to accept our invitation, we will be leaving the middle of November. Josefa, all five kids, and Helen will travel in the coach we are bringing. Anna or Yolanda will be with them in the coach, so things will get a little crowded. I recommend you both start spending a couple hours minimum in the saddle every day to get your riding muscles built up. I'll be bringing plenty of guards so security shouldn't be an issue either."

When I was done talking I glanced at my hand before picking up the deck. "Let's play cards, gentlemen. Will you be taking cards or staying pat?"

We played the next three hands with Tom grinning like a Cheshire cat and the other two with a glazed distant look in their eyes. After the third hand, I stopped the game for the day.

"Gentlemen, your minds are obviously no longer on the game. We've given you a lot to think about, I know. Tom and I are going to call it a day and go get something to eat. We have some things to do tomorrow but why don't we plan on having supper together here tomorrow night?"

The Judge readily agreed, as any bachelor would, and Hiram agreed moments later. We all left the gentleman's portion of the club, and said our goodbyes for the evening. Tom and I walked around to the club's family entrance and enjoyed a well prepared supper, for the first time in almost three months.

At breakfast the next morning Tom asked what I had planned for the day.

I gave him a grin and said, "Today we are going to enter the world of women the world over." At his puzzled look I said, "We are going shopping."

Tom groaned, and I barked out a short laugh. "It's not that bad, Tom. We're looking for coach trunks. When we come back in November with a coach, you can bet the ladies are not going to accept having their family's clothes and baggage carried around in burlap bags like we've been doing. So, let's surprise them with coach trunks."

He nodded thoughtfully and grinned. "I like the surprise Yolanda part. It's the shopping part that makes me want to face the comancheros again."

We were still laughing as we walked into the bank to see if Hiram could recommend a couple of stores in town. We found Hiram sitting at his desk, staring at a large map of the New Mexico Territory.

We stood in the doorway trying to figure out if he was actually seeing the map or not. After a minute of standing there, Tom looked over at me and shrugged. I cleared my voice startling Hiram from his trance. He turned his head seeing, us as if for the first time before a smile spread over his face. He got up and greeted us warmly, while ushering us into his office and closing the door.

"I was just thinking about you two," he said before rushing on in a demanding tone. "Tell me more about this railroad you want to build."

I had been half expecting a grilling on the railroad but not quite so soon. "Relax, Hiram. The railroad is only a part of what we are trying to do. A large part to be sure but still only a part. It would take much more time than we have just to explain the background much less go into any details. Suffice it to say we are building a railroad from Las Cruces to Santa Fe, and let's leave it at that until Steve sets up the meeting after he gets back. We're not going to start building it tomorrow so there's time."

Tom and I watched as Hiram's enthusiasm visibly deflated.

"You'll have to forgive me, Paul, but this is damned exciting and I want to be part of it. So does the Judge and we're sure Lucien will, too."

"You'll all have an opportunity to play a part in both the railroad and the bigger plan, Hiram, but now is not the time. You need to understand though that the secondary reason for the railroad is to help move the products produced by the Estancia, mostly cattle and produce, to a larger market. I will not give up control of the railroad to anyone, if for no other reason than that," I told him in an even but serious voice.

He nodded once again, and then it was like a switch turned off and he smiled and asked how he could help us today. I explained about needing to buy some coach trunks, and asked for recommendations on places to start.

"Now that I can help you with," he said with visible enthusiasm. "The Altamirano Wainwrights builds the finest coaches in New Mexico. In addition to building coaches they also carry a wide selection of coach trunks. I suggest you start there."

We followed his directions and soon found ourselves at the storefront of the Altamirano Wainwright Shop. Inside was a dazzling array of coach trunks in every imaginable size, shape, and internal configuration, as well as a high-end selection of other coach accessories. Tom and I browsed for a few minutes before a clerk approached and pleasantly asked if he could help us find something. We explained our needs, and he took us over to a side by side display of three almost identical looking large trunks.

He explained the differences succinctly. "This

style is best for a growing family. We make and sell three different versions, each having its own price. The least expensive trunk is our most popular and is built from a good hardwood but is our least durable and will probably not stand up to regular sustained use for any long period of time. The next most expensive is built from a better grade of hardwood with a soft padding and cloth lined interior and includes a removable top tray for toiletries and other smaller items. Our most expensive trunk is made from solid mahogany with the padded cloth lined interior and two removable trays. The price for this trunk includes a custom paint scheme of your choice."

Wow! Who knew buying trunks could be so difficult? I shrugged my shoulders and pointed at the most expensive version and told him we'd take six of them. His eye's widened and he took us over to the counter to write up the order.

We told him we'd pick up two plain trunks just like the one on display in five days. The other four we would pick up the second week in November, after they'd been painted in the Estancia color scheme with our seal on the front of all four trunks. Each trunk would also have one set of our initials AM, YM, TM, and PM with one letter on each side of the locking mechanism. We went through the signing and countersigning folderol, before receiving a copy of the receipt.

With an hour to kill we strolled the streets of downtown Santa Fe, doing some window shopping to see if anything caught our eye. Nothing caught our interest, so after a light lunch at the club we went to visit the Judge.

The Judge greeted us in the small reception area before ushering us into his small rather cramped office. He called in his clerk, explaining that his family had lived in Santa Fe for over 150 years. When he told the clerk what we were looking for he immediately nodded his head telling us the Maes family library had been for sale for almost ten years, but no one appeared to be interested in it.

I asked how many books there were, and he gave a shrug of his shoulders saying he didn't know. He did know the Maes family agent though, and agreed to try and get us an appointment to see the library so we could examine the books. He also told us of two other private libraries from before the war that were for sale, and we asked to see those collections as well. The clerk told us he would send a note to the hotel, when he had the visits arranged.

With that task out of the way we retired to the club where we relaxed in comfort reading the collection of newspapers the club had accumulated since my last visit, and drinking coffee. We joined the Judge, Hiram and Helen for a really good supper in the main club, as planned.

Everyone was on their best behavior with no mention, at all, of the railroad. Instead we talked about Joseph and JJ, and told Helen they would be coming up with us at the beginning of November. We also spent a great deal of time talking about schools and public libraries. Helen was almost as excited by those, as she was the news about the babies.

When Tom and I returned to the hotel late that evening, we found a note from the clerk telling us he'd arranged for us to see the three collections starting just after lunch the next day, beginning with the Maes family library. He included directions to the Maes house from the hotel, and said he would meet us there, and escort us to the other two collections from there.

The next afternoon we arrived at an old house to find the clerk and an older gentleman waiting for us, near the front door. It was quite apparent that at one time the house was one of the best homes in Santa Fe, but years of neglect were beginning to take their toll.

The clerk introduced us to the older man who

opened the door and led us inside. He lit an oil lamp sitting on one of the tables. With the lamp lit, he led us down a hall into a long fairly narrow room set up as a family library. The man told us the Maes family had used it as both a school room for their children, and to entertain guests.

The far wall and one of the short side walls were covered in floor to ceiling bookshelves full of books. I couldn't help but wonder as I looked around, how many of the books had actually been read. At a guess there were over 1,000 books, all covered in layers of dust, but otherwise in good condition. Tom and I randomly pulled a few books off the shelves and, after blowing the dust off, opened them up. All the books we pulled out were in Spanish, which was no surprise.

I spent a few minutes negotiating with the agent before we agreed to a price of $300 for all the books. We also negotiated a separate price to have all the books cleaned and packed in wooden crates, ready for pick up in four days. The agent appeared to be happy with the results, and the clerk led us to the next house on the list.

By the time we walked into the club for supper, Tom and I had sneezed our way through both of the remaining houses, and were both covered in dust. Despite the dust we had purchased another 450 books between the other two collections, with about half in English. All the books would be cleaned and packed in crates ready to be picked up with the Maes collections. We'd made a good start on the Village School Library as well as the Las Cruces Public Library, so we were both happy.

Two days later Tom and I were both bored to tears. We were sitting in our room having some late morning coffee, just passing time as we waited for lunch time to roll around, when there was a knock at the door. I opened the door and found Steve grinning at me. I invited him inside, and offered him coffee which he accepted before excitedly saying he had much to tell us and asking when we were leaving to go back to the Estancia.

"We plan on leaving in three days, Steve," I replied. "What's got you so excited?"

Steve answered my question with another question. "What are your plans between now and then?"

I gave him an exasperated look. "We have absolutely nothing planned between now and the afternoon, day after tomorrow, when we have to pick up two coach trunks from the wainwright and a wagon load of books we bought from three different houses. Oh, and we have to pick up the quarterly shipment of scotch and wine from the warehouse, too. Now what gives, Steve?"

"That's perfect. It gives us two days to go over everything I've done, and make any changes you want made. As far as what gives, let's have lunch at the club and then come back here where we can talk in private, and I'll fill you in on what I did," Steve said gleefully. "By the way, Anna sent two teams to escort me home and escort you back to the Estancia. They're staying at the hotel down the street. They'll be joining me for supper at the restaurant downstairs."

That last bit was really good news for Tom and me. We were both very tired of driving the freight wagons, which had proven to be even more uncomfortable than a farm wagon. It was obvious that we weren't going to get anything out of Steve until after lunch so we acquiesced, and headed to the club.

During lunch, we talked about our trips and the physical stress they took. Despite our curiosity at what Steve hadn't told us yet we found ourselves spellbound as he recounted the trip to Austin, and back to the Hacienda.

They hadn't had any problem with raids or robbers, but they'd seen plenty of signs that both were active. They'd come across the results of both raiders and robbers within hours of their occurrence, and spent time burying the dead or helping the survivors. Steve was amazed that he'd ever thought he could make the trip to Austin and back in a buggy by himself.

Tom and I headed back to the suite with strict orders from Steve to order coffee, and be ready to talk as soon as he got there. He needed to stop by his office and pick up some papers before we talked. We did as he asked, and were sitting in the suite drinking coffee when Steve walked in carrying a large overstuffed portfolio full of papers. Steve saw the coffee, nodded to himself, and locked the door, coming into the room and sitting down across from Tom and I.

He poured himself a cup of coffee and took a long drink while looking at us.

"Gentlemen, Governor Pease turned out to be exactly as advertised. If we had someone like him as a Territorial Governor, statehood in a few years would be assured. Governor Pease was convinced we were trying to pull a fast one, buying the salt flats; but after reading the Trust documents, he changed his mind.

"We talked at some length on the reasons you were doing this, and he agreed completely with Paul's analysis. He was very impressed with the forward thinking you displayed on this. In fact, he was so impressed, he cut the price to a third of the original price which helped us buy the entire salt flats instead of just the third we'd have bought otherwise."

"A third? What in the world are you talking about Steve?" I asked incredulously.

"The maps we used were wrong Paul. It's as simple as that. The salt flats cover roughly 60 miles by 10 miles. That's 384,000 acres. The original price was three dollars an acre. Governor Pease cut it to one dollar an acre, so the Trust now owns all of it. Before I left Austin, I got a bank draft for $190 Thousand which I later redeposited in your account in El Paso."

"So, the trust now owns the entire Salt Flats, which is three times the size we thought it was, and it cost us two hundred thousand less than we thought it was going to cost? And the trust has been registered in Austin and Santa Fe?" I asked.

Steve swallowed a mouthful of coffee. "Yes, to all that, Paul. I also registered it in San Elizario, so that anyone who cared to look would know it was owned by a registered Public Trust."

"Well done, Steve!" I said enthusiastically. Then the rest of what Steve had said hit me. "Wait a minute, Steve, what about the rest of the money? What happened to the other twenty-six thousand dollars?"

"I'm getting to that, Paul. Give me a few minutes to explain and all will be clear," Steve said with some exasperation of his own. "Now, something had been bothering me since you arrested the Mayor and the Probate Judge, but I couldn't, for the life of me, figure out what it was. It bothered me all the way to Austin.

"We'd been in Austin for a few days when it finally dawned on me what it was. Paul, what's going to happen when word makes its way around the territory that someone bought up most of a strip of land between Santa Fe and Las Cruces?

"I'll tell you what's going to happen, the price of land is going to go much higher. Other speculators are going to see the land you didn't purchase near Socorro and Albuquerque, and they'll buy it up. When you finally get around to buying it, the value will be so high it will eat into the material costs of actually building the railroad not to mention all the rolling stock and other things we'll need.

"That's not all though. How about the land for depots and stock pens? How about the land going west to Colorado City, or east to wherever it is out there we're going to go?"

I softly groaned to myself as I realized he was right. What had we been thinking?

"Okay, Steve, you made your point. It will eventually get out but we have time yet, I think. The only one who knows about the land we bought is the land office clerk in Las Cruces and his report isn't due here in Santa Fe for another few weeks," I said reasonably.

"That would be true except for one important fact Paul. Who is the best friend of the land office clerk in Las Cruces? The land office clerk in Socorro is his best friend. And people talk, Paul! The land office clerk in both places will talk to their friends who will talk to their friends and before you know it a land rush has begun," Steve said excitedly before rushing on.

"When I got back to the Hacienda seven weeks had already passed. I explained the problem to Anna and Yolanda as soon as I arrived. They thanked me for bringing it to their attention and then shut themselves in the study for most of the day. The next morning, they told me to travel as fast as I could to Socorro and Albuquerque and see what, if anything, I could do to get the land we need to complete the route.

"That's when she assigned the two teams to escort me. She told me to use the twenty-six thousand dollars I'd brought back with me and gave me another twenty-four thousand dollars in case I needed it. To make a long story short, I ended up needing to use some of it, not much, but a fair amount.

"The two farmers who owned the land we're interested in near Socorro and Albuquerque weren't interested in selling. They hadn't heard about the land we'd bought yet but they liked what they had.

I got both of them to agree to sell the land in exchange for two acres of land for every acre they sold me as well as the right to farm the land they sold me as long as they or their family owned the adjoining acres," he finished with a grin.

"I don't know what to say, Steve," I said, flabbergasted at what he'd accomplished. "Thank you seems so inadequate but: Thank You."

He waved off the thanks before continuing. "We still have a problem guys. The rumors have already reached Santa Fe, and people are buying or holding the last seventeen miles of land we intended to buy to connect where you finished buying land to the east side of Santa Fe."

I heard a big groan from Tom, that I wholeheartedly agreed with.

Steve held up his hand with a grin. "It's not the

end of the world, guys. I have a plan that will end up costing you less than what you originally expected to spend anyway."

At our look of puzzlement, he took out the territorial map from the Hacienda that showed the route from Las Cruces to Santa Fe, and refolded it to show the area around Santa Fe.

He pointed to the end of the route we'd already bought the land for.

"Instead of going into Santa Fe from here as originally planned you continue north for another twelve miles," he said tracing the route he was proposing. "As of this morning no one had bothered to buy this land because of these two gorges, here and here." Pointing at the two gorges on the map as he was talking. "The twelve miles ends between the two gorges. This first gorge is the smaller of the two but it's still just over a hundred yards wide. We'll have to span that before turning into this small valley here," he said pointing again.

He took a large drink of coffee before continuing with a large grin on his face. "If you buy this small valley, it's about six square miles by the way, and offer to exchange it for the right of way across the next valley, I can guarantee the owner of the connecting valley, here, will be more than happy to agree. That puts us just outside of Santa Fe on the West side of town, which as of a couple of hours ago was still available. That's where we build the depot complex."

"What makes you so sure the owner of this second valley will agree to the swap you're talking about?" Tom asked with a snort.

Steve's grin got even bigger which I didn't think was possible. "Because I'm the owner of that second valley! I've had my eye on that other valley for a few years now. It would complete the little ranch I've been dreaming of."

I picked up the map and stared at what Steve had drawn in with his pencil. The more I looked, the more I liked it. The route he was suggesting was actually easier than what we'd originally envisioned in spite of the gorge we'd have to cross.

I put the map back on the table and nodded at Steve. "Okay, you convinced me. Let's make this happen," I said with a burst of enthusiasm.

Steve held up his hand. "There's more, Paul. Anna figured that you'd go for it when I explained it to her in anticipation of the news already being out. She told me to remind you that you had two more routes you were interested in and that others were going to be able to figure out what you were doing if you continued the piecemeal approach. She recommended you buy everything now and be done with it."

I rubbed my chin thoughtfully for a few moments. "I'd love to Steve. It would be much more convenient to get it all over and done with, but I don't have the routes memorized, and everything I need is back at the Hacienda," I said regretfully.

Steve laughingly replied, "Anna thought of that too, Paul. She gave me these and told me to use them for buying the land for the other routes you wanted."

As he was talking, he reached into his portfolio and pulled out several pieces of onion skin and laid them next to the map. I picked them up and glanced at each one, smiling as I did. Now I knew why she and Yolanda had locked themselves into the study. They'd used the road map to map out the routes to Colorado City, and where Roswell would eventually be. They'd also mapped out the Mescalero Reservation and the town of Tularosa. What a woman!

I looked over at Steve and asked, "Have you figured out how much we're talking about for everything?"

Steve nodded his head. "Yep, I figured it all out this morning after stopping in at the land office. We're talking a total of just over 750,000 acres at a cost of about $740,000. That's an average cost of just under one dollar an acre. That includes everything. The land to finish the route into Santa Fe, the Santa Fe depot complex, the route west, the land in Tucson and Colorado City for the depot complexes, the route east and the three parcels of land. I don't know why you want those three areas of land on the route east but those are what's driving the cost."

It was my turn to grin. "You'll find out soon enough, but none of them have anything to do with the railroad. Okay, let's go talk to Hiram and get this done." I rose from the chair I'd been sitting in, and started walking towards the door.

Tom quickly followed suit and caught me at the door while Steve scrambled to collect the map and onion skin papers. Tom and I waited patiently at the door while Steve put everything neatly away in his portfolio, and when he joined us at the door we left to see Hiram.

We walked into the bank to find Hiram at his desk. I ushered everyone inside the office, and closed the door behind me. Hiram looked up as we walked in and welcomed Steve back from his trip before noting the closed door and raising an eyebrow.

"Hiram, based on what Steve's been telling us, and orders from Anna, we're getting ready to buy a bunch of land," I said without preamble.

I motioned to Steve who gave a very quick recap of the situation without going into details about what we were going to buy, or how much it was expected to cost.

Hiram listened patiently with no sign of his previous excitement.

"The land situation is worse than you think, Steve. That new land office clerk Meriwether appointed before he left last year likes to talk." Hiram glanced over at Tom and I before explaining. "The old land office clerk you dealt with apparently got a case of gold fever and left for Colorado last fall. At least that's the rumor. Governor Meriwether's term was up shortly after that, but before he left he appointed a new interim land office clerk until the new Governor arrived.

"Unfortunately, President Pierce has decided to wait until after the election to appoint a new Governor. The new clerk is supposedly a relative of someone Meriwether knew, but no one seems to know anything about his past. He seems to know the business and as I said, he seems to like to talk about what goes on at the land office. There have been some complaints about land that should have been available, suddenly being bought by someone else."

Damnit! Why did everything have to get so complicated? I heard Laura's soft sweet laugh in my left ear followed by her voice.

"Self-importance and greed have been powerful motivators since the dawn of time. Put your big boy pants on and deal with it my love."

I gave a deep sigh and looked at the three men. "We are going to spend about $750,000 on at least 7 different land transactions Hiram. What do you recommend?"

Hiram responded without hesitation. "I'd bring the Judge in on this if at all possible. If he's available for supper, book a private room at the club. We can all meet tonight for supper, discuss what you're trying to do, and come up with a plan to make it happen."

Another delay. If there's anything I hate, it's kicking the can down the road, but I didn't see any readily available alternative.

"Alright, Hiram," I said with an air of resignation. "I'll get back with you after I see the Judge and get the room booked."

We talked for a few more minutes about a good time for supper and the three of us left Hiram's office. Outside the bank I told the other two that there was no need for all three of us to go traipsing around town. They both hesitated, and it was Tom who reminded me that 'the Boss' was still a threat and was based here.

He was right.

Again, damnit!

Tom and I went on together while Steve went back to the suite and waited for us there.

At the Governor's Palace, I passed by the land office and found it closed with a note on the door saying it would reopen tomorrow morning. That made me feel a little better and I walked into the Judge's office in a much better mood. I told the Judge that we had a problem we were hoping he could help us with and that we could discuss it over supper at the club this evening if he was available. He readily agreed to supper at seven. We quickly left to arrange it, and to let Hiram know before going back to the suite.

In the suite, I let Steve know the arrangements. Steve gave me a small grin and then left saying he had to let the escort teams know that he had to change their supper plans that night to breakfast in the morning. Tom and I stewed in the suite, the rest of the afternoon.

We arrived at the club just before seven, and

found the other three already in the private room, waiting for us. We kept the discussion to pleasantries until after our meals had been served and then got to the specifics as we ate. The Judge listened carefully to everything we had to say, asked a few questions, and then thought for a few minutes as the rest of us finished our meals.

The Judge waited until after the table had been cleared, drinks served, and the door closed again before giving us his thoughts.

"Gentlemen, this is potentially a complex problem. However, like many other such problems, it has a simple solution. We simply use overpowering force to deal with it. In this situation 'overpowering force' is in the guise of a Federal Judge with two US Marshals to ensure everything is done above board and legal, while a bank president stands by to authorize the transfer of funds. If we arrive as the clerk is opening the office, there's no reason that the transaction won't be complete by the end of the day."

After some thought and discussion, we all agreed to the plan.

The next morning, after breakfast with the two teams from the Estancia, we met the Judge and Hiram in the Judge's office before walking to the land office together.

The clerk seemed more than a little surprised to see the five us enter the land office right behind him. The Judge took the lead as planned.

He pointed to Steve and told the clerk, "This gentleman is here to fill the territorial coffers, with some much-needed funds. You will conduct no other business today, and you will not leave this office until you've finished with his transactions. These two US Marshals are here to see my orders are carried out, as I just directed. Mr. Greenburg, the President of the 1st Territorial Bank of Santa Fe is here to document and authorize the immediate transfer of funds to the territorial coffers as soon as you've determined the price of all the land this gentleman is buying. Do you have any questions?"

The clerk swallowed once and shook his head before saying "No," in a high, tight, stress filled voice. The Judge nodded to Tom who picked up the closed sign from the counter and put it back on the outside of the door before closing it.

Steve moved up to the counter and began buying the land in separate transactions. By the time we were done, at noon, we had spent just a few thousand dollars over the price he'd estimated. Hiram left to arrange the transfers from my private account to the territory's general account, and Steve left to have the new deeds processed by the county clerk.

Tom and I were in the Judge's office when Steve returned with a grin, telling us that, with one minor exception, everything was done. The minor exception turned out to be the contract for the land for the right of way swap which I signed after reading it. As with all of his legal documents the terms were straight forward and clear.

CHAPTER 18

O ur final day in Santa Fe was hectic as Tom and I, with the ready assist-ance of the escort teams, gathered supplies for the trip home in the morning, and picked up the trunks, booze, and books that afternoon.

With little fanfare, we departed Santa Fe the next morning after a good breakfast with the Judge, Hiram, Helen, and Steve. We assured all of them but most especially Helen that we'd be back the first week in November with the la-dies and babies.

Pushing the animals hard we travelled from 'can see to can't see' hoping to get home before the rainy season started. We had no problems with raids or bandits but at this time of the year we hadn't really expected any. No one, good or bad, wanted to be caught out during the unpredictable and often deadly rainy season. Still, we'd delayed our departure a few days longer than prudent, so we weren't surprised when we were caught by rain two hours out from the Estancia.

Despite the rains we travelled the last few miles of the trip extremely quickly as Giuseppe had completed the new paved portion of the Camino Real and seamlessly diverted the road from its old course through the Estancia. Tom and I had been amazed both at how difficult it was to tell that the route had been changed, and at how smooth the macadam road was to travel on.

We arrived at the Hacienda very wet and uncomfortable, just as the rain ended for the time being. Anna and Yolanda were at the door to greet us and all my attention was focused on the huge super megawatt Anna smile I was receiving.

I scooped Anna up in a long drawn out hug and kiss before setting her down, and listening to her laughing admonishment about getting her wet. Tom and I helped unload the wagons and then disappeared into the Hacienda for long hot showers and some time with our wives and kids.

All the kids were doing great. Beth and Izabella were of great assistance in keeping the younger ones under control and out of too much mischief. Mike and Alejandro were growing like weeds. A strong bond had developed between the two, further strengthened by their fast friendship with Antonio and Carlo. Manuel and Sierra remained the most physically active and able of all the kids in the Hacienda although Sierra was beginning to lose her tomboy disposition in favor of more domestic activities.

Sierra was also beginning to notice boys. She spent much of her indoor time with Beth and Izabella instead of Manuel now. Izabella hadn't formed any close relationships with boys her age yet but apparently had her eye on a couple. The relationship between Beth and Maco also continued growing stronger although Beth remained concerned that it was going too slow.

Of course, after supper that night, Anna led me by the hand to the piano. I played some of my favorite instrumentals quietly to warm up while listening to the various conversations going on. Shortly before the kids were sent to bed I sang them "Do-Re-Mi".

After they'd all gone to bed I sang a new mix of songs I'd been saving up. I started with "All I Have To Do Is Dream", moved right into "I Do, I Do, I Do, I Do, I Do", followed by "My Girl", and ending with "Southern Nights".

The Padre asked for anything Irish, so I gave him the classic, "Danny Boy" which he really appreciated as it was one of his father's favorites. I ended the evening at the piano with "Anna's Song" as expected and then led Anna upstairs giving our goodnights to all as we walked up the stairs.

As I'd half expected Anna had prepared our bedroom for a little intimate time. She had a bottle of opened wine on the fireplace bench with glasses, a small fire going in the fireplace, and the guitar she'd given me shortly after her quinceanera leaning against the wall.

With a smile I picked up the guitar and softly sang "Getting You Home" just to set the mood for the remaining activities before we fell asleep.

After breakfast, the next morning we showed off our treasures from Santa Fe. All the ladies of the Hacienda were very appreciative of the trunks and amazed at the number of books. We opened all the crates of books and asked the ladies to decide how to divide them between the Hacienda, the village school, and the Las Cruces Library. While that was going on, Tom and I retired to the study to catch up on all the work going on within the Estancia by reading the monthly reports.

Construction activities continued apace with the school/community center scheduled for completion by the end of November. Giuseppe had received a reply to his letter about pumps and windmills along with a sample of both pump sizes he had questions about. Early testing with the larger pump indicated it would be more than satisfactory for our ice making operation. The smaller pump had been set aside until my return.

The initial work preparing for construction of the storerooms and stable complex on the upper plateau had already begun. Work slowly continued on the North and South boundary walls which Heinrich was using as training areas for a handful of older boys from the village who had expressed an interest in becoming masons. Preparation for paving the road from the bridge to the village as well as the village streets themselves would begin as soon as the rainy season ended.

The Estancia was awash in cattle again thanks to another better than normal calving season. Deliveries to the forts continued and Hector reported that the vaqueros were starting to hear rumors of increases in future deliveries at all the forts. He was extremely concerned about the potential for over grazing. In support of Hector and Ranch Operations, Tomas had increased the area of alfalfa and feed corn production along the base of the Doña Ana Mountains and was advocating for larger and deeper cisterns to capture more run off water. Between sales to the forts, the butchers in Las Cruces and Mesilla, and sales to our own villagers, Ranch Operations were showing a modest profit again this year.

Finca Operations had taken off this year as expected. The pecan trees had arrived and were planted with 60 of them covering 5 acres on the upper plateau and the remainder covering almost 80 acres at the north end of the Estancia.

Tomas had planted 3,000 acres with a mix of sweet corn, lettuce, chile, beans, tomatoes, peas, and carrots. All had produced large crops with the bulk of the lettuce and chile still to be harvested. Tomas reported little loss from spoilage as sales to the forts' commissaries as well as stores and individuals in Las Cruces and Mesilla were not only brisk but the demand outweighed supply.

The Hacienda vegetable gardens had also produced well and between them and the crops along the river everyone on the Estancia was well supplied with preserved vegetables. Overall, the Finca Operations were expected to show a profit after the lettuce and chili were harvested.

George had been busy on two fronts. The first front was actually protecting the Estancia from Indian raids. The Navajo, Comanche, and, something we hadn't seen much of the last two years, other Apache, had been very active this year starting shortly after we left and continuing until about a week before we returned.

None of the raids ever penetrated far enough into the Estancia to threaten the village, ranch area, or Hacienda thanks to the Scout/Sniper teams, the observation/signal posts, and the Estancia's signaling system.

Most of the Apache and Navajo raiding parties were ten men or less, sometimes on foot and sometimes on horseback. The Comanche raiding parties, on the other hand, were anywhere from twenty to sixty warriors and always on horseback.

The Estancia had lost a wrangler and two farmers fighting off these raids and Anna, with Yolanda's support, had issued George the only order she gave him while we were gone. Her order was simple and directly reflected her Apache heritage. All raiding parties were to be attacked outside the Estancia when at all possible. Further, the intent of the attacks was to leave only one survivor who would take back the tale of another failed attack on the Estancia. I not only agreed with her order but was quite proud of her for giving it.

The second front George was busy with was organizing various types of training including horsemanship for the farmers, supply and logistics planning, and deployment, as well as marksmanship. He was strongly pushing for building an area to be used by the rapid response force. He was hoping for what amounted to a small military style post where the teams assigned to the rapid response force would be headquartered and conduct their daily training.

His vision included a small headquarters building, a large covered open-air training pavilion, as well as nearby rifle and pistol ranges. He was supported in this by both Yolanda and Miguel.

Stable operations were going well with the animals healthy and well cared for. However, Raul needed more of everything. More saddles, tack, harnesses, leather for tack repair, more wood for the cooper, more iron and steel for the blacksmiths. He also wanted to see less hay and more seed feed for the horses and mules. He was working with Tomas and Juan to identify possible sources.

Anna had talked to me over a private breakfast on the terrace about the Rivera's accepting her offer of employment as landscapers after visiting the Estancia for a week. Two of the sons remained in Mesilla to continue the courtyard and house landscaping business the family had been developing while the rest to the family moved to the Estancia.

So, it came as no surprise when I saw that Anna had added a new section on landscaping activities to the report. This new section, written by Francisco Rivera, covered landscaping plans, activities, and status for the Hacienda, village and ranch area.

The initial plans were to focus on trees, principally acacia and crepe myrtle, in all three areas. Francisco was working with Tomas for manpower, Giuseppe for impacts to and from engineering activities, and Jesus, who had formed two volunteer committees in the village and ranch area to advise Francisco on their thoughts regarding specific locations and colors.

Finally, Jesus reported the villagers remained happy with few problems outside minor personality related squabbles and the inherent family issues that crop up in any village.

When we were both done reading, Tom looked at me with concern and said, "We need to spend more time digging gold if we're going to get everything done on the Estancia, the Mesilla Valley Trusts, and the railroad."

I had reached the same conclusion. We didn't have answers to the problem yet, but it was clear we were going to have to do something and time was running out for the La Paz site which was, by far, the richest of the known sites.

Tom and I quickly settled into a routine after our return. A morning ride, joined again by Anna and Yolanda, followed by working on some aspect of our planning, working on the ice making machine, refining the prototype ice boxes and ice chests, or working on the swamp coolers.

At the beginning of October, we took a family trip to Las Cruces with our two ladies and the three babies. Tom and I had to go to El Paso to pick up the new coach and prisoner wagon while the two ladies wanted a little time with the Mendoza clan. We also needed to see how the two Trusts were doing and determine how much money to bring back from El Paso to fund their estimated expenses for the coming year.

As was usual by now we were escorted to Las Cruces by two mixed teams led by Rodrigo who was the de facto head of our personal security force. He and his two teams had been training with Miguel and George while Tom and I had been gone and all the men were armed identically to me and Tom so there was plenty of firepower if we needed it.

The first four miles of the short trip to Las Cruces were extremely pleasant. The new macadam road through the Estancia was a joy to travel. All too soon, however, we left the Estancia and it was back to the rutted wagon road. Still, that first four miles of paved road had served to speed up the trip and we arrived in Las Cruces well before lunch.

Tom and I spent an enjoyable hour with Mr. Mendoza showing us the results of the work he had done with the coach team as well as the custom harnesses and tack that Delores and Francisco Delgado had made. After that it was back in the saddle again for a quick trip to Mesilla to check on Esteban and Ed.

Both men were curious about the trip to El Paso. I had sent a note to them via Juan giving them our plan and asking one of them to accompany us but hadn't told them anything about the custom prisoner transport wagon we were picking up.

I told them we were bringing back a surprise to make their life a little easier and then settled down with coffee in the office courtyard to get caught up on their activities. Esteban mentioned he had a letter for me from the Judge and while he went back inside to get it Ed told us about the three minor felons they had arrested over the last few weeks during the daily visits to the saloons.

None of the three had put up a fight and were now in the county jail waiting for transport to Santa Fe. Both Esteban and Ed felt that making the trip to Santa Fe this time of the year for three minor felons was unnecessary and suggested making the trip in the spring when it was much warmer up North. I quickly agreed with them and our discussion turned to their weekly circuits around the valley. There were a few Indian raids but no holdups or comanchero raids, so things were relatively quiet from their perspective.

The Judge's letter wasn't much more than a note giving me formal authority to hire two more full time deputies at least one of which needed to be stationed in Tucson or Colorado City. I already had two people in mind for the positions, I just had to find them and decided that was a task for next year.

After some discussion, we decided that Esteban and Ed would leave in two weeks to finally make a circuit of the Western part of the territory with the primary purpose of being seen as well as pick up any prisoners Tucson and Colorado City might have. We

P. C. Allen

returned to Las Cruces after our short visit knowing we'd see Ed for breakfast in the morning before we left for El Paso.

Tom, Ed, and I along with our escort team left for El Paso the next morning as planned, herding the coach horses and four mules we'd brought from the Estancia to pull the coach and wagon back from El Paso. With no wagons, we were able to shave a half day off the trip and arrived in El Paso early the next afternoon going straight to the Rivera Brothers wagon yard.

The coach and the prisoner wagon were everything we could have hoped for. Both were true works of art in vastly different ways.

The coach was luxurious in every way imaginable. The outside was the light dusty rose with green trim we had requested. They'd even used the green to highlight what I had taken to calling privately our coat of arms on both doors. The interior was as plush as it could be. The leather seats, seat backs, and side walls were thick and well-padded, again continuing the rose and green theme. Interior storage was provided under the seat with both large empty spaces as well as small drawers.

At the brother's insistence, we harnessed up the horses and took a short ride around the wagon yard. While it still had the characteristic sway of a coach the ride was much smoother than any of us expected. The second coach we'd ordered was well under construction and we were assured it would be ready in December as planned.

The prisoner wagon was at the other end of the extreme in virtually every way. It too was solidly built with comfortable accommodations for a driver and guard up front but any similarity to the coach ended at that point. The wagon bed had stout, thick, high sides and a tailgate with the driver and guard separated from the prisoners by a thick wall. A sturdy wooden bench ran along both walls and seven eyebolts had been sunk into the floor in front of each bench. Attached to each eyebolt was a complete set of hand and foot manacles that the brothers assured us was just long enough to allow the prisoners to remain seated but yet short enough to prevent them from standing up straight. The wagon was clearly marked on both sides with a US Marshal's badge and lettering. Ed was ecstatic with the security features and the built-in storage compartments underneath, but his main enthusiasm was for the well-padded driver's seat with its separate springs.

We must have looked a site as our strange little parade made its way across the river to the hotel where we were staying the night. We gave Levi a tour of the coach after which he joined us for a long supper. Tom left us shortly after supper to spend the night with his father. While Rodrigo and the escorts drank beer, Levi helped me sample the latest batch of available scotch, none of which was up to par with what I was getting from Santa Fe.

We arrived back in Las Cruces the evening of the fifth day after we'd left. Ed left us near Mesilla thanking me profusely for the new wagon and us wishing him and Esteban a safe journey on their upcoming circuit of the southern Territory.

Anna and Yolanda brought the babies out with them to see the coach. I'm not sure which Anna was more impressed with, the coach or the team of black horses. We drove them around town for a short ride and they exclaimed their pleasure at its look and ride.

When the short ride was over, Tom and I escorted them back to the restaurant. Along the way Anna told us that she and Yolanda had met with both Trusts and approved their plans. They had also given their grandparents two thousand dollars each, as the leaders of their respective Trusts, to begin implementing the approved plans. I asked what the plans were for the next few days and a grinning Anna told us that while Las Cruces was a nice place to visit it was time to go home.

Tom and I exchanged a quick look and silently reached agreement that the hot bath we'd planned tomorrow morning could wait until we got to the Hacienda tomorrow afternoon.

We returned to the Hacienda the next morning. The coach was a hit at the Hacienda and everyone wanted a short ride. The driver and guard graciously gave everyone who wanted a half mile ride as much to experience the coach as the road. Tom and I watched the first ride from the terrace before parting ways to enjoy our much-anticipated long hot shower.

We were scheduled to leave for Santa Fe in three weeks and there were still plenty of things that I wanted to get accomplished before then. While Anna and Yolanda finalized our travel plans and did some additional work on our long-range plans Tom and I were busy on two other tasks.

Our first task was to build the ice making machine now that the building and windmill was completed. I found I'd really missed building things and getting my hands dirty building the machine was both back breaking and extremely enjoyable. With the assistance of Giuseppe and Rafael we had all the pieces Rafael had made in the blacksmith shop assembled and working in six days. Another two days and we had the pump connected to the windmill and integrated with the rest of the machinery.

The next morning, with all of us watching and holding our breath, Giuseppe engaged the windmill. Machinery started moving and clanking and we could hear the sound of water moving through the pipes but there really wasn't much to see. Everything appeared to be working and we didn't find any leaks so we settled down to wait. Two days later, after four failed attempts, we succeeded in producing solid ice. The ice came out of the machine in a single, long, thin rectangle scored to give us fifty individual, ten pound ice blocks, measuring five inches by five inches by eleven inches which was the standard size we'd come up with.

The final test of the prototype ice box we'd built proved successful with a block of ice lasting three days keeping the interior frosty cold the entire time. With our testing completed we wasted no time getting the word out that ice boxes and ice were now available through the village store. Until we could come up with enough young men that wanted to make and deliver ice for a living we simply included this as one of the rotating tasks for the teams to do.

Tom and I split our time building and testing the ice making machine with the other task, loading gold bars. We spent an hour or two each evening in the cave loading burlap bags with 80 bars each. When we were done with that we had a wagon parked next to the Hacienda and spent two hours every morning hauling gold from the cave to the study to the wagon after everyone had finished breakfast and gone their separate ways. I'm almost positive we didn't fool anyone, but no one asked any questions about the wagons and for that I was thankful. It took some time but two days before we left we had four wagons sitting next to the Hacienda loaded, covered with tied down canvas, and ready to leave for Santa Fe.

The day before we left for Santa Fe an almost palpable sense of excitement permeated the entire Estancia. What was causing it I couldn't tell. Perhaps, as Anna and Yolanda believed, it was a combination of the ice making actually producing ice, the availability of ice boxes, and a long trip being made by a significant amount of the Estancia's population. And make no mistake, it was a significant portion of the Estancia's population.

Besides the four of us and the three babies there were Rodrigo and his two teams plus the coach driver and guard, forty additional escorts, five pairs of wagon drivers and guards, and a cook with two helpers. Beth was coming with us to help care for the babies which meant Maco was coming as well.

By the time it was all said and done there were seventy-four people making the trip. I had a fleeting thought that perhaps things had gotten a little out of hand but then I remembered my comment a few trips back about this trip making a statement about the Estancia.

Between the numbers in our party, the coach, and the amount of gold we'd be depositing we were certainly going to succeed in making the statement I wanted made. The Estancia Dos Santos was a major power in the territory and it was here to stay.

CHAPTER 19

It seemed like the entire Estancia had turned out to wish us all safe travels. Both sides of the road, from the bottom of the slope to the bridge were lined with people, as were both sides of the road from the opposite side of the bridge to the Camino Real.

Anna and I sat on our horses at the top of the slope, watching the procession of ten outriders, twenty escorts, the coach, four gold wagons, a supply wagon, and twenty more escorts move down the slope, across the bridge, and up to the Camino Real.

Mixed in somewhere among them were Tom, Maco, as well as the cook and his helpers while Yolanda and Beth were in the coach with the babies. The way it was set up, almost made it look like a military formation. At that thought I suddenly realized what I was seeing.

It looked like a military formation, because that was the way I'd originally trained them. George had trained them even further, of course; but there really wasn't much difference between this trip, and the original trip each family had made coming to the Estancia. On top of the formation structure, was the fact that every visible person was wearing what amounted to a de facto Estancia travelling uniform.

Everyone, including me and Anna wore camouflage pants, dark brown Apache knee high moccasins, a tan shirt, and a dark brown leather coat. All the men, except myself, were also wearing wide brimmed straw hats. Anna and I waited a few more moments and then rode down the slope to catch up with the procession.

I had known intellectually that traveling long distances with this many people and animals was much different than the way I usually traveled. While safer, it was much more difficult. Knowing I wasn't equipped with the right experience, I turned it all over to Rodrigo as 'road segundo', making him responsible for finding appropriate places to stop for lunch as well as overnight camps.

He was a senior vaquero, after all, and had much more experience judging the suitability of potential overnight stops, to provide the grazing and water needed for the animals, which was my biggest concern. We had two days of emergency feed grain in case we needed it but otherwise we expected to find sufficient grazing for all the animals.

For the bulk of the fourteen-day trip Tom and I rode where we pleased in the formation. Most of the time either Anna or Yolanda was with us, as they had decided to take turns riding in the coach with Beth. When Beth wasn't in the coach with the babies, she could be found riding next to Maco who was enjoying both the trip, and Beth's company.

We were less than five miles outside of Santa Fe, when we stopped early in the afternoon, for our final camp. As soon as camp was set up we turned to cleaning our clothes and gear. The dust and dirt was washed off the coach and wagons, clothes were cleaned and dried, tack was cleaned and oiled, and the animals were brushed and combed.

We intentionally broke camp later than normal the next morning so that we arrived in Santa Fe just before ten. Our procession of riders, coach, and wagons made its way through town to the expected stares, comments, and wonder.

The coach pulled up outside the hotel. The

ladies, escorted by the driver, guard, and one team of escorts, entered to start making arrangements for our stay. Everyone else continued down the street.

All five wagons pulled up in front of the bank. As we'd discussed at breakfast, Rodrigo sent one team around to the back of the bank to guard the back door. Four teams spread out around the wagons facing outward while three teams dismounted joining the drivers, guards, Tom and me, as we unloaded the wagons, and carried the bags straight into the bank. Hiram came out of his office as I led the long line of men back to the weighing room.

I set the bags I was carrying down on the floor near the weighing table and the others followed suit before turning and going out for more. Hiram walked in with a small smile on his face.

"You weren't kidding about using the front door from now on, I see. It's good to see you again, Paul," Hiram said before asking in rapid fire. "How was the trip? How are Anna and the babies? How much did you bring this time?"

I couldn't help but laugh. "It's good to see you as well, Hiram. The trip was long but not too bad. Anna and the babies are fine, and the ladies are all down at the hotel making arrangements for our stay. We brought four times more on this trip than we brought last time, so you'd better get some help in here and start weighing. Oh, and please tell your guards that I have five men out back, guarding the back door. I wouldn't want anyone getting nervous."

With a startled look the smile left his face to be replaced by his serious business face. He nodded once, and hurriedly left the room as the line of men returned to drop off more bags. Hiram and one of the tellers watched from the hall as the last of the men dropped their bags and left for more.

"Good lord, Paul!" Hiram exclaimed as he entered the room with his assistant. "Did you bring the entire Estancia with you on this trip? There must be forty men outside from what I saw out the window."

This time my laugh was much louder. "Hiram, there are seventy-four of us total on this trip, and, no, it's nowhere near the entire Estancia."

Hiram simply nodded as both he and the teller began setting the scales up, to start weighing. I started stacking gold bars on the table as more bags were coming in. As we worked I couldn't help but watch the amazement on Hiram and his assistant's faces each time more bags were brought in. With twenty men, each carrying two bags per trip, it took twenty trips, and over a half hour to empty all four wagons.

Tom left two teams to guard the bank after the wagons had been unloaded, taking everyone else with him to the hotel. The two teams guarding the bank rotated every hour for the three hours it took Hiram and his assistant to finish weighing the gold and I had a deposit slip. I released the two teams to continue settling in, and met Hiram in his office.

"Well, Paul, any real doubts about you having the financing needed to build a railroad have certainly been laid to rest, today," Hiram said handing me a glass of scotch.

"It's a drop in the bucket compared to what I need to make all my plans come to fruition," I said taking a long appreciative sip of scotch. "I've got enough for now, though. We'll see what happens as times goes on. On a different subject, Anna asked me to make sure to invite everyone to supper tonight at the club at seven. So, consider this your and Helen's invitation."

Hiram gave a small laugh. "Helen would never forgive me if I turned down a supper invitation at the club, much less one from Anna! I think you can count on us being there."

Finishing my drink, I put the glass down on Hiram's desk. "Thanks for the drink, Hiram. I'd stay for another but right now I have a date with a hot bath, clean clothes, and a shave," I said as I opened the office door.

"Paul, your use of the front door, and the time it took to unload the wagons will have been noticed. You need to be careful while you're in town. Santa Fe is normally pretty peaceful, but we do have our unsavory elements, just like any town, not to mention 'the Boss'," Hiram warned as I was walking out.

I stopped, turned, and with a hard look, said, "Thanks for the warning, Hiram; but everyone on the Estancia has learned to be careful, no matter where we are. Anyone who tries anything with us will quickly wish they hadn't."

He gave me a quick nod, and with a wave of my hand goodbye I walked out of the bank. I walked into the hotel lobby and found Tom and Maco sitting with Kit. I walked over and exchanged greetings with Kit.

"Kit, it's good see you again. How long have you been in town?" I asked as I dropped his hand.

"We've been here two days, Paul, and it's damn good to see you again. I've heard some stories about you from the Judge and Steve since we got in and I'm mighty interested in finding out just how much of the stories are true," Kit said with a grin.

"Well, that's going to have to wait a bit Kit," I said and waved my arm indicating Tom, Maco, and myself. "The three of us have our marching orders from the ladies. A hot bath, clean clothes, a shave, and a haircut. You're welcome to join us if you'd like," I finished as I accepted the bundle of clean clothes and the burlap bag of dirty clothes from Tom.

"Josefa gave me the same orders when we got here Paul. Thanks, but I'll meet you at the club when you're done. It's Wednesday after all and I don't think we'll be seeing the ladies anytime soon the way they were talking up a storm when we got kicked out," he replied with a low laugh.

The four of us left the hotel together, talking until we neared the club when Kit left us. Once ensconced in our tubs, Tom caught me up on the arrangements Anna had made for the week. The escorts were spread out among our hotel and two others nearby. We had a suite on the second floor with connecting rooms on both sides. Maco was in one room and Beth was in the other. Kit and Josefa were across the hall in another suite with their two young ones, William and Teresina. Maco and Beth would be having supper in the suite, minding the five kids, this evening while everyone else was at the club.

I gave Maco a glance with a cocked eyebrow.

"I just can't seem to tell her 'no'," he said with a grimace.

I gave a sigh. It seemed like the time had come. "Maco what are your intentions towards Beth?" I asked with a straight face.

I struggled to keep a straight face as Maco stared at me in horror, while on the other side of him Tom was fighting just as hard to swallow a laugh.

"I love her Paul. I'm just not sure that's enough," Maco finally replied.

"Have you told her you love her? Have you talked with her about your doubts?" I asked quickly. "Because if you haven't, you're running out of time. Once she decides that you aren't serious about her, it will be too late."

With a resigned sigh Maco said, "I know that, Paul. I'm just trying to figure out what to say exactly, and find the right time."

Both Tom and I erupted into laughter. "Maco you need to man up, and tell her how you feel about her. Look her straight in the eye and say those three magic little words. 'I love you'. That's all you need to say. All the other doubts and fears will become less meaningful, once those three words are said by both of you. As for the proper time, it sounds like tonight while everyone else is at supper would be a perfect time."

Maco glumly nodded, and sunk further down into the tub thinking about what I had said. A few moments later he sat up straight, and looked over at me with a smile on his face.

"You mean it's alright with you if me and Beth get married?" he asked.

"That's a topic for a different day Maco. Whether we approve of the marriage or not won't matter one bit, if you and Beth don't get things clear between you. Once you've expressed your love for each other and talked things through; then, and only then, will it be the right time to come ask for her hand," I told him with a straight face.

It was evident that Maco saw past my words, as he just nodded his head and sank back into the tub much more relaxed.

Washed, wearing clean city clothes, and with fresh haircuts and shaves we dropped off our well-worn, dusty, and stained travel clothes at the laundry before heading for the club. Inside the club I arranged for a temporary week's memberships for the three of us, as well as a private dining room for supper tonight, before heading to the dining room where we found Kit, The Judge, Steve, Lucien, and Hiram having lunch. We joined them after a complete round of introductions, and ordered almost immediately from the server who magically appeared at our sides.

Lucien looked askance at Maco after the server left. "Paul make sure you or Tom are with this young man whenever he's about town. Many establishments won't serve Indians, and even those that do, can be gruff. Not to mention the reaction he'll get walking down the street."

With a laugh Tom responded before I could. "Lucien, anyone who tries to mess with Maco is going to quickly learn two things. First, they're going to learn that Maco is one hell of a fighter, with or without weapons. Second, they are going to learn what it feels like to have a minimum of twenty guns pointed at them."

In an even tone Lucien said, "Tell me another one, Tom. This young man is still wet behind the ears. And who would be pointing the twenty guns?"

This time Maco responded for himself as he felt behind his ears. "No. I dried behind my ears carefully after our bath a short time ago." Looking directly at Lucien now he smiled and continued, "You Anglos have so many idiomatic expressions that it takes a while to learn them all. You'll find that besides Apache I am fluent in both English and Spanish, and have a passing knowledge of Latin.

"More importantly, you'll find that every man on the Estancia is more than capable of defending themselves in a fight, with or without guns. I know because I help train them every morning. As for who would be holding the guns Tom referred to, that would be the seventy men from the Estancia who made the trip with us.

"As for your unspoken question of why they would be defending me, that would be because I live and work on the Estancia, just like they do. Most of them are farmers, vaqueros, or wranglers. My job is to protect the Estancia so they can do their job. I take my job seriously, as do my cousins from the other sixty-eight Garcia Apache families living and working on the Estancia. You could ask Flat Nose and his comancheros how well we do but all ninety of them died when they tried to attack the Estancia this spring."

By the time he was done talking Tom, Steve, and I were sporting large grins. Lucien had lost all traces of equanimity and was sputtering while Kit, Hiram, and the Judge were giving Maco open mouthed stares. Before they could recover, lunch was brought out, and we focused on eating.

Lucien put down his knife and fork about half-way through lunch. It seemed that he'd been thinking about what Maco had said.

"You have sixty-eight Apaches living and working on the Estancia? You brought seventy men with you on this trip? You wiped out a very large group of comancheros this spring? How many damn people do you have on this Estancia of yours, Paul?"

I gave Lucien a glance, swallowed what I had in my mouth and washed it down with a large sip of coffee before responding.

"You got the first part wrong Lucien. Maco said there were sixty-eight Garcia *families* of Apache. That means they are all cousins to each other and to Anna, Yolanda, me, and, by extension, Tom. An Apache family generally includes multiple generations so there are roughly 150 or so Apache warriors living and working on the Estancia.

"Yes, I brought roughly seventy men, the actual number is sixty-eight but why quibble? Yes, we wiped out a very large comanchero gang this spring. The actual number that attacked us and died straight out was just over eighty. We captured seven prisoners that were later transported here for trial by the Judge.

We captured another two prisoners when we took their main camp a few days later. They were also transported here and tried by the Judge. As for how many people live on the Estancia, I've kind of lost track. Do you have a number, Tom?"

Tom gave me a grin and said, "Well, let's see. There're 150 cousins, give or take. There're 80 vaqueros, 274 farmers, 8 wranglers, 7 stable/wagon yard workers, the 3 Segundos, George, the 15 masons, the Padre, and the two of us. So that's a total of 541 men. Figure an average family size of six and you get a total of just over 3,200 people on the Estancia, give or take a few at any given time."

"Thanks, Tom," I said before turning to Lucien. "Any other questions Lucien?"

Steve was quietly laughing as he continued eating. The other four were looking at Tom, Maco, and me, like we had two heads as we returned to eating. Finally, Lucien just shook his head, and started eating again.

The rest of lunch passed quietly with little conversation. When we were done with lunch we left the others to their afternoon game of cards, reminding them as we were leaving, that supper was in the club at seven, and walked back to the hotel.

We found the ladies in the suite chatting and drinking the ever-present coffee. Anna beamed me one of her smiles before the greetings and introductions were made.

"You'll need to order more coffee my love, there's not much left."

Just as I started to tell her that I'd ordered some on the way up, there was a knock on the door.

"Your wish is my command, my sweet Dulcinea," I said as I walked over and opened the door gesturing the young lady carrying fresh coffee and cups inside.

Anna's smile grew brighter and with a twinkle in her eye holding the promise of a later reward, made a deep curtsey. "Your thoughtfulness is always appreciated, my Don Quixote."

With a bowing sweep of my arms I gestured the giggling young lady who'd delivered the coffee back out the door. At that point, the women all broke into giggles, while Tom and Maco shook their heads and poured themselves some coffee.

We recounted our lunch at the club, with Maco telling the bulk of the story. As usual, when he was telling a story, he had everyone in stitches as he imitated the facial expressions of the various participants. He had just finished the story, when William, Josefa's oldest came walking out of Beth's room, followed closely by the sounds of crying, waking, hungry babies, from behind him. That was our cue to leave.

I stood up and with a deep sweeping bow to Anna said, "My two apprentices and I shall leave you now, my sweet Dulcinea, as we hear the sound of women's work beckoning you. They have much yet to learn about the proper tilting at windmills and now seems the perfect time to expand their understanding of this almost mystic activity. But never fear, we shall return, anon."

A laughing Tom and Maco followed me out the door, to the sounds of the ladies giggling. As we walked downstairs I suggested we get a wagon or the coach and go see if the trunks we'd ordered on our last visit were ready. At their head nods we headed out to the stables behind the hotel, where the coach, wagons, and their teams were stabled.

The first thing I saw was the coach and giving Tom a quick glance said, "You know, I've never driven a coach. How about you?"

Tom stopped and rubbed his chin. "It's been a while since I drove a six in hand, but I think I can do it without too much trouble." He got a big grin on his face and said excitedly, "Let's do it."

The stable boys hurriedly hitched the six black horses to the coach, and as Tom climbed up to the driver's seat, I gave another sweeping bow as I opened the coach telling Maco, "Your coach awaits Don Maco."

Maco laughed, assumed a regal bearing, gave a haughty nod, and entered the coach. I closed the door behind him, joined Tom on the driver's seat, and told him to show me how it was done.

Grinning, Tom gave the reins a quick slap, and the horses moved out of the stable yard smartly. A few minutes later we pulled into the Altamirano Wainwright's yard and Tom smoothly stopped the coach. Maco let himself out, joining us as we walked over to the store.

The clerk we'd talked to on our last visit was admiring the coach from the door, and greeted us as we walked up quickly ushering us inside.

"That is, indeed, a very handsome coach. Your color choice for the trunks makes much more sense now, and I think you will be pleased with them. If you'll wait here just a moment, I'll have them brought out for you."

At my nod, he disappeared through a curtained doorway into the back of the store. While we waited, I browsed through the shelves of travel related gear. Near the area used to display the trunks I found a simple but well-made set of wooden travel brushes, combs, and mirror neatly packed in a leather case. The set was designed to fit into one of the compartments in the lift out tray of the larger trunks. After some discussion, the three of us decided they would be great gifts for the ladies.

When the clerk finally returned, he was followed by four men each carrying a trunk. After we'd examined them and admired the finish for a few minutes I told the clerk we wanted to add three of the traveling comb and brush sets as well.

The clerk nodded and said while turning, "Let me get them, it will only take a moment." He stopped after two steps, and turned back to us. "The wood sets you've asked for are good for travel, and are what most people who need them buy. However, we also have them in tortoise shell, as well as silver. Would you like to see those before you make a decision?"

I quickly stifled the laugh I felt bubbling up at his up-sell attempt. The man would definitely have been at home on a twenty-first century sales floor. I looked at Tom and Maco before giving a shrug, and telling him we would certainly like to see both.

We followed him over to the counter, where he pulled out two admittedly nicer leather cases and opened them up fully before laying them on the counter. The silver set with mother of pearl inlay immediately caught the eye and was very beautiful to look at but I couldn't see Anna ever using it. It was just too ostentatious. As a matter of fact, it took a good thing just a little too far and bordered on gaudy. The tortoise shell set was just as well made and, while nice to look at, retained the functional look of daily use items.

I asked Tom and Maco which they thought the ladies would prefer and without hesitation both said the tortoise shell set. Grinning, I told the clerk we'd take three of the tortoise shell sets. He pulled out two more sets from underneath, laid them on the counter, and put the silver set away.

I paid for them and started to pick them up, when Tom asked the clerk if he could wrap them up as gifts. The clerk agreed and pulled out some plain butcher paper and twine wrapping each set up individually, before handing them to us and thanking us for our business.

The four men carried the trunks out to the coach, loaded them into the boot, and tied them the leather boot cover down. We thanked them, and with a slap of the reins we were on our way back to the hotel.

We were met with appropriate oohs and awws when we walked back into the suite carrying the trunks assisted by one of the valets. When the man had left the three ladies took seats on the couch.

"My ladies, this is an auspicious day in the annals of La Mancha Oeste, otherwise known as Estancia Dos Santos. For, on this day, my two apprentices have displayed full mastery of the art of tilting at windmills. I therefore proclaim this day as National Tilting at Windmills Day to be henceforth celebrated annually with the giving of gifts by the Knights of La Mancha Oeste to their ladies, in appreciation of having received their favors," I haughtily proclaimed.

By the time I was done the ladies were quietly giggling again. I imperiously put out my hand, and Maco handed me one of the wrapped packages, and gave Tom one as well.

I stepped in front of Anna and went to one knee before presenting the package with a flourish, and a bow to Anna. Tom and Maco followed my lead with their ladies. Maco, a natural ham, made a much more credible job of it than poor Tom, but at least Tom tried. Anna beamed me one of her special Anna smiles, before regally lifting the package from my upraised palms.

The giggling had stopped to be replaced by curious looks as they went about the very serious business of opening their gifts. The soft gasps, oohs, and awws, as they examined the leather cases, were soon much louder as they opened up the cases and laid them out flat on their laps. Anna beamed a huge super megawatt Anna smile in thanks for the gift as she returned to examining the tortoise shell brushes, combs, and mirror. The party atmosphere was interrupted a few moments later, when the coffee I'd ordered on the way upstairs was delivered.

Supper that night was a lively affair, what with all the people involved. The conversation was lively and wide ranging without any undue focus on my activities as US Marshal, the railroad, or the Estancia. Before we left, I did take the opportunity to arrange a private lunch at the club, with the men, particularly Lucien, to discuss the railroad.

In bed, with the door closed, I told Anna about my talk with Maco. We talked about that relationship for a few minutes, before reaching a mutual decision to explore some more possibilities.

The next morning, we were met by a very different Beth than we were used to seeing. The Beth who greeted us was bubbly, almost giddy, constantly smiling, and very attentive to Maco, who was also wearing a pleased smile on his face. At one point during breakfast I whispered to Anna that things must have gone well during their talk while we were at supper last night. Anna gave me a grin, and a small head nod in agreement.

Tom, and I spent most of the morning in the suite giving Kit an overview of everything we'd been doing, including some of our longer-range plans. He was quite surprised to learn that he had a minority non-voting position within our little railroad scheme and objected at first. He only quieted down, when I explained to him how he was going to earn the stake we'd given him.

The afternoon was spent with the three of us teaching Maco how to play poker. He proved to be a quick study, particularly after we explained it was largely a game of chance, and included bluffing your opponents. Once he understood the rules and the rankings of hands, he quickly got better and better. By the end of the day he was the best player of the four of us and we judged he was ready for an afternoon at the club.

With two exceptions, the rest of our time in Santa Fe followed the same pattern. In the morning, following breakfast, sometimes with Hiram and Helen, the four of us would follow the ladies around town as they shopped for family and friends. By the time we returned to the hotel for lunch, we were all loaded down with various parcels and packages. After lunch, the four of us would join Lucien at the club, spending the rest of the afternoon playing poker.

The first exception to our routine was Sunday with a visit to the church, and more socializing with Steve, Hiram, Helen, and Lucien. The second exception was the Monday lunch meeting I'd arranged with all the men, which stretched out well into the afternoon.

The meeting didn't really start until after lunch had been cleared off the table, and the door closed. I stood up and when I had all of their attention I started talking. I gave them the same type of speech I'd given the two Trust groups earlier in the year, covering the same items with more of a focus on the northern part of the Territory and the role I saw them playing influencing legislators on schools and other social issues.

I did explain what we were doing in the Mesilla Valley, with the two trusts. I also gave them my vision of splitting the Territory into two territories, as well as my reasoning and urged them to exert their influence to make it happen as soon as possible.

Everyone at the table, except Maco, was familiar with bits and pieces of everything I was saying, but this was the first time most of them had heard so many pieces fully explained, and the relationships between the various components. I answered all the questions and responded to all the comments that were thrown out before calling a break to get fresh coffee delivered, and to give everyone a chance to process everything I had said.

With fresh coffee and the door closed again I continued. "As you all know, we're planning to build a railroad. Tom, Yolanda, Anna, and I own a majority of the railroad with Kit and Steve holding a minority non-voting position. The reason for the railroad is three-fold. First, and most importantly from our perspective, the Estancia produces so much beef and food we need to expand our markets to remain profitable. Second, we want to significantly cut the travel time between the major population centers in the territory and encourage settlement. Finally, we want a convincing sign of civilization to encourage acceptance of statehood. We already own all the land we need for the first three stages of construction."

I stopped there and spread out the map of the Territory I'd brought with me on the table.

"The first stage in building and operations will be from Las Cruces to Santa Fe. The second stage is Las Cruces to Colorado City, via Tucson. The third stage will be Las Cruces to the northeast about 200 miles. This stage of the railroad will be solely to encourage settlement in an otherwise under populated area of excellent farm and cattle country. We've already ordered the first three steam engines from back east, with the first scheduled to arrive here in Santa Fe in about eighteen months.

I looked at each man around the table before finally letting my eyes settle on Lucien. "Lucien, there is another part of the second stage, that is completely up to you. Assuming we can agree on an acceptable price, the second stage will include construction of a route from Santa Fe up through Raton and onto the prairie.

"We'd prefer not to buy the land through your grant outright if we don't have to, although we are prepared to go that route if you insist. Instead, we'd like to buy a two hundred yard right of way from where your land starts east of Glorietta Pass, and up through Raton Pass to where your land ends on the prairie."

Lucien sat in his usual slumped position staring off into the distance, as I patiently waited for him to respond. A few moments later he looked up at me.

"I like what I'm hearing so far Paul but what are you going to do, once you've reached the prairie?"

I smiled to myself as I'd anticipated just this question.

"What we do will ultimately depend on two things. First, at some point in the next few years, there are going to be enough people in and around the Rocky Mountains that someone is going to stumble on the gold that I know is there. When that happens, we'll solidify our plans to run a line to Pueblo.

The second thing we will have to consider is the coming war, and the impact it will have on the nation at the time we get out of Raton Pass. Our initial plan is to turn east and build through Kansas eventually joining with one of the larger eastern railroad lines, but we'll just have to wait and see."

Lucien sat thinking and a few moments later nodded his head once.

"Alright, Paul. I'll sell you a two hundred yard right of way through my land for twenty-five cents a mile, a private car stored here in Santa Fe, and free passage of that car when attached on one of your regular runs."

I looked over at Steve who was pulling some

papers out of his portfolio.

"Thank you, Lucien. Those terms are acceptable. I had Steve draw up the papers with just those conditions. He's filling the price in now, and once he's done he'll give them to you to review and sign when you're comfortable. I want to make sure, though, that you are aware that this is a contingent offer."

Again, I looked around the table. "It's contingent on us buying either the land or right of way from Santa Fe through Glorietta Pass to Lucien's land. I'm hoping Lucien, Hiram, and the Judge can help us with that.

"I don't have the time or inclination to get involved in the local social and political structure and negotiate either buying the land outright, or buying the right of way through the various pieces of land. Steve won't have the time either, as he'll be busy doing some traveling for us.

"What I propose is that the three of you work together to buy the land or the right of way, and either sell it to me, or give it to us in exchange for a minority stake in the railroad. It's your choice. Either way, we won't be exercising the contract or filing the covenant on Lucien's land grant, until we have the rest of the land or right of way we need from Santa Fe to Lucien's land.

"You all also need to understand that I'm not interested in a speculation event. I am willing to pay up to an average of four dollars an acre. If the average cost goes above that then the route east and north won't be built. Not by us, anyway."

From the looks on their faces it was clear to me that they needed time to discuss my proposal among themselves. "We leave for the Estancia after breakfast, Thursday morning. Hopefully, that will give you enough time to think about my proposal, talk about it among yourselves, and reach a joint decision. I think I've covered everything I wanted to discuss, so unless there are more questions or concerns I think we're done for now."

There were no other questions, so we broke up; with Hiram, the Judge, and Lucien all going directly to Hiram's office at the bank, to continue the discussion among themselves.

The four of us walked back to the hotel where we relaxed and gave the ladies a brief update, before resuming our usual routine.

CHAPTER 20

Thursday morning dawned sunny with a crisp chill in the air, as Tom and I carried the last of our things out, and loaded everything in the wagons or coach as appropriate. We joined everyone else in the restaurant, and were surprised to find Lucien sitting at the table.

I sat down in the empty chair next to Anna, as she handed me a cup of coffee. Glancing around the table I greeted everyone and suddenly realized that Hiram, Lucien, and the Judge were all sitting together across the table from me.

I raised a questioning eyebrow in their general direction, and Lucien began talking, being very careful to not give away any specifics.

"Paul, we've all agreed to your request and have come up with a plan to get what you talked about. I'll start working that plan while these other two reprobates are down south, relaxing in your warm weather. They'll pitch in and start working their parts of the plan when they get back. Between us we should have what you want, ready to turn over to you at the stated average price, by late spring of next year."

I gave a small smile to all three of the men. "Thank you, gentlemen. I wish you the best of luck. Your success will ensure the success of our phase two plans. Lucien, I wouldn't worry too much about Hiram and the Judge. They'll be kept plenty busy during their visit. I doubt they'll even notice the warmer climate."

We were enjoying our last cup of coffee after breakfast, when Rodrigo stuck his head just inside the door and gave me a quick nod before backing out into the lobby. I let everyone know we would be leaving as soon as we were done with the coffee.

I took my last sip, and reminded Lucien that he was invited to the Estancia anytime he wanted to visit. I knew he was concerned his family was too big to be comfortable on the Estancia, so I didn't push it. Instead I suggested he talk to Hiram and the Judge when they returned, and make any future decisions based on their recommendations.

Our cavalcade rode out of town a half hour

later, preceded by the two scout teams who left five minutes before we did.

As we rode out Tom nodded with his chin at a building we were passing.

"Remind me the next time we're here. I want to visit that place. It looks mighty interesting."

I gave him a quick glance to see if he was serious. "Okay, Tom but I'm not sure what TJ's Haberdashery and Millenary Emporium could have that would interest you so much."

Yolanda gave a small giggle from her horse on the other side of Tom.

"Anna, Beth, and I bought some hats and other accessories there the other day, Tom. You should have come with us. Most of the store is women's hats and accessories but there are a few men's hats."

Tom snorted and reiterated that it just looked interesting.

Our trip home was much like our trip up to Santa Fe, only with more ladies and babies. All the ladies except Helen took turns riding horseback. The Judge and Hiram were also taking turns riding horseback or on the wagons, when the babies were feeding at mid-morning and mid-afternoon. Just as on the trip up, Rodrigo was responsible for managing the lunch and evening stops.

Our last night on the road, the Judge walked up rubbing his rump.

"Paul, how much further is this Estancia of yours?" he asked as Hiram came walking up to join us.

With a smile, I said, "We're about fifteen miles away from the Estancia and twenty miles from the Hacienda."

"This is the last time I visit you until the railroad is running. I'm too old for this kind of travel," he groaned.

Hiram nodded his head in agreement. "It's not age that's my problem, it's the fact I don't ride much, but I agree with the Judge. You did try to warn us, Paul, but the reality is very different than the expectation."

We came to the northern boundary of the Estancia early the afternoon of the next day. Once we hit the paved section of road we picked up speed, no longer having to worry about wagon ruts or holes in the road. Less than two hours later we rolled over the bridge, and our escorts waved as they turned for either the village or the ranch, taking the wagons with them.

We let the coach pull up outside the courtyard door, and we pulled up behind it. There were ten of the older boys waiting to help unload the coach and individual horses, before taking everyone's horses and the coach away. Right behind them, came everyone else from the Hacienda. We all greeted one another, and quick introductions were made.

Kit, Josefa, the Judge, Hiram, and Helen looked around in wonder. We all knew that they would get the full effect tomorrow after taking a ride to the village and ranch, but for now they just stared.

Anna led the ladies inside with the men following carrying the trunks and baggage. She led the procession through the Hacienda, and pointed at rooms giving the name of the person assigned to that room. She waited for the trunks and luggage to be placed inside before moving on to the next room.

When that was done, she asked Steve to show the five new visitors the bathroom, and explain how everything worked, while the rest of us took our trunks and luggage to our rooms.

We were all on the terrace less than ten minutes later, enjoying fresh coffee and biscochitos as we waited for Steve to finish explaining how things worked in the bathroom and lead the other five up to the terrace.

Anna and I were standing quietly at the railing

with our arms around each other, looking out over the Estancia as Steve finally led the others out on the terrace. They all walked over and joined us standing quietly looking around.

After a few moments Anna turned to them with a smile.

"Welcome to Estancia Dos Santos and to our Hacienda. We'll take a ride to the village and ranch tomorrow, but from here you can see most of the Estancia. It runs four miles north and south of here and extends from the other side of the Doña Ana Mountains you see in front of you to the backside of the Robledo Mountains behind us."

Kit gave a low whistle. "I still don't understand what you need all that land for, Paul."

I waved my hand out over the Estancia. "Most of the land from the road east is for cattle, Kit," I turned towards the table. "Hector, what's the latest cattle estimate?" I asked.

Hector came over to the railing. "Roughly 16,000 head Paul, and by the end of next summer probably over 20,000 head at the rate it's going."

I shook my head, wondering out loud how we were going to keep that many cattle fed without overgrazing before turning back to Kit. "Does that answer your question?" I asked.

"Why haven't you sold any?" Kit asked in a perplexed voice.

I gave a snort, while Hector barked a short laugh. "We've sold over 10,000 head the last three years Kit," Hector replied.

"Well, hell, Paul. I don't know what cows go for around here, but I'll take all you can deliver to Taos at fifteen dollars a head," Kit said in a firm, no nonsense voice.

"What in the world would you do with that many cows, Kit? You've got buffalo if you need meat and Lucien's herd is a lot closer to you than we are," I said in disbelief.

Kit shook his head at me. "Paul, buffalo are migratory, and they never seem to be around when we need them. Lucien owns a lot of land, but he doesn't have that many cattle. You know I'm the agent for the Jicarilla Apache and the Ute's. I could have really used your beef last October. As it stands now, you'll probably have to wait until March to start driving them up to Taos so you don't arrive before enough snow has melted to get through."

"Hector, get with Kit after the meeting Monday morning and work everything out with him. Make sure Steve is with you and he can write up a contract with the terms you two come up with," I said with a smile at Kit.

Anna chose that moment to ask, "Kit, whatever happened to those sheep you were going to look at for us? I sure would like have some on the Estancia."

"Well, I keep looking Anna, but I haven't been able to find the combination of sheep and herders you talked about. Just before we left Taos to meet you in Santa Fe I got word that a flock of 1,000 sheep had arrived with five families of herders but the man who hired them and brought them over from Spain, died before they arrived. I heard that they were looking to sell the sheep, and their services to someone, but I don't know that for sure," Kit replied.

I groaned inwardly, knowing what was coming I quickly turned to Hector. "You better plan on taking at least six teams when you deliver the cattle, Hector. You'll need at least that many to escort all those sheep back it they are still there."

I turned back to Kit and said, "If they are still available when you get back, Kit I would appreciate it if you would let them know we're coming, and will buy the sheep and their services. Hector knows the standard rates we pay our men, and will discuss that with them, but I'll ask you to negotiate the price of the sheep please."